He frowned. "I have no intention of ravishing you, if that is your worry, if that is what makes you vicious as a snake. Have you looked at yourself? You're about as tempting as a field of trampled onions. You are thinner than a starved goat. How old are you? Twelve? Surely no more than twelve. I have no taste for children, none of my men do either. Rest easy now. Rest your mouth as well. This will hurt but I will be as gentle as I can."

Merrik realized his mistake when he pulled the ragged breeches down her legs, off her feet, and threw them outside the tent. She was on her belly, her legs slightly spread. He stared at the long legs, very thin, that was true, but shaped well enough to give promise to what they would look like when she'd gained flesh. And those hips of hers surely weren't a boy's hips, he'd known that, but these hips were not a girl's hips either.

These hips hadn't been twelve years old in a long time. Too long a time.

They were a woman's hips.

Merrik cursed.

LORD of RAVEN'S PEAK

CATHERINE COULTER

JOVE BOOKS, NEW YORK

LORD OF RAVEN'S PEAK

A Jove Book / published by arrangement with
the author

PRINTING HISTORY
Jove edition / April 1994

ISBN: 0-515-11351-4

A JOVE BOOK®
Jove Books are published by The Berkley Publishing Group,
200 Madison Avenue, New York, New York 10016.
JOVE and the "J" design are trademarks belonging
to Jove Publications, Inc.

PRINTED IN THE UNITED STATES OF AMERICA

10 9 8 7 6 5 4 3 2 1

To my sweet sweet cat, Gilly,
Who's the same age as my marriage.

LORD of RAVEN'S PEAK

1

The Slave Market of Khagan-Rus
Kiev, A.D. 916

THE SLAVE RING was as sweet-smelling as it would ever be, Merrik thought. It was early morning and still cool; a breeze off the river Dnieper rustled gently over the scores of unwashed bodies. It was July and the water below the embankment flowed smoothly and serenely within the Dnieper's broad banks now, the ice floes having finally melted early the month before. The consequent flooding had eased now as well, sending cleansing river smells upward.

The sun had just risen behind Kiev, showing bright gold behind the endless stretch of barren hills and jagged mountains to the east. The stench of winter-dirty furs and scrawny bodies too long unwashed wouldn't offend the nostrils until later in the day, even here in the slave ring. The only thing here to offend anyone was the abject human misery, and that was a condition so familiar in a place like this, it hardly bore notice.

Merrik Haraldsson had unfastened the pounded silver brooch and slipped its sharp point from the soft otter fur cloak. He'd slung the cloak over his arm as he walked toward the slave market's perimeter. He'd come from his longboat, *The Silver Raven,* moored below at a long wooden pier that lay in a protected inlet of the Dnieper just below Kiev. He wasn't sweating now, but the climb was a hard one, and he'd walked briskly, wanting to be here as early as possible to find a slave his mother would approve before they'd been picked over and only the sick and wasted were left.

The Khagan-Rus slave market was set apart from the town. Its name was the same as that of the prince of Kiev: a reminder that there was a tax at each purchase that would go directly into Prince Khagan-Rus's capacious pockets.

Merrik turned to Oleg, a man he'd known since they'd both been boys—wild and passionate and eager to best their older brothers and acquire their own longboats to trade and fight and grow rich, rich enough to buy their own farmsteads sometime in a future that they pondered only rarely, richer even than their fathers and older brothers.

"We will leave after I buy a female slave. Keep a sharp eye, Oleg, for I don't want a drudge for my mother's longhouse, or a sloe-eyed maid that would unduly strain my father's faithfulness. He has had no concubine for thirty years. I don't want him to begin now."

"Your mother would break his head open were he ever to gaze fondly at another woman and you well know it."

Merrik grinned. "My mother is a woman of strong passions. Very well, then, I think of my brother's wife. Sarla is a shy little thing and could easily be governed by a clever female, slave or no."

"And your brother is a man of strong appetites, Merrik. A female doesn't necessarily have to be toothsome for Erik to want her. Look at Caylis, I'll grant you she's a beauty even though her son is close to ten years old now, but Megot, whom he beds just as much, is a plump pullet and her chins shake when she laughs."

"Aye, 'tis true. We must consider many factors before I pick the right female. My mother needs a female slave who will be loyal to her and work only for her. My mother wants to teach her to spin, for her fingers stiffen and give her pain now. Roran told me this should be an excellent selection this morning, many slaves were brought in just last night from Byzantium."

"Aye, and the great golden city of Miklagard. How I should like to voyage there, Merrik. It is the greatest city in the world, it is said."

"Aye, 'tis difficult to believe that more than half a million people live there. Next summer we will have to build a stronger longboat, for the currents and rapids below Kiev are vicious. There are seven rapids and each is more deadly than the last. The one called Aifur kills more men than all the others combined. Even the portage is dangerous for there are many vicious tribes living along the Dnieper waiting for men to come ashore with their longboats to drag them overland to beyond the rapids. Aye, we'll join an armada of other trading ships for protection. I don't wish to die just to see Miklagard and the Black Sea."

"The Aifur, huh?" Oleg grinned at Merrik. "You have been talking to other traders, Merrik. You are already preparing this in your mind, aren't you?"

"Aye, I am, but Oleg, we grow rich trading in Birka and Hedeby, for we are known there and trusted. The Irish slaves brought more silver than even I believed possible. And this year we grew even richer trading our Lapp furs in Staraya Ladoga. Remember that man who bought every reindeer comb we had? He told me he had more women than he wanted and all of them begged combs from him. He said their hair would beggar him.

"Nay, we will wait to travel to Miklagard next year. Be content."

" 'Tis you who aren't content, Merrik."

"Very well, I will be patient. We return home with more silver than our fathers and brothers have. We are rich, my friend, and there is no one to gainsay us now."

"Forget not that lovely blue silk that came from the Caliphate, at least that's what Old Firren claimed."

"He's a liar who has grown over the years to believe his own words, but the material is beyond beautiful."

"Aye, and you will continue the lie. Will you give it to your bride? You plan to buy your own farmstead now, Merrik? Or perhaps return with your bride to her father's?"

Merrik said nothing, but he frowned. During the winter, his father had negotiated with the Thoragassons, not bothering to tell his son until the two fathers had come to agreement. Merrik barely knew the seventeen-year-old Letta. He'd felt anger at his father at such interference, for Merrik was, after all, nearly twenty-four years old, but he'd said nothing. The girl was lovely, appeared gentle, and her dowry would be impressive. He would look closely at her when he returned home, then make his decision. But if he wedded her he would have to leave his father's farmstead, for already his eldest brother and his wife of two years, the gentle Sarla, lived there and would continue there after their parents died. Surely they would have many babes, and soon it would be too crowded, what with all his father's and brother's people and his own men and slaves as well. He shook his head. He disliked thinking of leaving his home, but if he wed, he would have to take his wife somewhere, and there was no more land in Vestfold that could be farmed. His brother, Rorik, had gone to Hawkfell Island, just off the coast of Britain, and had prospered. Ah, but to leave his home, it was something he didn't yet wish to do. He also disliked knowing he was now rich enough to leave.

He said only to Oleg, "A farmstead and a wife are two decisions a man must weigh carefully."

"That is what my father says, but he is always smiling at me when he says it. Think you he wants me out of his longhouse?"

There were at least eighty slaves in the pit, as it was called. They were of all ages, both sexes in nearly equal numbers, some few still proud, their shoulders squared, but most stood still as stones with their heads bowed, knowing what was to come, perhaps praying to their gods that the men or women who bought them would be kind.

Merrik walked slowly through the rows. The young women were lined up on one side, the older women behind them, and the boys and men on the other side of the pit. There were guards only behind the men, whips in their hands, watching, ever watching, silent and menacing, but they really weren't concerned. None of this group would cause any problems. They'd been broken sufficiently since they'd been captured on raids, some of them had been slaves for decades, some even born of slaves.

It was a sight Merrik had seen since he'd been a boy when his father had first taken him to York to buy slaves. This was nothing new, save that this slave market wasn't as grim or as dirty and didn't smell yet since it was so early in the day and they were in the cool fresh air of Kiev and not in the Danelaw where the Saxons smelled as bad as the slaves, and their stench filled the air. Here a man could breathe as he made his selections.

Many of the girls were fine looking and appeared clean enough. They were from all parts of the world, some with yellowish skin and beautifully slanted eyes and the thickest black hair he'd ever seen, long and board-straight. They were slight, and all had their heads down. There were redheads and blonds from Samarkand, some very tall and broadly built, others squat with heavy torsos and short legs who hailed from Bulgar and beyond. Merrik saw a girl who pleased him. He realized she pleased him too much, for she had the pale golden hair of his people, pale clear flesh, and a long slender body. He felt a mild spurt of lust and shook his head. No, she wouldn't do for his mother. His brother would soon have her flat on her back, if Merrik didn't take her first. He wouldn't provide another concubine for his brother Erik, for unlike his brother, he saw how much it hurt Sarla when her husband ignored her at night, then took himself off to bed with one of his women.

He must search for a comely face, but not too comely, certainly no more than a pleasant face, perhaps one on the broad, flat side. His brother disliked thin women; Merrik searched out females with hollow cheeks, showing bones. He selected three possible young slave girls, turned to search out the slave-auction merchant, Valai, to bargain. As he waited for Valai to finish with a Swedish merchant who smelled of rotted fish and stale sex, he realized he'd seen that same merchant—so obese he wheezed even as he spoke—the night before with a dozen more merchants at the house of a man who had many female slaves to sell. Each merchant was given a girl and they had, each one in turn, with all the others looking on, stripped the girls and had sex there on the wooden benches that lines the inside wall of the great hall. Merrik had felt immediate lust, for he saw that there were still half a dozen girls left and one would be his, until he saw a merchant over a girl, and the girl was lying there, her eyes closed, so still she could have been dead, and the fat merchant had shoved into her, huffing, his great belly shaking, until, finally, he'd spilled his seed inside her. She'd never opened her eyes. Merrik saw tears seeping from beneath her closed eyelids, streaking down her face. He had left.

He turned away from the fat merchant, and looked indifferently at the long line of men and boys. He froze.

He didn't know why that of all the scores of men he looked directly at the boy, but somehow, once he had, he couldn't seem to look away. The boy was perhaps twelve years old, not older than thirteen. He was so thin Merrik could see the long bones clearly in his bare arms, the knobby scabbed elbows, the wrists so thin he could wrap his fingers about them twice over, long narrow hands held loosely to his sides. His legs, bare from the knees down were just as thin and very white where they weren't blackened and streaked with filth and scabs from cuts. He could even see the pale blue veins. The boy was pathetic and would die soon if he weren't bought by a master who would at least feed him properly. He'd doubtless been mistreated in the past. He was wearing rags and a ripped filthy sealskin.

Not that it concerned Merrik. The boy was a slave and would be sold, perhaps to a cruel master, perhaps not, perhaps to a master who would let him buy his freedom someday. It was a common practice and perhaps the lad would be lucky. It didn't matter. Ah, but there was something about him that held Merrik very still, that wouldn't allow him to look away. But he forced himself to look away. He wanted to sail from Kiev this morning and there was much he still had to do before leaving. He turned to go when the boy sud-

denly looked up and their eyes met. The boy's eyes were
a gray-blue, two colors that sounded normal, even common, particularly in Norway, but this boy's eyes were
different. The gray color was deeper than the rich pew-
ter bowl Merrik's mother had received as a gift upon
her wedding to his father, and the blue darker than a
sea in winter. He could tell that the boy's flesh was very
white despite all the dirt. His brows were dark and
well-drawn but the tangled, filthy mat of hair on his
head was too dirty and oily to determine its true color.
It was simply dull and dark and filthy. The boy was
beneath notice were it not for those eyes. They caught
Merrik cold. Eyes weren't made filthy; but eyes could
reflect a man or woman's thoughts, and the boy's eyes
were drained empty, dull, accepting. Certainly that
wasn't odd. But then, quite suddenly, there was a remarkable shift—where there'd been emptiness, there
was now coldness and a look of defiance that would
probably get the boy killed or beaten to death if he
didn't learn to mask that spark better. In a flash that
look of defiance turned to one of anger, immense anger
that held such violence and rage, it shook Merrik. Then,
just as suddenly, the boy's eyes became blank again, all
that fury and passion buried beneath hopelessness and
awareness that his lot in life was that of a slave and
probably would remain so until he died. It was as if
Merrik could see the boy withdrawing into himself. He
could see him dying and accepting death before his
eyes.

Merrik roused himself from this ridiculous revery.
The boy was a slave, nothing more. It didn't matter if
he'd been captured from a hovel in a small village or
from a rich farmhouse. Merrik would never see him
again after he left the slave pit. He would cease to think
about him the moment his hand was on the rudder of

his longboat and the wind from the sails was sharp in his face. He shrugged and shook his head. He turned then when Oleg tugged on his arm to point out another slave.

He heard an agonized cry and turned back. The very fat merchant, the same Swedish merchant Merrik had seen the night before, the same merchant who had just been dealing with Valai, had grabbed the boy's arm and was pulling him away from the line of other boys and men. He was shrieking that he'd paid too much silver for the filthy little *garla,* or puny pig, and he would shut up now or be very sorry for it. But the shouts and cries weren't all coming from the boy. The most piercing ones were from a small child who had a death grip on the boy's other hand. By all the gods, Merrik thought, it was the boy's little brother and the man hadn't bought him. The child was screaming, terrified cries that were pathetic, and it made something deep inside him twist and cramp and he didn't understand it. He took a step forward, then saw the fat merchant slap the boy, for he was now trying to grab his little brother. The merchant then kicked the child hard. Merrik watched him fall onto his face and remain still, saw him just lie there, huddled into himself, sobbing. The boy hit the merchant, not a hard hit, for Merrik doubted he had the strength, but a fist in that oaf's fat belly that surely had to hurt. The merchant raised a fist, but then lowered it. He cursed, threw the boy over his shoulder and walked away.

The child rose slowly, holding his ribs, and just stood there, not crying out now, just staring after his brother, and suddenly, quite without warning, Merrik couldn't bear it. Something gave way deep inside him. No, he couldn't bear it, he wouldn't bear it. "Wait here," he said to Oleg.

He was on his knees in front of the child. He gently cupped the child's chin in his large hand and lifted it. The tears were still streaming down his dirty face, leaving obscene white marks in their wake. "What is your name?" Merrik said.

The little boy sniffed loudly. He stared at Merrik, his small features so drawn with fear that Merrik said, "I won't hurt you. What is your name?"

The child said quite clearly, his words only mildly accented, "My name is Taby. That fat man took my—" His voice died, just stopped cold. He looked at Merrik and the tears were thicker now and the child was sniveling and hiccuping. And there was such fear in the child's eyes that Merrik wanted to snarl like a wolf, but he didn't. He didn't want the child to fear him more.

He said only, his voice low, slow, "What is your brother's name?"

The child ducked his head down and said nothing.

"Is he your brother?"

The child nodded, nothing more. He was very afraid. Merrik didn't blame him.

Merrik had looked up as he'd spoken, but the merchant was gone. The child was alone. He looked down at that bowed head, saw the child's thin shoulders heave and shake with his crying. He knew well what became of children who were alone and were slaves. Most of them died, and if they didn't, well, perhaps what became of them was even worse. Suddenly, Merrik didn't want this child to die. He took the little boy's hand, felt the filth on the child's flesh, felt the delicate bones that would snap like twigs at the slightest pressure, and something lurched inside him. The child wasn't as thin as his brother, and Merrik knew why. The older brother had given what food he'd gotten to the little boy. "You will come with me, Taby. I will take you from this place. You will trust me."

The child shuddered at his words and didn't raise his head or move.

"I know it is difficult for you to believe me. Come, Taby, I won't hurt you, I swear it."

"My brother," the child whispered, and he raised his head then and looked at Merrik with pathetic hope. "My brother is gone. What will happen to him?"

"Come," he said, "trust me." He walked away from the line of slaves, the little boy's hand tucked firmly in his large one.

Merrik knew he would buy the child for a very small weight of silver, and he was right. Soon he had completed his business with Valai, a small man with a twinkling eye and a shrewd, ruthless brain. Valai wasn't, however, necessarily cruel, just matter-of-fact and spoke his mind when it couldn't hurt his trade. He said to Merrik, "I know you aren't a pederast, thus the child will bring you no pleasure and will be only a burden to you."

"Aye, but it doesn't matter. I want him."

"It's possible that someone would buy him and he would be raised well, used only to service his masters. Not a bad life for such as he. Better than dying, which is what would happen at many other places."

Merrik said nothing but he felt his guts surge with rage. Aye, the best that could happen would be that the child would be raped endlessly, then trained to pleasure men, those damned Arabs who kept both sexes in their keeping to pleasure them at their whim. After Taby grew up and no longer had a boy's allure, he would be thrown into the fields to work over crops until he died. And Merrik couldn't bear that. He looked down at Taby. No, he wouldn't allow that to happen. He didn't question what he would do with the child. He paid Valai, then went to find Oleg.

If Oleg believed him mad, he said nothing, merely stared at the small boy, then grinned and nodded, rubbing his hands together. Oleg always loved an adventure. Merrik realized he was thinking he would grant him one this day. And Oleg would probably be right, Merrik thought.

2

THRASCO, A VERY rich fur merchant of Kiev who prided himself on the quality of his miniver and his judicious use of bribes, looked down at the boy, smiled grimly, and nodded to himself. He tossed the whip to his slave, Cleve, who was also looking at the thin bloodied back, at the shuddering skinny body.

Thrasco was too fat to come down on his haunches, so he merely leaned down a bit, breathing hard even with that mild exertion, and said, "Now, boy, you will know that any disobedience from you, any hesitation in doing whatever I bid you to do, and I will flay the flesh off your pretty back. Do you understand me, boy?"

The boy's head finally nodded.

Thrasco was pleased; he was also relieved. He'd paid a goodly amount for the boy and he didn't want to kill him, but he'd had to discipline him for the blow in the belly he'd given him at the slave market. Now he was broken. Thrasco straightened. Aye, it was good now. Once he'd fed the boy for several weeks, he would be repaid many times over for his investment. He said his plans aloud to Cleve. "This boy will be a fine present to Khagan-Rus's sister, Old Evta. She is fond of young boys, and I know once this one is bathed and given a bit of food, he will please her. She will gain much enjoyment from him. If he shows her a bit of spirit, why then, she will enjoy whipping it out of him."

"Aye," Thrasco's man said, one eye on that whip. He said nothing more because he had no wish to taste the whip on his own back, and Thrasco was unpredictable.

"I know what you're thinking," Thrasco continued, still staring down at the boy. "You're thinking that the boy is a pathetic scrap and even clean will still look a pathetic scrap. I am a man of experience and I know that the boy has a fine-boned face. He is slight, delicate even. Just look at those hands and those feet, long and narrow. Aye, it's good blood he carries in his skinny veins. His parents weren't slaves. No, this one is different, and I will use his differentness to my advantage. See to him now, bathe his back and use some of that cream my mother sent me from Baghdad, 'twill prevent scarring. Leave him filthy for the moment, leave him clothed in his torn rags. He deserves to wallow in his dirt for the blow he struck me. All saw it and Valai laughed, others too. If he obeys you completely, you will bathe him on the morrow."

Cleve nodded. Poor little boy, he thought.

Thrasco said as he walked to the door, "Old Evta will appreciate the little squirrel. Did I tell you that she likes to call her boys animal names? Perhaps if he comes to answer to squirrel here, she will like that and reward me even more. I will send food for him, just some broth, I don't want him to puke up his guts. Feed him, Cleve, and keep feeding him."

Cleve nodded again, turning back after his master had left the small chamber to once again look at the lad. At least he wouldn't be sodomized, and that was something. Cleve had been sodomized regularly for nearly two years until finally he'd been sold to a woman with hair so pale it seemed white, a woman who looked like one of the Christians' angels, but she wasn't. He unconsciously fingered the jagged scar on his face. After her, he was bought by a master who didn't like boys, and that master was Thrasco, bless the gods. He was cruel but he wasn't a pederast. He was occasionally even generous. He'd given Cleve a patched beaver fur to wear this past winter. Cleve knelt down and said quietly, "Are you awake, boy?"

"Aye."

"The pain is bad, I know it. Thrasco enjoys wielding the whip, but his mother disapproves of it so he can only do it when she is visiting her family in the Caliphate. You are unlucky she is not here. Now, Thrasco ordered me not to bathe you or change you from these rags you wear. I dare not disobey him, but I will bathe your back and fetch this cream he just spoke about. He will send you food and you will fatten yourself."

"I heard everything he said."

"Then I won't repeat anything else."

"There is nothing else to repeat. I'm not a squirrel. Your master is beyond foolish. He's also ugly and fat."

"Nay, it is Old Evta who would call you an animal. Thrasco merely tries to select the animal before she does."

"They are both foolish."

Cleve frowned. The boy was still arrogant; Thrasco wouldn't like that at all.

"You heard Thrasco speak of Khagan-Rus?"

"Aye, he will give me to this man's sister. But who is this Khagan-Rus?"

"How can you be so ignorant? Why, he is the prince of Kiev. He is rich, and Old Evta is even richer, a fact the prince hates, but she controls him. She calls him her proud bull when he pleases her. When she wishes to hurt him, she calls him her little swamp beetle.

Thrasco wants to supply her with furs, mostly miniver, and she requires many. She is very fat, you know, nearly as fat as Thrasco. You will be his means to succeed."

"Have you looked at me?"

The tone of voice was odd, but Cleve said only, "Aye, you're a miserable offering, but with food, you will improve, at least Thrasco believes so. I hope you're not really ugly under all that filth."

"I am."

Cleve frowned. "You're in pain yet you speak back to me as if I would not do anything to hurt you further. I am Thrasco's slave. You are the foolish one."

The boy was finally quiet.

"Good," Cleve said. "Keep your mouth shut and I will attend you. Thrasco won't tolerate his wishes being ignored."

"He will die soon of gluttony."

"Aye, mayhap, but you won't be here to see it. Now, boy, you will allow me to help you. No, don't shrink away from me. I know your back hurts, but you must let me get you onto the cot."

"I would allow it, but I really can't move."

Cleve stretched out his hand and gently turned the boy's face toward him. He lifted that face and saw that the pain had leached the very color from the boy's flesh. He saw, too, immense rage in eyes that should have grown accepting. Cleve lifted him as gently as he could, propping him up, actually, and half dragging him to the narrow bed. He eased him carefully down onto his side. Then he just stood there, staring down at the thin figure. And Cleve said quietly, "I can see your breasts."

The girl said nothing, made no move to pull together the shreds of her tunic. The pain was simply too great.

"What is your name?"

"Laren."

"A strange name and you speak with a stranger accent. You will tell me soon enough why you play the boy. In this land being a boy can lead to your rape as quickly as being a girl. Come now, I must help you. Nay, I shan't tell Thrasco, but know he will learn the truth soon enough and then I will suffer for saying naught to him."

"I know," she said, and bit her lip until it bled when he picked away bits of the filthy sealskin from her back and began to bathe her. "Thank you."

Cleve grunted, calling himself more stupid than a naked man in winter, but he was gentle, and each time the girl tightened in pain, he felt it inside himself. After her back was clean and the thick white cream coating it, Cleve stood over her and said, "You will lie still. I will bring you food. Broth, Thrasco said, else you'll puke up your guts you're so skinny."

"I know," she said. "I heard him say it." She said nothing more, merely waited until the man had left the small chamber. She looked about. The room was all clean whitewashed walls. She was used to dark timbered chambers with smoke-blackened beams, not this stark whiteness. Huge chambers that smelled richly of men and women and scented candles. Here it was so very different. There was only the bed she lay upon and a small table beside the bed. There was a single candle on the table. A high window, its fur covering drawn back, let in bright sunlight, and for that Laren was grateful. She looked at the bright light and wondered what had happened to Taby, trying for a moment to keep it a question even though she knew well enough. She felt the pain grip her chest even as it twisted and roiled in her back. She'd failed him.

She wasn't stupid. She knew what happened to chil-

dren left in the slave pit. They died. She had already
seen it happen. Or here, in this strange savage land,
they were used sexually until they no longer pleased
their masters. Taby wouldn't survive that.

She didn't cry. Tears were a long, long time in the
past, in a past that was vague and whispery and gray
now, the blacks and whites having faded quickly, so
very quickly in the press of hunger and cruelty and the
absolute will to survive.

She wondered if she should simply end it now, for
there was no reason to go on. She'd forced herself to go
on in the past, for Taby's sake; she'd tell herself, I will
survive for Taby. But it was difficult. Although the hatred inside her still burned as brightly, the need for
vengeance still gnawed fiercely in her belly, it seemed
all that was left of her. Ah, but there was Taby, always
her little brother. He'd kept her spirit alive, kept her
determined upon life else she might have simply closed
her eyes forever if he hadn't been there, if he hadn't
needed her, if she hadn't known that if she died he
would surely die as well. And now, Taby would die.

But not right now, not immediately.

If he hadn't been bought today, he would be in the
slave pen, a filthy enclosure near to the slave market.
He would be alone and hungry and terrified. She realized she was his only hope. But because she'd been stupid enough to strike Thrasco, he'd beaten her, and now
she was sprawled on her belly, helpless as a pup. At
least a pup was better than a squirrel. She shook her
head at that and raised herself on her elbows. The pain
shot through her back, curving around her chest, making her gasp. It even hurt to breathe, but she did, and
she realized that she could bear it. Odd how she could
bear things now that before would have surely killed

her. Had she once been so soft, so delicate, such a use-less creature?

She was so hungry. She smelled the rich beef broth before she even heard Cleve come into the small chamber. She felt saliva pool in her mouth.

"You will remain on your belly but I will put a pillow under your chest to raise your mouth."

Soon he was spooning the hot broth into her mouth. It burned all the way to her belly. She felt light-headed at the taste of it, felt her body warming and strengthening. But she knew that it was an illusion at best, that her body would betray her, for she'd denied it too long.

She ate until the bowl was empty. She raised her eyes to Cleve's face. "I want more."

He shook his head. "Nay, you'd puke if you ate more. Thrasco knows about these things."

"I don't know how he could know. He looks as if he's never stopped eating in his life." But she knew it as well, even as she spoke, but her belly was still rumbling, and she didn't care if she vomited up her guts if only she could have more of that broth to eat.

"You will sleep now, 'tis best for you."

"What is the hour?"

"It is noonday."

"You're very ugly, Cleve. What happened to you?"

He was silent a moment, then he laughed, a raw, hoarse sound, obviously a sound he hadn't made in a very long time. "It is a worthy story, one that makes women cry and men sigh with envy. Aye, it is a tale that makes the soul take flight."

"I've given you pain. I'm sorry. Did someone slash your face when you were that young?"

"Aye, you've good eyes, little girl. Hush now."

"Your eyes are beautiful. One is gold and the other is blue. In my land, many would believe you a devil's get."

He grunted even as he pulled a cover to her waist. "If I were devil's get, believe you I would be Thrasco's slave? Nay, I would rule this damned Kiev had I the power. What you see in me is the way of life and men, naught more, naught less. At least I have enough food in my belly and my ribs don't stick out. Right now, you're uglier than I am."

"And I smell worse."

"Aye, that too." Cleve paused a moment, rubbing his chin. "Do you have much pain?"

"It is less now. The cream is magical."

" 'Tis because Thrasco's mother is a witch. Even the Arabs fear her. She goes wherever she wishes to and no man tells her no."

"You've been kind to me. If you didn't have the scar, you would be beautiful. Your hair is golden, like a god's, and your body is well made."

"Aye, you've the right of it, little girl. Be quiet now. Thrasco ordered me to care for you. Aye, I find you unusual for a slave. Is Thrasco right? Are your parents not slaves? Is your blood unlike mine?"

She looked at him, then said slowly, "I have a little brother, Cleve."

"Aye, I did, too, once long ago, only he was my big brother and he was sold and I wasn't. I cannot bring his face into my mind now."

"Then you must understand. I must save him."

Cleve laughed in genuine amusement. "The little boy won't die here, not in Kiev. Nay, he'll be sold to an Arab trader from Miklagard, or even farther to the south, and he'll be used, aye, I won't lie to you about that, but it won't be so bad. I survived it."

"I'm sorry that you were used in that way. I cannot allow that to happen to Taby."

"You are helpless to prevent it. You are a slave yourself. It matters not if you have royal blood flowing through your veins. You're nothing now, less than nothing, a pawn in Thrasco's endless games."

"You speak very well for a wretched slave, Cleve!"

He grinned at her. "The master who used me also educated me. It gave him pleasure to discuss philosophy with me whilst he raped me. Also, when he was done with me and well sated, he enjoyed lying there, toying with my hair, speaking of the ancient Greeks and their strange ways. Your spirit will get you beaten to death, if you do not measure your words. Keep your mouth closed, little girl, else this magical cream won't be able to heal you."

She thought furiously, but gave it up, saying, her voice slurred with sleep, "Aye, you're right. I'll forget about him. What is one little boy? Naught to anyone."

Cleve frowned at those words. Even after such a short time he recognized them as not sitting well on those thin, scrappy shoulders. Still, he said nothing. He rose and stared down at the girl's back. "There is no more bleeding. Thrasco said I could bathe you on the morrow and give you clean clothes. He will come and inspect you himself. You will mind your tongue."

"Clean clothes would be nice," she said, and nothing more.

Still frowning, Cleve said, "He won't think to demand you appear naked in front of him since he has no liking for boys, so you will be protected for a little while, but I cannot imagine that you will look much like a boy once you're clean."

"I've been a boy for a very long time. No one has guessed. It was my only protection and it worked."

"Then you have been in a land of stupid people." Cleve turned to leave her, though he worried, and wondered why he did so. She was naught of anything, just a slave, and she would be gone soon to Old Evta—that or Thrasco would discover her sex and she would probably be sold to a brothel or beaten to death.

"Thank you, Cleve," he heard her call after him. Aye, if Thrasco discovered her sex, he just might kill her for ruining his plans. He knew the sister of Khagan-Rus, Old Evta, would never want a girl in her household. She had only female slaves who were older than the murky swamp that lay just to the west of the Dnieper.

It wasn't his problem. What would happen would happen. She had courage, but of course she was stupid to show it. Look what it had gotten her. Flat on her belly with a raw back. It just made him sad to think of that girl dead, or worse.

Although what could be worse than death? He could not even bring the image of his long-dead mother's face to his mind. Death was the last thing anyone could wish for.

It was dark, finally. From the single narrow window in the chamber, she could see only blackness. There was no moon and the stars were laced over with billowing dark clouds. Aye, it was very dark, thank the gods.

Laren had finished another bowl of broth, spoken only briefly to Cleve, for Thrasco needed him to serve at the evening meal. She begged him to leave her the basket of soft bread for the night. He'd left it, the fool. She wrapped it in a bit of torn cover from the bed. She wished she had something other than her rags, but she didn't. At least she'd wrapped the rest of the cover around her body beneath the rags. She looked like a boy now, no one would ever suspect. She was thin, her breasts weren't all that lavish and she'd flattened them to almost nothing with the cover, and her hair was short and ragged. Too, she was so dirty, smelled so rancid, she doubted anyone would even notice what sex she was, or care. She wished her back didn't nearly send her to her knees with pain, but she locked it away from her, this pain that wouldn't stop, and gritted her teeth against any sound she wanted to make, any moans that would attract attention.

The door wasn't locked. If it had been, she would have managed to ease through that narrow window. She eased out into a dim narrow corridor like a dark shadow. Beneath her feet was a rough wooden floor, not packed earth, and overhead was a low ceiling of white-washed beams. There were no furnishings in the corridor. She tried to remember being brought into the household. She pictured it in her mind and took a left turn when the corridor forked.

She heard men talking—surely they were guards—and pressed her back against the wall. It was rough and she gasped with the pain in her back. How many were there? The boards creaked beneath her feet.

"What was that?"

"What? You're hearing yourself eat, you fool, naught else."

"I'd best go see. You know Thrasco."

Laren forgot the pain in her back. She was as still as a stone. She saw the shadow of a man. She didn't move, didn't breathe. He took a step toward her, then paused, listening.

Another man called out, "You see, I told you there was naught. Be quiet and drink. Or give the ale to me. No one is there, no one is ever there."

There was a grunt, followed by a deep belch. Another man laughed.

She slowly let out her breath. She waited and waited still longer. Then she walked as quietly as she could, skimming against the wall, always going left when she had a choice. She heard many voices now, even Thrasco's, if she wasn't mistaken. If it was Thrasco, it had to be the dining quarters, the gluttonous heathen.

Finally she reached a narrow door. She turned the iron handle, and eased out into a foul-smelling alley. She smelled fetid water and wondered how Thrasco could have such a clean house and such filth at his doorstep. It didn't matter, she'd managed to escape. She nearly yelled with relief. She did let out a huge pent-up breath, jerking at the pain it brought her. She stopped a moment, just standing there, trying to gain control again. Her back burned and throbbed. She thought she felt damp stickiness and wondered if some of the slashes were bleeding again.

She was nearly free. It didn't matter. Her back would heal, only not here, not in Thrasco's house, not in Kiev. She would get Taby and they would travel north to Chernigov, a town just on the east bank of the Dnieper—she'd heard a slave speak of it. Surely it was not more than three days' walk from here. She would steal them clothes; she would become a widow, Taby her child. She would survive, and she would see that Taby survived. It was her first opportunity to escape and she intended to succeed. In the past she would never have managed to get this far. She supposed she had the beating to thank. Thrasco would never imagine that anyone would try to escape with a back in shreds.

Suddenly she heard men's voices. They were speaking quietly, from just down the way, to her right. They were sneaking toward her. They were thieves. Or they were Thrasco's men. It didn't matter. She closed her eyes a moment, wondering if every god of every country were against her, then she shrank back into the blackness, knowing she was trapped against the house. She couldn't run, she couldn't move, else she would run into the men. She wouldn't go back into Thrasco's house.

They were silent now, but she could hear their soft footfalls. There were two of them. No more. Just two men. If they were thieves, surely they wouldn't be interested in her. She was nothing, less than nothing. Ah, but she would be there and thus they would probably kill her.

She wanted to scream at the unfairness of it. She was trapped and any second now they would see her and that would be the end of her. And of Taby. She crouched down, trying desperately to press against the house, to become just one of the shadows that clung to the night.

She heard one of the men speak, his voice deep and quiet. He said, "We will go through this small door I was told about."

The other man said, "Told, Merrik? You were told naught until you gave the weasel that silver armlet."

"It matters not. The door should be close now. I understand the boy isn't being kept in the slave quarters but in a small chamber in the house—"

They were on her. She couldn't simply stand there, pretending they didn't exist, pretending they wouldn't see her. No, she would surprise them, she would attack, and then she would run, for surely she was smaller and faster and . . . She leapt upon the nearest man, striking his face with her fists.

"What in the name of all the gods—! 'Tis a boy and he's trying to kill me!" Oleg was big and strong, a warrior, and within seconds, he grabbed her arms, whirling her around, shouting in her face. "Hold still, you damned little sod! Stop fighting me!"

The other man whispered, "Keep him quiet, Oleg, and yourself! The last thing we need are Thrasco's guards on us."

In the instant the man spoke, she broke one arm free

and struck her fist into the man's belly. He only grunted, then grabbed at her again. It was a silent struggle then, for Laren didn't want the guards any more than these men. But she had no chance. Her arms were finally pinned to her sides. She looked up to see the man's hand raised and fisted. He would strike her. She looked at that fist and knew that when it hit her, it would be over. His other hand still held her upper arm.

What did it matter now? She jerked down her head and bit down on his hand as hard as she could. He grunted in pain, but she knew he wanted to scream, for she tasted his blood in her mouth. She didn't let go.

The other man was on her then, and his hands were about her throat and he was squeezing, saying low in her ear, "Release his hand or I will strangle you."

She let the man's hand go. He swore quietly, stepping back from her. The other man kept his hands around her throat and slowly turned her to face him.

He said, staring down at her, "Look who we have here, Oleg. We are blessed or cursed, depending on the pain in your hand. Ah, I'm not mistaken, for there is a bit of light coming over my left shoulder. Aye, Oleg, it is the boy we were coming to fetch. He came to welcome us. Well, boy, how did you get out of the compound?"

Laren didn't move. She felt the other man's blood trickling from the side of her mouth. She just stared up at the man. He was the one she'd seen at the slave market.

3

SHE HEARD THE other man cursing in a furious whisper as he hugged his bloody hand against his chest. She stared up at the man who still held her by her throat, saying not a word, just staring. Then suddenly, she drove her fist into his belly and jerked up her knee to his groin.

That knee came up fast, too fast, and Merrik knew, even as the bony knee struck him, that he wouldn't like what was going to happen. And he didn't.

He sucked in his breath when the inevitable nausea struck, and clutched his belly as the pain washed through him.

Oleg cursed, then grabbed the damned boy by his neck before he could run, squeezing even harder than Merrik had because his hand hurt and was bleeding, and the damned little savage had kicked Merrik in his groin and sent him to his knees.

She saw blackness, and she cursed herself for not immediately running, but she'd stayed there, frozen, watching the man she'd struck, the man she'd recognized from the slave market, wondering what he was doing here. In her hesitation, she missed her chance to escape. The blackness filled her mind then until she saw nothing at all.

* * *

Merrik stood very still, breathing deeply, until he could finally stand straight once again. Oleg was looking down at the boy in an unconscious heap at his feet.

"I should have killed the little sod," Oleg said. "He bit down to the bone."

"Well, he kicked me down to the bone," Merrik said.

Suddenly, with no warning, there was a fearsome growl and a man, a man both tall and slender, a man not a warrior, jumped on Merrik's back.

Merrik, still dazed from the blow to his groin, didn't react as quickly as he normally would have. Oleg jerked his knife from its sheath at his waist and raised it to strike at their assailant. In that instant, Oleg's leg was jerked from under him. He teetered, astounded, for he saw the boy staring up at him, and knew that the waif had done it to him yet again, and he just couldn't believe it. He was off balance when he felt the boy's fist in his gut, and fell against the timbered wall and over into a bush.

No one said anything. There were no curses, no grunts, no yells. The fight was a silent one for no one wanted Thrasco or his men to come bursting from the house.

Merrik managed to jerk the man's arms free of his throat. He lunged forward, pulling the man over his shoulder. He flung him to the ground at his feet, knocking the breath out of him. He drew his own knife and was on his knees in a moment, the knife tip at the man's throat.

"No, don't hurt him!"

The boy was scrambling to the fallen man who was trying to sit up, shaking his head.

The boy grabbed his arm and shook it. "By all the gods! Cleve, what do you here? You didn't come after me, did you? Is Thrasco close? Cleve, answer me!"

"Hurt this ugly beggar?" Merrik said, his voice low, but filled with surprise and sarcasm. This was the strangest rescue he'd ever attempted. "Why would I want to hurt him when he would have killed me? Would kill me even now if he could. Surely that makes no sense."

Cleve came to his knees slowly, shaking his head, and reached blindly for Merrik.

"No, Cleve," the boy said, coming to his knees beside him, clutching at his arm. "Wait, there are two of them and they are both armed. They will kill you. No, don't move. He is here and he has a knife."

"I am not here to kill you," Merrik said, staring at the two of them. "I am here, actually, to rescue you, boy. I have your brother, Taby."

She stared up at him then, unable to believe her ears. "You what?"

"I am here to rescue you. I am Merrik Haraldsson, from Norway, and I'm here to take you away."

Take her away? He had Taby? None of it made any sense to her. She was nothing but a slave, as was her little brother. She just looked at him stupidly. "But why?"

Merrik just shrugged. "Because I have suddenly become crazed. I looked at your little brother after Thrasco had taken you away at the slave pit, and lost what few wits I possessed." He didn't add that he'd lost his other wits when he'd looked at the boy and couldn't look away. "Come, boy, let's get out of here before your owner comes howling from that door with a dozen armed men. I would rescue you but I wouldn't want to die for you."

"He's too fat, but you're right about his men. There are many of them. They're drinking in a chamber off the inside corridor." The boy rose slowly, but his hand remained on the ugly man's shoulder. "Cleve must come too. He must." The boy stared at Merrik, then added, "Please." It was a word Merrik suspected the boy didn't often say.

"Why not?" Merrik said. "Oleg, arc you alive or did the lad bring you low again?"

"If you weren't bent on rescuing the little beggar, I would kill him."

"I'm bent on it," Merrik said. He stared at the man with the hideous jagged scar on his face and his long golden hair tied at the back of his neck. The man stood quietly beside the boy, his arms at his sides. He was slight, but lean and fit. He obviously knew nothing about fighting, thank the gods for something. Merrik sighed and said, "Come along. We're sailing the moment we get back to my longboat."

Oleg looked at the filthy boy, stared down at his bloody hand, and said, "I should beat you."

"No need," the boy said. "Truly, there is no need." He weaved where he stood, looked helplessly toward Cleve, then crumpled to the ground.

Cleve tried to catch her, but Merrik was faster. He lifted the boy in his arms. "By all the gods, the lad is naught more than a few bones held together with filthy flesh and filthier rags. This sealskin smells as if it's rotted in the sun for years."

"Aye," Cleve said. "Thrasco let me feed him broth, but he wouldn't let me give him a bath or clean clothes. Here, my lord, I'll take the boy."

"No need." Merrik lifted the boy onto his shoulder. He felt his pelvic bones grinding against his chest, and wondered if the lad would live long enough to see his little brother. And if he died, what would Merrik do with Taby?

Cleve wondered at the sudden turn of fate. He'd crept

through the huge compound hoping to find Laren before the guards caught her, for he knew she would never make good her escape; she was too weak from the beating and from the lack of food. Thrasco, of course, had believed the same thing, and thus, she hadn't been guarded. But she had escaped, at least she'd made the good beginnings of an escape. Cleve looked at Merrik. This man had come to save her? To save *him*—a boy, actually. He shook his head. He refused to believe that any good could come of this. The man was probably a savage out to capture slaves from others to save himself silver. This Norway, a place Cleve had heard daunting tales about, was a savage land, much farther to the north of Kiev, and thus it had to be savage and violent and barbaric. It bred not only men who explored, traded, and stayed to build settlements, but it also bred warriors who raided and plundered and killed without mercy. And now one of these Vikings had three new slaves and all without paying out a pinch of silver. Surely the man had lied. Rescue a boy because he'd felt sorry for the boy's little brother? It was ridiculous. Cleve wondered what the man really wanted. And he wondered how long it would be before Merrik discovered the boy was a girl.

The Silver Raven moved swiftly and silently in the dark smooth waters of the Dnieper. It was Merrik's pride. He'd had the sixty-foot craft built three years before by Torren, a builder in Kaupang, whose renown had reached even to York in the Danelaw. The longboat was a good fourteen feet across, nearly flat bottomed, not made for extended travel, but rather for sailing on rivers, and held a deep cargo hold for goods. The sides of the boat came out of the water only six feet, curving gracefully. Loose pine planks lay across the cross-

beams. In rough water they could be raised easily to
bail out the bilgewater, or now, as the longboat glided
under sail through the calm waters of the Dnieper, beneath those planks lay silver, gold, and jewelry and
other goods they'd traded for here in Kiev, as well as
tents, cooking utensils, and food for their journey home.
The rudder was large and worked smoothly, Old Firren
moving it tenderly and gently, as knowingly as a
mother would her child. The water was deep so the rudder held its eighteen inches below the keel line. The sail
was hoisted high on the yard, for the breeze was sharp,
and would carry them northward in good time; still the
men remained seated on their sea chests, their hands
near the oars as they spoke in low voices to each other.
They were too close to Kiev, too close to men who would
kill them without a whisper of regret, and if the wind
died, they would be rowing within seconds. There were
twenty-two oar holes, but on this trip Merrik had
brought but twenty men.

The dim light given off by the few rush torches along
the fortress perimeter in Kiev grew faint in the distance. The thick black smoke given off by the torches
could still be seen, curling into the clear summer sky.

The men began to row steadily now, for the wind had
died as suddenly as a man's lust caught in a sudden
belly cramp. Merrik spoke to each of them, encouraging
each to pull hard on his oars until they were well beyond the reach of all other warships and trading vessels. He wanted no trouble, no confrontations. There
was wealth on the longboat, and thus they were a mark
for pirates, though Merrik sincerely doubted anyone
would be fool enough to attempt an attack with twenty
armed Vikings.

Merrik made his way back to the stern and sat next
to Old Firren, whose hand never left the rudder. He

looked down at the boy huddled at his feet, wrapped in a thick wool blanket, then nodded toward Cleve, who had just taken his place at the oars. He sat on a wooden bench near Old Firren, who said naught, merely let his hands guide the longboat, his rheumy eyes taking in their current speed, the shadowing of the dark clouds overhead, the set of the few visible stars, the landmarks on the stern side of the longboat. Merrik would kill for Old Firren, not really all that old, but at least forty, an age to be respected. He had no family, but was wont to say that Merrik would do if he needed a son in a hurry.

The boy groaned, then tried to fling himself over onto his back. Merrik gently held the thin arm, keeping him on his stomach. Taby, his little brother, was crouched next to him, saying nothing, merely stroking his small dirty hand over his brother's shoulder.

"He will be all right, Taby, I promise you. He's just very weak from hunger and from a lot of exertion. We'll row to shore in a few hours and camp until dawn. I'll see that he's fed then and that he continues to rest until he gets his strength back. You too, lad."

"It's very dark," Taby said. He raised dark blue eyes to Merrik's face and once again, Merrik felt that twisting and burning deep inside him. "I'm afraid of the dark."

"No need to be afraid now," Merrik said, feeling that damnable pain in his gut at the child's words. He forced himself not to reach out to the little boy and bring him against his chest. No, it would frighten the child, but he wanted to hold him, very much, and Merrik didn't understand it. He said only, "I'll keep the dark at bay. It's important that we put a goodly distance between us and Kiev before we stop. You're safe now. So is your brother. Trust me."

The child nodded, very slowly, and Merrik doubted

that he believed his words. He doubted he would believe them himself if he were Taby. He stared at the small dirty hand on his brother's shoulder.

Now he had three slaves and hadn't paid a gram of silver for two of them. He hadn't gotten his mother a female slave, but no matter.

Slaves.

He looked from Taby to his brother to the man, Cleve, with his magnificent golden hair and his scarred face, who was rowing clumsily, obviously unused to the task. He was young, not more than twenty, Merrik thought, but he was strong, just untrained in fighting.

What was he going to do with the three of them?

The boy accepted the water skin from Merrik and drank deeply. Then he began to shake uncontrollably, and he dropped the water skin. Merrik reached out his hand to the boy's forehead. He was hot to the touch. He had the fever. Merrik frowned. Because he was hungry? Because he'd kicked Merrik in the groin and belly and bitten Oleg's hand to the bone? It made no sense. Merrik cursed, knowing he could do little, save soak the boy with cold water to bring the heat down. It seemed a strange thing to do since the heat was on the inside, but it sometimes worked. It was something his mother always did. He prayed the boy wasn't sickening of something that could kill all of them.

"Taby," he said quietly to get the child's attention without frightening him. "Tear off a bit of the cover your brother has wrapped around him. Hand it to me so I can wet it in the river."

The child did as he was told.

Merrik slipped his hands beneath the boy's armpits and lifted him over his legs, saying, as he looked down into the vague pain-blurred eyes, "Don't move. For some reason you have the fever. I must soak the heat out of you."

The boy said nothing. Merrik could feel him trembling and shuddering and wondered at it. It was more than that, he knew, but he refused to let that fear, or whatever it was, into his mind.

The night was cool. There were cloud-covered stars above the smooth dark waters of the Dnieper, gleaming dully off the opaque surface. The wind was still naught but a whisper of a breeze scarce rippling the surface of the water. The men were bent low over the oars, pulling, pulling, their motion smooth and powerful. He could see the boy clearly in the sudden shifting of the clouds that showed a quarter moon. He could see Taby's face just as clearly.

He yelled to Cleve, "Do you know what could be wrong with the boy? He has the fever. He's shuddering like a virgin."

The boy began to struggle. Merrik merely tightened his hold around the boy's back. He moaned and jerked. Merrik felt something wet and sticky against his arm. Frowning, he slowly lifted the boy on his legs, bending him over his left arm. He jerked off the filthy sealskin, then pulled away the ragged and torn tunic. Beneath was a clean linen sheet. When his hands closed over it, the boy jerked. Then he tried to scuttle away from him, but this time Merrik was ready for him. He pressed his hand against the boy's back to hold him still. The boy keened deep in his throat. It was then Merrik saw the dark wet shadows on the white linen, felt the stickiness against his hand. He lifted his hand in the star-dim light and saw the blood on his palm.

He winced. By all the gods, no. He was careful not to touch the boy's back again, saying close to his ear, "Hold still or I will hurt you without intending to. He beat you."

"Aye," the boy said between gasping breaths. "Thrasco beat me."

"For striking him at the slave market."

"Aye, for that, and to teach me obedience."

"Hold still," Merrik said again. "I have to see how bad it is. You have the fever and now I know the cause."

He slowly peeled down the sheet, much of it sticking to the bloody welts. He knew the pain must be very bad, but the boy didn't move now, didn't make a sound. He had guts.

He finally managed to get the linen sheet down to the boy's waist. He looked at the narrow white back covered with bloody welts. He cursed softly. Taby was standing beside him now, his face bloodless, tears streaming down his face.

"Nay, Taby, he will be all right. I promise you. Sit down, I do not want you to fall overboard."

Merrik looked down again at the narrow back, at the flesh scored with the long raw whip slashes. It was a very narrow, very white back that curved to a waist. Something wasn't right here. He looked at the thin arms, at the shoulders, at the slender neck, at the filthy tangled hair. Very gently, he laid the boy on his belly over his thighs. Slowly, he pulled at the ragged breeches, drawing them down the boy's hips. The boy tried to rear up again, striking Merrik's legs with his fists, but it did no good. Merrik just pressed him back down, holding him still with his palm against his waist. He pulled the breeches down further, baring the boy's backside.

These weren't boy's hips. This wasn't a boy's backside.

Merrik closed his eyes a moment. He didn't need this.

By all the gods, this was too much, more than too much.

He heard Cleve call out, "Nay, lord. Don't strip the lad. He needs his clothes. He must have his clothes!"

Merrik said for both Cleve and the girl over his legs, "I understand. I'll keep the boy covered."

He jerked the breeches back up to the girl's waist. He leaned down and said close to her ear, "Hold still. Now that I know what I've got here, I'll try to keep you covered." And then he cursed and cursed some more until he saw the fear in Taby's eyes, and he stopped.

"I won't hurt her," he said low to the child. "I won't. Keep seated. I don't want to have to worry about you as well."

What he would do with her, he had no idea.

He cleaned her back as best he could. The river water was clean, ah, but the pain of it against the welts, the harshness of it, and she was naught but a girl. He'd never been beaten in his life. He'd never whipped a slave. He'd cuffed shoulders and heads when he'd needed to gain obedience, particularly when a slave was newly captured, but not the whip, not to flay the flesh from a back.

He gently pressed the wet cloth against her back, holding it there, hoping to leach out some of the pain, to cool the fever. The longboat rocked with a sudden shift in the current sending a wave to slap against the starboard side, and she nearly slid off his legs.

He called out to Oleg, "Find a good place on shore for us to remain the rest of the night. The boy here needs to have his back tended. Thrasco beat him badly."

Roran, one-eared and black-eyed, an unlikely looking Viking in his darkness, said, "This is all very strange, Merrik."

"Aye, I know it well. You must keep your nose on watch, Roran, for I have to see to the boy here. I don't remember any savage tribes along this stretch of the Dnieper, do you?"

Roran shook his head, saying, "I will sniff them out if they are stupid enough to think of attack." He looked toward Old Firren, a master trader as well as a master rudderman. Old Firren shook his head. "Nay, 'tis safe enough. We're drawing close to Chernigov though, and that filthy place is filled with savages."

"Aye, I know."

"We are but one longboat, though only a fool would attack us. Since you have the children, though, we'll take care where we go ashore."

Merrik merely held her until they pulled the longboat ashore on a narrow strip of beach, not a beach really, just a shoreline littered with black rocks and driftwood. Tightly packed fir trees and pine trees pressed toward the water, and the gods knew what or who could be hiding in that dense forest.

He leaned down and said, "I will lift you over my shoulder now and we will go ashore. Don't fight me. Say nothing."

She was limp over his shoulder and he wondered if she were unconscious again. He gave Taby over to Oleg and watched Cleve pace back and forth along the narrow strip of rocky land until Merrik strode to him, the girl still over his shoulder.

"Help the men raise the tents, then spread covers and furs inside mine. The men will build a fire and we will eat. I will see to her. What is her name, do you know?"

"Laren."

"A strange name, as is her accent. Do you know where she comes from?"

"I am not dead," she said, rearing up slightly, and he could hear the pain mixed with a natural arrogance in her voice. "Cleve knows nothing. Leave him alone. Let me down. I don't want your heavy hands on me."

"You aren't strong enough to fight me," Merrik said mildly, "at least not enough to make me fall to my knees, so it's best you shut your mouth."

"Let me down."

"I will as soon as there is a fur to let you down upon."

She said nothing more. He imagined it wasn't because she didn't want to but because she wasn't able to. He winked at Taby but realized the boy couldn't see him for the light from the stars wasn't as bright here as it had been on the water. The heavy dark fir trees seemed to steal all the light.

When the furs and wool blankets were spread inside his tent, he bent his head and walked inside and laid her onto her stomach. "Don't move," he said shortly, rose, and helped fetch firewood. He wanted to bathe her as well. Her stench was as heady as his brother's dog, Kerzog, in the early summer, after a long winter. So was Taby's.

It was Cleve who fed her the bits of flatbread soaked in hot water and a handful of pecans and hazelnuts. It was Cleve who bathed Taby and black-eyed Roran who collected an assortment of odd clothes to cover the child.

But it was Merrik who decided he would care for the girl. He looked at each of his men in turn as they sat around the campfire, eating cheesy curds, dried beef, flatbread, and nuts. He nodded as if to himself, and said, "This boy here was beaten badly by Thrasco. He isn't a boy, he's a girl. There is no reason not to tell you. Her name is Laren and I know nothing more about her save that Taby is her little brother. I will tend her. She is very young, no older than your little sisters, so you will not think rutting thoughts about her. Eat now, drink only a cup of ale, and get some sleep. Roran, bend that nose of yours to the night sounds. Begin the first watch."

Merrik had heard Cleve suck in his breath when he'd spoken, but now he turned to him and said, "They would find out soon enough. There was no reason not to tell them. They are all good men. I trust them with my life."

They were still Vikings, men who were raw and violent, and Cleve wasn't sure how good that made them, but he said only, "She told me she'd been a boy for a long time and I said that the people where she'd been were stupid. She has no look of a boy."

"No," Merrik agreed.

He walked back into the tent and stared down at her raw back. He said matter-of-factly, "You will think of me as your father or your brother or even your mother, if it pleases your modesty. I am going to take off these rags and bathe you, then I will cover your back with some clean cloths. I have a clean tunic you will wear and Eller, my smallest man, will give you some breeches. Oleg, the man you bit, will even give you some cord to keep the breeches at your waist."

"I don't want you to. I want you to go away. I will take care of myself."

"Your mouth lies even to you. Close it. If you fight me, I will leave you here and take Taby. You will never see him again. Your escape to save him will have proved worth naught. Do you understand me, girl?"

She said nothing.

He frowned. "I have no intention of ravishing you, if that is your worry, if that is what makes you vicious as a snake. Have you looked at yourself? You're about as tempting as a field of trampled onions. You are thinner than a starved goat. How old are you, twelve? I have no taste for children, none of my men do either. Rest easy now. Rest your mouth as well. This will hurt but I will be as gentle as I can."

Merrik realized his mistake when he pulled the ragged breeches down her legs, off her feet, and threw them outside the tent. She was on her belly, her legs slightly spread. He stared at the long legs, very thin, true enough, but shaped well enough to give promise to what they would look like when she'd gained flesh, and the hips that surely weren't a boy's hips, he'd known that, but these hips weren't a girl's hips either. These hips hadn't been twelve years old in a long time. Too long a time. They were a woman's hips.

Merrik cursed.

4

MERRIK SAID NOTHING more. He bathed her legs and back quickly, matter-of-factly. She was very thin, pale and bony, and that helped. She was older than he'd first believed, but she was still pathetic, beyond pathetic, and he refused to let himself see anything save a bloody back and what should have been a boy. He was careful that the wet, soapy cloth covered his hand well when it washed her hips and between her legs. She was sick, she was dependent on him. She was a slave, nothing more.

He even washed her hair, three times, rinsed it twice, and spread his fingers through it to pull through the knots and tangles. It took him a very long time. She was very dirty and he wasn't done yet.

"I got most of you clean, but you will need another bath tomorrow," he said, and slowly turned her over onto her back. "Now I'll wash the front of you." He wished he hadn't turned her over.

Her eyes were closed, her face white with fatigue and probably pain as well. He could see her ribs, sharp and ugly, her flat belly with her pelvic bones sticking up. But he also saw very nice breasts that surely didn't belong on such a thin body. He got hold of himself and set himself to work. Her eyes were closed and remained

closed even when he finished washing her face and
moved on. When the cloth went over her breasts, she
didn't move, but he saw her hands clench at her sides.
He closed his own eyes when he bathed her belly and
her woman's flesh. He worked as quickly as he could
for he feared the onset of the fever again. The air was
getting cooler as the night grew later and later.

"The skalds will write great songs about me," he said
to her even as he eased his hand between her legs to
wash her. "I am a man with a Christian monk's control
and a warrior's honor, surely a combination that brings
on a pain as great as the one in your back."

She opened her eyes and stared up at him. "What are
you? Why are you pretending to be gentle with me and
Taby? What is it you want? Will you give me to your
men or to a friend to gain you something? Thrasco was
going to give me to the prince of Kiev's sister, who likes
young boys. What will you do?"

"You must get well again to find that out," he said as
he rinsed her as quickly as he could, then covered her
even more quickly, drawing the thick soft wool to her
chin. He said instead, "Does it hurt you too much to lie
on your back?"

"Aye, it does."

He helped her to turn onto her stomach. He patted
her back with more hot water, then laid clean linen
cloths over it. He pulled the wool cover to her neck. Her
hair was thick, curly, short, and very ragged.

"What color is your hair?"

"Red."

He sat on his haunches and frowned down at the back
of her head. Her voice was arrogant again, just that one
simple word and yet it sounded like a royal announcement from a royal mouth. He said, "The light is dim
and I could not tell, and before it was so dirty, it could

have been green. So it is red. I do not like that color, and our women at home don't have it."

"Do you think I care, Viking?"

He smiled more widely at the back of her head, adding, "It is too strong a color for a woman, it is perhaps indecent, not quite civilized. No, it is a color I do not like. How do you know I am a Viking?"

"You are from Norway. Are you so witless you remember not what you say? Also, you have blond hair and blue eyes. You are larger than the men I've seen in other lands. All Vikings are big. All Vikings look alike. There is nothing about you that sets you apart from any other man of your country. You are common."

He laughed. "And where you come from, do all women have red hair, red hair so dark it looks nearly black in the dim night?"

"Nay."

"I did not think so. All the women from your land don't have skin as dead white as a new snowfall in Vestfold either, do they?"

"Nay, but more than a few do, if one looks closely, which the Vikings don't, since all they do is raid and kill and steal whatever they can carry, including people."

He ignored that, saying, "Ah, you are even different from those in your own land. I thought as much. Red hair and white flesh, surely the Christian devil's curse on a female, one that bespeaks a god's punishment."

"It wasn't a god or a devil who cursed me," she said, and he heard the pain in her voice and the utter weariness, and something else, rage, banked but still there, so deep it would remain with her the rest of her life, hard and strong.

He frowned again at the back of her head, only this

time there was no mockery in his voice as he said, "Do you wish for more bread?"

"Nay, but Taby is always hungry, always more hungry than I. He would want more bread."

"Cleve is seeing to the boy, both he and Oleg—the man whose hand you bit—are tending to him. They will feed him until he can't move. There is enough food for both of you. Neither of you will starve."

"You will then sell him?"

"I can't believe Taby would bring me much silver," Merrik said, his voice thoughtful even as he felt anger at her for her deep distrust. By all the gods, hadn't he saved her? "He is only a small child, of little account. Aye, I should probably sell him."

"I will buy us from you. Cleve too."

"Are you hiding your silver somewhere I haven't looked? Surely not, for I was thorough in my bathing of you."

She was quiet as a stone.

"Yourself as well?"

"Aye, all three of us."

He laughed, marveling at her. "You are flat on your belly, my girl, with naught to cover you but the clothing I and my men give you. The food in that skinny stomach of yours is from me. Everything is from me, including your clean hair and your clean hide. You wouldn't have Taby if it weren't for me. Mayhap you should caution yourself to guard your tongue before you speak. I think it would serve you better."

She was silent for a very long time. Merrik rose and stretched and tossed away the dirty bathwater and threw her rags into the forest. He doubted even the animals would scavenge those smelly rags. He then came back to her and stretched out on his back beside her.

He snuffed out the candle, throwing the tent into blackness.

"You are right," she said, nothing more, then she turned her face away from him, and soon she was asleep.

Merrik didn't sleep until the sun was beginning to rise. Right about what, exactly? That she should guard her tongue around him? He thought it a good idea, but doubted that she could maintain such a guard for very long.

Oleg shouted, "Merrik, Eller smells something!"

Eller's nose was all Merrik needed. Within moments, all the men were carrying their supplies to the longboat. Merrik had jerked trousers to the girl's waist and a tunic over her head and was carrying her over his shoulder. Within another minute, they were pushing the longboat into the current and hoisting themselves over the sides. In the next instant, at least fifty men rushed onto the narrow beach, yelling and shouting at them, waving spears and rocks. One spear came arcing through the air and landed solidly in the wooden bench, not a hairsbreadth from Old Firren, but he didn't move nor did his hand recoil from the rudder.

"Eh?" he said only, and spit over the side, toward the shore.

"We could have killed most of them and taken the rest," Oleg said, his voice wistful.

"They don't look like a likely lot for slaves," Merrik said. "We would have to kill most of them and the others look too savage."

Oleg shaded his eyes with his hand from the bright sun overhead. "Aye, you're probably right."

It was then that Taby eased up beside him and looked at him with his child's clear eyes. Merrik watched the shifting expressions on Oleg's face, then saw him sigh and lift the child onto his lap. He said not another word, merely bent to the oar.

Soon they could no longer hear the shouting from shore or see the small men in their ancient animal skins jumping about, hurling curses at them in a strange tongue.

Merrik looked down at the girl. She was soundly asleep again, not that she'd ever really awakened earlier when he'd dressed her and grabbed her up over his shoulder and run to the longboat with her. Her flesh was very white and he feared the sun would roast her. He leaned over her, trying to protect her. It was something, but not enough.

It was Cleve who silently handed him a hat of sorts fashioned out of a shirt covering a wooden plate.

Merrik had bread waiting in his hand when she awoke. She was asleep one instant, and the next, she was staring up at him, making no movement, no sound.

"How do you feel?"

"Clean."

He grinned at her. "You should. Do you remember my bathing you last night?"

She merely nodded. Somehow, though, he knew that in a very short time, she would have something to say about it, something sharp. No, she would not guard her tongue. He tore off a piece of bread and stuck it in her mouth when she opened it.

"I'm glad you're alive," he said, watching her chew the bread. There was an expression of sheer bliss on her face. Her eyes were closed.

He was sorry the flatbread was stale, though to look at her he'd never know it.

He fed her until she said at last, "Nay, I wish no more. It is remarkable, but I don't." She sighed. "I've been hungry for longer than I can remember. To be full-bellied is a wonderful thing. Thank you."

"You are welcome," he said. "Would you like to sleep some more?"

"Nay."

"Perhaps you will want to close your eyes anyway, for I want to look at your back and bathe you again if it's necessary."

She just looked up at him. He knew she wanted to refuse him, but she didn't. She kept her mouth shut. She was learning; she was showing control. He supposed he knew she had to have some control, else she never would have survived any time at all as a slave.

He gently turned her onto her belly over his thighs and drew the tunic over her head. He looked up briefly to see that all his men were at their oars, faced away from him. He scooped up river water and set to work. Her makeshift hat fell off but he didn't retrieve it just yet.

How could anyone have ever believed her a boy? Her hair, as red as an early fall sunset over Vestfold, nearly as bright as the bolt of bloodred silk he'd seen from Baghdad two years before, curled in ragged clumps around her face and down her neck. A pretty face, he thought, never a boy's face. But so very thin. He still feared she would die. Not from the beating Thrasco had given her, but from knowing hunger for too long.

After he'd bathed her back, he dressed her again in Eller's tunic. She slept again. He gave her over to Cleve and took his turn at the oars, for he was restless. Taby still sat on Oleg's thighs and when Merrik looked toward him, he saw fear, not so much now, but it was still enough to make him want to clutch the child to him and protect him forever. He smiled painfully and said, "Your sister is sleeping. I bathed her again and tended her back. The fever is nearly gone."

He hoped it was the truth. He could do no more for her. He nodded to the child, and bent back to the oars. The day remained calm and hot, with scarcely a breeze to cool the men. They let the longboat drift close to shore in the mid-afternoon to rest and drink ale from the barrel Roran had dangled from a rope overboard to cool in the river water. The silence was absolute, save for the soft slapping of the water against the sides of the longboat and their low conversation. They were well beyond Chernigov now and drawing to within a half day of Gnezdovo and Smolensk where the Dnieper ended just beyond, curling eastward. They would sail to the far shore at roughly the mid-distance between the two towns before the sun set tonight, then early tomorrow morning, they would drag the longboat ashore to begin the portage overland to the river Dvina. The portage wasn't overly difficult, the ground was mostly flat, a wide road worn down over the years by hundreds of traders. Viking traders in the past years had killed most of the savages who had attacked trading vessels, or taken them as slaves, but if there were still some of the savages nearby, Merrik didn't want to alert them, and that was odd of him, for he always relished a good fight. But now he wanted no trouble and it was because of the small boy and the girl who were helpless and in his charge.

When she awoke again and yawned deeply, it was Merrik's face above her. He smiled at her and stuffed some bread into her mouth. She chewed silently, then opened her mouth again. He fed her until once again she shook her head, a look of pleased amazement on her thin face. He gave her cool ale to drink. Then she said, "I wish to go ashore for a moment."

He stared at her. "What?"

"I wish to go ashore."

"You cannot. There could be danger. We will continue northward for three more hours, then we will go ashore and camp for the night."

"You are a coward then."

He shook his head at her. "Were you truly a boy, you would surely be dead by now. You forget again that you are alive only because I decided to intervene."

She winced. He didn't know whether it was from pain in her back or from the reminder of what she owed him.

She looked at him straight on and said, "I must relieve myself."

He said matter-of-factly, "You have seen the men relieve themselves. It is more difficult for you, a female, but nonetheless, you must do it. I will stand in front of you to give you some privacy. Do you wish to do it now?"

She nodded.

Once she was finished, he helped her sit down beside him. "That wasn't so very bad, was it?"

"It was bad," she said, not looking at him. "It's always been bad. At first I couldn't bear it, it was more humiliation than I thought one could endure. Then I realized that all regarded it with indifference, save for those who enjoyed shaming the slaves. They enjoyed watching closely and laughing. When I became a boy it was all the more difficult." She sighed, then grinned. "I became quite good at aping the boys. I would turn my back, position my arms just so, and all would think it a boy relieving himself. It was an act, of course, to lull any suspicions."

"How long were you a female before you changed to a boy's garb?"

"Not long, it was too dangerous. I didn't wish to be ravished. Being a boy was safer."

"Not in Kiev and to the south," he said.

"Then I was lucky not to be in the south," she said, and her voice was cool and he wondered if she were lying. He couldn't tell.

He said, "If ever I intend to humiliate you, it will not be in that fashion. I gave you what privacy I could. I could do no more for you."

"I know."

"How do you feel?"

She looked surprised, then said, "Much better."

She squared her skinny shoulders, winced, and let them relax again. "Perhaps not all that ready to kill your enemies," he said.

"No, not quite."

She was different, from her red hair and white flesh to the natural arrogance in her that should have been beaten out of her a long time ago. "How old are you?"

"I am eighteen."

"How old is Taby?"

"He is nearly six now."

"How long were both of you slaves?"

"Nearly two years—nay, I forget. It isn't important. There is no reason for you to know, no reason for you to be interested."

"It matters not that you told me. Had it been longer than two years, you would probably be dead, at least Taby would. It is amazing that you managed to keep him alive for two years. He was naught but a baby. Where do you come from?"

She shook her head and said, "I am from a place much like the place you come from. It is a place I will return to, in my own time, when I am ready to return. And I meant it, Viking, I want to buy the three of us from you." She drew a deep breath. "I will pay you for the clothes, I will pay you for what you paid for Taby, for—"

He wanted to cuff her. Instead he grabbed her arm and jerked her around to face him. "My name is Merrik. You will use it. You will also learn to mind that tongue of yours. No wonder Thrasco beat you. How many other masters have flayed the hide off you for your insolence?"

She shook her head, looking at him straight in his eyes. "Only one, the first one. I kept quiet after that. But I did win, for she bought Taby as well."

"And why has your learning failed you now? Do you believe me too soft to beat you?"

Her eyes shifted and she looked over his left shoulder, toward Cleve, who was holding Taby's hand, looking down at him and listening to him speak. "You aren't like the others," she said. "You are not soft, but you are different. I don't fear you, at least I don't fear that you will beat me or Taby."

"You should fear me only if you find obedience to me difficult."

She shook away his words. "You are different, aren't you? You won't sell us or hurt us or give us to your friends? When I asked you before, you mocked me."

"I will think about it. Perhaps one of those choices you named will suit me. I will eventually determine some gain the three of you will bring me, but I will have to think about it, perhaps discuss it with Oleg, whose hand you nearly chewed off. In any case, I must fatten you up first, for now no man would want to grind his body against a woman with more bones than soft flesh."

She said matter-of-factly, "I have learned that men will grind themselves against any female who is not dead. I became a boy after I saw a man rape a girl. He cuffed her until there was blood streaming from her nose and mouth and then he tore off her clothes and raped her. I don't know if she lived. When he was finished with her, she was bloody everywhere. If I'd had a knife I would have killed him. If you decide to sell me to a man who would do that, I would kill him."

"Then perhaps you should consider more gentleness of word and manner toward me." He supposed it pleased him that she didn't consider the possibility that he would rape her. But he could if he wished to, surely she knew that. Surely she knew he could do whatever he wished to her. On past trading voyages, he'd been given slave girls to pleasure him, thus making him more apt to spend his silver and trade his goods with the men providing the girls. Would she believe he had raped the girls? They'd never fought him or cried out. He'd never raised his fist to any one of them. He'd never hurt any of them. Or had he? And hadn't he simply left that merchant's house in Kiev when he'd seen Thrasco plowing that girl? Aye, he'd left, disgusted with what he'd seen. Still, a female slave was for the use of her masters, wasn't she? He frowned, disliking the way of his thoughts. He dragged his hand through the fresh, cool water, wondering yet again why he had rescued these three from Kiev. Surely he had been struck by a madness, a strange sort of malady that would leave him soon enough. His hand fisted in the water, spewing a light rain upward to his chest and throat.

"Why did you stare at me at the slave market?"

5

H<small>E DIDN'T LOOK</small> at her, rather at the huge sail that was flapping wildly overhead. He held his hand up to dry and to feel the exact direction of the wind. He said with complete indifference, "Why do you think I would stare at you?"

"You did. I remember feeling that someone was staring at me and that's why I looked up. There you were, standing there as if you'd been frozen and you were looking hard at me."

He shrugged. "It's true, no need to quibble about it. I don't know why. I simply saw you and I couldn't look away. Then you looked at me and I thought you defeated, utterly, then just as suddenly, your eyes held such anger, such bitterness, that still I couldn't look away from you. I didn't understand you. You intrigued me."

She said nothing.

"Then there was Taby. That is truly odd. I have no particular liking for children. But these feelings for him went deeply within me the moment I saw him. I did not understand them then nor do I now, but I will keep Taby safe."

"That is why you came to save me, then, isn't it? This feeling you have for Taby, you wanted only him but you had to save me, too, in order to make him happy."

"Aye, that's more the way of it than not, though you did interest me as well."

"You will get over these odd feelings for my little brother. You're a man; men don't love children, not as women do. They are proud of them if they show prowess in something a man admires, but to have love for them, to give them attention, it's more a thing of words for men, not of action, as it is for women."

"You appear to be knowledgeable beyond your years," he said, sarcasm thick as he looked toward the shoreline and not at her. "Your words are perhaps true for the men in your country but I doubt it. Men are men. My father loves me and my brothers. His affection for us isn't to be questioned. He also cuffed us and praised us in equal amounts, and taught us endlessly when we were boys. As to my feelings for Taby, you have no idea what kind of man I am or what I will or will not feel for him in a year or in five years."

"He is no kin to you. He doesn't carry your blood. I know this is important to men. You will easily forget Taby once you are home again. What will your wife think of a child you bring back to her?"

"I have no wife."

"Men must have wives to have heirs. You will have a wife soon enough. You are still young, but not that young. Men must breed when they are young else their seed loses its potency. Aye, you will have a wife and then will you expect her to care for Taby? What if she were cruel to him? It isn't fair, Merrik. This is why you must let me buy him back from you, before you come to care nothing more for him, before your wife hurts him, before you come to sell him."

"You spin better tales than a skald, and none of it has a footing in truth. Also, you will stop asking that question. You have no silver, you have nothing to buy anything, much less three people."

"I can get silver, a lot of it, more than a man like you could possibly trade for or ever steal."

"Do I scent a ransom in your insult? Do you have rich parents, relatives? Is that the silver you speak of?"

"Perhaps."

"*Perhaps* is a word for weasels. Truth slithers about on your agile tongue like a toad through swamp grass. If there is someone who would ransom you, tell me. I will consider it. At least I can send a man to this person and ask him if he still wants you back, if he still even remembers you or the child. Since he is a man, perhaps he will have forgotten you since he would have no particular love or affection for you."

He could see her mind squirreling about madly, see the myriad shifting expressions on her face. He waited to see what she would say. He awaited lies. He was a bit surprised when she let out her breath in a gasp, saying, "I cannot tell you anything. There is someone, but I'm not certain. Perhaps that someone is no longer there. But, heed me, I buried silver long ago. Aye, that is it. I have a buried treasure."

Ah, at last the lie, but not at first, no, that was truth of a sort. He raised an eyebrow. "For just this emergency?"

"You mock me, Viking. A man like you could never understand."

"A man like me? I thought you said I was different."

"You're still a Viking. You are a warrior even though you are a trader as well, and you kill without hesitation, if killing would gain you something you want. I accept the manner of man you are. I know more of your practices than you could imagine. Also, during the past two years I have learned to recognize the way of things. I have learned that if you don't at least pretend acceptance, you will rot in a ditch quickly enough or be beaten to death."

"So you do have people who would ransom you if you could but get a message to them, people who would want you back." He stared thoughtfully at his feet, big feet, as brown and strong as his hands. He leaned down and scratched his toe. None of the men, she'd noticed, wore boots or shoes whilst in the longboat. All their belongings and clothes were in the chests upon which they sat. He said slowly, not looking up at her, "This is curious. You don't wish to tell me anything because you're afraid any message I sent would reach the wrong people." He looked up then to see her face whiten, if such a thing were possible. Perhaps getting her to tell him the truth would present something of a challenge, but if he guessed the truth, it was as apparent as a maiden's blush in her expression.

He said nothing more, merely leaned over to speak to Old Firren. It was a long time before he spoke to her again, and when he did, it made her start, so deep and strangled was she into her own thoughts.

"Your name—Laren—it is odd. Where do you come from?"

She was wary now, very wary, and said only, "Far away from Kiev."

"But not that far away from Norway? From England? From Ireland?"

"It is not of concern to you."

He chose to let the arrogance of her amuse him. It was either that or wring her neck. "Your eyes have more gray than blue in this bright light."

"Not all that common a color in my land, is that what you want to know? It is common enough. As for your eyes, Merrik, the blue is like the clear summer sky overhead, too clear and pure to be guileless. Aye, they could hide deceit in their depths, they could lie cleanly to the one looking at you. Your eyes are just like those of every other man from your country. Just look at Oleg yon. His eyes are darker, but nonetheless, enough the same."

"Roran has black eyes."

"The man with one ear? He looks like an Arab. Surely he is not a Viking."

An Arab, he thought. Where had she come from before she'd reached Kiev? Miklagard? The Caliphate? Perhaps as far away as Bulgar?

"Surely he isn't one of your countrymen."

"He's from the Danelaw, near to York. His mother is a Saxon, but his father a Viking merchant."

She nodded.

She knows the Danelaw, then, he thought, or at least she has heard of it.

Oleg called out, "Merrik, Eller smells something."

"What does that mean?" she asked.

"Eller's nose is magical. Sit still beside me, for we must get into the center of the river quickly."

"I don't see anyone on shore. No one, nothing."

"It doesn't matter. Once I ignored Eller's nose to my great cost. Never again. Be quiet and keep your head down."

The men were silent now, once again concentrating all their energy on getting the longboat back into the strong current and moving swiftly away from the scent that reached Eller's nose. The wind picked up as they reached the middle of the river and they tightened the huge wadmal sail, its squares of black, green, and gold vivid in the afternoon sun. Four men held the lines, making them taut when they sailed too close into the wind, and slacking off when the sail flapped too wildly away from the wind.

She looked back and saw men now lining the shore, waving spears and rocks at them, yelling. They didn't look friendly. Still, how could they have harmed the Viking longboat?

She leaned back her head and breathed in the clean air. She felt he was toying with her, and doubtless he was, but she wouldn't tell him more, she couldn't afford to. He was too close to the truth and she was too afraid. No, what would happen in the future would be what she would make happen. She would be responsible, she alone. Still, as she felt the river breeze cool her forehead and make her eyelids droop, she knew again something of the taste of freedom. Perhaps, at last, she was free. Both she and Taby.

She looked at her little brother, sitting on Cleve's knee, pressed against his chest. She looked at the hideous scar on Cleve's face and wondered what vicious mistress had ordered this done to him and why. What offense could warrant this? Ah, but without the scar, he would be a handsome man, with his thick golden hair and bronze flesh. And his smile was full and laughing, his teeth as straight and white as the Viking's.

She frowned and looked at Merrik's back. The wind had slackened and the men were rowing again. He was big and obviously he was very strong. He was bare to his waist, his tunic lying over his legs, his flesh deeply tanned, and the muscles in his back and arms worked with the strength of youth and health, deep firm muscles that glistened with sweat beneath the sun. She'd seen many men in the past two years—men old enough to die, men too young for the power they held, men who were broken in their spirits and bodies, men who were so fat like Thrasco they wheezed just getting a spoon to their mouths.

This Merrik was a beautiful man, she would give him that. His body was splendid in its vigor and shape, his very leanness purifying the lines of him. His face was well looking, strong in its features, his jaw showing his boldness and determination. He could be as stubborn as a pig, she didn't doubt that, not a bad thing if one wanted to survive.

But he was a Viking, like all other Vikings, and she didn't know the sort of man Norway bred. She'd told him he was different and so he was. She'd never met a man like him, but that didn't mean she could trust him. That was something the past two years had taught her well. She'd quickly come to know perfidy and treachery and the smell of lies. Her nose was as good as Eller's when it came to recognizing the cruelty and selfishness of people, and thus she now well understood the need for caution. Trust was something for fools. She was no longer a fool.

Ah, but he had saved her and Taby and Cleve. But he wouldn't say what it was he intended to do with them.

He was a trader before he was a warrior. He now had three human beings to trade. Surely he didn't intend to keep them for himself, and if he did, what would that mean? His reasons for saving her and Taby sounded true to her, but still she couldn't credit it—just this look at Taby and he'd been compelled to save both of them? Men didn't behave like that. Vikings would impale a child on their swords before they'd consider saving them, being burdened with them.

She was shaking her head even as she watched him quit the oars, rise and stretch, and walk back to where she sat, the crooked cloth-covered wooden bowl on her head. He was wearing only a loincloth, and it rode low on his lean belly. The hair on his chest and belly was golden, crisp, and thick. She looked away from him. He was too big, too intimidating.

He sat down beside her as he pulled his tunic over his head and she smelled his sweat and the scent of him that was dark and pleasant. He said something to Old Firren, who just spat into the river, and then turned to her. He just looked at her for a very long time, at the exhaustion that still blurred her eyes, lining them beneath with faint purple shadows. He said nothing, just patted his thighs.

She fell asleep with her face on his thigh, her hands pillowed beneath her cheek. Merrik moved slightly to give her more protection from the afternoon sun.

They pulled the longboat out of the river at dusk. There were many marks and blurred footprints on the ground from other boats that had left the river at this point, for it was the shortest land route to the river Dvina. It would take them nearly four days to reach the river Dvina, longer if it rained, untold nightmare days if it rained heavily. It was backbreaking work and there was always danger from tribes who hid between the two mighty rivers, waiting for unwary traders to come along.

Merrik didn't use rollers for the simple reason that the longboat wasn't large enough to carry the rollers and trade goods and men, not without making any voyage more miserable than need be. No, they used brute strength. They were young. They had a lot of it.

The first time Merrik had voyaged to Kiev, he'd made it a point to search out a tribe during the portage and to kill every man he captured. He didn't kill any of the women or children nor did he take them as slaves, though he could have made something of a profit in Kiev. No, he let them remain in their village and he made certain that all the women and children knew his name before he and his men were on their way again. He showed them all the silver raven carved in rich walnut that stood high on the prow. No other longboat, he told them several times, had this same figurehead. He hoped this would gain him a reputation and cause other tribes to stay away from him. On a trading voyage the last thing he wanted was to lose any men.

He'd now made three voyages to Kiev. There had been only one attack, and that one halfhearted, a brief testing of his strength. He'd lost only one man and killed twenty of the enemy. Another message to hostile tribes.

All prayed to Thor for dry weather and, more times than not, the god had listened to their pleas and given them heat and sun. He heard Roran asking Eller why he couldn't smell out rain. It was a near litany, for all could remember a portage when Thor hadn't heeded their prayers. It had rained so hard that it had taken them nearly eight days to drag the longboat through the slogging deep mud.

"I remember this," she said, looking around her. "That is, I remember the doing of this but it was a different route."

He tucked away that bit of information. "Do you now?"

She looked at him quickly, then away.

"So you came by way of Lake Ladoga and Novgorod."

She shook her head. "It isn't important. Perhaps that was it, or perhaps it was just a dream that came to me from another's mind. I will see to Taby."

"Stay close. These next four days will be dangerous."

He looked at her a moment, wondering if she had

indeed been brought by way of the river Neva to Lake Ladoga and then to Lake Ilmen. That would mean that she'd been brought by way of the Baltic. But many more traders and merchants voyaged through the Baltic to take that route, all of them carrying slaves captured from every land imaginable. It was a route that took much longer, but it was less dangerous than this route. Merrik remembered his brother Rorik laughing at him, saying, "You would journey by way of the moon if one were to assure you that it would be more deadly. Your taste for danger will bring you low." As much as he'd told his brother he didn't seek out danger, particularly when he had valuable furs and goods to trade, he wasn't believed. His brother remembered how easily heated his passions could become and how quickly his temper would erupt when he'd been younger. But growing into his manhood for five years had made him different.

He and his men steadied the longboat just off balance, not wanting to put all the weight on its keel for the portage. He looked around, then looked at Eller, who sniffed and shook his head. Oddly enough, now he was worried as he had never been before. Always before he felt anticipation, excitement, a vague longing that there would be a tribe to attack them, an enemy to test himself upon, particularly when they were on their way back from their trading ventures. He much preferred protecting silver than he did slaves or goods or furs.

But now he was worried and he knew why. It was Laren and Taby. He had to keep them safe. He didn't like it one bit. He enjoyed fighting, had never sought to avoid it, but since he'd gotten her away from Thrasco's house in Kiev, he'd done nothing but choose the safest route. Except now. But he didn't want to take the extra weeks just to avoid possible trouble.

He looked over at her. She still wasn't standing

straight because of the pulling pain in her back, but her chin was up. She stood like a princess—a very thin, a very ragged princess—staring as the men worked the longboat up onto the rough trail made by so many longboats before them. Taby moved away from Cleve to stand beside her. He saw the child smile up at her. It was just a simple smile yet it pulled at him. He looked quickly away before he saw her expression.

They pulled the longboat over the pitted path throughout the morning, stopping only briefly to eat and rest. The weather held hot and dry.

The men were exhausted by the evening, for Merrik had pushed them hard. They couldn't waste the good weather, he'd told them again and again. He himself was breathing heavily, his shoulders and arms cramping, his legs feeling like great weights dragged at them.

He looked over at her to see that she was also breathing hard, as if she'd been running a long distance, only she hadn't, she was still very weak, both from the bone-deep hunger that had gone on far, far too long, and the beating. He looked over at Taby, standing quietly beside her, saying nothing, merely staying close, nearly touching her, and suddenly he felt a new spurt of energy. His men went about their tasks, all very familiar with what they had to do.

Eller oversaw the gathering of wood for a small fire and built it up. Old Firren hooked the iron pot from a chain he attached to the three iron poles that were fastened at the top, and prepared to serve up the dried meat and cheesy curds and boil some vegetables.

Oleg set up the perimeter so that they could guard the longboat and themselves. Roran and three other men went hunting. As for Merrik, it was his job to oversee things, but now he didn't. He walked to her and said, "You are very tired. I have spread furs in the tent for you and Taby. You will rest now, both of you. Cleve will bring you food when it is prepared."

She looked at him, at his blond hair plastered to his head with sweat, at the rivulets of sweat streaking down his face, at his arms, still wet with sweat, the muscles still flexing. "Did we come as far as you wished to?"

"Aye, a bit farther even. I don't trust those clouds building to the east of us. Rest now, both of you."

"I know how to cook."

Merrik stared at her as if she'd said instead that she practiced some sort of old Celtic magic. Old Firren usually cooked and what he prepared was edible, but no more. "Do you really?"

"Aye, I cook very well."

Still he just looked at her.

"I learned from a woman just last year. She said I was apt, for a slave. She cuffed me every time I prepared something not to her liking. I learned quickly. It was either that or go deaf from the blows to my head."

"Very well. You will speak to Old Firren. We have vegetables from Kiev—cabbage, peas, some apples, rice, and onions. Roran is hunting. Mayhap he will bring in a pheasant or a quail."

"I will make a stew."

She made, with Old Firren's nominal help, a rabbit stew, with Cleve and Taby also helping her. She stood over the huge iron pot, stirring the stew with a long-handled wooden spoon. The men sat about the fire, cleaning their weapons, or paced the perimeter, always on the lookout for enemies. The sky darkened and Merrik worried, but kept silent about it. Soon his mouth was watering at the smell of the stew. His men looked ready to do battle for it. They were all moving closer to the pot, all staring at it intently.

His first bite made Merrik close his eyes in absolute wonder. His second made him grunt with pleasure.

There was no talk from the men, just the sounds of chewing and swallowing, and the sighs of satisfaction.

She looked at them and smiled. She filled her belly quickly, too quickly, and she looked sadly at the rest of the stew in her wooden bowl. She had made more stew than ever before and yet it was eaten, all of it, not a bit left. Old Firren looked at her and grinned, showing a wide space between his teeth.

"I hate the taste of my cooking," he said. He heard laughter and agreement from the men. "My belly is singing."

"Your belly sings a simple tune," Oleg shouted. "My belly believes it's gained Valhalla and is being caressed by the Valkyrie."

The men laughed, and each one of them thanked her. When Merrik told her it was the best meal any of them had eaten since leaving Norway, Taby said, "Before she didn't know anything. All the servants did that, but then when we were—"

She clamped her hand over his mouth, hissing, "Merrik isn't interested in that, Taby. Say nothing more."

The child looked at her, frowning, but he slowly nodded.

Merrik merely smiled. He held out his hand to Taby. The child looked at his hand, then very slowly, tentatively, he placed his own small one in Merrik's. Merrik said easily, "My mother cooks well. Travelers and kin hate to leave just because of her cooking. Now there is pain in her fingers and it is a chore for her, but Sarla, my brother's wife, is learning." He paused a moment, then added with a slight frown, "You cook as well as my mother." He said nothing more, just lifted Taby into his arms and carried him to the campfire. The men were talking low, sporadically, for the most part just content to sit there before the fire, their bellies satisfied.

"I would hear a story," Merrik said. "Deglin, have you a new one to tell us?"

Deglin smiled up at Merrik, a sly smile that made his cat's chin even more pointed. He looked at Taby and said, "Have you heard tell of the great warrior Grunlige the Dane? No? Then sit with Merrik and I will tell you of him before you sleep."

All the men settled back, for all loved the tales they'd heard since their own childhood.

Deglin had been the Haraldsson skald for nearly four years. He knew well his audience. He spoke slowly, emphasis on the words he deemed most important, his eyes on the men to see their reaction. His voice was deep and low as he said, "Ah, listen all of you to this tale. It is of Grunlige the Dane, a man who could break the neck of a cow with one hand. He was so strong that he wrestled with four bulls and then slaughtered them all for the winter solstice feast. Even with his mighty strength, he knew honor and never did he hurt those who did not deserve it. When he and his men were voyaging back to Denmark, they were caught in huge ice floes that threatened to crush their vessels to sticks of wood. Grunlige leapt upon the first ice floe and began to tear it to little pieces with his bare hands. His men pleaded with him to wrap his hands in skins and furs, but he didn't heed them. He broke up the ice floe, then leapt to the second and then to the third. When all the ice floes were but shards of ice in the sea, as harmless as grits of sand on a shore, he swam back to his longboat. He looked at his hands, those hands that had strangled a ferocious bear in Iceland, and saw that they were blue as the frigid water from the cold. And he said to his men, 'I cannot feel my hands.'

"And his men wrapped his hands in furs and skins, but it was too late. His hands were frozen. When they thawed with the coming of spring, they were withered and looked like small animal claws, the fingernails still the blue of the sea, and there was no more strength in them. All grieved for Grunlige's plight, save his enemies who rejoiced in secret and feasted and plotted against him." Deglin paused, then smiled toward Taby. "And that is all I will tell you tonight."

Taby, as well as all the men, were sitting still as stones, bent forward, toward Deglin. There was a collective sigh and moans, for all knew he couldn't be cajoled or bribed to finish the tale until he wanted to.

" 'Tis a new tale just for you, Taby," Merrik said to the child, who was lying in his arms, his cheek against Merrik's chest. "Thank you, Deglin. You will tell us more soon?"

"Aye, Merrik. The boy needs to sleep now. I did not wish to waste my words on these sods when Taby is so sleepy he can't appreciate my greatness."

Laren slipped back into the tent, her heart pounding with excitement at the story she'd just heard, and with words and ideas of her own that jostled and tumbled about, words that wanted to spew out of her mouth. She hugged them to her as she eased down between two thick wolf hides to sleep. What a wondrous tale, but it was important that it continue with . . .

"Taby will sleep with us," Merrik said, easing the child down beside her. He said nothing more, merely arranged himself to his own comfort and was soon asleep.

When she screamed, he had his sword in his right hand and his knife in his left hand within seconds.

6

H<small>E WAS LEANING</small> over her, so close to her that she
could feel his breath hot on her face and smell the stale
wine he'd drunk.

She wasn't afraid at first, no, just confused, for it was
the dead of night, and she'd been sleeping soundly and
who would want to come into her chamber in the dead
of night to see her? His face was very close now, she
could hear his breathing, and she forced her eyes to
open to stare up at him, and in the dim light. She saw
him clearly, and what she saw sent bile into her throat.
For an instant she was frozen with fear. She wanted to
scream, but there was naught but desert dryness in her
throat. His hands were on her then, rough hands, and
it jolted her. She reared up, trying to jerk away from
him, to run, but his hands were hard around her arms
now, holding her down, his fingers digging so deeply
into her flesh she felt the pain to her bones. He was
grinning at her, and she realized this wasn't a dream
or someone's jest and that this man was here to hurt
her.

Taby!

He'd been lying beside her, his child's restless nature
having sent him into her chamber, and she'd held him
close and soothed him and sung to him of the valiant

deeds of his uncle and his father until he'd fallen asleep again.

"Aye," the man said, "I've got her."

Fighting him now would gain her nothing. It was the hardest thing she'd ever done, but she forced herself to go limp. To her unspeakable relief, the man's hands eased and he grunted, "I think the little girl fainted from fright."

Another man said, "She saw your ugly face. It's good she fainted. I was told she's wild as a wolf. I have the child. He's no larger than a loaf of flatbread. Tie her arms and legs, then bring her. There are too many guards about for my liking, more than promised. Not close, but still, I want to finish this quickly."

She waited another moment, forcing herself to be utterly slack, just for a brief instant. She counted slowly, each second, feeling the terror cramp her muscles, feeling her throat close, wanting to suck in air, but she didn't dare, not yet. Finally the other man had moved off with Taby. She grabbed the bronze candle holder beside her bed, lifted it, and smashed it against the man's head. He yowled, hurtling away from her. She was on her feet then, and she was kicking him in his belly and his legs, striking him again and again, sending him to his knees. She saw blood gush from a blow against the side of his head. Then the other man whirled about, stared in astonishment at the scene, and came running back and she knew she had no chance against the two of them. He dropped Taby on the bed, then turned to her, his hands out toward her. She leapt back away from both of them, hurled back her head and screamed as loud as she could, screamed and screamed . . .

But they were both on her now, their hands digging into her flesh, making her screams real cries of pain, and it wouldn't stop for they were violent with anger and still she screamed and screamed. The man struck her hard in the jaw, but still she cried out until the blackness covered her mind, and she wondered even as all thought slipped away from her: *Why hasn't anyone come to help us?*

"Damnation, wake up!"

The scream broke off, dissolving into a deep moan. Merrik dropped his sword and knife and grabbed her shoulders, shaking her. "Wake up!" he shouted in her face.

"Don't you hurt my sister!"

Taby was suddenly on Merrik's back, beating his fists against his shoulders, jerking at his hair. Laren awoke fully, saw the man over her and screamed again. She raised her fists to strike at him. No, no, wait, wait . . . It was Merrik and Taby was on his back, yelling at him, hitting him, all the while sobbing, tears streaming down his thin cheeks, sounds so ragged she wanted to howl with the pain it brought her.

Now she'd terrified him with her stupid screams, illusion screams that had no meaning, that had naught to do with anything save her fear from that long-ago night. She felt the humiliation of it go deep inside her, that and her anger at herself for succumbing and crying out like a fool. It had been months since she'd dreamed of that night, but it had come again, more intense this time, but still she was used to it, should be used to it enough that she wouldn't squeal like a stoat. Aye, she should be used to the terror it brought her, terror still as fresh in her mind as the night it had been real. Only this time she'd awakened Merrik and frightened her little brother. She drew a deep breath, tried to make her voice calm, and said, "Taby, it's all right, sweeting. No, don't hit Merrik. He was trying to wake me up. I had a nightmare and it was so very real, but it's over now. Come on, Taby, it's all right. Come to me."

Merrik hadn't moved. He simply waited until she had the child in her arms, unaware until that moment that he had been straddling her, his bare thighs locked against her sides. No wonder Taby thought he was attacking his sister.

Slowly he eased off her and came down on his side to look at her in the dim light of dawn. She was facing him, holding Taby against her, rocking him, and singing to him, her face buried in the child's neck. She sensed him looking at her, and gazed over at him.

"Tell me," he said.

She ducked her head down and continued to rock Taby. The child pulled away from her, and came up on his knees beside her. He leaned down and touched his fingers to her face. "Was it the bad men again?"

"Aye, but still just a dream, Taby, just a dream."

"What bad men?" Merrik said.

"It was only a dream, a dream that comes to me when I'm very tired. I'm sorry I woke you. I'm a fool. But it was just a silly dream, nothing more, Merrik."

"I see," he said, and stood. He looked down at her in the pale light, saw that chin of hers go up so high that by all rights she should be forced to stare at the top of the tent, then left her.

She heard the men grumble when Merrik shouted at them to wake up. She hugged Taby tightly against her, then said, "You mustn't say anything to Merrik about that other time. Besides, you don't remember it very well. He wouldn't understand. It was a long time ago, Taby, a very long time ago."

"Why do you still have bad dreams about it?"

A child, she thought as she kissed his cheek, always went directly to the hidden core. "It was a bad time," she said honestly. "A very bad time, but we are safe now."

"Merrik will take care of us."

She hated the confidence in his voice, his child's utter certainty. She also hated having to rely on a man, particularly this man who was a Viking, surely one of the most ruthless and vicious of men on this benighted earth. Aye, she didn't want to rely on him, not for her safety, not for all her needs and Taby's needs. During the past two years, she'd learned men were vicious and brutal, not to be trusted, taking what they wanted, feeling no remorse, having no conscience. Also she'd learned that to trust in anything or in anyone could leave one dead or worse, though at the moment she couldn't think of anything worse than death. She remembered Thrasco's beating. That had been close. She unconsciously flexed her shoulders as she stood, and leaned first to the right and then to the left. There was only a little pulling, nothing to draw her down into that choking pain.

She said to Taby, "I don't want him to take care of us." Her voice was too sharp and Taby flinched back from her. "Nay, sweeting, it isn't Merrik's responsibility to care for us. He is a man and men don't feel comfortable about caring for those who aren't part of their blood family. He's caring for us just for now, that's all. Then I will take care of both of us. We are still a long way from home, but soon, perhaps very soon, we will return."

She wondered if she believed it herself. How could she return when she didn't know the face of her enemy? She wondered, as she had countless times during the past two years, what home was like now.

* * *

With loud cheers and equally loud prayers of thanksgiving to Thor, the men finally shoved the longboat into the Gulf of Riga six days later. They'd been slowed by a violent storm that had shredded the men's tempers and tested their strength, but it had only lasted a day and a half, nothing all that dreadful, but dreadful enough. When the longboat slid smoothly into the clear blue water of the gulf, she and all of the men breathed a deep sigh of relief.

No one had attacked them.

Thor had given them a safe portage, they'd earned a lot of silver from their trading, and all were thankful. When they camped that evening, she decided she would make them a delicious dinner.

Her back was healed now, but still, she tired too quickly, and it angered her, this weakness, this continued betrayal by her body. Merrik had merely laughed at her that morning when she'd cursed her weariness in language as colorful as the brightly plumed birds they saw in the forest. As for Taby, she could now look at him without pain. His cheeks were no longer sunken, but were rounding out again. He walked upright, no longer bowed down with hunger. There was light in his eyes, not the dull blank acceptance, or silent questions to her that she couldn't answer. And his laughter, that was the best of it all. Just a few moments ago when the men were cheering their safe portage, Merrik had suddenly lifted Taby high in the air, swinging him over his head. Taby had shrieked with laughter. Laren had simply stood there, watching them and listening to her little brother's joy.

They brought her venison for supper. She cut the meat into thick steaks and seasoned them with snow berries and juniper roots, then wrapped them in wide maple leaves rubbed with venison fat.

After the meal, the men, their bellies full and content, shouted for Deglin to finish his tale of Grunlige the Dane.

But Deglin was sulking. Merrik had told him earlier that he would be in charge of keeping the furs brushed and clean, and most importantly, to make certain they were kept dry in the hold of the longboat. Deglin had thought himself above such a chore, but Merrik had held firm, and Deglin had grumbled endlessly as he'd done it, making the men want to yell at him and Merrik want to break his neck.

So Deglin refused to do anything now, telling Merrik and the men that it was his genius that enabled him to tell them stories and that the genius had been overworked by brushing and cleaning the furs, a task that didn't merit his skills and talent. He was a skald and was to be revered, not worked like a slave, and he'd looked at Laren, who was busy adding vegetables to the buck the men had killed and said she was a slave, she should have tended the furs. Merrik said, "There are few furs, only those we are taking back to our families as gifts. Your tasks were light, Deglin, and the furs important."

But Deglin sniffed and said his bowels weren't happy with the foul offal *she* had made them eat. He took himself off into the pine trees and relieved himself for an hour. The venison steaks had been delicious, but she didn't say anything. The men grumbled at Deglin's perversity. Several began throwing pebbles in a test of their accuracy. After a while, though, they were bored.

It was then she said, "I have thought about Grunlige the Dane. Perhaps I can continue the story in Deglin's stead."

The men looked at her as if she'd lost her wits. She could cook. She was a woman. They stared at her.

She merely looked back at them gravely, saying nothing more.

It was Taby, sitting between Merrik's legs, leaning back against his chest, who said, "Do tell us, Laren, your stories are wonderful."

"Aye," Oleg said, with no real conviction. "We've naught else to do. Tell us what you can."

"I'm full with venison and care not what comes to my ears," Old Firren said. "Go ahead, girl."

Merrik said nothing. He held Taby. But she knew that he, like all the other men, believed that no woman could spin a tale to hold a man's interest, for all knew women had no talent for it. The skalds were men, only men, and all knew . . .

Laren pitched her voice low and smooth and leaned slightly toward the men to gain their full attention, something she'd seen her uncle's skald do many, many times. "When Grunlige said, 'I cannot feel my hands,' and all his men were saddened at the sight of the hideous shrunken claws his hands had become, it seemed that all his mighty strength, his miraculous courage, would be no more. It took not many months for him to grow shorter, for his shoulders and head were always bent, his eyes on the ground, since there was no hope in his heart to look to heaven.

"All his friends fell silent when he was near. Not long thereafter, Grunlige went off by himself and many believed that he had gone off to die, for what reason was there for him to continue? He had no more strength and, thus, no more pride, and therein lay his own knowledge of his worth and his sense of his own greatness. But after three days he returned, blank-faced and silent.

"His enemies rejoiced, but in private, for they knew that Grunlige was popular with many people, far and near, and it wasn't wise to speak happily of what had befallen him. Some of them began to make their plans. Evil men they were, and they knew not honor. They weren't Vikings, not valiant warriors, but rather Saxon raiders, mean-spirited and petty, and they knew only betrayal and treachery. They decided to raid his holdings.

"Thus in the months that followed, they seized his warships, stole his slaves, his silver and gold. They would kill his people and steal cattle and sheep. One even wanted to kidnap Grunlige's beautiful wife, Selina.

"And so it began and continued. His men cried out, begging Grunlige to help them, but Grunlige said nothing, merely bowed his head and drank his ale until he was senseless and his slaves had to carry him off to his bed. Then one day, ah, it was just after dawn on a hot morning in the summer, Parma, an evil Saxon raider from Wessex, managed to steal into the main farmstead where Selina lived. He was a tall man, dark visaged, his eyebrows so thick they met over his eyes. He hated Grunlige and knew his best revenge on him wouldn't be his own death but the loss of his beloved wife. Grunlige had killed his brother when the man had been drunk on mead and flogged to death one of Grunlige's favorite horses. Thus the reason for Parma's hatred. On that morning, Parma saw her and she was alone, sitting quietly beside a stream, staring at nothing really, thinking about her husband, and the ill fate that had befallen him. He snuck up on her, making not a single sound, and when he stood right behind her, he said, 'My name is Parma and I have come to take you, Selina, wife of Grunlige. I will treat you as I would treat Grunlige were he my prisoner. I will have you on your knees begging for mercy. Then I will flog you just as Grunlige flogged my brother.'

"She showed no fright, but turned to look up at this evil man and said, 'If you touch me, Parma, you will regret it until the moment breath leaves your lungs.'

"He laughed loudly, for she was but a woman, slight, of no account at all. Just a woman, but she was Grunlige's woman and thus Parma wanted her. He leaned down to grab her. But when his hands touched her arms something very strange happened."

Laren smiled and turned to Merrik. "My brother is very nearly asleep. I will continue the tale, if you wish me to, tomorrow night. I trust I haven't bored you."

The men were staring at her. Then they grumbled. Then Roran called out, "Aye, but what happened? The only thing strange when a man touches a woman is that he wants her and that isn't strange."

"Taby isn't tired, are you, boy?"

"What magic is this?"

Merrik said nothing. He just looked at her, a small smile on his mouth. Then he laughed. Then he raised his voice and cheered, and suddenly all of them were cheering and shouting. Before she went into the tent for the night, four small silver coins had been pressed into her hand. She stared down at them lying brightly on her palm.

Four coins for telling them a story. As she fell asleep, she wondered what it was that Parma felt when he touched Selina's arms.

They rowed into the Baltic Sea a day later, for there was no wind, the water as calm and unruffled as Merrik's temper. He was quiet, thoughtful, perhaps thinking of new adventures, Old Firren thought, as he carefully steered the longboat past a nearly sunken log.

"We will be at my home in five days if a good wind rises," Merrik said to her late that afternoon when she came forward to stand beside him. He'd been teaching Taby how to row and now the child was fast asleep on Merrik's legs. He rested his elbows on the huge oar and turned to face her, saying, "The men have decided that Thor demands a sacrifice from us to give us wind enough to fill the sail. I have decided it will be up to you."

She nearly tripped as she lurched backward.

She felt a man's hand on her back and jumped forward to escape him. She fell against Merrik. He didn't touch her, merely looked at her and grinned.

"The sacrifice isn't a virgin one. You must continue the story of Grunlige tonight else Thor won't cooperate and give us wind for our sails."

"After you finish preparing our meal," Eller said. "We cannot decide which we prefer if we have to choose."

"You can already smell that meal, can't you?" black-eyed Roran said, and laughed.

"Aye, I dream of some pheasant, perhaps stewed with greens and peas and mushrooms."

All they thought about was food, Laren thought, smiling now, her fear, surely ridiculous, well tamped down. "I will fill your gullets," she said, then stopped cold at the sight of Deglin's face. There was cold fury there and she knew fear of him because she wasn't stupid. A man's fury could quickly turn into violence. Deglin wasn't a warrior as Merrik was, but he was just as frightening, for he was a man and a skald and the two were together in his mind, and she had poached on what was his. She had as good as attacked him physically. She thought of the four silver coins that lay snug in the lining of her trousers. She could only buy her freedom from Merrik with silver. Not with sweet womanish smiles and good cooking. No, only with silver.

She said slowly, "I will tell you what happened next only if you promise not to snore so loudly outside my tent."

Old Firren laughed so hard he swung the rudder deep and sharp and accidentally swiped another sunken log. The longboat shuddered and rocked.

"What do you mean *your* tent, girl?" Deglin called out, his skald's voice deep and clear and cold as the layers of water beneath the longboat. "Merrik sleeps there with you. We should ask you not to cry out so loudly when he plows your belly at night."

Merrik said very calmly, "That is enough, Deglin. Your own vanity and conceit deprived you of the men's interest. You went off to sulk, to punish us by refusing to continue the story. Blame not the girl."

"She is no skald!" Deglin yelled. "She is nothing—a slave, a pathetic scrap you should have killed and left in Kiev! I don't wish to hear her befoul my skills with her foolish attempts. She is naught but a woman and a woman has no use save for what is between her legs and the skill she brings to the cooking pot. She shows those skills, 'tis enough."

Very slowly Merrik rose. He handed the still-sleeping Taby to Cleve, who'd been silent as a tomb.

He loomed over Deglin, who now looked uncertain, though there was still fury and hatred in his eyes and he was looking toward Laren.

"I told you not to blame her," Merrik said again.

"But she—"

Merrik leaned down and grasped Deglin's tunic. He drew him upright and held him very close. "No more else I will make you regret it."

Deglin said, his skald's voice soft now and pleading, filled with deep sincerity, "Nay, my lord, I wish no insult to you, but she . . . ah, you have the right of it. I should have done what you wished without showing my displeasure, without showing vexation. I will continue the tale. I don't wish to deprive the men further. There is no need to listen to her again."

Merrik was in a quandary. He released Deglin and returned to sit down on his own sea chest. He looked at Laren, but her head was down and he couldn't see her expression. Deglin was the recognized skald. He saw no choice. He said then, "Tonight Deglin will continue the tale of Grunlige the Dane."

No one said anything. Merrik seated himself again. The longboat righted and ran along smoothly in the water. Aye, everything was just as it should be again and Laren felt rage build within her. But she'd learned during the past two years to hide her rage, though with Merrik she hadn't succeeded very well. But now she must. She didn't want to, but she looked toward Deglin. He was smiling at her and it wasn't a nice smile.

The four silver coins. There would be no more to add to them.

That night, she worked beside Old Firren and Cleve to prepare the evening meal. She paid little attention to the men's talk as they went about their familiar tasks. She worked, saying nothing, knowing she must be grateful because she was alive and Taby was alive. The night was clear overhead, the stars brilliant, the moon nearly full. They were camped close to shore, the longboat pulled onto the narrow beach and covered with pine branches. The tents were up, several fires lit, and now the smells from her venison stew filled the soft evening air.

After the meal, when the men lay about on their furs, warm by the fires, their bellies full, Deglin rose, stretched to his full height, which wasn't all that im-

pressive, then coughed behind his hand to soothe his
voice and took a small sipping drink of ale. He stared
at all the men, gaining their full attention, then he said,
"When Grunlige the Dane killed his hands with the ice,
he knew that he had failed himself. He had believed
himself safe and secure in his own strength and now he
had killed part of himself; not his enemies, but he himself had done it. He was a proud man, a man without
rival, a man with great strength and skills, but he had
only himself to blame for the death of his hands. He
looked down at them, saw the withered claws, the fingernails that were blue and ridged, curling up about
the edges. He called his son to him and said, 'Innar, it
is over with me. I bequeath all that I have to you. Do
not kill yourself as I have done.'

"Then he hugged his son to his chest and dismissed
him. Three days later his men found him dead at the
bottom of a ravine. He'd had one of his men chop off his
hands and they lay there in the morning sun, shriveled
and blackened, and all knew he'd stared at his hands
until he had lost all his blood and died.

"His son, Innar, did not weep, for he believed his father to have done the right thing. Like his father, he
was proud and sure of himself, but he held no great
respect for the old man whose seed had created him. He
had no wish to cleave bulls in half, no wish to use great
strength to bend those to his will, for he had not the
great strength of his father in any case. Instead, he
wanted to go araiding and amass wealth. What his father had left him wasn't enough. He gathered his father's men together and told them that they would sail
to Kiev. On their way there, they would gather slaves
and sell them in the slave market of Khagan-Rus. He
was brave when he was surrounded by his father's men
for they were seasoned warriors and knew well how to

kill and plunder. They would protect him because it was their duty to protect him. They killed many tribesmen on their voyage and portage to Kiev and captured many women. And Innar, secure in his prowess, had all proclaim that it was he who had killed the tribes and had them tell all they knew of his skill and cunning."

The men were looking at each other, furtive looks that showed anger, embarrassment, uncertainty. There were murmurs.

Deglin continued quickly, "Innar became well-known for his skill in dealing at the slave market. One day he chanced to see a girl there who was bowed and thin and dressed in rags. He decided he wanted her and thus he bought her and brought her with him back to his home. He didn't know that she was filled with evil, that she hated being a woman, that she wanted to be a man with a man's talents and skills and a man's genius. She tried to do the things the men did and she failed and her rage grew for she knew she was inferior."

The talk was louder now, drowning out Deglin's words. The men were looking toward Merrik. His face was still. He said nothing for a very long time, merely looked at Deglin thoughtfully. He raised a hand finally to quiet the men and said, "You do not wish to continue the tale as it is now going, Deglin." His voice softened now, and Laren felt a shiver of sheer terror at the feel of it. "Tell us what became of Innar, this man who had no respect for his father."

"Why, my lord," Deglin said after a moment, "he changed, certainly he changed. He became his own man and thus gained respect for his sire who had given him all the gifts he now used to make himself successful. He won himself great honors and respect from the men, for he was a trader above all other traders. He killed the evil slave. He brought home much silver and became richer than ever his father had dreamed of wealth. He wed the girl his father had picked for him and he had many sons. Thus Grunlige the Dane was followed by men who did not shame his name."

There was a long silence, broken finally by Oleg, tall and lean and menacing, who loomed over Deglin and said in a voice of disgust, "Your tale is unworthy, Deglin. I found it filled with ill-disguised venom and lies. You are like a gnat that buzzes about—you dart in to strike, then you're off again, hiding in your cowardice of words. I would prefer to hear the girl tell us what happened to Grunlige the Dane."

Deglin's beautiful skald's voice shook with anger as he said, "The girl will tell you nothing! She has not the wit nor the skill. She pretends to it, aye, but she has it not. She is a slave, nothing more, just a miserable slave. She would not dare to speak her foolishness, for I will not allow it. Do you not see it? She is evil, she brings discord. She makes us angry at each other. She has cast spells on Merrik, weakening him!"

Oleg slipped his knife from his belt. He took a step toward Deglin. There was no expression on his face, nothing to show his intent. He stopped when Merrik said, "Hold, Oleg. Again Deglin has allowed his mouth to rule the logic of his brain. Is that not true, Deglin?"

Deglin drew a deep breath, gaining control. "I have been careless. Aye, my lord, I have not heeded what I should heed. I will tell you another story, one that you will find more to your liking."

Oleg just shook his head at Deglin, sheathed his knife, and eased himself back down on the wolfskin, crossed his legs, and said, "Come, Laren, what happened? Parma touched Selina's arms and he felt something strange. Continue."

She was silent, wondering what to do. The men were

all looking at her expectantly. She could tell nothing from Merrik's closed expression. Taby was drowsing in his arms, his head against Merrik's chest. The men all nodded at her now, some telling her to begin again, aye, tell them about Parma and what Selina did to him. She continued to look back at Merrik. Finally, he nodded at her. She smiled. She rose. She opened her mouth to speak, the words brimming in her mind. She saw his arm rise but she didn't move back quickly enough. Deglin hit her cheek hard with his fist, knocking her sideways to the ground, and into the fire.

7

Merrik dumped Taby onto the ground and leapt to his feet, but Cleve was faster. He raced to Laren and dragged her from the fire. She was still senseless from the blow Deglin had struck her. Her right trouser leg was burning, sluggish flames that were seeping into the dry wool, seeking better purchase, billowing up black smoke from the material. He knocked her onto her face and dug dirt up with his fingers, flinging it onto her leg. Then he pressed the dirt into the trousers, rubbing furiously. Merrik pulled Cleve aside, jerked off his own tunic, and flattened it against her leg. He raised it and looked down at the burned wool, peeling back, now gaping about her flesh. She turned slowly onto her side and he looked at her face.

"Are you all right?"

She stared at him a moment, her face without color, her fingers digging into the earth, spasmodically, with no reason, just digging and digging. She winced, lightly touching her fingertips to her cheek where Deglin had struck her. Then she shook her head, as if to clear it. The blood pounded deep and hard, fear clogging her brain, and she smiled and said, "I wasn't fast enough."

Merrik just stared at her, shaking his head. "Is your jaw broken?" Even as he spoke, he touched her cheek, his fingers light and gentle, then nodded. "No, but there will be a bruise." He looked at her leg again. "Sit up," he said. He was aware of the men's angry voices all around them. Good, they wouldn't stand behind Deglin, not that it mattered to Merrik.

She did, saying nothing.

He ripped back the wool, baring her leg. Her leg wasn't too badly burned, but the flesh from her ankle to her knee was dark red. He imagined the pain must be great, but when he looked at her face again, he saw only blankness, and realized she hadn't yet given over to it, hadn't yet realized fully what had happened and what the consequences were going to be. "Stay still," he said and rose. He turned. Oleg was holding Deglin.

The skald was panting, struggling against Oleg, but Oleg was strong, as strong as Merrik, and he was very angry.

Merrik walked to him slowly. He stood there in front of him, saying nothing, merely stared down at him. Deglin stopped struggling. He said, "I did not mean to harm her, just to punish her. She deserved the blow to her face, but she tripped into the fire, it wasn't my fault. She is a slave, my lord, there can be no retribution."

Cleve snarled behind Merrik, his hands fisted, his body tensed, ready to leap. The men were all on their feet, their shock at what had happened quickly changed to fury. But they were willing to wait to see what Merrik would do. It was his decision, not theirs.

Merrik heard Taby crying and turned to see the child crawling toward his sister.

He said calmly, "Cleve, take the child to his sister. Oleg, bring our skald here, to the fire. He is doubtless cold, at least he's proved his brain is cold and without reason or sense. I will warm him, as he did Laren."

Oleg smiled and dragged Deglin to the fire. The men

all drew near, making a circle about them, saying nothing now, waiting.

"Give him to me," Merrik said. Oleg shoved Deglin to Merrik. Merrik grabbed him about his neck and forced him to the ground. Without warning, he grabbed Deglin's right leg and shoved it into the flames, holding it there.

Deglin stared in horror at the flames lashing upward around and through his leg. He felt the awful scalding heat, felt the material burn from his leg, felt the flames go into his flesh. He screamed and thrashed, struggling wildly against Merrik.

Merrik released him only after the cloth had burst into flames and turned to ashes. He watched him dispassionately as he scrambled away, rolling in the dirt, screaming, gasping for breath, choking.

He just looked at him, then said, "You have less sense than a snail, Deglin. Your lack of control is offensive. I won't kill you this time. But heed me, never again harm another without my permission. Do you understand me?"

Deglin was filled with pain, filled with the shock of the pain, the disbelief of what had happened, of what Merrik had done to him simply because he'd struck a slave. He smelled his own burned flesh. His craw filled with vomit and loathing. He said on a gasp, "Aye, my lord, I understand you."

"Good," Merrik said, then turned away from him. He saw that Laren was sitting up now and staring down at her burned leg. Her fingers were hovering above the reddened flesh. She was afraid to touch herself. Cleve was beside her, holding Taby, who was gulping down tears, speaking quietly to both of them. Merrik said to Eller, "Fetch me the healing cream my mother sent along in the herb pouch in my tent. Quickly."

Merrik came down on his haunches. He grasped her chin between his fingers and lifted her face. "The cream will leach out the heat and pain. It is the same cream I put on your back, and it eased you, did it not?"

She nodded, words stuck in her craw. She couldn't keep from staring at her burned leg.

"You are doing well."

And he expected her to continue doing well, she thought, and knew that she would. She smiled again, more difficult than she would have thought, and said, "I should have been faster. During the past two years I've learned to duck quick as a flea and dodge blows with the spryness of a horse about to be gelded." She sighed, and he saw color come back into her face, too much color on her cheek. It was now turning a pale purple. He knew that she was calming, that her mind would tell her quickly enough that there was a goodly amount of pain to come.

It wasn't fair. She'd suffered too much already, and now this.

Eller handed him the cream. "I have only one other pair of trousers, Merrik."

"Bring them. She cannot be naked around an army of men."

Merrik saw that she was just staring at that cream and she was afraid of his touching her burned flesh, afraid of the pain, and he didn't blame her. When he'd rubbed it into her back, it had hurt, and she remembered that, too well.

He said nothing, merely took the cream in one hand and grasped her beneath her arm with the other. He half carried her to the tent. When he laid her onto her back, he said, "I'm going to pull these trousers off you."

She didn't want him to for she was naked beneath the trousers. But her leg was hurting now, throbbing, the pain deep and becoming deeper and stronger by the moment. What did it matter? He'd already seen her body, already tended to her back, bathed her. She said nothing, merely turned her head away. He was kneeling over her now, his expression intent. She couldn't look at him. She closed her eyes as she felt his hands at her waist, unknotting the rope that was holding up Eller's trousers. She felt the cool night air on her bare flesh as he pulled them down. He was very careful, she'd give him that, but when a bit of charred wool clung to her leg, she lurched up, crying out with the sharp pain of it.

"I know it hurts. I'm sorry. Lie down." He pressed her back down, his fingers splayed on her bare stomach.

She lay there, feeling pain, feeling helpless, and she hated it. He laid a blanket over her, leaving only her leg bare. She wanted to thank him for that, but she couldn't. It took all her resolve to keep cries buried in her throat, not to moan or whine, not to let him see that she was weak.

Suddenly she felt his fingers on her burned flesh, felt his fingers lightly rubbing in the cream. She wanted to scream as loud as a blast of thunder, but she forced herself to lie still, to bear it. The cream brought the strangest mixture of pain and relief, of hot and cold, then blessed numbness, just as it had on her back. She held herself still, concentrating on keeping her mouth shut.

When he was finished, he sat back on his heels. "You will be all right. The burn isn't that bad. My mother makes the cream, with elderberry juice, she told me. You will like my mother, she can be fierce as a warrior one moment and gentle as a child the next. She knows all about potions and medicines. When I was a boy, I was fighting with Rorik, my older brother, and fell in the fire pit and she . . . "

She was aware of what he was doing, distracting her, trying to make her focus on his voice and his words, not on the pain from the burns. She did hear his voice, deep and soft, and she tried, she truly tried to think about what he was saying, but it was beyond her. Finally, when he was quiet a moment, she said, "You love your mother."

"Aye, she and my father are the finest parents I know. Even when they hate, they do it better than anyone else. They are not without flaw, don't misunderstand me. I remember how they hated Rorik's Irish wife, believing her evil. But they changed because they saw the justice of it, realized they had been wrong about her."

She nodded, then said, "I have few body parts left unscathed. Thank you, Merrik. You are kind."

"Keep those parts sound. This was the same cream I used on your back. After this I don't wish to use it again on you. I haven't much left, for my mother can only make the cream in the fall months."

"What else could happen? You are not that far from your home now, are you?"

"Aye, 'tis true. Still, you must learn to be faster."

"Aye," she said, feeling the flesh grow cool and numb. "Next time I will be the one to inflict the pain."

"A slave doesn't inflict pain," he said in an utterly emotionless voice. He turned and called out, "Oleg, bring a cup of mead."

When Oleg came into the tent, he said nothing, merely stared down at her, then nodded. He handed the mead to Merrik and was quickly gone again.

When he put the cup to her lips, she drank.

"All of it," he said. "It will make you sleep."

And she did.

They survived a storm of two straight days in the Baltic Sea before turning northward up the Oslofjord to Kaupang. Oddly, Laren hadn't been particularly frightened. She was too busy trying to keep Taby reassured. He was as wet and miserable as they all were, there was naught she could do about that. She told him one story after the other. Her cheek had turned purple and yellow from the blow and had swelled. It didn't hurt, just made her look a witch, she imagined. It was her leg that hurt and throbbed, but then again, so did Deglin's and each time she thought of that, the pain seemed to lessen. Merrik made him row as long and hard as all the other men.

Laren wondered if he would die, for he moaned over his oar and complained endlessly, but the men ignored him. But he was tough, and on that fifth morning when the sun was hot in the sky and the winds had quieted into soft breezes that were just heavy enough to fill the sails, she saw that he hadn't sickened, nor was he complaining anymore. He was silent, and she distrusted that. Silent men, in her experience, usually were thinking of revenge. He saw she was looking at him and she quickly looked away. Since that night, none of the men had asked her to tell them about Grunlige the Dane. She wondered if she would continue the tale if they did ask her. She was nodding even as she wondered. Deglin deserved nothing from her.

There were seagulls overhead, screeching as they dove close to the longboat, then swooped away at the last instant. She heard one man yell when a seagull's wing hit his face. Scores of cormorants flagged their progress, the large birds in loose formation off their bow. There was a new quickened vitality to the men's conversation. All their talk was of home, of their wives, their children, their crops. And they spoke of their wealth, each man richer than he was but four months earlier.

As for Merrik, he would look at her cheek and frown. At night he continued to rub more cream into her leg, even though she could do it now, and she told him that she could. But he had merely shaken his head and continued with the task.

The trading town of Kaupang was protected by a wooden palisade made of lashed-together sharply pointed wooden poles, set in the shape of a half circle. There were a good half dozen wooden docks that stretched out into the inlet and it was at the nearest one that Merrik had the men row the longboat. When they stepped onto the dock, there was a loud cheer. They were home, or very nearly.

They would do no trading here this time, but the men wanted women and there had been no slave women for their use on the trip back from Kiev. They were hungry and they wanted one last night of wildness and freedom before they returned to their families. Laren saw it and understood it. They were men and that was simply the way they were. She didn't hate them for it, she was simply relieved that none of them wanted her. And that was thanks to Merrik.

She said to him even as he set her down on dry ground, "Thank you for protecting me."

"I didn't," he said. "Deglin hurt you badly."

"That isn't what I meant. The men—they will relieve their lust here. They didn't relieve their lust on me. I thank you for that."

He said nothing to her, merely turned to shout to the

men remaining on the longboat to protect their silver, "Keep sharp. We will be back in six hours and 'twill be your turn."

He looked down at her. "Can you walk?"

She nodded.

"Cleve will keep Taby close. Would you like a bath?"

They were allowed through the large double gates, and she found herself in a bustling area crammed with people and small wooden dwellings and shops, all connected with wooden walkways, and it seemed that everyone was busy selling something or making something to sell or yelling with another to buy or trade or barter. It seemed that everyone was talking. She smiled, wanting to stop, just a moment, just long enough to look at the beautiful soapstone bowls displayed in front of one wooden shop, but Merrik didn't pause. She saw a collection of weapons, and wished she could buy a knife, but she imagined her four small pieces of silver wouldn't be enough, and she had nothing else. Merrik took her to a bathing hut where an old woman looked not at all at her face, but only at her worn trousers and dirty tunic, tsked through her rotting teeth, and told Merrik to take his wife inside.

It was difficult, but within an hour, she had managed to wash her hair and her body and keep her leg dry. She was wearing only the same dirty tunic when Merrik entered the dimly lit bathing hut. He tossed a linen shift in her lap.

"It's clean. Put it on. Here is a dress and an overtunic. I don't wish to arrive at my home with you looking like a starved boy."

She just stared up at him. "Thank you," she said.

"When you are finished, we will see the cobbler. You need shoes."

When they returned to the longboat some three hours

later, her belly was full, she was well clothed, and there were soft leather shoes on her feet. She hadn't felt like this for two years. She felt like a . . . She couldn't find in her mind how exactly she felt.

"I'm afraid," she said to him finally as he walked slowly beside her. She was limping, but he made no move to carry her or assist her. She appreciated his restraint. The soft wool of the gown didn't hurt her healing leg, for which she was grateful.

"Why?"

"What will you do with me and Taby? What will you do with Cleve?"

He frowned then, but said only, "You will know when I tell you. I wish to see if Cleve bought Taby the proper clothes."

Her little brother looked clean and as well garbed as she did. But what surprised her was that Cleve also was wearing a new tunic and new trousers and there were leather shoes on his feet with soft leather straps crisscrossing up his calves. He looked magnificent. He grinned at her and puffed out his chest. It was the first time she had ever seen him smile. She was overwhelmed. She scarcely saw the scar that was even more hideous when he smiled. It wasn't important. It wasn't Cleve, this was, and she was glad, so very excited.

She couldn't have prevented it even if she'd thought about it. She turned to Merrik and shouted. Then she threw her arms around him, squeezing his back tightly. "Thank you," she said, her arms still around him, but she was looking up at him now and she realized in that instant what she had done, that she had touched him, that she was, in fact, holding him hard, treating him as she would a trusted friend, a relative, a husband. And what she realized fully in that moment was that he was a man, a big man, a handsome man, and to be pressed against him, to feel his flesh beneath her fingers, brought her pleasure, a strange pleasure she'd never felt before, but it was there and it was deep within her, and she was shocked at its intensity. But she didn't release him. If anything, she pressed closer, feeling him, feeling the pleasure it brought her.

He didn't touch her. If anything, he stiffened. His arms remained at his sides. He said nothing. Finally, Laren realized that he was still as a stone. She had shamed him with her actions. She was nothing but a slave even though he had protected her. She was nothing at all to him. She quickly released him and stepped back, her head down.

But Taby wasn't aware that anything was amiss. Cleve put him down and he took Laren's place quickly enough, tugging on Merrik's tunic until he leaned down and picked him up. The child hugged his thin arms around Merrik's neck, squeezing him as hard as he could, laughing and laughing. "I'm a prince," Taby said. "You bought clothes for a prince. Someday I will reward you."

Merrik felt something sharp and sweet unfold deep inside him. He held the child close, smelling his child's sweet scent, loving the sound of his laughter. He wanted this child and he would never let him go, never.

"I thank you, Prince Taby," he said against the child's soft cheek, a cheek not so thin now.

He looked at Laren. She was standing there, Cleve beside her, and she was just looking at him and at Taby and he saw something on her face that he didn't understand. It was fear, he realized at last. Was she afraid of him? Surely not. She had thrown herself at him, no fear there. Or did she realize that Taby was his? What he had felt when she had pressed herself so willingly and completely against him, he discounted. It didn't matter. He'd felt a shock of lust only because he hadn't had a woman in a very long time. He looked away from her and caressed Taby. He kissed his cheek, felt him with his big hands and frowned because he was still too thin, his small bones still too prominent, his ribs too sharp.

He closed his eyes a moment, just feeling the warmth of the child seep into him, filling him with a sense of rightness, a sense that this small human being had been born for his care, for his guardianship. As for Laren, she was naught more than Taby's sister. He wondered yet again who Laren and Taby were.

Vestfold was a huge land. Steep cliffs hugged the fjord, soaring upward, drowned many times with low-lying clouds. The hills and mountains were covered with firs and oak, many so steep and sharp that she couldn't imagine ever making her way to the top of some of those tall peaks. The fjord was like smooth glass, but the current was with them and the men spoke and jested whilst they rowed.

The air was warm and smooth, the sun high and brilliant. It was an incredible land. She'd never imagined anything like this. She couldn't look away from the endless stretch of cliffs, seemingly larger with the rounding of each turn in the fjord.

"This is my home," Merrik said. "Soon we will pass Gravak Valley. I have many cousins who live there."

He fell silent, but she saw a smile tug at his mouth, and he shook his head.

"Will we stop?"

He shook his head. "Nay, I wish to return home. It is odd but I've felt something, a strange feeling that gnaws at me when my thoughts aren't focused. I don't like it."

Laren had learned not to discount such feelings when they came. "What are these feelings?"

"They make my flesh itch. They make me want to hurry faster, for there is something not right at home." He shook his head. "It is nothing, surely nothing. I grow as foolish as a female."

"I am not foolish."

"Very well. I grow as foolish as a female who is not you."

"Has your home a name?"

"Aye, for generation upon generation my father's farmstead has been called Malverne. The name is older than these mountains on either side of us, and none know what it means or from what language it comes."

"Malverne," she said. " 'Tis an odd word and not one I recognize either, except that it—" Her voice fell like a stone dropped from one of the huge towering cliffs.

He raised an eyebrow at her, waiting.

She shook her head, then said brightly, her voice so false that he wanted to shake her, "Tell me about your cousins."

"One of my cousins is wed to a woman without hearing. Her name is Lotti."

Laren couldn't imagine such a thing. "And she is alive? She is grown?"

"Aye. Egil, her husband and my cousin, has taken care of her since she was Taby's age. She can read the words from your lips as you speak, but Egil has also devised signals with his fingers so they can speak together more easily. It is fascinating to watch their fingers fly about and then hear them laugh, for they can even jest in this finger language. They are very happy and have four children. Lotti is special."

She nodded, then fell silent. The men rowed more closely to shore and the cliff loomed over them, casting shadows when it momentarily blocked the sun. "I don't know if I should like this in the winter. I've heard of the winters here, of course. I've been told that they . . ." Again, she stopped herself and he didn't frown this time, merely waited, impassive, looking at the mountains they were passing. She said, "They sound difficult."

"No more difficult than most things. It's a different sort of beauty," Merrik said. "But you're right, when the days are short, the mountains and trees covered with snow, there is a sameness that soon bends your thoughts. We spend much time inside during the winter months, for the snow can be so deep you could step outside and sink into snow that covers your head." He paused a moment, then said, "Ah, but to stand alone in the midst of a forest of pine trees, and there is nothing but silence and the utter white of newly fallen snow. That is something that moves the most remote of men."

"I have heard it said that the Vikings keep the animals in their longhouses during the winter."

"Aye. In the winter months, else they would freeze to death. The extra animals are slaughtered, their meat smoked and dried so that we will eat well during the winter. Aye, the remaining animals are brought into the longhouse." He grinned down at her. "The smell isn't too bad. One becomes used to it. But when the snow stops and the sun burns overhead, and fresh air fills everything, ah, that is what makes everything perfect here. Where do you come from, Laren?"

"From Nor—" She stopped and began to slowly tug on her meager braids. "It is not important, Merrik, truly. Thank you for the clothes. I no longer feel like a man, and 'tis a foolish feeling I didn't like. Though the freedom to run and move quickly is something I will miss."

He let her be. He would learn everything about her and Taby soon enough. He watched her fidget with her hair, hair thick and curly that she'd somehow managed to braid—even though her hair was still too short for much plaiting—pinning the meager braids with two wooden clasps on top of her head. Tendrils of shorter hair curled about her face and several long, loose strands trailed down the back of her neck. Even with the shorter spikes of red hair sticking out of the braids, she still looked very female, and he admitted to himself, in her woman's clothes, she was lovely. Indeed, despite the still pale yellow-and-green bruise on her cheek, she looked quite acceptable. By the gods, he thought, she looked beautiful, that violent red hair of hers glistening in the bright sunlight.

He looked away from her, to the shoreline that wasn't really a shoreline at all, for the cliffs crashed from their heights right into the deep waters of the fjord, all of it continuous, without the interruption of sand or loose rocks, without break. He thought of Malverne again and felt that now familiar gnawing in his belly that left a coldness and a dread. He hated it for there was nothing he could point to, nothing to focus upon. There was nothing to do but wait.

Eller shouted, "I don't smell anything, Merrik, but there is Malverne! I see it yon!"

The other men craned to look and shouted.

Oleg came to stand beside Merrik. " 'Twas a good trading trip," he said. "Our chests are full with silver. The women will show us much appreciation for the beautiful furs we brought them."

Merrik grinned, dismissing his foolish feelings, now as carefree as a boy. "Aye, and the brooch I brought my mother will make her smile and feed me all her delicious meals until my belly puffs out."

Oleg laughed. "I brought Tora an arm bracelet," he said. "I am so skinny she will have to feed me well for a year. What did you bring your father?"

"Ah, I brought my father a knife of great value, its handle an odd ivory from beyond Bulgar."

Oleg only laughed louder. "And I brought Harald a cask for his jewels and I will have the runemaster engrave it to him."

Merrik punched his arm. Oleg hit him in the belly. The longboat rocked. The men laughed and shouted advice.

The two men grappled, grunting from each other's blows, and the longboat tipped first one way and then the other.

Laren watched them, smiling, until she saw that Merrik was perilously close to a loose sharp-edged oar. She called out just as Oleg shoved him and he lost his balance. He flailed at the empty air, looked utterly astonished and went overboard.

The men hooted with laughter even as they fished him out. He came dripping into the longboat, and shook himself as would a mongrel dog.

"You think it funny?" he said to Laren, who was holding her sides with laugher.

"Aye, you have the look of a drowned god."

His own laughter died in his throat. A god? She believed he looked like a god? He turned quickly, uncomfortable with her words, at the sound of Taby's laugh. The child was laughing and pointing and trying to get to Merrik. "Keep your distance, Prince Taby," he called. "I do not want you to become as wet a god as I."

When they arrived at the long single dock that lay at the base of a winding pathway up to the huge farmstead atop, the men could no longer contain their excitement, for there were their wives and children awaiting them on the dock, shouting to them.

Merrik scanned the gathered people for his father and mother. He saw his brother, Erik, and from this distance he didn't see any welcoming smile on his brother's handsome face. His heart began to pound, slow deep strokes. The foreboding he'd felt, no, it couldn't be true.

But it was. Both his father and mother were dead of a virulent plague that had struck the farmstead a month before.

8

MERRIK SAT SILENT and still, hunched over on the long bench, a cup of mead between his cupped hands.

His brother Erik sat beside him, silent as well. Finally, Erik said, "Their passing was swift. They did not suffer overly. It struck so quickly, I cannot tell you how it was, not really. Death was here and you could smell it and feel it in the very air around you, and there was naught anyone could do, save look on and watch the ones we loved die." Erik paused a moment, shaking his head. "Sarla was ill but she recovered. I believe it was she who gave the illness to our mother, for Mother tended to her. And then it struck our father who wouldn't leave Mother's side for an instant. Aye, and Sarla survived it."

Merrik wanted to tell him not to be stupid, that it wasn't Sarla's fault, but words stuck in his throat. He felt his control slipping and swallowed, lowering his head even more.

Erik continued after a moment. "The older people, well, they were struck hard and most of them died. Our parents were amongst the first. Ten of our people died, eight slaves. It wasn't a good time. I wish you had been here, but perhaps it was better that you were not. I would not wish to have lost you."

"Did it strike any of the other farmsteads?"

"You mean our cousin Egil? Nay, he and his family were spared. It came here and stayed, then was gone suddenly like a ghost that fades away in the stark light of day. All of Gravak Valley was spared, save us."

Sarla appeared at Merrik's elbow, and said quietly, "You must eat, Merrik. I have prepared the stewed venison you very much like, at least that is what your mother told me. I have not her skill, but it is tasty enough, I think."

He smiled up at her, this shy wife of his brother's, so slight, quite pretty really when one looked at her closely, but she was so quiet that it was easy not to notice her. Her hair was a dark, rich blond, her eyes more gray than blue, her skin fair and pure. She was also dominated completely by Erik, as most were. He was glad she had survived. "Thank you, Sarla, but I have no hunger. Please see to the other men." He realized then that he had forgotten about Laren and Taby. "Sarla, please see as well to the woman and child I brought with me. The man's name is Cleve. They will sleep here in the longhouse."

She nodded, touched his sleeve, and asked if he wished more mead. Before he could reply, his brother said, his voice cold with impatience, "If he wishes you prattling about him, Sarla, he will tell you. Get you back to your duties."

She said nothing, merely bowed her head and left the brothers. Erik said, "You bought them in Kiev, so Eller told me."

"I bought the child. The woman and man came to me free." For a moment, his grief fell away from him and he smiled at his brother. "Actually, we had to flee Kiev before an enraged merchant discovered he'd just lost a boy and a man."

"Boy? She is very obviously a girl."

"Aye, but then she was a boy, thin as a stick and dressed in ragged breeches and tunic. Even I didn't realize she wasn't a boy until I had to tend her back. This merchant Thrasco had beaten her very badly."

"She is a slave, then," Erik said, satisfaction in his voice. Merrik said nothing, indeed, he hadn't heard his brother, for his thoughts were on his parents again.

"She is still thin," Erik said, and Merrik looked up to see his brother's eyes on Laren, seated near the fire pit, Sarla standing beside her. "But she doesn't look sickly."

"No, she doesn't. You should have seen her when I managed to flee with her. She was naught more than bones covered with white flesh. The child, too, was so thin it would make you cry, Erik."

"The child?" He looked toward Taby who was playing with a leather ball. "Surely he is more a burden than anything. Did the girl beg you to buy him? Did she promise to be your whore if you bought him? But none of that would matter, for a man does as he pleases with a woman, and a slave is of no account at all. Why in the name of the gods did you buy a child, Merrik?"

Merrik said slowly, "I don't know. I saw him and I knew I had to have him. Laren had nothing to do with it. She'd already been bought by the merchant. I bought Taby." Merrik shrugged. "Aye, he is mine now. I saved her because she is Taby's sister."

"Ah," Erik said and fell again silent. "Why is there a bruise on her cheek? It is nearly gone now but still I can make it out. Was she insolent? Did you have to strike her?"

Merrik didn't want to answer his brother's questions. He wanted only to feel his grief and not be further distracted from it. "No," he said shortly, rising, "I did not strike her. I am going outside for a while, Erik. I must be alone. I suppose I need it for a little while."

Erik thoughtfully watched his brother walk to the wide oak doors of the longhouse and go outside. He looked again toward the female Merrik had brought with him from Kiev. She was laughing softly at something the child said. Her face lit up as she hugged the little boy close to her. She stood back again to toss the ball to him.

Erik rose. He looked about the large outer chamber that was filled with the soft blue haze of smoke from the fire pit. A thin thread of blue smoke trailed upward, disappearing through the small circular hole in the roof of the longhouse. As a child he'd stared and stared at that slender blue line that seemed unreal, so steady was it and so unchanging, and so very blue. Some things didn't change, he thought, just the people looking at them did. He felt tears burn his eyes, but they didn't overflow, not now, not in over a week now.

The large outer room was warm, filled with conversation. Some laughter, but quickly muted, some angry words, children being scolded, so very normal, all of it. Erik let it flow about him, scarce touching him, but there and comforting nonetheless. He could hear the tenor of the voices, hear the sorrow in the voices, so much sorrow, deep within everyone, so close to the surface, so very close. He sighed. Unlike Merrik, whose pain he understood well, he'd had a month to accustom himself to his father's and mother's passing. And, unlike Merrik, he'd had to live with them here at Malverne, never leaving as Merrik did on trading voyages since he, Erik, was the eldest son. Ah, and he'd argued with them even when he'd reached his man years and they'd had no reason not to agree with him, not to let him have his way, and thus his memories were tempered with the bitter quarrels, the shouting, the bone-deep anger he'd sometimes felt toward them. They'd disliked his keeping Caylis and Megot, though they'd treated his son by Caylis, Kenna, well enough. They'd taken Sarla's side when he'd become angry at her and struck her. Aye, there was much to temper his memory of his mother and father. But not Merrik, not the favored younger son who was never here at Malverne.

Now Malverne was his and his alone. There would be no more arguments with his father on something he wished to do. He was the master now, he was the lord. Only what he said mattered. There were none left to gainsay him. He looked over at his wife, Sarla, knowing in his belly that she was barren, knowing that he would have to rid himself of her if he wished an heir. Or, if he kept her, then one of his other sons could be made legitimate. Probably Kenna, Caylis's son, a handsome boy of eight who looked just like Erik had at that age. Certainly Sarla would never say anything to him that might displease him enough to dismiss her. She was little more than a shadow, a quiet child whose body he still enjoyed, but not all that much, for she lay there, cold and silent, waiting for him to be done with her. And he had hurt her many times because he'd wanted her to cry out, wanted to hear something from her, whether it be pleasure or pain.

The smell of venison was strong, too strong. He frowned. When his mother prepared the venison stew, the smells were wondrous, the smell of the meat never overpowering the other ingredients. What could he expect? Sarla had not his mother's skills.

Sarla gave Laren two blankets and told her in her quiet way to sleep close to the fire pit, for the night would be chilly and the still-glowing embers would keep her warm throughout the night. As for Cleve, Sarla merely handed him a blanket and said, "Any place you wish to rest is fine." Then she smiled at him. Cleve looked down at the slight female in front of him. Didn't she see the hideous scars on his face? How could she smile at him? Was she nearly blind? He merely nodded to her as he took the blanket.

"Sarla!"

She raised her head to see her husband standing, hands on hips, his handsome features cold with impatience. It was always so with her. He was always impatient, always displeased with her about something. She supposed she couldn't blame him. She did little that was like his mother did, though Tora had never scolded her or treated her meanly. But her husband did. She sighed, feeling her body retreat inward. He wanted her to come to his bed and she didn't want to. He wanted her to see to his pleasure. She didn't want to do that, either, but she supposed she preferred that to lying on her back and feeling him invade her and sweat over her, making those ugly grunting noises. Whatever he wanted, she had no choice. She lowered her head, not looking at anyone for she knew that all the men would realize what her husband wanted of her. She couldn't bear their knowing.

"Sarla," Erik called to her again, more of an edge on his voice now. "You will come to my sleeping chamber now."

It had always been his sleeping chamber, never *theirs*. Thus it was now with Malverne. Since his father had died, Malverne was his and he enjoyed saying it aloud, for she'd heard him saying it, savoring the taste of it on his tongue. Now his parents' sleeping chamber was his. She supposed Merrik would take his former sleeping chamber, but as yet he'd said nothing about it. Probably it hadn't even occurred to him, for he was so immersed in shock and in grief. As for her, she was here only because she was his wife and she doubted he would send her away. For what reason? She thought of her parents' farmstead, not too far to the north of Vestfold, and shuddered. She saw her father, his wide leather belt wrapped around his hand, saw her mother bowed, her back naked, saw the belt come down again and again, saw her mother fall and lie huddled on the ground. She saw her father turn to her, and she saw the smile of rage on his face. She shuddered again. She preferred Erik. Besides, he had his women so he didn't bother her all that often. Never had he struck her.

She walked slowly to him, stopping in front of him, her head still bowed.

His hand closed over her upper arm. "I have need of you tonight," he said.

Laren watched the two of them, frowning. Taby said, "Merrik's father and mother are dead, just like ours. He is very sad, Laren."

"Aye, he is. He was so excited about seeing them again." She remembered the strange feelings he'd had and wondered at it.

She set about unfolding the blankets and arranging them on the packed earthen floor. She looked up, but Taby had left her. She saw him ease between the great oak doors of the longhouse. She started to call after him, but saw that many of the Malverne people were wrapped in their blankets on the benches and the floor. She rose instead and followed him.

Taby saw Merrik standing near the palisade wall, utterly silent and unmoving. He was looking upward at the brilliant display of stars overhead. It was very quiet. The huge expanse of water below, the tree-covered mountains on the opposite side of the fjord, all was silent, eerily so.

"I'm sorry they died," Taby said to the big man who towered over him, the man he trusted more than anyone he'd ever known in his short life, other than his sister.

Merrik turned to look down at the child. Words clogged in his throat. He knew his cheeks were wet but he didn't care. His grief was deep and his pain at his loss deeper.

"I don't remember my mother and father," Taby said after a moment. "I was too young when they died, but Laren tells me about them sometimes. She tells very good stories."

"I know."

"Sometimes she cries, just like you're doing. I ask her why and she says that the memories of them are so very sharp and sweet that crying makes her almost feel them and taste them again. Sometimes I don't understand what she means."

Ah, but Merrik did. He leaned down and lifted Taby into his arms. He carried him to an oak tree that was probably as old as the cliffs that the fjord had cut through below and eased down, leaning back against the trunk. He settled the boy against his chest. He began to rub Taby's back in wide, soothing circles.

He said quietly, his voice deep and low, "I am lucky, for I grew to manhood with my parents. But that makes their passing that much more difficult, for I knew them first as parents, then as a man and a woman I could trust beyond life itself, and as my dearest friends. My father was a very proud man, but he was a man who loved his children, a man who loved his wife dearly, a man who would never act unfairly or hurt another out of anger."

"He is like you," Taby said, settling in against Merrik's shoulder.

Merrik smiled and lightly kissed the top of Taby's head. "To be like my father would be a great accomplishment," he said. "You would have loved my mother, Taby. All children flocked to her and she gave them all equal measures of love and attention. She was warm and strong and my father never tried to make her into a submissive female."

"She sounds like Laren."

That made him frown. "Hardly. My mother was very different from your sister. She had not your sister's pride, her vanity, her arrogance." He remembered telling Laren that his mother was a warrior one minute and gentle as a child the next. He frowned more deeply.

"I don't understand what you mean," Taby said. "Laren is my sister. She would kill to save me. She would die to save me too."

"That may be true," Merrik said. He didn't want to speak of Laren. She was only important because she was Taby's sister. He didn't want her to be important in any other way. He thought of her throwing herself against him at Kaupang simply because he'd bought clothing for both Cleve and Taby. He clearly remembered the feel of her, the touch of her warm breath on his cheek. He said now, "I must leave Malverne soon, for now it is my brother's home, and he and Sarla will have children, surely, and it is not large enough for both of us. Aye, I had thought of it before, thought that I must leave soon and build my own house, farm my own land. My other brother, Rorik, owns an entire island off the coast of East Anglia called Hawkfell Island. It's a beautiful place and it is his alone. I must make my own way as he did. What do you think, Taby?"

Taby was asleep.

Laren said quietly, stepping into his line of vision, "A man must be his own master, tread on ground that is his alone, farm land where he spreads his own grain and tends and reaps it."

Merrik was silent for a moment. He was taken off guard, and he didn't like it. She'd come upon them, silent as a shadow, and overheard him. He didn't like that, for he'd also been thinking of her, and he didn't want her to get close to those thoughts, to guess about them, perhaps. His words to Taby were really meant for himself, not for anyone else, for Taby was a child without a man's reason. And yet she was here, coming upon him like a silent shadow, listening to him without his knowing it.

"I like it not that you hide yourself and listen to words not meant for your ears. It is true, though, and I will repeat it to your face: your pride is overweening. You are as arrogant as a warrior, which is absurd. Your belief in your own value is more than a female's should be."

She only shrugged. "I had not heard you say that, but if that is what you believe, why then there is little I can do about it."

He sighed, wishing he'd not spoken. "Does your leg pain you?"

"Not so much now. The cream is wondrous."

"There won't be more, for my mother is dead. Perhaps she taught Sarla how to make it. We will see." He stared off into the nothingness beyond her, and thought, first she is starved then beaten and then burned. His anger at her died. Her damned pride and arrogance had brought her through it; she'd survived because of it. Aye, he thought, that part of her was like his mother, or more like his sister-in-law Mirana, Rorik's wife, perhaps, a woman he'd hated at first, for he saw her tainted and befouled with a villain's blood as had his parents. He'd distrusted her, feared for his brother. Ah, but she'd been strong and loyal and as stubborn as his brother.

He sighed now, saying, "I hate the suddenness of death. The finality of it. To die in battle—a man is ready for that, at least he is in his heart, if not fully in his mind, because he knows that if he falls, he will go to Valhalla and live there for all eternity. But to be felled by an illness that is unexpected, to be helpless against it, to know there is nothing you can do, that is frightening. It strips a man of dignity, of honor."

Her voice was hard, as was the line of her mouth. "That is life. Honor and dignity have nothing to do with death. I see being cleaved into two parts in battle as no more a virtue than being struck down by an illness or an assassin's knife. There is so much death in life that soon you cannot think of one without the other. Death is always riding on your shoulder. Always. It all ends in the same thing. You are no more."

"You speak harshly and you don't understand the virtues of a man's passing in a certain way, in a way of his own choosing, in a way that proclaims his valor, his worth. My father did not choose this plague."

"Neither did your mother. Remember, Merrik, women do not have the chance to be butchered in battle as do men. Do all their deaths lack honor and dignity?"

"I don't know. I hadn't thought of it in that way. But women—they are different."

"Aye," she said slowly. "They are." She started to say something else, then just shook her head, obviously changed her mind and said, "Aye, they are, and men are lucky to be larger and stronger."

He said, thinking again of her burned leg, "You survived."

She laughed, but it wasn't a joyous laugh. "Without you I would not have survived much longer. I think that Thrasco was the final link in the chain. When he discovered I wasn't a boy, he would have either sold me or killed me. Since Taby was gone from me, since I'd failed to keep him with me and as safe as I could keep him, why then it wouldn't have mattered."

"You would have killed yourself?"

She was silent for a very long time, just standing there close to him, the moonlight at her back now and he couldn't see her face, just a nimbus of light around her head. "I don't know," she said at last. "I had no time to dwell upon it. I was intent only on finding Taby. And then you came. I am very sorry about your parents, Merrik. I am sorry for your pain."

He said nothing, merely leaned back against the rough bark of the oak tree and closed his eyes.

"Leave Taby with me," he said, his eyes still closed. "I will bring him into the longhouse when I wish to return."

"As you will. What will you do now, Merrik?"

"I want an island like my brother Rorik's."

She laughed. It was a pure, rich sound, no mockery in it. He realized he'd never heard her laugh before, not like this, honest and open. Not that she'd had reason, of course. He opened his eyes. "I amuse you?"

"Where would you get an island?"

"I don't know, 'twas just a thought, just a quick answer to your insolent question."

She stiffened, but he didn't care. She deserved his sharp tongue. She turned away from him and walked away. He closed his eyes again and pulled Taby closer. He felt the child's palm on his heart.

There was a feast to celebrate Merrik's return, but it wasn't like the one of the year before or the year before that. There was mead and beer to drink, cheese, cabbage, onions, peas, wild boar steaks, dark pink salmon

well smoked and delicious, flatbread and rye bread and
apples both sweet and tart. Sarla spread a beautiful
pale linen cloth on the wide wooden table. Laren looked
at it and felt a sudden unexpected surge of tears. There
had always been such finery in her life until that awful
night: beautiful cloths to spread over surfaces, exquisite furnishings, huge spaces, not dark and low and
filled with smoke like this longhouse. She remembered
her own mother's laughter as she spread a beautiful
linen cloth on a table, how she'd complained that the
men didn't care, but she did, so it didn't matter. Such
beautiful cloths, their edges beautifully embroidered.
She hadn't thought of her mother in more months than
she could count. It was strange. Her mother's name was
Nirea, a soft name, a name that was like music to say.

"What may I do?" she said.

"You will eat, Laren, that is all you may do until you
are stronger."

"She is a slave," Erik said, coming up behind her.
"Give her tasks to perform, Sarla. You are mistress
here, it is time you acted like one."

Sarla said calmly, without hesitation, "There are
spoons in the soapstone bowl on the ledge yon. Please
place them beside the plates, Laren."

Erik grunted and went out.

Laren felt anger rise from deep inside her. Erik was
like Helga's husband, Fromm. He was a tyrant, a bully,
proud because of his bloodline. He was a man who
would be beyond dangerous were there not others to
restrain him. She wondered how much Erik had tempered his swaggering and commands when his father
had been alive and master here at Malverne.

The feast passed off well enough, Merrik supposed,
sipping on the sweet mead that Sarla made so very well.
His mother had taught her just about everything else,

he remembered, but not how to make mead. He complimented her.

Erik said, "There is too much honey in it for my taste."

"It is perfect," Merrik said. "What think you, Oleg?"

"I will drink ten more cups and then tell you."

There was only a chuckle or two, but it was a start. Erik said, "After we have supped, Deglin will tell us a tale, perhaps about my young brother's brave exploits in Kiev."

There was silence, brutal cold silence, uneasy silence, with darting glances. The men murmured and fidgeted, waiting for Merrik to speak.

Erik raised a blond eyebrow, staring first at Merrik, then down the long table to Deglin.

Merrik said mildly, "Deglin tells us no more tales, Erik. He has discovered he no longer enjoys being a skald."

"Aye," Eller said quickly. "He trained another, this girl here. It is she who now tells us stories."

Erik said, "That is nonsense. She is a girl, naught more. She cannot—"

"You will listen to her before you make your pronouncements."

Erik looked as if he would clout his brother, but he didn't. He subsided in his chair—what had been his father's chair—his face flushed, his eyes narrowed. He now looked at Laren, who was sitting beside Old Firren. "You fancy yourself a skald, girl?"

She looked up at him, and regarded him dispassionately, as though he were of little account at all. She shrugged then and it enraged him. "I fancy myself nothing at all. You will tell me, aye, doubtless you will tell me what I am."

Sarla sucked in her breath. She was seated next to

her husband, and felt the quick rage pulsing through him. She said quickly, her voice too loud, fright sounding through, she knew it, but couldn't prevent it, "Do you like the herring, my lord? Roran Black Eye caught it just this afternoon."

Erik forced his eyes away from the female slave. "Roran always has luck with the fish," he said, and drank deeply of the mead.

So it was that after the interminable meal, Laren was asked to stand before them and begin the tale of Grunlige the Dane from the beginning. She saw Deglin leave from the corner of her eye and was relieved. Just looking at him brought a wave of pain to her burned leg. She noticed that he limped and knew that he blamed her for it.

She thought of silver coins, took a sip of beer, smiled at all the assembled company and said, "Once there was a valiant warrior whose name was Grunlige the Dane."

She embellished the beginning of the story so that all of Rorik's men were sitting close now, listening carefully, all their low conversation stilled.

" . . . And when Parma leaned down to grab Selina, when his hands touched her arms, something very strange happened."

She paused apurpose, looking at each man and woman and child—those children who were still awake. Her eyes sparkled, she leaned close, as if about to tell a secret, she wet her lips with her tongue.

It was Oleg who said finally, "Enough, girl! Tell us else I will steal your beer and you will have no more for two seasons!"

The men cheered and Eller said loudly, "Give the girl a chance. I smell a good tale acoming."

9

LAREN SAID, HER voice low and filled with emotion, "Aye, when Parma touched Selina's arms, he felt as though Thor himself had sent a bolt of lightning through him. He fell back, trembling, and suddenly he was brutally cold, his hands shaking. His hands felt seared, pain surging through them, yet there were no marks on them. They felt numb, then they ached and throbbed. He looked from his hands to Selina. She said quietly, 'I told you not to touch me.'

"As the moments passed, so did his memory of his fear, the memory of the strange scorching pain in his hands, the cold that was surely colder than death itself, and he was angry now, unwilling to believe that something strange had indeed happened, something that he hadn't seen or understood. He snarled at her and leapt upon her, throwing her to her back on the rocky ground. Still, she didn't scream, didn't try to struggle against him. He lay on top of her, grinning now, spittle pooling on his lips, for his was an evil grin, a triumphant grin, and he said, 'There was nothing strange, to well up within me, nothing foreign. 'Twas just a momentary dream, an instant of uncertainty, nothing more. I will plow your belly now and then I will take you back to my farmstead and you will become one of my concubines and know a life of servitude.'

"No sooner were the words out of his mouth than he felt himself lifted bodily off her. What man had the strength to lift him and hold him like this? Like he were naught but a small child? He tried to jerk free, but could not. No, he hovered over her, not more than six feet above her, looking down at her, stunned, unspeaking, words clogging in his throat. He didn't drop back down to the ground as a man should when falling from a height. No, he wasn't falling at all. He was going higher and higher, until finally he saw Selina still lying there on her back on the ground, just looking up at him. She smiled and called up to him, 'Go higher, Parma, 'tis your ambition, isn't it? Aye, as high as the clouds. Go, Parma. Your fate awaits you.'

"He kicked and thrashed about, but he continued to go higher and there was naught he could do about it. He was shrieking now with fear, struggling wildly against the unknown force that was holding him, yet even as he tried to turn onto his back, he was not able to. His body seemed frozen there, staring down at Selina, who was growing smaller and smaller, and he knew she was still smiling at him.

"He shrieked and shrieked. He wanted his release but he knew, too, if he were released he would die, for he would plummet back to the ground and be crushed against the rocks. Suddenly, without warning, he felt himself heaved forward, as if shoved by a mighty hand, and now he was no longer hovering over Selina, he was moving swiftly to the east. Then there was water beneath him, a vast sea of water, and his fear was so great that he couldn't begin to understand what was happening to him. She must have cursed him, he thought, clinging to that, aye, she was a witch and none of this was really happening, it was a vision, an illusion brought on by her witch's curse. He would find her and he would kill her, but all he did was move more quickly, shoved southward now by that mighty force. He was in the clouds and he couldn't see through the white haze, and he was cold, shivering, his flesh blue, as blue as Grunlige's hands had been after he'd shredded all the ice floes. He remembered Selina's words. He damned her for a witch just as she'd damned him. He would die here, high above the earth, frozen to death in the clouds all because of a curse from a woman he would kill if only he could find her again.

"Then, very slowly, he began to descend from the sky. The air grew warmer and he felt himself once more able to think, to see, to reason. He could see the earth clearly, the rocks, a narrow stream, the brilliant green of the grass. He was not plummeting downward, but gliding smoothly and slowly, ah, he felt like a magician, and began to wonder if it had been he who had raised himself, if he had finally come into his own. Aye, it had to have been he who had climbed upward and begun to fly.

"He believed this, now smiling as he drew closer to the ground. He was warm again, feeling the blood course through him. He waved his arms about to change his direction. He changed direction. He laughed aloud with his marvelous discovery. Ah, there was nothing he couldn't do now. The gods had granted him the power. He kicked his feet and rushed forward through the silent warm air, then slowed. He laughed aloud and set about to test his new abilities. But before he could wave his arms again or kick his feet, he fell like a stone the remaining short distance to the ground, as if he'd been released and thrown downward, landing at the feet of a large bearskin-clad man, a warrior, perhaps even a *berserker,* huge and strong, a mighty sword held in a bandaged hand.

"That warrior was Grunlige the Dane. His hands were still bandaged, but he seemed to hold that sword easily. He stood straight and tall, as proud as he had been before the tragedy had struck him. And he said, 'You are Parma and you dared to touch my wife. Do you know what I will do to you?'

"Parma stared up at Grunlige, openmouthed in disbelief. He shook his head dumbly, unwilling to believe it was really Grunlige. It couldn't be Grunlige. He gained courage. He said, his voice brash and arrogant, 'You should be dead. You went off to die. You *are* dead. You are merely some remnant of a man, some lost shadow that has yet to fade into oblivion. This is naught but your shell, for you are nothing, just a voice and an illusion propped up by the air that surrounds us. I have raided your holdings, stolen your cattle, and plundered your ships. You were not there when your men cried out for your help.

" 'Now we are far away from your homeland and mine. What is this place? Where are we? You cannot be Grunlige, for he stands not tall and proud anymore. He is pathetic, probably dead now by his own hand.'

"Grunlige stared down at him, unmoving, and smiled. 'Shall I tell you, Parma, exactly what I am and where we are? What would you like to hear first, you vile coward?'

" 'I will fly away from you, and then I will come back and slay you!' Parma jumped to his feet, flapped his arms, but nothing happened. He climbed atop a high rock and jumped off, flailing his arms wildly, kicking his feet. He heard Grunlige the Dane laugh, a laugh as wicked and frightening as a laugh from the Christians' hell. Parma didn't soar into the heavens, he fell hard once again at Grunlige's feet. He screamed with rage, 'It is the witch again! She has stolen my powers. Damn her for all time!'

"Grunlige said very softly, even as he raised his foot above Parma's head, 'Heed me, fool. You have no powers, only vanity and guilt and a stupid man's arrogance. Now you will gain what you deserve.'"

Laren stopped. She smiled at the men and women and children, all of whom were staring at her, their attention focused solely on her. Cleve was smiling and nodding at her, Taby asleep on his lap.

"Continue," Erik bellowed. "I grow tired of your waiting! Damn you, what happened? What did Grunlige do? Did he send his foot into Parma's skull? Where in the name of the gods are they?"

She shook her head. "I am but a woman, my lord Erik, and must rest now. Forgive me. My brain and my throat are sore and need to recover. Perhaps by tomorrow night I will be able to continue."

There were murmurs of protest, and Erik looked as though he would explode, for even as a child, he would sit before the skald listening so intently that their mother could call him and he would not hear her. Merrik laughed as he rose, and said quickly, "Nay, all of you be quiet. It is her way. She stops not because she has any supposed weakness of a woman, nay, she leaves you purposely dangling, hooked like bait on a fishing line. Don't wriggle about. Yawn and tell her she did fairly well but you really don't care what happens next. It will drive her mad with doubts and make her less arrogant in her skills."

He laughed again and turned to Erik. "Well, brother, what do you think of my new skald, my female skald?"

Erik just looked at Laren. Suddenly, Merrik didn't like the way he was gazing so intently at her. He didn't want that kind of trouble. By all the gods, he didn't want to have to quarrel with his brother, tell him to leave her alone, but he would have to if Erik decided he wanted to bed Laren. He didn't know why he would have to, but he knew he would. He looked at Sarla, who was, in turn, staring at her husband. She knew, Merrik thought, she knew. Indeed, it was difficult for her not to know. Two of Erik's bastards were here in the longhouse, both boys, although the youngest had not yet gained a year. But Kenna was strong and healthy and the very image of his father. And their mothers were there, too, and as far as Merrik knew, both Megot and Caylis still shared his brother's bed.

But Sarla had no children as yet. She and Erik had been wed for two years now and as yet her belly hadn't swelled with child. Merrik sighed. He didn't like this. He walked to Cleve and held out his arms for Taby.

He gathered the child to him, then went to search out some blankets, Taby held securely in the crook of his arm. He saw Laren looking at him. It was the first night he had kept Taby with him. He walked to her and said, "I will see to Taby tonight." He paused a moment, studying her upturned face. Her face was flushed from the heat and from her success. He smiled at her, and to his surprise, she smiled back. It was a lovely smile and he felt the warmth of it all the way to his belly. Yet he wanted to see her smile again and yet again. But not now, not at him. So he turned away, saying as he did so, "You will stay close to the longhouse. Remain by Sarla's side. I will decide where we will go soon."

In her hand were seven small silver pieces. She closed her fist over them, holding them close. They tingled against her flesh. Perhaps they were enough to buy her freedom and Taby's and Cleve's. She said, "I would speak to you, Merrik, perhaps on the morrow. It is important." Then she was uncertain. She had eleven pieces of silver. Surely that was a lot of silver, but she had no idea what she or Cleve were worth in the slave market. "Perhaps I can speak to you not tomorrow, but later, perhaps in three or four days. Or perhaps I can question you about certain things, about the value of things."

She'd said nothing about Taby, sleeping soundly, now cupped in one of his arms against his shoulder, and that surprised him. "Your meaning is as clear as a piece of bog ore. Nay, don't try to confuse me or yourself more. Now, I would have a promise from you. Do you swear you will stay close to the longhouse and to Sarla?" She frowned at him, then nodded, not understanding. He knew she didn't, but said nothing more.

Early the next morning when she went to relieve herself, she came out of the privy to see Erik standing there, his hands on his hips.

"I have been waiting for you," he said, and he smiled at her.

"Why?" He frowned and she quickly added, "My lord."

"That is better. I am the lord of Malverne and you are naught but a slave. It is good you don't forget that. You are comely, Laren. You are still much too thin, but I shall take care not to grind myself against your bones."

"Why would you wish to do that?" But she knew what he wanted now, she recognized the lust in his eyes, and his supreme confidence. He wanted her and he would have her, and she recognized the certainty in him. But she would feign ignorance until she could think of something, anything . . .

"Actually, Merrik tells me you are still very thin but you don't look thin with your gown and tunic covering you. I will remove your clothes, look at you and study you and decide for myself."

Still, she merely cocked her head to the side and looked at him like a questioning half-wit. "My lord, I will go assist your wife now. I make an excellent porridge."

"You will assist no one but me, Laren." He took a step toward her now and Laren quickly took a step back. He frowned. "What are you doing? I am lord here, and if I want to bed you I will bed you. You have no say in the matter. But still, I am a man of handsome parts and there is no reason why you wouldn't want me to touch you and caress you."

Ah, she thought, but the parts didn't add up into a handsome whole. She said hesitantly, looking beyond his left shoulder, "I cannot, my lord. I am Merrik's slave, his possession. I am his concubine. You must ask him if you wish to share me with him."

That drew Erik up short. He frowned. "My brother said nothing about keeping you. You haven't slept with him. By all the gods, he sleeps with your little brother, or alone. You lie, wench. He doesn't want you. He even told me so. He said he took you only because you were the child's sister."

She felt a shaft of pain at his words, a pain so deep she thought she'd strangle with it, but she managed to say calmly enough, "It is my monthly flow. Merrik doesn't like to touch me at those times."

"I am surprised my brother would let such a simple thing deter him. As for me, I don't care." Erik took another step toward her.

She shook her head even as she eased to her left, toward the longhouse. To her unspeakable relief, one of Erik's men, Sturla by name, a huge man with arms larger than her legs, bulging with muscle, came striding from the longhouse. He said, "The men are ready, Erik. The boar was seen just late yesterday and I know we can find it. I have promised Sarla she will have it to make us boar steaks this very night."

She wanted to kiss the huge man, who could, if he wished, kill her with one blow from his immense hand.

Erik looked at her, saw the relief in her eyes, and cursed quietly. It was obvious he'd forgotten about the boar hunt. He said nothing, merely turned to Sturla. "Let us be off, then." He said over his shoulder to her, "I will see to you this night. You will not gainsay me."

Laren said not a word. She waited, unmoving, until Erik disappeared through the palisade gates with six of his men.

A woman said from behind her, "I heard Merrik warn you, yet you came out here alone. Do you not heed your master's warnings?"

Laren said nothing, just continued staring after Erik and Sturla until all the men were gone from view.

The woman continued, "Erik will have you, despite your wishes, despite his brother's wishes."

Laren turned slowly to face a young woman with brilliant blue eyes and blond hair that looked filled with the morning sunlight. She was taller than most women, deep bosomed and well garbed. Laren said, "I had to relieve myself. That is not a thing done with others. Who are you?"

"I am Caylis. Erik has kept me for nine years now. His father bought me when I was only thirteen years old to assist his wife and to be a companion to their niece Sira. Erik wanted me and took me. My son is eight years old now. He is Kenna, a good boy, strong and proud. If Sarla has no children, then Erik will doubtless make him legitimate. I pray it will happen. I have borne him three other children, all girls, but they died."

"But Erik is wedded to Sarla."

"Aye, the poor little weak fool. Over two years now. 'Twas a marriage arranged by Erik's father, Harald. She hasn't the guile to hold him, to make him do what she wants him to do. She is timorous as a newly foaled calf." She paused, looking Laren up and down. "Erik was careful whilst his parents still lived. He only visited my bed and the other women's after his parents had departed to their sleeping chamber for the night. He knew they were fond of Sarla, so he did nothing untoward toward us whilst they were about. But now he has no reason to deny himself anything. He can do whatever he pleases, and for whatever reason, he wants you. I suppose it is because you are new, and like all men, Erik will seek to bend you to his will until he has bedded you and discovers that you are but like the rest of us, only not as pretty or as well made."

Laren didn't say anything, but as she lifted her skirt, she smiled at the woman. Caylis sucked in her breath. "Your leg—it's horrible!"

"Aye, I burned myself. I will show your lord Erik. Perhaps that will cool his ardor."

Caylis just shook her head. "So you are Merrik's mistress, just as I heard you tell Erik. Merrik is a beautiful man, I have many times remarked on it. Is he a good lover or does he just want you to pleasure him and watch whilst his face flushes with his own passion? Does Merrik care what you feel?"

Laren stared at her. Caylis laughed. "So, you haven't bedded with him. Resign yourself, then. It is Erik who will have your virginity. It isn't bad, if he is in a pleasant mood. If he isn't, you will know much pain. Sometimes he enjoys pain, sometimes not. You will learn soon enough what it is he will want from you.

"It is a pity that Merrik has no power here now. Erik

will grant him none. If Erik wants you, he will have you. Do you really make an excellent porridge? Sarla doesn't. Come, then, for I am quite hungry."

That night, replete with the delicious boar steaks that Laren had helped Sarla to prepare, Erik called for the end of the tale of Grunlige the Dane.

Laren thought first of the silver coins, then of what would come after. She knew that Erik would come to her tonight. She simply didn't know what to do about it. First, she would tell her story, then she would decide.

She rose and rubbed her hands together, saying nothing until all attention was on her. " 'I will tell you who and what I am,' Grunlige said, his foot poised over Parma's neck. 'I am still myself and none other. I am not a shade from the nether regions. I am flesh and bone, but I have gone beyond a mere man's flesh and bones to a higher realm. But mistake me not, Parma, I am still myself and Selina is still my beloved wife. You see my hands are still bandaged. That was for you to remark upon and feel superior about.'

"Grunlige slowly unwrapped the bandages from his hands. Parma could but stare. No longer were Grunlige's hands shriveled like claws, fingernails twisted and blackened. No, his hands were whole and clean and strong, and the sword handle fit well into his palm.

" 'Your witch wife, she brought you back,' Parma gasped, so frightened now, he felt his bladder loosen and knew great shame for his fear.

" 'Nay, 'twas Odin All-Father,' Grunlige said matter-of-factly. 'He deemed me worthy, deemed my people worthy, and thus restored me. You are a fool, Parma, do you not recognize where you are?'

"Parma gazed about him, but he recognized nothing. Then he saw Selina walking toward them, her white robe flowing, her shoulders proud, her walk confident.

" 'You have gone nowhere, Parma. You are still here where you attacked my wife. Odin but played with you, teased you, and you were a fool. Now, what have you to say for yourself?'

"Parma thought furiously, and knew he had but one chance to keep his life. He said, 'If you are truly a hero, if Odin All-Father truly deemed you brave and worthy, why then go perform a deed that would prove your greatness. Do not crush my neck with your foot. That would be nothing, it would be more the act of a coward. Aye, go, Grunlige, and prove yourself. Go in a vessel into the seas east of Iceland. Once again, shred the ice floes, once again, aye, and see if you are truly the gallant hero you believe yourself to be.'

"Selina cried out, 'Listen not to him, Grunlige! His tongue is wily and he wants only to mock you, to make you lose your sense of what is right! Don't heed him!'

"But Grunlige had lifted his foot from Parma's neck. He stepped away from Parma, who didn't move at all, who resembled a statue, so still did he lie. Grunlige gazed upward at the heavens. He threw back his mighty head and shouted, 'Odin! Hear me, oh mighty lord of the heavens and of all warriors! I will go again to prove myself and when I return you must grant me what it is I deserve!'

"Suddenly, a great white flash of lightning streaked through the sky, turning the air itself to vapor. Again and again there was that sheer white filling the air, filling their lungs. It was followed by crash after crash of thunder that shook the ground itself. Selina fell to her knees, burying her face in her hands. Parma felt fear, but now he also felt hope. He stared at Grunlige.

"Grunlige was smiling. 'I hear you, Odin. I go to prove myself yet again to you.'

"Before he strode away, he grasped Parma by the

throat and hauled him upright. He shook him until
Parma believed his neck would break apart from his
body. Grunlige said, 'If you touch my wife again or any
of my belongings or any of my people, I will peel the
flesh from your body. I will then fling you onto an ice
floe and there your seeping blood will freeze and you
will know more agony than a man can bear.'

"He strode to his wife, drew her to her feet and em-
braced her. Then he was gone, his shoulders straight
and strong, his stride quick and sure."

Laren stopped then, and smiled, first down at her
clasped hands, then at each of her audience in turn.

"I will not accept this dithering," Erik shouted at her.
"Finish the damned tale! Finish it!"

She just shook her head.

It was Sturla, Erik's huge warrior, who said now,
"Nay, my lord, leave her be. I like this suspense, it
teases my wits and makes me wonder what will happen
next. Aye, perhaps tomorrow night she will continue
the tale. Mayhap she will even finish it for us."

Erik subsided. He sat in his lord's chair, fingering the
magnificently carved chair posts that had come through
the family for two hundred years. The oak was smooth
as silk with the many fingers that had stroked it, but
the images of Odin and Thor and Frey were still clear,
the expressions on their carved faces still sharp.

He waited, was content to wait. He watched Sarla
dismiss the slaves, watched all the children herded off
to the small sleeping chamber where they slept,
watched his men and Merrik's men roll themselves into
blankets. He waited until all was nearly silent. He prepared to rise, but stopped. Merrik was walking to where
Laren was lying near the fire pit, her blanket wrapped
closely around her, Taby tucked in the curve of her
belly. He came down beside her on his haunches.

He said low so as not to awaken Taby, "You are my concubine, I have heard said today. I think it is the only thing that might save you from my brother's lust. You will give Taby to Cleve and come with me. We will sleep in my sleeping chamber."

She stared up at him in the dim light cast by the dying embers. "Will you hurt me?"

"I will look at your leg and at your back and probably apply more healing cream to both. Then we will see."

"I don't want you to see," she said. "I don't want to be your concubine, Merrik, 'tis just that I could think of nothing else to say."

"I know, but you are the one who said it. Therefore we must continue as you began, else Erik will be beside you within another instant. Well? What do you wish?"

She didn't look at him, just said calmly, "Where is Cleve?"

Merrik smiled at her. "I will fetch him."

10

ERIK STOOD OVER her, oblivious of his brother and their people who stood near. "Give the child over and come with me."

"I fear she cannot, brother," Merrik said. He turned to Cleve. "Take Taby for the night. I would keep his sister with me."

Cleve said nothing as he gathered up the sleeping child, nor did Laren. She waited there on the floor, wrapped in her blanket, watching the two men.

"I want her," Erik said, and she heard the petulance, the covetousness in his voice.

"She is my concubine and she is my slave as well, Erik. When I tire of her, I will consider selling her to you. Come along, Laren."

"She said you didn't want her because it was her monthly flow. She said you wouldn't want her until she had finished it. And I've watched you, Merrik, you haven't touched her, even scarce looked at her since you came home. All you care about is that damned boy."

Merrik said slowly, consciously relaxing his hands from fists at his sides, "It is true that I like not taking her at those times, but I am in much need and thus will make do. I try not to look at her, because whenever I do it makes my lust rise. I do not like to torment myself.

But tonight I will not wait longer. It is my will that prevails here, for she is my slave, not yours. I bid you good night, brother. I see Sarla awaiting you."

"Damn you, Merrik, 'tis not just that I want to plow her belly, I would have her tell me what happened to Grunlige the Dane!"

If she hadn't been so afraid, Laren would have laughed.

"She will tell you tomorrow night, Erik." Merrik reached out his hand, and without hesitation, she placed her own in his. He pulled her upright. She fell forward, against his chest, and he laughed a little, stroking her hair with familiarity as he did so. He held her there as he said, "I told you she was thin. She is. So thin you would look at her only once and tell her to leave you. Also, her hair is short and ragged, as you see, not as full and thick like your wife's or your mistresses'."

Laren heard a laugh and knew it was from the woman Caylis.

She saw Sarla from the corner of her eye. How could Erik shame his wife like this? It enraged her. Before she could say anything, Merrik leaned down and kissed her hard.

The shock of it rendered her immediately silent. He laughed again, gave his brother a small salute, and picked her up in his arms. She didn't move, barely breathed in fact until he laid her upon the box bed that had belonged to his brother before their parents had died.

The chamber was small and dark. Merrik cursed under his breath, left the chamber, and soon returned with a lit oil lamp. There were wool blankets on the bed and atop those were otter and reindeer skins traded from the Lapps in the North. There was a beautiful large chest at the foot of the bed, nothing else.

Merrik walked to the entrance of the chamber, pulled the skin aside and looked out. Erik was nowhere to be seen. Hopefully he was with Sarla. All was quiet, save for the snores from some of the men and the few moans and giggles from the men and women enjoying themselves before sleep came.

He cursed again, and once more left the chamber. Laren didn't move, just stared at the bearskin that covered the entrance. When he came back there was a soapstone jar in his hand.

He said briefly, "The cream for your back and leg. Take off your clothes."

She didn't move. "Why did you kiss me?"

"For my brother's benefit. To show him my possession of you."

"But everyone was watching."

He shrugged, and said matter-of-factly, "I know. It will keep Erik's men away from you as well. Obey me now. I am tired and wish to sleep."

She didn't want to take off her clothes in front of him, didn't want to repel him with her thinness. It hadn't mattered to her before but it did now for the simple reason that now she cared what he thought. No, she didn't want to have to obey that command. It was as if she didn't matter, who she was and what she was—it was entirely unimportant to him. It was Taby he wanted, not her, Taby he cared about, not her. Erik was right about that. She said nothing to him, nothing at all. She tried to remember that if he hadn't saved her from Thrasco, she would surely be dead now. But that wasn't true. She had escaped from Thrasco on her own. She would have managed. She owed him only for saving Taby.

She didn't know what to do.

She wanted very much for him to kiss her again, but of course he would never kiss her freely, never because he wanted to, never because of desire for her. Quite simply, there was no one for her, no one save a five-year-old child.

Suddenly the terror of the last two years, of the endless weeks that had flowed into months and beyond, that endless time of hopelessness, of rage and fury that had eaten at her deeply and more deeply still as time passed, it all welled up in her then and she felt herself crushed under the weight of it. It erupted and she couldn't prevent it. She began to sob, deep ugly sobs that shook her whole body. She buried her face in her hands, hating the ugly sounds that showed him her weakness, but the wave upon wave of grinding pain wouldn't cease. The helplessness, the fear, the bitterness, all were there, pulling at her, defeating her. She tried desperately to gain control, for she didn't want him to see how pathetic she was, she didn't want anyone to see it, but the sobs were deeper now, a part of her, and they wouldn't stop.

Merrik stood by the bed simply staring down at her. His first thought was that Erik had terrified her. Then he knew that wasn't the case. She wasn't some gutless female. No, she was a survivor. Surely Erik's lust would have no effect on her, at least not this effect. But she sounded as if her very world had ended.

He set the cream on the bed, sat down, and without a word, pulled her into his arms. He rubbed his large hands down her back, only to remember that her back must still be sore from the beating Thrasco had given her. He rubbed her scalp, just holding her with one arm loose around her back. He said things to her, words that had little meaning to him, to her, just words, but their tone was gentle and reassuring, and he supposed,

vaguely, that was what was important. He realized he
might be holding Taby, stroking him, telling him everything would be all right because he, Merrik, was here
now and he would take care of him, he would protect
him with his life.

She moved against him and then he felt her breasts.

She wasn't a child and he felt like a fool. No, she
wasn't a child and he felt a surge of lust for her. It was
unexpected and he didn't like it. She was Taby's sister.
It was just that it had been a long time since he'd had
a woman, too long. But, of course, he remembered the
softness of her, the feel of her when she'd hugged herself to him in Kaupang.

He didn't intend it, but he kissed her temple, felt her
soft hair tickle his cheek, his nose.

"It's all right," he said again, but now his voice was
deep and hoarse with his burgeoning need. "I won't hurt
you."

Her breath caught in her throat and she hiccuped.
His hands came around to close around her chin and he
lifted her face. Tears were wet on her cheeks and she
was gulping for breath. Her eyes and nose were red, her
hair was loose from its braids and straggling over her
forehead. She looked as appetizing as a gutted herring,
and he thought she was the most beautiful woman he'd
ever seen.

And he wanted her.

In that moment, he forgot Taby, forgot that this was
Taby's sister. He leaned forward and kissed her. The
second time. He tasted the salty tears, and something
else, something sweet and dark and mysterious, something that had no part of either of them separately, but
something that was both magical and an odd enchant-
ment when he touched her mouth, when the two of
them came together. It was something he'd never ex-

perienced before; it was something he wanted for himself, and he wanted it badly. He was a man with a man's needs and she was here alone with him. She belonged to him.

She wasn't moving. Yet he wanted her even more now. He kissed her again, harder this time, willing her to part her lips, but he realized suddenly that she very probably had no idea what to do. And that stopped him cold. She was innocent in deed, if not in what she had witnessed during the last two years.

She didn't know how to kiss him. He started to say something, to pull away from her, but suddenly, she leaned forward, her hand came up to touch his cheek, and she kissed him. Her lips were soft and firmly together and she just pressed them to his mouth, but it was a kiss and it was she who was freely offering it. A virgin's kiss.

He opened his mouth slightly and let the tip of his tongue lightly touch her mouth. She jumped. Then, to his surprise and pleasure, she leaned into him, and this time her lips were sightly open as well.

He felt the surge of lust throughout his body, not just his groin. He was swelled and ready, but that wasn't all there was to it. He felt that mystery again, felt that something deep and still hidden from him, felt it moving within him, pushing him toward her, and knowing even as he felt those odd feelings that coming together with her would change his life. He fought it even as it swamped him, lured him toward her. Surely she was just a woman, and he'd known many women, but at the same time, she was just herself and like none other. He drew away from that. It struck fear in him, for he believed a man must remain unto himself and not give himself over to anyone else, particularly a woman, particularly this woman who was scarce a woman really, just a girl who was so thin that surely she wouldn't have the strength to take him as a man, and she was Taby's sister. He had not saved her to ravish her. He had not saved her to hurt her.

No, he saved her because she was Taby's sister, nothing more, nothing less. Suddenly, he saw her as he'd seen her so long ago now, aye, ages ago, it seemed, yet not really, but he saw her very clearly in his mind's eye—the ragged boy, defeated yet as proud and defiant as he was himself, standing there, helpless, in the slave pit of Khagan-Rus. No, he'd looked at her and looked again and he knew now that what he had felt was different, for she had touched him with the essence of herself. He would never be free of her just as he would never be free of Taby.

He supposed that right now, at just this moment, he didn't want to be free of her, didn't want to rail against it and try to protect himself, for his lust for her was grinding him down. When her tongue lightly touched his, he gave it up.

There was no rape here. If he hurt her because of her thinness, so be it. He would try not to, but . . .

He pulled her down and came over her. The feel of her beneath him made him want to shout and groan and come into her, all in the same instant. His hand was wild on the skirt of her gown, and he was jerking it up, his movements frantic. His fingers scraped against her bare leg and she jerked and cried out.

At first he didn't realize what had happened. Then he knew. He'd hit her burned leg and hurt her. He drew a deep breath, feeling his whole body shudder with the force of the control he was trying to find within himself.

Her breasts were heaving against him, but now it wasn't desire or even a girl's excitement in the unknown, it was the pain he'd just brought her. He gathered her up against him and whispered against her ear, "I'm sorry. Damnation, I hurt you. I have the cream. Hold still and soon the pain will lessen."

Laren lay there, breathing hard from the curious mixture of intense pain and feelings that she herself couldn't begin to describe. She just knew that she'd never felt such things before, in such places, and it was wonderful and she wanted them again. She didn't want them ever to stop. She didn't want him to stop, but he had because he'd hurt her. She looked at him now and he was flushed, his hands none too steady.

She felt his fingers, chill with the cream, lightly touch her leg and she gasped, the pain making all the other feelings recede. She tried not to cry out, but she couldn't help it.

He said nothing, just looked up at her and saw that she was crying and her eyes were closed, the tears just seeping from beneath her lashes and trailing down her cheeks.

He saw the print of his fingers on her still-red flesh. He gently rubbed in the cream. Actually, her leg looked much better. If there would be scarring, it would be slight. He began a gentle rhythmic motion and stuck to it. His desire was nearly gone, and for that he was grateful. He would find a woman this night and drain his desire so this wouldn't happen again. Then he realized he could not leave her, could not leave this sleeping chamber. He was in here with his concubine and none must doubt it, least of all his brother.

"How is your back?"

She got control of herself. No more damnable tears, no more weak moans and groans. The cream was leaching out the pain. She could manage it now. "My back is fine, Merrik. My leg is better too."

He should look at her back, but the thought of her

naked made his belly seize with cramps. But he'd seen
her naked before and it hadn't particularly moved him.
But that had been before he'd kissed her and held her
hard against him and touched his tongue to her lips, to
her tongue, breathed in the scent of her, felt the wondrous feelings that had passed between them, locking
them together in that brief instant of time. It was beyond what he could understand or accept. He hadn't
come inside her; he hadn't spilled his seed in her and
come to his release. No, it was just the simple kissing,
the holding of her close to him, and those simple acts
had brought him to the edge. He had never lost himself
before, certainly not with the simple matter of sex, certainly not in the simple things that came before sex. It
wouldn't happen to him now. It would never happen to
him. He wouldn't allow it. He would look at her back,
rub in more of the cream if necessary, and it would be
as it had been before.

But he wouldn't kiss her again. He wasn't that great
of a fool.

He said, his voice so stiff and cold it surprised him
more than it did her, "I will help you off with your
clothes. I will look at your back. You know nothing, for
you can't see yourself. Now, stop arguing with me."

Actually, she hadn't said a word. He helped her sit
on the side of the box bed. He untied the knots of the
tunic at her shoulders and pulled it over her head. He
unlaced the front of her gown and eased it down to her
waist. She wore only a plain linen shift beneath, the
one he'd bought for her at the market in Kaupang. He
didn't want to notice but he did. It was tight on her, her
breasts crushed against the material. He knew he had
to get her onto her stomach quickly.

Once she was facedown, he pulled her gown and her
shift down to her waist. He brought the oil lamp closer.

The marks from Thrasco's whip were still clear, long narrow marks that crisscrossed her back. The ugly redness had given over to pale pink now, there was no puffiness, no red angry or dark lines radiating out from the marks, or any other sign of illness. Still, the cream couldn't hurt. He scooped up two fingers full of cream and began to massage her back. She was stiff as a board, but he said nothing, just continued to rub her, his touch lightly stroking. Soon, he felt her ease. Soon after that she moaned with the pleasure of it and he had to smile.

He should rub in the cream every night. Her body was tense too and he rubbed her shoulders. She moaned again.

He pushed the gown lower on her hips. He didn't know why he'd done it, for he knew that Thrasco's whip hadn't struck that low on her body.

He just wanted to see her, see how much flesh she'd added during the weeks she'd been with him. He could still see her ribs, but there was a woman's softness there now as well and her white hips were full enough, and he thought he'd spill his seed.

From laughter to such lust he thought he'd yell with it. Quickly he pulled her gown back to her waist and rose. He put the cream on the floor beside the bed.

He would sleep in the same bed with her, next to her, he had to, else he had no doubt that his brother would be there in an instant. He would not allow Erik to rape Taby's sister. It was that simple. Nor would he allow himself to seduce Taby's sister.

He said very quietly, "I am going to pull your gown off you and your shift. I will lay one of my clean tunics over your back. All right, Laren?"

She said nothing, merely nodded. Her hair had fallen over her cheek so at least she knew he couldn't see her face, nor she his. She'd felt exposed and she'd felt excited. She didn't understand why she hadn't yelled or hurled curses at him when he'd pulled her gown to her hips, but she hadn't said a word, hadn't made a single sound. And now she felt like a fool, a blind, quite stupid fool. Her back and leg were beyond ugly, and she'd forgotten that. She was still too thin. Aye, about as appetizing as a goose carcass. He'd wanted her only as long as he'd forgotten what she really looked like.

She felt tears sting her eyes again, but these weren't tears that had built and built inside her for two years. These were tears that showed how miserable she felt right at this moment, with this man who didn't want her, in this hopeless situation.

She let him strip off her clothes. She felt the soft tunic spread across her back. Then, very quickly, she felt him smooth a wool blanket over her.

When he eased down beside her, he said, "I won't do that to you again."

And she knew what he meant. She said, her voice devoid of all feeling, "It is because I am so very thin and ugly."

"No," he said. "It is because of Taby."

And again, she knew what he meant.

He knew he hadn't spoken the truth. No, it was not just because of Taby. He had no intention of shaming her and that is what would happen if he took her. Ah, but let Erik believe she was his concubine, let him listen, hoping to hear moans from her to prove that she was. Erik had to believe it. He didn't want to have to face the situation that would result from any doubt.

The following day passed quickly. At every opportunity, Merrik was giving her food, standing over her until she'd eaten every morsel he'd dished out.

Taby was playing with the other children now. Kenna, the eight-year-old son of Erik's concubine, Caylis, was a particular hero. He followed Kenna everywhere. Kenna, a handsome lad who didn't seem to have his father's meanness or arrogance, treated Taby with good-natured tolerance. The other children followed his lead.

Cleve was the one in an odd position. He was a slave, yet he didn't sleep in the slave hut, nor did he perform menial tasks. Merrik kept him with him and his men when they hunted that afternoon.

Laren counted her silver coins. She now had eighteen. Soon now, she would ask Merrik. She'd forgotten to speak to him the previous night. Too much had happened, far too much, and she knew she and Taby and Cleve had to leave soon. In weak moments, like right now, she didn't want to leave Merrik any more than Taby did, but she had to get them away from here. Neither of them belonged here.

She cooked that evening, making a stew from boar meat that brought satisfied nods from Merrik's men and grunts of surprise from the Malverne people. After the meal, Erik looked at Laren, and there was lust and meanness in his eyes. He said, "We won't have the girl continue her foolish tale tonight. I have other matters I wish to see to."

So Laren would gain no more silver pieces that night. She assumed that Erik believed he was punishing her. She didn't care. Sarla touched her sleeve. "The stew was the best I have ever eaten. You must teach me, Laren, you must."

Sarla had spoken sharply, urgently, and Laren turned to her, frowning. "It is simple, truly. Your cooking is just as good, mine is simply different."

"Nay, you must show me."

Laren looked at her closely, very closely, and for the first time she saw the faint bruise that was beneath Sarla's right eye. Fury curdled her belly. "By all the gods, he struck you!"

"Hush! Be quiet, Laren, please just be quiet. It's nothing of anything, truly. It doesn't hurt, and you can't see it unless you look very closely. Be quiet."

"Why did he strike you?"

Sarla said nothing. She merely shrugged.

"Why?"

"Erik doesn't need reasons for his actions. I displeased him and he hit me."

"Has he hit you before?"

Sarla looked at her then, and there was pity in her fine gray eyes. "I seem to displease him more and more as the days and weeks go by."

Laren knew that men hit women—their wives, their concubines, their slaves, it didn't seem to matter. But Sarla was so quiet and kind. How could she possibly displease anyone? And then she knew why Erik had struck his gentle wife. It was because he'd been thwarted; he'd wanted her, Laren, and Merrik had forestalled him.

"Your look is violent, Laren. I beg you, please say nothing. Please just forget this. Besides, I saw him speaking earlier to Caylis and then to Megot—she is the beautiful girl over there near the loom speaking to Ileria, the one with the pale brown hair. It is likely he will leave me alone now."

Laren held her peace, but it was difficult.

"You are angry."

Laren was making bread the following morning, for the men had eaten every single loaf she'd made the previous day. She plunged her hands in the trough full of dough, up to her elbows. She looked up at Cleve and forced a smile. "Nay, not really angry. It's just that Sarla is very kind and gentle. Her husband isn't."

"He is a man who enjoys being the master. He dislikes any to disagree with him. I have heard that since his father died, he has become more reckless in his actions. It makes him feel important and powerful to know he can hurt or kill any man or woman at any time, at his whim."

"At least Sarla was spared his attention last night."

"Aye, she was. She slept in the outer chamber. Near me."

Laren sighed and dug deeper into the dough, kneading it furiously. The flour hadn't been ground as well as it could have been and she felt the grit between her fingers. She would have to see about that. She remembered her owner in Staraya Ladoga, that foul-tempered old woman who had, at least, taught her how to cook and grind flour properly and make beer and ale. She'd learned quickly, just as she'd told Merrik, for the woman had struck her hard for each failure. Actually, she'd also occasionally hit her if she prepared a dish perfectly, saying she didn't want her to become conceited. Laren said now, "You and I have seen so much, Cleve, lived through so much. I don't know why a bruise on Sarla's face would make me so angry, but it does. It makes me nearly as angry as that horrible scar on your face. If I could I would kill both men who caused each of you the pain." She paused a moment, then said, "I am afraid of Erik."

"I know. It is a pity that your body isn't as strong as your spirit. Would you truly kill the man who scarred me, Laren?"

"Aye, I would enjoy causing him great pain."

"It was a woman."

She could only stare at him, then she shook her head. "I don't know why I am so surprised. I have seen equal cruelty from both men and women. Why did she do it?"

"I wouldn't bed her."

She just shook her head at him. "Did it matter so much to you?"

"Aye," he said shortly, "it mattered greatly to me."

She saw that he would say no more and held her peace. Of all people, she knew what it was like to keep the darkness of the past close and quiet. "Do you hunt with Merrik today?"

He shook his head. "Nay, I am here only to eat some of your porridge, then I will work in the fields. Harvest is not long in coming now and there is need for every hand. Even Merrik will be in the barley fields soon."

"And Erik?"

Cleve shrugged as he spooned porridge into a wooden bowl from the iron pot hanging from its chain over the fire pit.

"I last saw him taking a woman into the bathing hut with him. I doubt washing himself is all that is on his mind. I believe her name is Megot. She is short and too fat for my tastes, but her hair is as rich a gold as the barley in the field."

"She's very beautiful. I have eighteen silver pieces."

He poured a bit of honey over the porridge. "That is a lot, Laren. I would give you silver if I but had any."

"You don't understand, Cleve. When I have enough, I will purchase all of us from Merrik and we will go home."

"Home?"

"Aye, my home."

He just looked at her, then shook his head. "How

would we get there? Where is your home? Have you people who would take us in?"

She kneaded more quickly. "I don't know. First I must have enough silver. Then I will worry about what comes next."

"You will gain even more silver tonight. I fancy that Erik will call for you to speak. He punished only himself last night. I, like all the others, want to know what will happen to Grunlige the Dane."

"Actually, I don't know myself much of the time until the words just pop out of my mouth."

He gazed at her in some astonishment. "You speak truly?"

"Aye, Grunlige is a wily man and sometimes he does things I never plan."

Cleve thoughtfully spooned the porridge into his mouth. "I begin to think of him as a real man when you speak of him. To realize that he is naught more than a figment of your mind depresses me."

"Don't tell the others, all right?"

"Nay," he said, grinning at her, "I shan't."

"Most of the time he is very real to me as well."

She worked in silence now, and Cleve stood there eating. She chanced to look up. He was staring at Sarla. There was such tenderness in his eyes, she wanted to weep.

"Oh no," she said.

He turned and smiled down at her. "Nay, Laren. I am no fool. Do you know that she doesn't seem to mind the ugliness of my face? Sometimes when she smiles at me I don't even think she sees the scar. There is only gentleness in her and kindness. And a liking for me, not that it matters. It is a great shame. She is wedded to that foul bully and I, well, I am not worthy to dry her tears."

She looked at him and saw his pain and reminded herself yet again that life held little enough joy, and that any joy at all that came should be savored to the fullest.

11

LATE THAT AFTERNOON, there was a great commotion
outside the longhouse. Men were shouting, but it wasn't
in fear or the kind of shouted orders before an attack.
She went outside to see that visitors had come to Malverne.

"It is the Thoragassons," Sarla said at her elbow.
"They live to the north in the Bergson Valley, some
three days' journey from here." She paused a moment,
then added, "Before Merrik's father died, he negotiated
a marriage contract with Olaf Thoragasson between his
eldest daughter, Letta, and Merrik. I do not know if
Merrik will honor it. It is expected that he will do so.
Perhaps he wishes it, I do not know."

"Oh," Laren said.

Sarla gave her a quick look. She looked off into the
distance, at the vivid green of the thick fir trees that
covered the mountains on the opposite side of the fjord.
"I know Merrik took you to his chamber last night, as
well as the night before. All know of it, Erik as well."

"Aye, Merrik made no secret of his intent."

"Erik was furious. He ordered me to remain in the
outer hall. He took both Caylis and Megot into his
sleeping chamber with him."

"He doesn't deserve you, Sarla."

Sarla shrugged. "He is a man and now he is the lord of Malverne. Whatever he wishes he can have. Me included. Other women included as well. I am glad he left me alone." She paused a moment, then added, a touch of surprise in her voice, "I speak so frankly with you and I do not understand why I do so. Many of the women here are my friends, they welcomed me here two years ago when I arrived at Malverne as Erik's wife, and yet I say nothing to them about, well, I speak of nothing save household matters. It was the same with Tora, Merrik's mother, and she was very kind to me."

"I will not betray your trust. I was not raised to do that."

"I never thought that you would. Somehow, I sense it. Perhaps you will confide in me. I doubt I can help you, but perhaps it would be possible. Did Merrik hurt you?"

"No."

"Ah, you are not like me. No, don't apologize to me, Laren, it doesn't matter. You are used to being alone and having no one save a child to share your confidences. Merrik is a man to trust. Perhaps you can bring yourself to confide in him."

"No, that would never gain me anything. He doesn't want me, Sarla, I will tell you that. He does want to protect me from Erik, and he has the last two nights, as I think he will continue to do. He does this because he loves Taby, and he feels he wouldn't be keeping faith with the child if he allowed me to be raped. He doesn't think of me as a woman, which is fine with me. As for trust, who can say? He is a man and a Viking and I have always known that Vikings seek profit, and that they only hold faith and honor amongst themselves, not with outsiders or slaves. Aye, I know this very well."

"But Taby—"

"He loves the child. But how long will that last?"

"I do not know him that well. But you are fond of him. You must sense something worthy in him. I have seen you look at him, Laren. Do you know that when you tell of Grunlige the Dane, you look nearly always at Merrik? Ah, say what you will, Laren, deny it until your tongue dries out with all your denials, but I will keep my own opinion."

"Your opinion is wrong, Sarla."

"We will see. Ah, I must greet the Thoragassons."

The Thoragassons had brought some dozen men and four women. They were a handsome family, Laren thought, but then again most of the Norsemen she'd ever seen and known were well made and pleasing to the eye, both here and at home. As for Letta, Laren thought she looked like a spoiled child. Oh, she was pretty enough, seventeen years old, with thick blond braids coiled atop her head, a full mouth that looked as if it pouted a lot, and breasts that were surely too large for such a small girl. Laren was only a year her senior, yet she felt like the girl's mother. She felt ancient and cynical and bone-weary. She could scarce remember now the times when she was happy and a child and there was nothing more than playing and riding her mare, Selje, to concern her.

Laren saw Erik eye those big breasts and quickly looked over at Merrik. He, too, was looking at the girl, but he wasn't looking at her breasts. He merely looked harassed. No pleasure at seeing his father's choice of a bride, just harassed.

When the Thoragassons learned of the deaths, there was consternation, and it wasn't due entirely to an overabundance of sorrow at Harald's and Tora's passing. No, it was because there were no negotiated ties now to hold Merrik Haraldsson to their family.

Still, the elder Thoragasson, a bluff, hearty man with white threaded through his blond hair, slapped Merrik on his back, inquired, discreet as a wild bull, as to his current wealth after his summer trading, and pointed out with a sly wink the lovely attributes of his daughter. "Aye, she's even more finely endowed than she was during the winter solstice when last you saw her," he said. "Aye, more than a handful she would give a man."

Merrik agreed that this was true.

Olaf Thoragasson frowned. "I wonder why her mother isn't so, well, bountiful."

Merrik wisely kept his mouth shut.

"You have reached your twenty-fifth year, Merrik," Thoragasson said, his voice fraught with meaning.

Merrik only smiled. "I am not ready to lose my teeth or my virility just yet."

"Ah, but to have children relieves a man's mind, for there are his progeny to succeed him if he falls in battle of if struck by illness. Aye, a wife and children make a man's life fuller and richer."

Merrik agreed that this was probably so.

"A man needn't just cleave to a wife," Olaf said, lowering his voice, giving Merrik an understanding leer. "I know your brother Erik surrounds himself with women and enjoys all of them. A man may do whatever he wishes if he has the silver for it."

"My father was always loyal and faithful to my mother."

"He was, but he didn't have to be. Heed me, Merrik, your father very much wanted to unite our families. He himself looked upon my little Letta and chose her for you. Surely you admired your father, surely you trusted his judgment."

"In most cases, certainly," Merrik said.

"Is not my little Letta a gem?" Thoragasson said, his voice sharp now, pressing, for he scented that things weren't going as he wished.

"Surely a gem of more value than to be wasted upon a younger son who has no land."

"Aye, but my Letta is a Viking woman. She would follow her husband wherever he wished to settle. Besides, there is more than enough land for you near our farmstead. The Bergson Valley is rich enough to support you and a family."

Merrik hated the Bergson Valley. It rained too much; fog shrouded the fjord most days. He didn't like the Thoragasson men. He looked over at Letta, who was seated next to Ileria, the old woman who had worked the loom for all his life. The soft gray tunic he was wearing she had woven for him during the spring from the finest wool. It was to be his lucky tunic for when he traded with the savages, she'd told him. Letta was helping Ileria, loading a shuttle with thread from a distaff. She looked competent doing it.

"Even now, she seeks more knowledge to make your life comfortable," Thoragasson said near to Merrik's ear. "She is always learning, always asking her elders what is right, what is good. She is a fine girl. She would be submissive to your wishes."

Merrik doubted that, but said nothing. He even managed to smile. Thoragasson, pleased with himself, took himself off to speak to Erik. It wasn't until after a quickly prepared feast that night that he sat back, patted his belly, and looked toward Deglin.

"Well, Deglin, what say you? Have you a special tale for me this night?"

Erik said in a loud voice that brought him everyone's attention, "Nay, it is the girl here who is now our skald."

There was immoderate laughter from Thoragasson,

his family, and his men. "Who?" one of the men shouted. "That thin little wisp of a beggar that I could crush with one hearty breath?"

"Your breath could fell an oak tree," one of his friends shouted.

There was good-natured banter, until one of Erik's men insulted one of Thoragasson's men with too much eagerness, and a fight broke out. It ended quickly, but one man's arm was broken and another's nose was bleeding profusely.

There seemed to be blood everywhere, not just from that single nose. Laren looked about the large room, at the havoc wrought in such a short time. Was it always so with men? Were they only content when they were eating, rutting women, or breaking each other's bodies? They loved to yell and curse and strike each other. Then, suddenly, Erik rose from the floor, where he'd been pummeling one of his own men, reached for Megot and fondled her breasts in front of everyone. He kissed her hard, then smacked her bottom and told her to fetch him more beer.

Laren watched Sarla oversee the bandaging, watched another woman, Bartha, tend to the bleeding nose. She watched Megot give Erik his beer. She watched him fondle her buttocks and smile at Thoragasson as he did it. She waited, silent, knowing that Erik would say something soon. She looked at Merrik, who had himself flattened several men, and had bruised knuckles. At least there was no blood on him. He was grinning hugely and had just taken Taby from Cleve and was hugging him then tossing him into the air. The child shrieked and laughed. He kissed him and held him close. She saw Thoragasson staring at him, and she knew he wondered if Taby was Merrik's child. He might as well be his child, she thought, for the bond between

them was strengthening each day. She had to get Taby
away from here soon, or losing Merrik would break the
child's heart. No, no, she told herself, children forgot
quickly, they adapted easily as situations changed.

Laren looked away from him to the Thoragassons,
and suddenly she saw them with new eyes. Now she
saw them as a source of more silver pieces. She saw
them as saviors. If they but knew it surely they would
find it funny.

When Erik called for quiet and told her to begin, she
rose, smiled at everyone, and began once again at the
beginning. In order not to bore the Malverne people, she
embellished the tale, giving more details, small new
twists. Then she paused, and said in a lower voice, in-
fusing new drama, new mystery into her words, "Selina
remained on her knees staring after her husband. As
for Parma, as soon as Grunlige had disappeared over a
rise, he rose and laughed, so proud of himself and his
cleverness that he did a little dance. He took a step
toward Selina, then stopped. 'Nay,' he said, 'I will only
take you when Grunlige is dead and I have seen his
body and spat upon it. I will cut off your witch's head
so all your evil will die with you.' He laughed again and
left her there, her body racked with her sobs.

"Grunlige felt filled with power and strength. Odin
had saved him once and when he again proved his
valor, Odin would reward him again, give him more
power than before, and then he would slay all his enemies. He strode back to his farmstead and called his
men together. They marveled at their lord who had
come back to them whole and strong. But when he told
them that they were voyaging to Iceland to trap furs
for trade at Hedeby, they looked furtively at each other,
fear scoring their faces. It was still winter; it would be

dangerous, just as dangerous as it had been the first time.

"But Grunlige was their master and they put their faith in him and in none other. Had he not come back to them, whole and strong? Aye, he was near to Odin, all knew it, and all trusted him completely. They left Norway and voyaged into the North Sea, past the Shetland Islands and the Faeroes, then straight toward the settlement of Thingvellir in Iceland."

Merrik stared at her. How did she know all these things? All these places?

"All went well, almost miraculously well. Their voyage took only two weeks, the wind pushing them quickly westward, more quickly than any would have imagined possible. It was as if an unseen force were shoving them toward their destination. The men's fear dissipated, for surely the gods had blessed this trip, and when they arrived at Thingvellir, they trapped more furs than they ever had before. The hold of the longboat was filled to overflowing. All were joyous. All would have died for Grunlige.

"They left Iceland and all cheered Grunlige. As before, the wind blew up at their backs and shoved them swiftly eastward. Suddenly, without warning, a terrible storm blew up. The weather was so cold even the warmest furs scarcely sufficed. Just as suddenly, not one day west of the Faeroes, a huge ice field moved down from the north and directly into their path. They were trapped behind it. They couldn't move forward. The men cried out that they must return to Iceland and they must row quickly for ice floes were breaking off the huge ice field and beginning to surround the longboat. They would soon be snared in the middle and they would die from the cold, far from home, forsaken by the gods. Grunlige said nothing. He smiled and then he laughed and spread his arms, shouting to the heavens, 'Odin, I am here. Test me!' "

Laren paused a moment, then said quickly, "Nay, this night you will all learn what happened to Grunlige the Dane, but first I must have mead to soothe my throat."

Erik grunted, subsiding in his chair. It was Letta, seeing that this girl had gained everyone's attention, including Merrik's, who said in a loud voice, "I am tired of this endless chatter. It is silly. You, my lord Merrik, never would you be so stupid as to venture out again onto an ice floe, as did this boastful Dane. I would that Deglin finish this tale, for it needs a conclusion worthy of a great man's skills."

There was utter silence. Laren stared at the girl, wishing she could slap her, the insufferable little twit with her big breasts, but she said nothing. It wasn't her decision. She thought of the silver pieces and wanted to cry.

Erik said, "She will finish the tale, Letta Thoragasson. Continue, Laren."

In that instant she smiled at Erik, so relieved that she would have smiled at a stone had it had given her permission. He stared back at her, his eyes gleaming, and she knew that smile had been a mistake.

She said quickly, looking directly at Merrik, " 'Test me!' Grunlige cried to the heavens, his arms outstretched. 'Aye, Odin All-Father, test me!'

"Then he leapt from the longboat to the nearest ice floe. He was smiling, then laughing. He shouted back to his men, 'Be not afraid, for I am not the fool I was before! Aye, I was vainglorious and thought not of myself as a man who could be hurt and could die. Trust me and know that Odin is testing my brain this time, and not my strength. Throw me the thickest of the otter furs!' "

There was a huge collective sigh of relief. Merrik nodded, and grinned at her.

"Grunlige shredded the ice floe, flinging the shards of ice wildly into the waters until, once again, nothing remained but slivers that wouldn't hurt a fish. He climbed back over into the longboat. He said, 'This is why I wanted so many furs trapped. I knew I would need them. I have demolished at least thirty of our stoutest furs in this battle. Aye, listen now closely, for I must speak softly. I didn't tell Odin what I planned, for I guessed it was my wits he doubted and wanted to test.'

"He then stared toward the sky. 'Have I gained your favor again, Odin?'

"There was a huge bolt of lightning that struck the center of the huge ice field that floated just off to the east. The ice field exploded, flinging shards of ice high into the air, causing the waves to swell and rock the longboat from side to side. The men fell to their knees, in fear and in awe.

"When they returned to Norway, Grunlige saw his wife and hurried to her. He held out his hands to her and said, 'I am not the fool you believed me to be. I am home and I am a man with new humility.'

"There was much rejoicing, until suddenly silence fell and all looked toward the open doorway of the longhouse. There stood Parma, and he was smiling. 'Do you come back with blackened claws again, Grunlige?' he yelled into the chamber. 'Come here and I will slay you this time and I will cut out your guts and throw them to the gulls that fly close to the shore.'

"It was Selina who answered, saying, 'Parma, you have heard aright. Grunlige is no more. This is his spirit, come to bid us all farewell. Come here and you will see what you have wrought with your guile and your cunning.'

"Parma swaggered through the chamber until he reached Grunlige. He stared at the warrior's hands, whole and strong and hard. He stared into Grunlige's face. He saw the truth and knew himself doomed. He paled and turned to run.

"Suddenly, a sword appeared in Grunlige's hand, a mighty sword of steel so bright and shiny that all would swear later that it was Odin's visage all could see in its reflection. Grunlige raised the sword slowly, in both his hands, high over his head. He smiled even as he lowered it, slowly, so very slowly, cleaving Parma's head into two halves, continuing downward until Parma was cut into two equal parts, each teetering, each searching for the other, for life that could no longer be. The parts fell to the earth. Oddly, no blood spurted from the severed body, no blood at all.

"All looked down, but there was naught but the two halves and they were empty. There was nothing at all inside the halves. The men pulled back in fear and consternation. They begged Grunlige to tell them what had occurred. Grunlige cried, 'I have smote the demon sent to test me, to strangle me with his fear.' He turned to his wife and said, 'He was Parma before he came into this chamber, but then Odin removed him and threw him into a coward's oblivion. He put the demon of air in his place. It is over now. There is no more.'

"There followed abundant good fortune for Grunlige the Dane and his children and his children's children. Each generation knew of his valor and his wisdom, and the tale was repeated so often that after many years it passed into legend and then into myth. But it is said that his progeny still live here in Norway—where, no one is certain. But you will believe it is a fact, if, on a stormy night, you listen very carefully, then you will hear the thunder boom out his name and know that Odin All-Father never forgot his warrior who was true to his honor and true to him, the god of all gods."

Laren stopped. She stood silent, her head down. She didn't look up when the cheering began nor did she move when the silver coins struck the ground at her feet.

A silver piece hit her toe and she felt nearly giddy with the joy of it. She kept her head down. She didn't want any of them to see the sheer hope in her expression, and she knew that if anyone saw it and understood it, it would be Merrik.

Not many minutes later Merrik took her with him to his sleeping chamber. He did it in full sight of the Thoragassons and the girl Letta. He left Taby with Cleve, telling him to put him to bed with all the other children when he had tired of listening to the child chatter on and on about Grunlige and how very wise he was. As if he were a real man who really lived, Merrik thought, and then realized that he himself had considered Grunlige to be as real as he was himself. Perhaps he had lived, perhaps Laren had been told of him, perhaps . . .

When he lay beside Laren, unmoving, he said, "You did well."

She thanked him, then drew a deep breath. "I would ask you something, Merrik."

"Aye?"

"How much did you pay for Taby at the slave market?"

He stiffened. She believed him stupid, curse her, believed him so stupid that he wouldn't remember all the silver pieces she'd been given since she'd begun her storytelling. He wondered how many pieces she'd col-

lected now. There had been at least twenty pieces at
her feet after she'd finished her tale this evening,
twenty pieces of silver and two heavy silver armlets,
one from Olaf Thoragasson himself.

"I paid fifty pieces of silver for him."

He heard her cry of distress, but he did nothing,
merely asked, "Why do you care? I would pay even more
for Taby. He is worth a great deal to me."

She said nothing, indeed words, for the moment, were
beyond her. She saw her dreams sinking swiftly into
the raging current of the North Sea.

Merrik chuckled. "Taby told me again this afternoon
that he was a prince. He stuck his chin in the air and
all but strutted when he said it."

Utter silence. That was odd, he thought. Surely she
should at least laugh or say something about Taby's
imagination.

"He told me he would allow me to continue taking
care of him. Then he ruined his princely image by jumping at me and winding his arms around my neck. I
nearly dropped him, for I was sharpening a scythe we
will be using soon in the barley field."

He heard her breathing, sharp and shallow. He said
easily, "The meal you prepared was beyond anything
our people have ever eaten. I imagine that Thoragasson, when he discovers who added girth to his belly this
evening, will want to buy you. Just imagine, Laren, he
would gain both a cook and a skald." He paused a moment, then added, "Your value rises with each passing
day."

"And I am your concubine."

"Aye, that too. I doubt there is much envy there, for
you are still too skinny."

"You allowed all the Thoragassons to see you take me
into this sleeping chamber with you. If you are be-

trothed to Letta, why would you wish to hurt her by doing it?"

"I believe a woman should know that a man will always do as he wishes. If I wed with her, she won't be surprised when I take other women to my bed."

"You are like Erik, then."

"Oh no," he said, then wished he'd kept his mouth shut. "What is wrong with my brother? Other than his wanting to bed you?"

"He strikes Sarla."

"Nay," Merrik said slowly, turning now toward her, for she had his full attention. "Erik is used to having what he wants, but to strike Sarla is absurd. He is a brave man and he is my brother. You are making that up because you dislike him so very much, because you fear him."

"Look at her face."

"You are wrong."

"She said that he hits her whenever she displeases him. He hit her three nights ago when you kept me from him. It was his disappointment, she thought."

Merrik struggled with her words, with the image her words provoked in his mind. Erik strike gentle Sarla?

Laren sighed. "If she proves barren, I doubt not he will kill her, that or simply send her back to her family. How long does a man give a woman to bear him children? Three years? Perhaps four?"

"No, he would not do that. Cease your tales, Laren, for I will give you no silver pieces for your stories. If you wish to, though, you could tell me who you are and where you come from."

"Perhaps once I am free of you, Cleve and Taby with me, I will send a messenger back to you, for then I would have nothing more to fear from you."

That nearly sent him over the edge. "Your damned

arrogance and pride! You gall me, woman. You fear me? For what reason? Have I ever hurt you? Damn you, I did not take you when you offered yourself to me, and you were more than willing, were you not? No, I didn't take you because—"

He seemed to realize that what he intended to say wouldn't result in the conclusion he sought. He shut his mouth.

She said flatly, "You didn't take me because you find me ugly."

"That is not true."

"The other reason you didn't take me is because of Taby. You love a child who isn't even of your blood. He could be the son of a savage from the stinking bogs of Ireland, stolen by Viking marauders just like you and your kind. I will accept that you care for him even though I will never understand the depths of your feelings for him. What did you do, Merrik, promise him you would protect me as well as him? Did you swear to him you wouldn't ravish me?"

"You should select another word. *Ravish* doesn't apply to us."

She sucked in her breath, fleeting memories of those incredible feelings whirling about the edges of her mind. "Even if I threw myself upon you naked, you would do nothing. You would cast me aside."

Merrik frowned into the darkness. He said slowly, carefully selecting his words, "You sound as if you want me to take you, make you my concubine."

Ah, she thought, here was the rub, here was the truth, unmasked, but she wouldn't admit it to him. She merely laughed, saying, "Perhaps I would want you to take me just one time so that I would know what it is all about. Then it would be enough. Then I could forget about it. But know this, Merrik, I would never want you for anything more than just a brief diversion, an amusement for just a single night that might please me as much as a good story."

He had saved her life, damn her. He had cared for her, protected her from his brother. He wanted to strangle her. He lurched toward her and came down on top of her. His hands closed about her neck, but didn't tighten. "You damnable witch," he said, then found her mouth in the darkness and kissed her hard, not caring if he hurt her. Let it be an amusement for him, and let her cry in pain at such a diversion.

His rage increased when she didn't move, just lay there, suffering his attack. He felt the softness of her belly, the giving weight of her breasts against his chest.

"Damn you, fight me."

12

SHE DIDN'T FIGHT him, oh no, fighting him was far from her mind. She lurched up against him, grabbed his face between her hands and brought him down to her. She found his mouth after kissing his chin, his nose, his cheek, and she kissed him hard, her lips parted this time, and he was so surprised, so utterly dumbfounded by her actions, that he froze over her, not opening his mouth, not doing anything at all, save trying to control the heaving breaths that bespoke his lust.

He jerked away from her, his heart beating so fast he wondered if he would survive it. He remained on top of her, but he was balancing himself on his elbows above her to keep distance between him and that wonderful mouth of hers. "Why did you do that, damn you? You were lying there as if you were dead, or suffering me until I would get done with you. And then you attacked me."

"I would do it again if you would only come back down to me. It isn't fair. You can force me since you are the stronger, but I cannot force you to do what it is I want."

Then she smiled up at him, hit the sides of both her hands hard against the crooks of his elbows and he fell flat on top of her, driving the breath from her. She grabbed his ears and held him there, kissing his throat,

his shoulders. Merrik laughed, he couldn't help himself.
He reared up again, still laughing.

"You forgot that I am very smart," she said.

"I won't forget that in the future. Now, answer me.
Why did you do that?"

She didn't say anything, just stared up at him in the
dim light. He wanted to demand that she answer him,
but that look of hers and the words she'd spoken flowed
over him like balm, soothing and so soft and deep, and
at the same time incredibly exciting. And her laughter,
by all the gods, her laughter was wonderful. And she'd
even knocked him down on her, she wanted to kiss him
so very much, and he said, surprising himself even as
the words came out of his mouth, "You won't have to
fell me again. I will allow you to do as you please with
me."

"Come back to me." She knew exactly what she was
asking. She'd thought about it for a very long time,
truth be told, probably since he'd cared for her on board
his longboat, at least thought about him as a man and
not an enemy who would hurt her. No, she'd thought of
him as a man, so very different from her, a man who
was kind to her, whose hands were gentle, a man who
would give her immense pleasure.

Her future had changed irrevocably that long-ago
night when she and Taby had been taken, and the future that would come had no meaning to her yet, for it
was shrouded in uncertainty, and in fear. She had become a realist and no longer believed like a credulous
fool that there could exist a future that would be sweet
and good. She had become a Christian because her uncle had demanded it of her, demanded it of all of them,
but she never called on the Christian God to save her,
to show her which path to take, which decision to make.

She knew she owed it to Taby to try to get back

home, to learn who had betrayed them, to restore to him what he'd lost and to herself what she'd lost as well. But that was the future, and she was here, and she wasn't at all certain that she even wanted to regain what she herself had lost, for there was Merrik now, and she wanted him.

She wanted something for herself now, and if Merrik was only willing she could have it. For just this one night she could have him. "Aye," she said again, her voice harsh with her growing excitement, "come back to me, Merrik."

He did, dipping his head down. Her hands again closed about his face, and her fingertips traced his brows, his nose, his jaw. He felt her warm breath fan upward as her breathing hitched. She wanted him. She truly wanted him. He felt at that moment as if Grunlige the Dane were naught but a gnat of a man in comparison to him.

"Come to me," she said again, and this time when he touched her, he opened his mouth just a bit and let her learn the feel and texture of him. When his tongue touched hers, she quivered, but then again, so did he, so he couldn't be certain who quivered first or the most, nor did he care. "Open your lips wider," he said and felt the heat of her when she did.

"Laren." He said her name, nothing else, just her name, and she responded to him fully and with no fear at all. She was eager for him and she was a virgin.

That stopped him, and he reared back just a bit. "Listen to me a moment before I forget who I am and what I am and what you are." Her eyes looked soft as his mother's butter in the dim light. She looked eager for him and ever so willing. She wanted him and she'd told him she wanted him. He forced himself to look away from her then forced himself to say the hardest thing he'd ever had to do. "Do you want to be my whore?"

He'd purposely chosen the crudest word he could, to shock her, to make her draw back from him, to make her think, by all the gods, surely she couldn't want this, surely. She had such pride, such arrogance, surely she wouldn't want to give herself to a man who wasn't her husband. She was probably some merchant's daughter from the Rhineland or cobbler's daughter from a village along the Seine in France, or perhaps even a local overlord's daughter from the dull, hot plains of Cordoba, Spain, but she deserved more than he could give her, deserved more than to be a vessel for his lust.

All that arrogance and pride sounded in her voice as she said, "No, I will never be any man's whore. I want you only for this night. I want you to teach me what I should know. I want to experience these feelings once in my life, 'twill suffice me. Actually, I am not even certain these feelings really exist. Perhaps they do but only to a certain point, just enough so that a woman would do anything for the man who makes her feel this way, and then the feelings stop and the man doesn't. But it doesn't matter. I want to know and I want you to be the one to teach me."

Now she was giving him permission to take her. He who should have told her then that he could have forced her the moment he'd gotten her from Thrasco's house, that there was naught she could do about anything. She was in his power and she always had been.

Instead, he said, "What if you want to have me again after this instruction I give you?"

She was shaking her head even as she said, "Even if it is possible that I might, I have more important things to consider in my life. No, just for tonight. I want you just this once, just so I may know why I feel this way about you, why you make me breathe more quickly when you're near, and when you touch me, why I want to fling myself against you and kiss you and stroke you with my fingers and never stop."

He wanted to strangle her and he wanted to make her take those words back, but not all of them, oh no, by all the gods, not all of them. He thought about kissing her and never stopping, and it didn't seem such a bad idea. He decided in that instant he would give her such pleasure that she would forget those silly words of hers—after all, what could be more important than he—forget everything but him and how he would always make her feel.

Always.

Oh no, not that. That couldn't be. He tried to calm himself. He wasn't forcing her. Truth be told, he was succumbing to her. He almost laughed at himself for his justifications. A randy man would force himself to believe anything in order to get himself inside the woman.

She lurched up again and now she was nibbling at his earlobe, her hands in his hair, tugging, kissing his chin, searching for his mouth, now kissing him, her tongue between his lips, probing, but not too deeply for it was still too new to her and she wasn't certain what to do. But just the touch of her was too much.

"I love your mouth, Merrik. I've never thought of a man's mouth like this, but with you, all I want to do is kiss you and touch your face." And then she was kissing him again, her fingertips feathering his cheeks, his chin, smoothing his dark blond brows, kissing him once more after that and yet again until he was drowning in her, the feel of her, the heat of her, the taste of her.

He wanted her more than he'd ever wanted another woman, except perhaps for Gunnvor when he'd been twelve years old and she'd been a magnificent fourteen and she'd let him kiss her and fondle her and caress her and she'd taken his rod in her hands and stroked him until he'd spilled his seed not once but twice, and he would have killed every dragon in the world for her on that day.

But this was different, he was a man now, and Gunnvor was only a boy's memory.

He was mad, he knew it in that moment, utterly mad, his judgment shattered, his reason flown to the four winds. Then he saw himself in his madness, saw her beyond the softness and yielding she was offering him. He saw the situation, and he saw Taby—all of it in one sharp moment—and he knew he would be beyond mad to take her. He drew a shuddering breath, even as her mouth kissed his, her tongue lightly touched his, making him shudder and heave with the pleasure of it.

But he wanted her, very badly. Just this once, aye, then he'd be free of her and her girl's idealized lust for him and she would be free of him as well. That was what she had said.

Aye, he'd be free. He wouldn't have her there in his mind, in his thoughts. His worry for her, his fear for her, would only be as Taby's sister, nothing else.

His eyes were dark and intense with need and control. He kissed her hard and deep, his tongue going into her mouth with a man's lust, and no gentleness. He felt her stiffen instantly at the assault, and he gentled immediately, furious with himself. He undressed her quickly, without care of her clothing, and when his clothes were off as well, when he was at last kissing her breasts, feeling them with his hands, holding them in his palms, trying desperately not to lose himself in their feel, their taste, he was forced to close his eyes at the joy she brought him, not just her breasts, but how her hands were on his chest, his arms, around his back, drawing him to her, moaning softly, not at all afraid of him. And kissing him. Even now her lips were nipping his shoulders, then licking where she'd nipped his flesh.

His hand went down to her flat belly, feeling her thinness, her still prominent pelvic bones, but not caring, for she was alive and that was all that mattered. His hand went lower until he was touching her woman's flesh lightly with his fingertips, and to his immense delight, she shuddered. She wanted him, he knew it, and she trusted him, at least in this, the giving of her body to him.

His hand trembled. He looked at her soft flesh, knew he wanted to taste her, but also realized in that moment that it would probably shock her, and the last thing he wanted to do now was make her retreat from him. He couldn't have borne that.

He closed his eyes, refusing to look at that thin body that was quivering for him, just for him. His mouth closed over her nipple and she lurched up, giving him more of herself, and her hands were wild on his back, his shoulders, his buttocks. She was encouraging him, not really knowing how to, and her ignorance was more exciting than any woman of more experience he'd ever enjoyed. His mouth was on her belly, then lower, and he didn't care if she was shocked, or frightened, he had to taste her, explore her, feel all of her with his fingers, with his mouth.

He pulled her legs wide apart, settling himself between them. He didn't want to look at her, but he had to, drawing her apart with his fingers, and then he caressed her with his fingers, his mouth.

She was stiff and still. Then, suddenly, she screamed with the power of it.

Quickly, he slammed his hand over her mouth, still fondling her as he did so, and she was twisting her head, nearly beside herself now, and he knew he couldn't wait another instant, another minute, for he would spill his seed on her belly, and by all the gods, he wanted to be deep inside her, have her holding him within her when he reached his release.

He shoved hard into her. He felt the tearing pain, for it was difficult to get into her, she was small, her flesh loosening and dampening, but it wasn't enough, and he'd known she wasn't completely ready for him, but he didn't stop, just kept pushing harder and harder still, until finally, with a deep groan, he burst through her maidenhead. He lowered his mouth over her just in time to catch her cry of pain, for he knew that if Erik heard her cry of pain he would know it had all been a pretense, at least until this night, until this moment. Merrik filled her with himself, touching her womb, pausing just a moment, because the power of it was making him shake and moan. He wanted to pull back, to caress her again with his mouth, but he knew he couldn't. He moaned, tensing, lurching more deeply into her. He pulled back, then drove forward, then once again. It took no more than that, just one final time and he felt his seed hot against her womb.

His heart was pounding madly, and he wondered if he was going to die with the impact of the release he'd just had. He thought to pull out of her, for he knew he was still causing her pain, but her arms closed tightly around his back and she held him tightly against her. He pulled her onto her side, facing him, still inside her, though not so deep now, but it didn't matter, he could feel the beating of her heart, the heat of her. He kissed her slack mouth, stroked her eyebrows, and smoothed her hair from her forehead. "I'm sorry for your pain," he said against her mouth. "It was your maidenhead. I had to get through it."

"You did," she said. "You did."

He'd not given her much pleasure, he thought, but there'd been some, before he'd come so urgently and deeply into her, and lost his reason. "Now, you have had me, Laren, but you didn't find the pleasure in our coupling that I did, and I am sorry for it. If there is to be no more between us after this night, then I must take you again, after you've rested, and show you what it is like between a man and a woman."

She said nothing. She was held tightly against him, and he wasn't inside her now, but he was so close, the scent of his warm flesh against her mouth, and she said, "I would like that except I hurt very badly, Merrik. And I'm bleeding. Will it all stop soon?"

He said nothing, merely pulled away from her, rose from the bed, and left the chamber, uncaring that he was naked.

It didn't matter in any case, for only a soft haze of smoke lit the outer room and no one was awake. He fetched an oil lamp and brought it back into the sleeping chamber.

He cursed as he held the lamp close to look at her, then said, "Hold still. I will see how badly I hurt you."

He looked up into her face then and saw not only her pain there, but confusion as well. Her blue-gray eyes looking nearly black in the light. There was a light sheen of sweat on her forehead. He said more sharply than he liked, "Don't look so lost. You will be all right, mating doesn't kill a woman, Laren, and it certainly won't hurt you the next time."

"This is something I wanted so very much, a mystery I wanted more than anything to solve with you—aye, and I solved it—but the solution to it is not what I expected. I know all this bleeding doesn't mean I will die, for you wouldn't slake your passion if you knew it could kill me. But it does hurt a lot more than I would like, and that is a surprise and a disappointment."

That was straight speaking, he thought, silent for the moment. The blood was trickling down her thighs, the flow slowed now, but she couldn't know that, and it was pooling on the blanket beneath her. He looked down at himself for just an instant, and saw her blood there, her blood and his seed. He drew a deep breath, and said, "It isn't bad. Now, hold still." She felt the wet of a soft cloth against her, cleaning her. Then he pressed the cloth firmly against her.

She looked away from him, from the intent look on his face as he tended to her. She had no idea what he was thinking, what he was feeling. She said, "I felt such strange things when you looked at me, when you touched me. When you kissed me, when I felt your tongue in my mouth, and on my body, I felt as if a small part of the world would be mine and everything would be well and good." Suddenly she gasped and tried to pull away from him. He flattened his palm on her belly, holding her still.

"Don't move," he said, and wrapped the wet cloth more securely around his finger and eased it again into her to see if he'd rent her. "No, keep still, don't tighten your body so. Try to let yourself ease. I'll be through soon."

She was silent, stiff, and he knew he was hurting her, but he tried, by all the gods, he tried to be gentle. He wished his damned finger were smaller, but it wasn't.

He eased his finger out of her, relieved that the flow of blood was nearly stopped, then rinsed out the cloth. He sat beside her on the bed, folded the cloth, then pressed it against her and held it there. He looked up at her face. She was pale, her eyes swollen from crying, her hair tangled about her face.

She'd wanted him; she'd offered herself to him.

And he'd done his best, surely he had, but still, he'd come into her before he'd brought her to a woman's pleasure. He remembered her scream when he'd closed his mouth over her. By all the gods, to make a woman feel like this. He shuddered with the power that memory brought him. He said, "You will be all right. I do not think I would come inside you again this night. But again, Laren, perhaps tomorrow or the next day when you're healed again."

She opened her eyes, and looked at him, never once letting her eyes fall below his face.

He said again, "I'm sorry."

"Why would you be sorry? I was the one who demanded that you do those things to me. You have been naught but honorable and kind to me. You did nothing that any other man does not do. It is my fault. I have nothing to cover me and I feel ashamed, for I am ugly and bony and I know it and I don't wish to have you staring at me. Could you cover me, Merrik?"

He covered her and his hand as well, for he still kept the cloth pressed firmly against her.

"You're not ugly," he said. "Stop saying that you are."

She smiled at him. She raised her hand to touch his face, then dropped it.

He wished she had touched him, was still touching him. "There," he said, looking away, "the bleeding has stopped. Do you still hurt?"

She nodded, not looking at him.

"You will be fine tomorrow," he said and rose. He stretched, then tossed the blood-dampened cloth into the soapstone bowl of water. When he came into the bed again, he said nothing more, merely drew her to him, and pressed her face down upon his shoulder. "No," he said, "don't move. I like you there."

"I do too," she said, unable at that moment not to speak the truth. His arm tightened around her back, then immediately loosened and she knew he was thinking about her back and the still tender welts. She wanted to tell him that she would rather have him hold her tightly, regardless of any pain, but she didn't. She burrowed her face against his chest, drawing in the scent of him, feeling his hair against her cheek, her nose, wanting to taste him.

She knew in that moment that her life had changed irrevocably. To have him inside her body, to have him hold her against him, had changed everything. What she'd been destined for meant nothing now. Only he was important now.

And Taby. What of her little brother? She had to try to set things aright for him. She closed her eyes, willing blankness to come but she couldn't close out the enormity of what lay just beyond the sleeping chamber. Her fingers clenched, and he grunted when she pulled the hair on his chest.

Forty silver pieces and two silver armlets. By all the gods, she'd much rather know that she could trust him. With her. With Taby.

The night was chill, the stars brilliant overhead. There was a half moon. Laren slowly turned back to the longhouse. She'd felt a very strong urge to simply walk through those palisade gates and keep walking, forever, for there were no solutions for her here, none.

She winced, remembering how Erik had stopped her early that afternoon, in plain sight of his wife and many of his men. He'd forced her face upward, cupping her chin in his palm, his touch hard, hurting her. He'd said, "Megot told me there was blood on the blanket in Merrik's sleeping chamber. And blood on a cloth and coloring the water in a bowl. So you didn't lie to me. It is your monthly flow and yet he took you anyway, my fastidious brother." He'd released her, and said over his shoulder, "You're still as skinny as a hen at winter solstice, so Merrik should tire of you soon. Then you will come to me. Then I will have you."

She shivered, not from the chill breeze blowing up from the fjord, but from his words. She was afraid of him, very afraid. And angry as well. Sarla knew what he did, and he didn't care.

He was very different from Merrik. At least Merrik would never raise his hand to her or to any one of his people. She didn't doubt that he could be violent and ruthless, that he could kill swiftly with no remorse, that an enemy would know no mercy at his hands, but he wouldn't inflict pain on someone weaker than he, someone in his care.

She walked slowly back to the longhouse. The huge doors were open and she saw all the men, women, and children inside, heard at least ten different conversations, the laughter, the arguments, saw two men fighting. But she didn't see Merrik. And she looked for him, she always looked for him, not feeling right until she'd found him. She'd seen little of him the entire day. He'd worked in the fields until it was nearly dark, then gone into the bathing hut with several of his men, laughing, jesting, punching each other. He'd seemed entirely untouched to her eyes, and it hurt her. The previous night had meant nothing to him. What had she expected? She was the one responsible for her own feelings, her own actions, not he.

She hadn't offered to cook the meal and Sarla hadn't asked her to. She'd sensed that something was wrong, but she'd said nothing, merely patted Laren's arm. With all the people here, Laren did help serve the din-

ner and she worked hard until it was done. Then she'd
left the longhouse. Now here she was dithering about,
and she hated herself for it. She squared her shoulders
and walked inside. No one noticed her, even Taby who
was howling with laughter as Kenna taught him some
wrestling tricks. Now, she helped herself to some venison, and some cabbage stewed with peas and apples.
It was a strange combination, but tasty.

She'd eaten only a few bites when Erik called out,
"Come here, girl, for all of us wish another tale."

Another story. She looked around at all the eager
faces. The men seemed as eager as the women, and the
children were already beginning to crowd around her,
Taby standing beside her, holding her skirt in one of
his small fists.

She'd thought of this on and off all day long. Aye, she
had a story and she prayed it would show her what to
do. She looked at the Thoragassons, and they, too,
looked eager, all except for Letta, who looked sullen.
Letta was also staring at Merrik, who had called Taby
to him and was now lifting him on his legs, tickling him
and smiling when he squirmed and giggled. There was
deep, very deep anger in Letta's eyes.

Laren smiled at all of them in turn, including Letta.

13

SHE'D SURVIVED ON her wits for two long years. Aye, her wits, and great doses of sheer luck, and that luck had almost run out by the time she'd met Merrik. She wouldn't fail now, she couldn't, it was simply too important. Everything hung in the balance now. She thought of her forty silver pieces, her two armlets, and knew they would make no difference to anything. She motioned the children to sit around her in a circle. She wanted to speak quickly, to get it over with, but she knew it was wise to begin slowly, for it gained everyone's attention and held them whilst she built her story, like a house. "I will tell you about Rolf the Viking who lived a long time ago here in Norway. He was proud and strong and fearless, a warrior of rare mettle, as are most of the men in Norway. Rolf was young, a man in his prime, and as handsome of mien as he was powerful of body.

"He had two brothers, both strong, both handsome, both ambitious. They were all in their prime, all as handsome of mien as they were powerful of body. Rolf was the eldest and he went araiding for the sheer joy of battle and he added to his wealth as the summers went by. Radnor, the second son, was a trader and he voyaged far and wide with his goods. He was wily and more quick-witted than an Arab in a bazaar. He became quickly as rich as Rolf. The youngest son was Ingor, a farmer. His farmstead prospered, for he had a magic way with crops and he, too, grew richer with each passing season.

"Rolf came home from raiding along the mighty Seine River. He brought with him twelve slaves, six men and six women, all of them captured from the three small villages having the misfortune to sit too close to the river.

"One of the male slaves was a man as proud and strong as were the Viking warriors who had managed to capture him. He'd been unlucky and the warriors knew it. He'd been ill and still he'd fought them until he'd collapsed with the wounds and the illness within his body. He was dressed more finely than the others captured, and all the warriors knew that as well. But whoever he was, what his real name was, none knew and he wouldn't say anything. He was also a man with talent—in short, he was a runemaster—but more than that, he was a scion of a proud family that had much wealth and power in that region of France. He'd just chanced to be in the village that fateful day because he was visiting an artisan from whom he wished to learn new methods to perfect his skill.

"But now he was a slave, just like the others. Rolf knew value when he saw it and kept him close. He made the man his runemaster and was astonished with the beautiful carvings the man accomplished along with his fashioning of magnificent writ. Visitors heard of the runemaster and visited Rolf from far and wide. Radnor, the second brother, tried to buy the slave from his brother, but Rolf refused.

"Ah, but the silver the slave gained from the visitors who came to Rolf's longhouse. He carved them magnificent chair posts, intricate designs on jewelry and on jewel boxes. He became renowned. Soon, he had as much silver as he thought he needed to buy himself from Rolf and thus regain his freedom.

"He offered all his silver to Rolf, but Rolf refused. He allowed the slave to keep all his silver, but he said he wouldn't sell him. He told the slave he admired him, he wanted him to be content in his new home, in his new land.

"He didn't abuse the slave. Some of his men wondered if it was friendship he felt toward the slave or whether he was afraid the slave would gullet him, for he was, as you know already, a valiant fighter and now he was back to his full strength.

"The slave held his peace until finally he could bear it no longer. Rolf assured him that whatever he wished to tell him he would keep in confidence; he vowed it on his honor. The slave wasn't stupid, but when Rolf told him if the truth meant he might lose him, then so be it. He was to trust him. The slave was still uncertain, but he leapt at the chance of going home. So he told Rolf who he was, told him that his family was powerful and wealthy and he was the heir and he asked Rolf to stand as his friend, as he'd just professed himself to be, and help him regain his proper station in life.

"Rolf clasped the slave to him and told him to trust him, that aye, he was indeed his friend. He told him he would most assuredly assist him to return to his home. Now, the question is, what did Rolf do?"

Laren paused, then looked at Olaf Thoragasson. "My lord," she said, bowing toward him, "what would you have done were you Rolf?"

Olaf Thoragasson leaned forward in his chair. He looked at his men, at the group of slaves who were clustered near the doors of the longhouse. He said loudly,

"I would flay the flesh from the man's back for such insolence! It means nothing to make a vow to a slave, less than nothing, despite his claims, despite his skills. Aye, Rolf should chain the beggar and let him starve until he declares his allegiance is to Rolf and to no one else!"

He sat back in his chair and his men cheered. Some of the Malverne people cheered as well, but not all.

Laren turned to Erik. "My lord, what would you have Rolf do?"

He smiled at her, a smile of superiority at her woman's ignorance, her lack of understanding of the way of men and of honor. He said slowly, "I would ransom the fellow from this powerful and wealthy family of his, and then I would keep him and chain him up. Olaf is right, it is just that I am not only right as well, I am also richer."

There was much laughter, Thoragasson not taking offense, guffawing loudly, praising Erik's wit.

Laren waited silently, standing motionless, outwardly serene and calm, then she turned to Merrik. "My lord Merrik, what would you have Rolf do?"

He said very slowly, his eyes never leaving her face, "Were I this Rolf, I would keep my word. It wouldn't matter if the man was a slave or a king. I would take the man back to his kin. I would restore him."

"You're a fool, brother!" Erik shouted. "You not only lose a valuable possession, you do not even make the possession pay for his freedom!"

"Aye," Thoragasson said loudly. "Honor comes not into it, Merrik. Your word given to naught but a slave means nothing, just as I said. Had Rolf given his word to one of his brothers, then it would have been different. But to this damned slave? Never! Let him be a captured king, it doesn't matter."

Laren waited until all the men and women grew silent once more, until one by one, they looked at her again.

"Tell us, girl," Thoragasson said. "What did Rolf do?"

"He went to speak to his brothers. Ragnor told him to treat the slave just as you said, Olaf Thoragasson. Ingor told him to do just as Erik said."

She paused and Thoragasson roared, "What did Rolf do?"

She looked at each man in turn, then said very quietly, "He could not decide. He trusted both his brothers yet he wasn't certain which was right or if either one of them was right. He muttered and tried to reason it out, but he couldn't. Time passed and his rage at his own weakness, his own failure to decide what to do, drove him nearly mad. Finally, in a moment of enraged madness, he took down his mighty sword, said good-bye to the slave, and ran his sword through the slave's heart."

There was a loud yell from Thoragasson, moans from the women, laughter from Erik, and nothing from Merrik, nothing at all. He didn't move, his expression didn't change. He did nothing, merely looked at her impassively.

Finally, when everyone quieted, Merrik said, "That isn't the end of the Viking though, is it? What happened next?"

"Rolf came to himself once again. He regretted deeply what he'd done. Guilt ate at him endlessly, never giving him respite, and he couldn't sleep nor could he eat, nor could he think about going araiding again. He withdrew from his brothers, blaming them for his loss of judgment. Soon he blamed them entirely for the death of his slave.

"The brothers were furious with his treatment of them. They bedeviled Rolf, telling him he was more a fool than the slave had been to trust in his word. Aye, they mocked him: he had lied to the slave, whereas they'd done nothing save offer their opinion, and he, Rolf, had asked for it, after all. But to kill such a valuable slave! It was madness and Rolf had done it, thus he was mad. They wouldn't leave him alone. On and on it went until, finally, Rolf could no longer bear himself for he saw at last that they were in the right of it.

"He'd betrayed the slave, then he'd smote him. He knew there was but one way to make amends. He threw off all his weapons and walked by himself deep into the forest. He knew that sooner or later a wild beast would attack him and kill him. He wanted death; he actively sought death to release him from the man he'd become."

Laren stopped because she didn't know what happened next. Her head pounded and she was thirsty. She became suddenly aware of the raw pain between her thighs. She looked toward Merrik, for he was the cause of that pain. He was looking back at her, his expression unreadable to her.

Aye, she felt the rawness between her thighs, but she knew it was the pain of his indifference to her during the entire day and evening that hurt her more. She lowered her head, waiting. The people were still silent, so silent, she fancied she could hear the thick smoke rising toward the hole in the thatch roof. They had hated her story. They would throw things at her. They would ask to have Deglin back. Then there were moans and complaints, demands that she continue, but she just smiled at them and shook her pounding head.

"I am very tired," she said finally. "Please, I must stop now."

There were gold coins amongst the silver, most pressed into her hand, and a beautiful pounded brooch, given to her by one of Thoragasson's two sons. "It belonged to my mother," he told her.

She tried to give it back, but he merely pressed it into her hand and closed her fingers over it. "I wish you to have it, Laren." She watched him walk away from her. She didn't even remember his name. He wasn't more than fifteen, but he would be as big as all the damned Vikings, and fair-haired, his eyes blue as the summer skies.

As for Letta Thoragasson, she stopped in front of Laren and smiled down at her. It wasn't a nice smile, it was filled with malice. "Listen to me," she said finally. She reached out and grabbed Laren's wrist and dragged her closer. "Don't ever think you will beat me, for you won't. I don't mind that Merrik uses you. You are a slave, a whore, and that is what you are good for. He is a man with a man's needs, and I admire him because he doesn't seek to dishonor me by coming to my bed before we are wed. You are nothing more than a vessel for his lust. Take him into you now, for soon, once we are wed, he will sell you and I will not have to see your ugly face again." She paused, then smiled more widely. "Oh aye, he will sell you for that is what I will demand for my wedding gift. Who knows? Perhaps my father will buy you and you will spend your miserable life telling him stories."

She threw Laren's wrist away from her. Laren stared after her.

"She is right, you know."

It was Erik and he'd heard Letta's words. "You are nothing more than Merrik's whore and it will stop when he weds that little fool. Merrik believes a man should cleave to one woman once that woman is his wife. He dreams of finding a woman who is like our mother was to our father. It won't happen with that one. He will bed Letta for a short time, even hold faith with her for a while, then he will realize that she gives him too little, and he will have other women, just as I have had to do. Sarla is different from Letta, but in many ways she is the same. No, you can believe Letta in this and you can believe me. Merrik will sell you once he weds. But it won't matter to you, Laren, for you will be gone.

"If you are nice to me, Laren, I won't let Merrik sell you to old Thoragasson. I'll buy you and keep you here with me. Merrik will wed her and he will go back to the Bergson Valley to live."

"Laren!"

Merrik was striding toward her. He nodded to his brother, then said, "Your story lacked force and passion tonight. Perhaps you are saving that passion for me. I trust so, else I will be displeased with you. Come along now, I wish to have you."

Laren heard a laugh. She turned slightly and saw that Letta was sniggering behind her hand. She saw Merrik's large hand extended toward her. Slowly, she placed her hand into his and followed him out of the outer chamber.

He released her hand the moment they were within the sleeping chamber. He didn't look at her at all, just began to strip off his clothes. He said as he pulled his tunic over his head, his voice muffled, "What are you, Laren, a merchant's daughter? An innkeeper's niece? I know you weren't a slave before two years ago. You're too proud, and you were a virgin, something you wouldn't have been beyond your childhood otherwise."

She said nothing.

When he was naked, he turned to see her sitting on the side of the box bed, fully clothed, her hands in her lap. She was staring at him, at his flat belly, furred with soft blond hair, then downward. Her face was flushed, her lips slightly parted.

"Stop looking at me," he said, utterly infuriated with her for testing him so. "Have you no sense? Do you so quickly forget what I did to you last night? Take off your clothes and go to sleep. You must still be too sore for me to have you again."

Still she didn't move. His sex began to swell, he could no more prevent it any more than he could the rising of the sun.

"You want more of the pain you endured last night?"

She shook her head, still silent.

"Then cease looking at me, damn you! I played my part in front of Erik, but now I wish only to sleep." His sex was jutting forward, hard and ready. His heart pounded; he ached with need for her, damn her.

She'd been looking at his face, but when she gasped, he knew she was staring at him again. He said nothing more, merely eased down onto the bed.

The chamber was dark now for she'd doused the oil lamp. He heard the rustle of her clothes, but didn't move.

"Your story is passing strange. Is it more than just a simple tale, I wonder?"

"That's all it is, Merrik, a simple tale." She could practically hear him thinking in the darkness, gnawing on questions about her and Taby. She sought to distract him, saying, "Letta told me that she didn't mind that I was your whore because you could use me. I guess she meant you could practice on me, but I don't believe you need practice. Well, perhaps you could have benefited from practice last night, but I don't really know." Ah, she heard him suck in his breath. She'd gotten her distraction all right. She hoped he wouldn't strangle her. She continued, her voice mocking, "I fancied myself as some sort of target and your coming at me as a mighty sword. You didn't miss the target, but it wasn't a clean kill either, speaking as the target, of course. I suppose swords don't mind so long as it is a kill for them. In any case, she is pleased that I will give you the use of my body until you and she are wedded."

"She is more a child than Taby." He was infuriated with himself that he'd spoken thusly to Laren. What he would do with Letta was his affair and no other's. "On occasion," he added, "most women are like children." He rolled onto his back, staring up into the darkness. He said after a long moment, battling with himself to just keep quiet and ignore her baiting words, but he found he couldn't, "I don't like your insulting comparison. What nonsense is this—you a target and I a sword? What do you mean, I need more practice?"

"I mean that I asked Sarla about how a man and a woman mated. She assured me it didn't hurt after the first time and even the first time it wasn't bad if the man was gentle and experienced. It was pleasant for a while, she said, then she became very silent and said no more. Thus, perhaps you do need practice, Merrik. At least for that first time."

He felt roiling anger at her, but more at himself. He'd been a clod. "Do you still hurt?"

"Aye."

"I won't practice on you again until you are completely healed and ready for me and ask me nicely. Now, you will cease your damned insults. Aye, they are insults, you just cloak them in your gentle guile."

"I told you, Merrik, that last night would be the only time. It is a pity that I won't ever know if mating can be pleasurable, but I won't allow myself to become more interested in you, as a man, that is."

"Then why were you staring at me, your eyes as bright as a child's staring at honeyed apple slices? I showed interest only because my man's body is like that. It responds when a woman stares, even you. There is nothing I can do to stop it. Not that I want to come inside you again, the gods know I don't." He stopped himself. He was making little sense, blatantly lying both to himself and to her. He was burying himself in a hole that would send him to the bottom of the fjord if he didn't shut his damned mouth.

She said nothing. Absolutely nothing at all, and he waited and waited, unwilling to say more. Then he heard her breath even into sleep. He wanted to strangle her. By all the gods, *practice*! He'd learned well to pleasure women, his father had seen to that, as had the wonderful Gunnvor when he'd been but twelve years old, when she'd taken him in hand, literally. Surely it wasn't his fault that he'd wanted her so badly he'd been forced to come into her before it was wise. Surely.

All awoke the next morning to a flood of rain. Tempers flared quickly at the enforced inactivity, men yelled at each other, fights broke out, children fought and shrieked with as great enthusiasm as the men. Even the animals were surly, a small goat biting one of Thoragasson's men on his ankle. It was Cleve who suggested to Merrik that Laren continue the story. "Aye," he said, grinning at the man he trusted with his life, "let her weave her magic around them. It will keep heads on shoulders, and hands from around throats."

"It will do nothing about the goat," Merrik said, but agreed.

And so it was still before noonday, when everyone had finally fallen silent, that Laren began again.

" . . . Rolf wandered deeper and deeper into the forest. The thick canopy of trees kept the sun from warming him. He knew he was searching for a beast to kill him, but none appeared. Aye, there were lynxes and rabbits,

even braces of pheasants that lurched into the air when
he came upon them suddenly, but nothing larger than
a fox.

"The third day of his wandering, he came to the edge
of a small meadow. It was the most beautiful meadow
he'd ever seen and he knew he'd never seen it before,
and he wondered at that, for he'd grown up here,
hunted in this forest. Yet here was this beautiful
meadow, carpeted with flowers of all colors, and the sun
warmed his face and his body. Suddenly, as he stood
there, wondering perhaps if his wits were failing him,
he saw on the far side of the meadow a beautiful creature that looked like a small horse. It didn't move, just
stood there, sniffing the soft morning air, its thick white
tail swishing. But somehow, Rolf knew the animal
wasn't the least afraid of him.

"The creature was ducking its head up and down, as
if inviting Rolf to come closer. Rolf slowly walked toward the animal. He realized as he drew closer that it
wasn't a horse at all, or any other kind of animal he'd
ever seen before. It turned to face him fully now, and
he saw a horn growing upward in the middle of its forehead. And the horn was gold.

"He walked to the creature and slowly reached out
his hand.

"The creature snorted, then stretched out his beautiful white head and laid his muzzle in Rolf's palm.

" 'Who are you?' Rolf asked, surprising himself that
he would speak aloud to a creature.

"To his utter astonishment, the creature said softly,
'I am a unicorn, Rolf, ah, but I am also more. You are
weak from wandering about in the woods. Go back to
your longhouse, then tomorrow return here.'

"The unicorn turned then, rearing onto its hind legs,
its beautiful white mane and tail arching and flying,

and galloped back into the depths of the forest. Rolf would swear he heard the voice calling to him, 'Do not forget your weapons tomorrow, for 'tis dangerous in the forest.'

"Rolf went back to his longhouse, stunned that it took him only an hour to return. His brothers were relieved to see him and gave him good food and wine and ceased in their bedeviling of him. They clapped him on the back and told him how happy they were that he'd come back. He found himself telling them about the unicorn and describing it and its beautiful gold horn. He told them that the unicorn had spoken to him and told him to return to it on the morrow. Didn't they think that curious? What did they think of this creature who had suddenly appeared to him?

"He then asked his brothers what they would do. Ragnor wondered if his brother had lost his wits and dreamed about this strange creature. He said only, 'You said the horn was of gold?'

"And Rolf said, 'Aye, 'twas of pure gold if my eyes weren't deceiving me.'

"Both brothers fell silent, deep in their thoughts."

Laren paused, then smiled toward Olaf Thoragasson. "If you were Rolf, my lord, what would you do about the unicorn?"

Olaf Thoragasson pounded his big fists on his thighs. "Why, I would kill the creature and cut away its golden horn. I would sell it to the richest prince in the world and become just as rich myself."

After the cheers had died away, mostly from Thoragasson's men, Laren turned to Erik. "And what would you do, my lord?"

Erik gave her a long, lazy smile. "I would not kill the creature. I would bring it back to my longhouse and I would treat it as tenderly as I would treat a woman. It

speaks, and thus I would gain its trust. It would have
a mate. I would find that mate, and keep them together.
Surely they would have offspring and then I would have
more golden-horned creatures. Thus I would become
even richer than Olaf Thoragasson."

The cheering filled the smoke-hazed room.

Finally, Laren turned to Merrik. "And you, my lord?
What would you do?"

Merrik was stroking Taby's hair. He looked up at her
as she spoke. He was silent for many moments, then
shrugged and said, "I would do naught of anything so
quickly. I would return to the meadow and see what the
magical creature had to tell me."

"A man of strategy," Thoragasson said, nodding his
head in approval. "Continue, girl. Tell us what happened."

"This time Rolf did as Merrik advised. He didn't want
to react so quickly. He'd already done that and lost himself a friend and a slave of great talent, and, he suspected when the night was at its darkest, some of his
honor. The following day, he returned to the meadow.
He'd wondered how he would find it, but just as suddenly, he stepped through a thicket of maple trees, and
there it was, the sun shining brightly down upon it, the
flowers wafting out sweet scents in a light breeze. The
unicorn stood on the other side of the meadow, calmly
watching Rolf walk to him. He allowed Rolf to muzzle
his head. He allowed Rolf to stroke his golden horn.

"Rolf said, 'The horn is pure gold?'

"If a unicorn could smile, this one did, and it said,
'Aye, of the purest, Rolf. Why do you ask?'

" 'My brothers gave me advice. They told me to either
kill you and steal your golden horn or capture you and
then your mate and thus have both of you and then your
offspring.'

" 'I do not think I like your brothers,' the unicorn said. 'What do you wish to do, Rolf?'

" 'I wish to speak to you, to learn who and what you are. I have never before seen a creature like you. Who sent you?'

" 'It's true I am magical,' the unicorn said. 'But I am also more. I am also your former slave, the one you smote with your sword.'

"Rolf stared at the creature. He drew his sword for he was certain the beast would try to kill him. He'd come back for revenge. He stood there, his sword poised in his hand, and the unicorn did nothing, didn't gallop away from him or attempt to protect himself in any way. Rolf raised the sword, then slowly, very slowly, he lowered it, and said, 'I cannot do it. When I killed you before, I knew such horror at myself that I came here to the forest to die. But you found me instead. Tell me what to do, for I wish to atone for taking your life. If you choose to kill me, I will make no move against you.'

"The unicorn nodded his beautiful white head, the golden horn glistening in the bright sunlight. Then, quite suddenly, he seemed to fade into nothing more than shadow and light, until Rolf knew he could see the sunlight through the creature's body, so pale had it become. He knew terror such as he'd never known. He fell to his knees, and clasped his arms around himself, waiting to die. But then as the unicorn was disappearing, something else was coming together and gaining darkness with the light and substance with the shadows. It was the slave he had smote with his sword. He held out his hand to Rolf and lifted him up. He said, 'The gods have granted us both another chance. Come with me, Rolf, and we will journey together back to my family, for they miss me sorely. Come.'

"Rolf's two brothers never saw him again. They

mourned him even as they believed him to have lost his wits, for surely the unicorn had killed him, and he'd trusted the beast, trusted him, and look what it had gotten him.

"But then there came a story into Vestfold told by a very old skald, toothless and scrawny, with thin bowed legs. All doubted he had anything worthwhile to say, but when he opened his mouth, all fell under his magic. He told about a man called Rolf the Viking, a man who was strong and fierce, a man to be trusted in all things, a man splendid of body and of face, and a man who was wiser than most men should be at such a young age. All honored him, all knew they could trust him, for it was known that once Rolf had been tested and had finally learned the way to true honor and worthiness.

"And his brothers wondered, even as they shook their heads in disbelief at their thoughts. Surely, they reasoned, there were many Rolfs who were tested and found worthy, but nonetheless, both wanted to question the old skald the next morning. When they went to search him out, he was gone, the men at the palisade gates said, gone with the rising of the sun, ah, but he hadn't disappeared with the sun, but rather into it, fading and fading, becoming as gold as the brilliance of the growing dawn light until he was simply gone. The brothers looked at each other. From that day onward, neither of them ever again mentioned either their brother or the strange appearance and disappearance of the old skald and his tale of Rolf the Viking."

Laren smiled directly at Merrik quite without realizing it. He looked at her, then down at Taby who was wide-awake, watching his sister, a frown on his small face. Taby said quite clearly, "Laren, I remember the unicorn."

14

S HE STARED AT Taby, then said, her voice as smooth as the soft hair on Merrik's belly, "That's because I've told you stories about magical creatures. I must have told you about a unicorn. Come now, sweeting, go play with Eila. See, she wants to throw the ball to you. Do play with her, Taby, it will keep her thumb out of her mouth."

Merrik started to say something, then stopped. He watched Taby run over to the little girl who was able to hold the feather-filled leather ball in one hand, and keep the thumb of her other hand in her mouth.

Laren quickly moved away from him, not wanting his questions, at least now. Olaf Thoragasson said to her, "You brought us into your story. It is good. No skald has ever before done that. I will speak to Merrik about buying you." Before she could say anything, before she could do naught more than shudder, he'd left her and was walking toward Merrik, rubbing his big hands together.

Letta frowned after her father. When she turned back to Laren, she said, "It has stopped raining. Merrik and I will go for a walk down to the fjord. I think I will let him kiss me. He will know what it is like to kiss an innocent virgin."

"Ah, so you will let him practice on you, Letta?"

The girl moved quickly, whirling about, the palm of her hand cracking hard against Laren's cheek. Laren stumbled back with the force of the blow, and Letta hit her again, this time shoving her onto the ground.

Laren knew she should accept the blows, knew indeed that she'd called them upon herself with her mocking words, but she couldn't stop herself. She jumped to her feet and was upon Letta in an instant. She wrapped Letta's two thick braids around her hands, winding and winding, until the girl was yelling and crying and but inches from Laren's face.

"Listen to me, you ill-bred witch. You will not ever strike me again. If you dare, I will remove all your pretty white teeth, one by one."

She quickly unwound the thick braid and gave Letta a shove. She fell back into Merrik's arms. Letta saw quickly who it was who was holding her, burst into tears, and whipped around, pressing herself against him, sobbing into his chest.

Merrik looked at Laren over her head. He saw the imprint of Letta's hand on her face, and the rage, and then he saw the instant she realized what she'd done.

Olaf Thoragasson lunged forward like an enraged bull. He saw Erik rubbing his hands together. Quickly, Merrik lifted Letta off the ground and handed her to her younger brother, the one who had so charmingly and witlessly given Laren his mother's brooch, and not, Merrik doubted, for the wondrousness of her tale. He stepped to Laren, grabbed her arm, and hauled her against his side.

He said both to her and to all who were staring at them, "She is my slave. I will see to her punishment."

Erik said, "And her punishment, brother? I wonder how severe it will be."

"Were she stronger I would whip her. But she isn't strong enough yet to survive it. She will cook for the next three days. Sarla, will you make her obey you when I am not present to do so?"

Sarla grinned widely at her and shook her fist. "Aye, Merrik, I will hit her with a pot if she doesn't willingly do the cooking."

"No insolence from you, Sarla!" Erik was flushed with anger as he strode toward his wife, his right hand a sudden fist.

"It wasn't insolence, brother," Merrik said, jerking Laren with him as he moved into Erik's path. "She was simply jesting. A simple jest, nothing more."

"Still, I won't have her speaking to you like that."

"If I took offense then I would tell her so. Forget it, Erik."

" 'Tis none of your affair, brother." Erik paused a moment, then turned quickly, sidestepped his brother, and struck Sarla open-palmed on her face. "There," he said, watching her struggle to keep her balance, her hand rubbing her cheek. "You will mind your tongue in the future." He turned to Merrik. "You see how you must treat a wife. No more will I have to bear her insolence, no more."

Merrik's hands were fisted at his sides. Laren ran to Sarla, but Erik shoved her aside. "Keep away from her, slave. By all the gods, you push me to violence."

There was no sound for several moments—just the sight of Sarla, tears running down her face, the men and women all still in their places, afraid to say a word. Even the children were quiet, staring at their parents, uncertain what to do.

Then Letta shrieked, "She said she would pull all my teeth out! One by one! Hit her, Merrik, she deserves it."

Merrik easily controlled the laughter welling up inside him, laughter mixed with his absolute fury at Erik. It was a helpless fury, for he knew he couldn't gainsay his brother in his own longhouse. He realized in that moment that he had to leave, he had to find a new home where he would be master. He turned to Letta and said, "You gave as good as you got, Letta. She is a skald. Of course she could frighten you with the imagery of her words. Hold your peace now, 'tis over."

He turned to look at the faces of his men; at Deglin, who looked disappointed that he wasn't whipping her right then, right there; at Old Firren who was whittling a chair post, his eyes fixed on his work; and finally at Cleve, whose face was white with the effort it cost him to keep still. Taby, thank the gods, as well as the other children, had turned away, all of them playing again, shouting and arguing, seeing nothing now. Thoragasson's men looked uncertain, many looking in any direction if Letta wasn't in it. He imagined they didn't have much affection for Letta, and they much more enjoyed Laren's stories. Merrik looked at Sarla. Her head was down, and he knew she was humiliated, crushed by her husband's actions.

He saw that Letta would say more, and quickly added, "Until it is time for her to sweat over the fire pit, I will take her to the fields and she can work there." He didn't add that he would be working next to her.

Without another word, he dragged her out of the longhouse. He knew she would have willingly gone with him, but he thought an impression of reluctance, perhaps fear, on her part, would calm everyone's ire.

The sun was bright overhead. The ground was still damp, but the sun had dried most of the mud puddles. She suddenly dug in her heels and yelled, "Stop dragging me!"

He turned and grinned down at her. "It was a good

act. But now there's no more need for it." He released her arm and said over his shoulder, "Follow me and be quick about it."

She moved swiftly after him. He said over his shoulder, not slowing, "Remove all of her teeth, one by one. I like that. It's a very effective threat."

"I thought so," she said, skipping to come alongside him.

He was silent.

She couldn't hold it in any longer. "I hate Erik. He is a bully, and without conscience. He struck her, Merrik, struck her just to prove he was the stronger and that she was nothing. I'm sorry since he is your brother, but I hate him. He is a bully and an animal. I know another man just like him."

"Who is he?"

She went still. Then she just shook her head, saying nothing more.

Merrik said slowly, not looking at her, "Erik has changed."

"I am relieved you didn't strike him after he'd hurt Sarla."

"I wanted to. It wouldn't have been wise. I have no say in his longhouse and I must remember that."

"I don't want to stay here."

"I have been thinking of that as well."

She waited, but he said no more. Laren said, with some reluctance, "I'm sorry I wanted to pull her hair from her silly head, but she enraged me and I lost my temper."

"One would think that after two years of retaliation and punishment, you would have learned to keep your tongue behind your teeth."

"Aye, one would think that would have happened."

"But it didn't. I remember too clearly your back after

Thrasco had beaten you for your lack of wisdom."

"Aye, 'tis a fault that will probably kill me."

"What did she say to you?"

"She said that she would walk with you and perhaps let you kiss her so you would know what it was like to kiss an innocent virgin."

"I see. I don't suppose you said anything back to her to make her slap you?"

Laren shrugged, not looking at him, but at the waving barley in the field. "Naught much of anything really, just something about her letting you practice on her. It made her very angry."

He laughed. "Aye, that was naught of anything. You mocked her apurpose. 'Twas not well done of you, Laren." He shook his head at her. He looked away from her then, and gazed upward where the fir trees were thick and full-leafed. "I had never heard of a unicorn before."

"As I told everyone, they're mythical creatures, magical."

"With horns on their foreheads of pure gold."

"Aye."

He paused a moment then said as he stroked his hand over a barley stalk, "Your tale interested me. I don't suppose by any chance it was a test?"

"Aye," she said, looking at him steadily. "I know you won't sell Taby back to me, no matter the amount of silver I have."

"You are finally right about something. I am pleased that finally you understand I will never let him go."

"And when you marry Letta? Merrik, please think. She would hate him just because he is my brother."

"You will not worry about that."

Laren said nothing more. When they reached the center of the barley field where others were working, he set her to looking closely at the birds flying overhead. "Keep them away from the crop." He said nothing more to her. She found herself staring at him, not wanting to really, but still she stared, watching him bend over, then straighten and stretch, his body strong and powerful, the sweat gleaming off his flesh beneath the afternoon sun. She wanted him. She knew a sharp feeling of hunger and knew it was him she wanted. But she held her peace. She had to hold herself away from him.

He dismissed her in the middle of the afternoon to eat. The sky was no longer overcast, the rain of the morning long before moved northward. The sun was brilliant overhead. Laren thought of food, realized there was something more important to her than warm bread for the first time in two years, and walked quickly toward the trail that led upward to the summit of an outjutting cliff that stretched out over the fjord. She'd looked at it several times in the past days, wanting very much to climb to the top to see the magnificent scenery, but knowing that her body wasn't yet strong enough. Her body was strong enough now. She set out at a brisk walk, keeping her eye on the sun. She didn't want to be gone too long from the field.

She didn't want to be gone too long from Merrik's side. She thought about that, thought about him smiling at her, laughing, stripping off his clothes, coming into her body, holding her close, giving her pleasure until he'd hurt her, but surely that wasn't his fault, but her own body's, unused to a man.

She wanted him again, very much. It was stronger now, this wanting. She looked at him and felt a quickening that was both frightening and exhilarating. But she would be a fool to allow herself the pleasure of him.

The path steepened; it was narrow with deep ruts and strewn rocks on it. Her breath was becoming labored. She hated it, this weakness of her body.

She looked at the top, not too far distant now, and kept looking until she was there, finally, breathing hard, a stitch beginning in her side. But she'd made it.

She straightened and walked to the edge. The view was more magnificent than she'd imagined. The fjord below made many turns, curving inward, then winding sharply outward, the dark blue flowing forever beyond the eye. She gazed at the fir-covered uplands opposite the fjord where no one had touched the land, for it was too steep, too irregular, with sharp faces falling hundreds of feet to the water. She turned now to gaze down at Malverne with all its slightly sloping or flat land given entirely over to farming. The wooden palisade looked like a near perfect circle from her vantage point, with its pointed wooden spikes standing high that would surely gut any enemy who tried to scale them. All the buildings within looked sound and solid, surrounding the large rectangular longhouse. Smoke snaked upward, a thin blue line that disappeared into the sweet air, and she fancied she could smell Sarla's cooking. Toward the back of the enclosure, she saw the burial site and the temple. She knew Merrik had visited his parents' graves many times, always returning to the longhouse quiet, his head and shoulders bowed. She knew he grieved deeply for them, but she'd said nothing. What could she say? She couldn't speak to him of her own parents' deaths because he would want to know who they were and he would push her and push her. She knew she would tell him soon. He'd been right about her tale being a test. She could trust him; she had to, it was that simple.

She sat down, not too far from the edge of the cliff, and leaned back against a rock. She hoped Sarla was all right. She hoped Letta's scalp hurt. Then she thought of Merrik and wondered if many lovers had come up here in the past, aye, many, she thought, as her eyes slowly closed.

"I saw you come up here. I waited to see if my brother would come after you but he didn't. Then I followed you."

She heard his voice in a half-sleep, far away, a caressing voice, one filled with satisfaction, but still only a voice and it couldn't hurt her, couldn't frighten her.

"No one else saw you, or me, come up here. This place is called Raven's Peak. In recent years there have been fewer attacks by other Vikings, thus it is no longer much used as a lookout point. No, it is a lovers' place now, and you are here, Laren."

More than a voice now. There was gloating in it and pleasure, the sort of pleasure a man would find if he caught a woman alone, unawares, a woman he knew was his for the taking. She felt her heart begin to pound.

"I know you are awake, Laren. I thought perhaps you were coming here to meet a man—as I said, it is that sort of place—but you are alone. I am pleased. You turned Merrik away or didn't he want you in the middle of the day?"

She opened her eyes and stared up at Erik. It was hard to see his face because the sun was directly behind him. If she didn't know him, she would have believed, briefly, that he was a god, golden and radiant, so very big. Slowly, Laren eased up, scraping her back against the rock. It made her wince, but she said nothing, merely moved up until she was sitting. Then, very slowly, she stood, her hand back against the rock.

"It is late," she said. "I must return to the fields. Merrik will expect me."

"Why did you come here?"

"I was told Raven's Peak offered the most beautiful view of your land. I wanted to see for myself."

"As I said, many men and women have come here to couple."

"I came only to look."

"I came to have you. I won't wait longer. Perhaps you knew I would follow you if only you managed to get away from Merrik. Is that what you wanted?"

"No, I don't wish you to hurt me, Erik. I must go now." She whirled about even as she spoke, but she wasn't fast enough. He was as strong as Merrik, and his long fingers dug into her upper arm. "You are still too thin. My fingers can wrap about your arm. Don't try to run from me again. I don't like it."

She turned back to face him now, looking up at his face, now brutal to her, its beauty masked by his lust. She remembered that long-ago night, how she'd managed to fool the one man by pretending to be faint. Somehow she didn't think she could succeed with the same ploy with Erik.

"I don't wish to couple with you. I belong to Merrik. Why would you want to anger your brother? Do you not love him? Is there not honor between you?"

His eyes narrowed on her face; his fingers worked on her arm, squeezing still, but not hurting her now. He said easily, as if to a half-wit, "You think yourself above Caylis and Megot because you weave a tale well. You are not. Listen to me, Laren, I am now the lord of Malverne, not my father, not my brother. I am the master of all you see from here. I have waited and waited for my turn and it was long in coming. I wanted to leave, to make my own way, perhaps voyage to Iceland, but my father begged me not to, told me that I was the future lord of Malverne and my duty was here. I am sorry that my parents died, but with all their damned words, their damned promises, I was still but a son, someone to be governed by them, naught more. But it is different now. Even Sarla now sees that she will be what I wish her to be. I had not struck her before, for my parents defended her, even though she is barren and useless to a man. At least now she will obey me without question and tread lightly around me."

"Erik, I am not a wife. I am naught of anything. I am useless as well. You have said I am too thin. It is true. Please, Erik, don't hurt me."

He smiled down at her and now he grasped her other arm. He pulled her against him and she realized he was as tall as Merrik, as strong and as big. She would have no chance against him, none. She didn't want him to rape her. She didn't think she could bear it.

She threw back her head and looked at him straightly. "Don't do this or you will regret it." The moment the words were out of her mouth, she knew she'd made a mistake. A woman didn't threaten him. She watched his eyes narrow until they were slits, she saw the pulse pounding in his neck. He was furious and now she would regret it. She did regret it. He slapped her hard, just as he had his wife. She caught the cry in her throat. She wouldn't give him the pleasure of hearing her cry out.

"Now," he said, and kissed her hard, his mouth grinding against hers, his teeth cutting her lower lip. One of his hands clutched her right breast and he kneaded her furiously, hurting her. His other hand was ripping her tunic, but the material was sturdy. He reared back, took both of his hands and grasped the neck of her gown and jerked.

She heard the rip even as she drove her knee upward into his groin. He loosened his grip just enough in his shock. She jerked away from him, running frantically down the narrow winding path. She heard him bellow behind her, but she didn't turn around. She heard him groaning, gasping for breath from the blow she'd dealt him. But still, she was terrified that he was behind her, almost upon her, and any moment now she would feel his hot breath, his clutching hands on her arms, spinning her around, and striking her hard. Then he would rape her and then he would kill her. She ran until she tripped, falling on the steep path until she struck a rock. She saw an explosion of white, then she saw nothing.

She didn't know how much time had passed when she awoke, slowly, her head spinning, her eyes unfocused. She shook her head, and felt the lump over her left ear. Pain coursed through her, striking hard behind her eyes. Suddenly she remembered. She grasped the edge of the rock and pulled herself upright. She stood there, weaving, trying to gain her balance and control the pounding in her head. She was listening, hard. There was no sound, nothing.

Erik wasn't in sight. Had she only been unconscious for an instant? Was he still there on top of the path, still on his knees, still holding his belly?

Fear rushed through her, clearing her head. She didn't wait, she stumbled down the path, not stopping until she reached the bottom and then she halted against a fir tree to catch her breath. Her heart pounded, her side ached, her back, nearly healed, was now pulling and throbbing. As for her leg, she felt nothing, which, she supposed, was a good sign.

"By all the gods, where have you been?"

It was Merrik striding toward her, yelling.

"I thought you'd gotten yourself attacked by a wild animal or you'd fallen into the water and drowned." He was utterly furious, but she saw it was from fear for her.

She tried to smile at him, a miserable effort, but still her best effort. "Nay, I'm all right. I wanted to see the view from the top yon. It is glorious, Merrik, so very beautiful, with the water winding like a snake and—"

"Damn you, be quiet! Who ripped your gown? Who?"

He was on her then and he grasped her upper arms just as his brother had done, but immediately he gentled. He stared down at her, gaining control of himself. He'd been frantic with fear, and he'd hated that damned fear that had driven him wild. He calmed. He saw then that she was heaving, that her face was without color, the pulse in her throat pounding wildly above the rent in her gown. "Who?" he said again. "Who did this to you?" He saw her wince, saw her make an unconscious gesture to her head.

He said more calmly now, more slowly, "Tell me what happened."

"I fell, nothing more, I just fell and knocked myself out for a moment. I'm all right now, Merrik." But even as she spoke, she was looking back over her shoulder, up the narrow path.

"And when you fell you ripped your gown? By all the gods, tell me who did this to you!" He felt her pulling away from him even though she wasn't really moving. He realized then that she was terrified.

He drew her close, his hands stroking lightly up and down her back. Then he remembered Thrasco's beating, and brought his hands up to her shoulders and her neck, massaging her, soothing her. "Tell me what happened."

"I want to go back to the longhouse. Please, Merrik, I wish to go now, I must!"

Her fear was palpable. He frowned down at her. "Neither of us is going anywhere until you tell me what happened."

She began to tremble, she couldn't help herself. She knew Merrik would fight his brother, he wouldn't hold back, she knew it. "He's up there, I know it. He ripped my gown but no more, nothing more, I swear it. I hurt him, kicked him just as I kicked you in Kiev, and I heard him screaming after me and then he was moaning loudly. But now he must be all right. He will come down and he will see me with you and he will take me away or you'll fight him and I can't bear that, not brother against brother!"

He said not a word, merely looked back up the winding, rutted path.

She struggled against him now, so frightened that she was trembling, her flesh cold beneath his fingers.

"How long were you unconscious?"

"I don't know! I don't know! Please, Merrik, let me go, don't let him see me!"

"Hush. Listen to me. You left me to return to the longhouse over an hour ago. I got worried and began to look for you."

"An hour?" She stared up at him blankly. "Oh no, that can't be right. No, that's too long. No, that isn't right, Merrik!"

Suddenly she felt his fingers tighten around her arms. She turned to see Oleg striding toward them, Old Firren behind him.

Merrik said, "Laren, you will remain here. Do not leave this spot. Do you understand me?"

"Why? Where are you going? Why?" Her voice was shrill and she was shaking. He cursed, then grabbing her hand, he pulled her after him. "Come, Oleg, Firren. We must see that Erik is all right."

They found him sprawled at the top, facedown, his

right leg dangling over the cliff edge. The back of his head was bashed in. He was quite dead. In his right hand he held a scrap of wool. Merrik recognized it before Laren did.

Erik had torn it from her gown.

15

"Aye, poor slave, you killed him and now you'll die.
I shall try not to smile when the last breath leaves your
miserable body. I will go away by myself and laugh and
know pleasure that you are gone forever. I won't fear
your ghost, for they will bury you so deep that even your
evil will die."

Laren stared up at Letta's face, barely discernible in
the dim light of Merrik's sleeping chamber. She'd been
sound asleep, deep in a frightening darkness that held
her unmoving and terrified. And now Letta's voice, low
and vicious and filled with glee. Still it was better than
that nothingness, those obscure shadows that would
have sucked away her life.

"Aye, now you'll pay, you miserable whore, you'll pay.
You're only a slave. Erik had a right to take you. And
you killed him and now Merrik will kill you, it's his duty
as Erik's brother."

"I didn't kill Erik."

"Liar. No one else was seen on the path. Just you and
Erik. No one else. You're naught but a slave. No one
believes your denials. Even now the men are discussing
what to do with you, and let me tell you, whore, Merrik
holds himself silent. He isn't taking your side."

"I didn't kill Erik," she said again, listening to the

hollow ring of her own voice, knowing that no one would believe her, no one at all.

"Aye, you've slept for a very long time. Sarla thought it would be best for you, the stupid cow. She didn't want the men killing you if you had dared to come to Erik's burial, ah, and they would have, they would have. She wanted you left alone, silent and asleep, to protect you, but it won't matter, because you'll be dead, as dead as Erik whom you killed."

"Is Sarla all right?"

Letta smiled then. "Aye, she is fine. She has lost a man who occasionally punished her for her insolence, but much more than that, she has lost Malverne, though she doesn't realize it yet. Now it belongs to Merrik, no one else, least of all that stupid cow, who is as barren as a fifty-year-old grandmother. There are only Erik's bastards, none of them legitimate because Erik was a young man and thus thought himself immortal and didn't even make Kenna legitimate. It was a pity, but not for me, not for Merrik, who now owns everything, as far as the eye can see.

"Aye, Malverne is Merrik's now. When we wed, I will be mistress here and both you and Sarla will be gone, I will see to it."

"Merrik would never make Sarla leave Malverne."

"He will want to make me happy. I will be his wife and thus he will do what I wish him to."

"What are you doing in here, Letta?"

It was Merrik silhouetted in the opening, his hand shoving aside the bearskin covering.

"I was just seeing if she was awake now, my lord," Letta said in a softly sweet voice. "Sarla sent me to rouse her. It is odd that Erik's widow would think so highly of the slave who murdered her husband."

Letta straightened, then walked slowly to Merrik.

She stood in front of him, gazing up at him, and touched her fingertips to his forearm. "I am so very sorry, Merrik. First your parents and now this slave killed your brother. I do understand, my lord, for I lost my older sister only two years ago when I was already grown. 'Tis a miserable thing."

"Go to your father, Letta."

She smiled up at him, patted his arm again, and left.

Merrik strode to the box bed and stared down at her. "At least there are no new bruises or burns or lash marks on you this time."

She merely shook her head. He hadn't seen her breast, thank the gods for that. Erik had hurt her in his frenzy, bruising her badly.

"It is over," he said. "My brother is surely gone from us now." He pictured his brother carried down from the steep path, he himself looking down at his bloodied head as he carried his shoulders, saw the women cleaning him and garbing him in his finery. His body wasn't brought into the longhouse, for all feared that a ghost would come and do them ill. Thus he was carried to the burial grounds and placed gently, feet first, into the deep hole dug beside his father's grave. His sword, his axe, and his favorite knife were buried with him, as were his favorite armlets and clothing. There was more shock than sorrow, the pain would come later. He wondered how much Erik had changed since their parents had died. Had he turned most of his people against him with his arrogance, his conceit? Had he made an enemy who would have crushed his head with a rock? It seemed unlikely. Sarla's face showed only shock, no sorrow, no relief, nothing, though it was difficult to tell since one cheek was nearly purple from the blow Erik had dealt her.

He himself had led the prayers to the gods—to Odin

All-Father, to Thor Redbeard, to Loki the Spirit of Evil, extolling Erik's bravery in battle, his honor, and to Saeter the underworld god, pledging his own word that Erik didn't belong there and so Saeter would gain nothing in this death. He begged them to accept Erik Haraldsson over the rainbow bridge and into heaven, to reward him for all eternity, to bless him in his final journey. As he'd spoken, he saw his brother's bloodied head. He had closed his eyes, words had been beyond him. So much death, too much death. His parents and now his elder brother. Had Erik spoken the words over their parents' bodies? Had he felt tears burning his eyes as he'd spoken? Had his voice broken and had he swallowed, trying to continue, to see all the rites and rituals done properly? Suddenly, Merrik had felt a small hand clutch his. He'd looked down to see Taby, the child's face filled with misery because he knew something was wrong with Merrik, he just didn't understand what it was. Merrik leaned down and picked up the child, bringing him against his chest. He kissed his warm cheek, felt the child's thin arms clutch around his throat. No one had said anything, even Letta, even Olaf Thoragasson.

No one had said anything about Laren to him either, but he knew that all wondered what he would do. He knew that all were speaking of her and her probable guilt. But he was the master of Malverne now. It was his thoughts that counted, his commands that ruled, none other's.

He looked down at her now. His silence had been long and she'd kept quiet. Her eyes were closed, but her hands were fisted at her sides.

"I didn't kill him, Merrik. I didn't. I kicked him in the groin and ran hard until I tripped and knocked myself out. Please, you must believe me."

"I can see you flat on your back, Erik on top of you, jerking at your gown, wanting to strip you and rape you. I can see you frantic to defend yourself. I can see you picking up a rock and striking his head. I do not blame you for that, Laren. You were a fool to go up to Raven's Peak by yourself. And now my brother is dead because his lust pushed him to rape the wrong woman."

"What will you do?"

"I don't know. All believe you guilty."

"I didn't kill him!"

"As a slave you have no rights at all. As a slave, killing a man of Erik's status, your death would be long and painful. It would be I who would kill you." He stopped then, staring down at her white face. He rose.

"What will you do?"

"I don't know. But I do know I cannot allow Taby's sister to die. He would never forgive me."

Relief that was oddly mixed with pain at his words shot through her. *Only Taby's sister?* "Why will you not believe me, Merrik?"

"Why should I? You have told me nothing since I saved your hide in Kiev. Not where you came from, not about your family, nothing. So little you've told me, and what I have finally pried out of you has been wrapped in mysteries and puzzles. Why should I believe you now?"

She heard a man's shout. Merrik said sharply, "Stay here!" He was gone from the chamber in an instant, Laren behind him, holding up her torn gown.

Two of Erik's men were holding Cleve, a third was beating him. It was Deglin who was shouting for them to kill the miserable slave.

Merrik caught one man's wrist and jerked him away,

throwing him to the ground. He kicked another man from his path.

"Let him go."

The two men looked at Merrik, but they didn't know him as well as they'd known his brother. His voice was low, very controlled. One of them said, even as he bent Cleve's arm nearly to the breaking point, "He came with her, Merrik. We'll beat the truth out of him, for surely she told him of killing Erik, surely he knows, perhaps he even helped her."

The other man struck Cleve hard with his fist in his belly.

Merrik said nothing more. He grabbed the man, swung him about and sent his fist into his throat.

"Release him or I'll kill you."

Erik's man was uncertain what to do. He saw Oleg running toward them and knew he would take Merrik's side. He shouted to Erik's men, "Come! Help me! It is justice!"

Merrik grabbed the man's throat between his two hands and squeezed. He stared into the man's face even as he bent him onto his knees, driving him slowly to the ground. The man tried to speak, but couldn't. His eyes clouded and darkened. He slumped unconscious on the ground. Merrik stood over him. "Are there others who wish to hurt this man?"

"He's a slave," Olaf Thoragasson said, his voice quieter now, for he'd seen Merrik's anger and his violence. "Aye, Merrik, naught but a slave. Let the men have their sport. Their master was murdered. This man is nothing, only a slave, and they're right, he came with her and probably knows the truth. Aye, let them break him. No one cares."

"I imagine that Cleve cares very much." He turned to him. "Are you all right?"

"My arm hurts, but he didn't break it. I thank you, my lord."

"He's a slave!" Deglin shouted.

"No he isn't," Merrik said. He faced them all now, looking at each face in turn. "He is now a free man. All of you heed my words. Cleve is a free man. He is now my man."

"Ah," Olaf Thoragasson said, "then if he is a free man, make him pay the Danegeld for Erik's death. If he doesn't have the Danegeld, then he must die, and by your hand."

"Wait!" It was Deglin again. "*She* killed Erik, not this ugly heathen. Get her, let her die, for she is a slave."

Merrik merely shook his head.

"Then he must pay the Danegeld!" Deglin shrieked. "He murdered your brother, she with him. All know it!"

"There she is, ask her, ask her!"

Laren stood in the shadows, still and silent. Merrik knew she had silver from her stories, and some jewelry, but surely not enough for Danegeld, surely not enough for both her and Cleve.

Cleve said to Merrik, his voice loud and strong, "My lord, Deglin is right. I killed Erik, not Laren. He had hurt her and she escaped him. I struck him with the rock in my anger. I alone am responsible."

"No!" Laren ran to him, grabbing his arms, shaking him, making him look at her. "You will not lie, Cleve, not for me! I didn't kill him and neither did you." She turned then to all the men and women standing there, staring at her, fury on some faces, uncertainty on others. She saw Sarla standing by the fire pit, slowly stirring a boar-meat stew, saying nothing, her hand turning the giant wooden spoon, evenly, smoothly.

"Of course you killed him, there is none other." This was from one of Erik's men. "He was much admired, a brave man, an honorable man."

"Aye, aye!"

Suddenly, Sarla called out, "Silence, all of you!" Slowly, she walked through the people to Merrik. She raised her voice then and said, "I will not allow Cleve and Laren to be blamed. I killed Erik. I alone. He struck me many times since his parents died, since he became the lord here, and I hated him. He followed Laren to Raven's Peak to rape her. All of you know how he lusted after her even though she belonged to Merrik, his brother. He cared not. His lust governed him. She fought him and managed to escape him. I saw her run away. Then I struck him dead. They had nothing to do with it."

There was pandemonium.

Merrik looked at her breast, at the streaks of purple and yellow, at the blunt outlines of Erik's fingers where he'd kneaded her flesh deep and hard.

He reached out his hand and lightly cupped her breast in his palm. She felt the warmth of him, the power of him, and she knew she wanted him more than she ever had, even now, when there was more pain and misery between them than ever before. She wanted to press against his hand. She wanted to lean into his strength, to feel him holding her, to know that he believed her and would stand beside her. She wanted to kiss him, to taste the heat of him, to experience again the incredible feelings he'd given her once, so long ago now, it seemed. But she stood frozen before him, unmoving, and he felt only the stiffness of her, the wariness. Now he knew that she watched his hand, watched as his fingers lightly moved over the bruises, then she looked up and he couldn't hide the fury in his eyes from her.

He'd come upon her without warning, and she'd tried to cover herself, but she hadn't been in time.

He said, "Your gown is torn beyond repair. I will ask Sarla to give you another."

He slowly lifted his fingers from her breast then and turned away from her. He said, not looking at her, "Does your breast hurt?"

She shook her head, realized he wasn't looking at her, and said, "No, not very much."

"A woman's flesh is very tender there. You are lying. I'm sorry my brother did that to you. But he is dead and that is more punishment than he deserved."

"I didn't kill him, Merrik. Neither did Cleve nor did Sarla. They were just trying to protect me."

He laughed then, a low, deep laugh, and he was still laughing when he turned again to face her. The laughter suddenly died. "Cover yourself," he said, and then she saw it—the hunger in him, the need. Was it just for her, or would any woman do?

She did, quickly, jerking the material up against her shoulder. She raised her chin, looking at him straightly. "Why? You do not wish Taby to know that you were staring at his sister? Would it upset him, this lust of yours, or do you merely look at me because there is no other woman who you believe belongs to you?"

"No, this time I had no thought of Taby," he said. He walked to the box bed and sat down. He leaned forward, clasping his hands between his knees. He appeared to be studying the woven wool mat that covered the ground. "Do you really belong to me, Laren?"

"You seem to accept me thus since I am Taby's sister."

"When I came into you, when I broke through your virginity and touched your womb, I had no thought of you as Taby's sister."

"You speak bluntly, Merrik."

"Aye, and you welcomed me until I hurt you. Your breasts are beautiful. I had forgotten."

"Many women have beautiful breasts, no doubt even Letta."

"I don't care about her breasts, truth be told. I wish she and her family would leave Malverne." He paused a moment, then smiled bitterly down at his clasped hands. "I am the master here now. I believe I will tell them to go. I dislike Letta's possessiveness and her father's interference. I dislike her conceit." He rose. "It is odd. I didn't want Malverne. I never considered that it would be mine. If Erik had a son, I would guard Malverne for him with my life until he was of an age to take it over. I cannot give Malverne to Kenna, though the boy is smart and brave. He is a bastard and none would stand for it. This is a damnable situation."

"I didn't kill Erik."

He sighed. "I believe you. However, I cannot be certain about Cleve. He is protective of you. If he saw that Erik was going to rape you, don't you believe he could have easily struck him down?"

"Yes, he could have, but he didn't. Don't you understand? If Cleve killed him, he would have run back down that same path. He would have seen me unconscious. He would have known that I would be blamed."

Suddenly Merrik raised his head. He smiled at her. "For that same reason, then, Sarla couldn't have done it either."

She nodded.

"That leaves us with a mystery, then, and I dislike mysteries. I thought the mystery of you and Taby would tease me into madness—your damnable lack of trust in me even though I passed your test—aye, that tale of yours was a test for me, to see if you could trust me—but this is beyond that, far beyond, for Erik, despite his faults, despite his growing conceit and arrogance, despite it all, he was still my brother. I must avenge him. You understand that, don't you, Laren?"

"Oh aye, Merrik, I understand vengeance."

He rose then and strode to her. He looked down at her, not touching her, just looking at her. "You have made a rare confusion of my life." As if he couldn't help himself, he gently lifted her chin in his palm, and stared at her. "Stay here. I will send Sarla to you with clothing."

"What will you do?"

"I will speak to all my people. I will speak to them of loyalty and show them Cleve's and Sarla's innocence. They are already doubtful, believing that they confessed only to save you. That will leave you, Laren, in their minds. None other, just you. I will deal with it, for by all the gods, I have no choice."

He left her standing there, her face pale, wondering what he would do, if he would be forced to kill her, a miserable slave who murdered his brother, despite Taby.

Sarla's gown hung loose on Laren, for she had no belt to fasten it to her waist. The overtunic hung nearly to her knees and even the two brooches couldn't make it drape properly.

When she walked into the outer chamber, only the women were there, not more than a dozen, all working: smoking herring just brought up from the fjord, cleaning cloth before dyeing it, working the large loom in the corner of the longhouse, kneading bread in the huge trough, so many things they were doing, all everyday, very normal household chores, and Laren realized she wanted to be part of it. She walked to the fire pit, to Sarla, and thanked her for the gown.

Sarla looked at her up and down and gave her a crooked grin. "You look passing strange, Laren. You are still so very thin. Come, eat some porridge."

"After I eat I want to cook."

"Aye, it is your punishment for your insolence." She paused, then added quietly, "Though I doubt the punishment is still in effect since Erik is dead."

"I want to cook."

"Do you feel all right?"

"I wish you had not fed me the drug, for my dreams were vicious shadows all concealed in darkness."

"I just wanted you to be safe. Now everyone is thinking beyond the obvious. Merrik is wise in his speech."

"You weren't wise, Sarla, neither you nor Cleve. You were foolish."

"I could not stand there by my fire pit stirring some ridiculous pot of stew whilst everyone accused you and Cleve of murdering Erik."

"You are very brave."

Sarla just looked at her. "Nay, I am weaker than you can imagine. Cleve is the one who is strong." She paused, opened her mouth to say more, then just shook her head.

"Have you seen Taby?"

"He is with the other children outside. I believe Kenna is teaching him wrestling." She shook her head. "I feel very sorry for Kenna. And for Caylis. Both she and Megot have nothing now. There is not much justice in that, I think."

"No, there isn't."

"I didn't realize until just this morning that Merrik is now master of Malverne. Oh, I knew Merrik was the master now, but I didn't realize what it would mean. Letta told me. She is very pleased about it. She made me feel as though my time here were nearly over. I wanted to slap her."

"Don't worry about that one. Merrik said since Malverne is now his, he will send the Thoragassons on their way. Perhaps he will do it today. Why don't you tell Letta that she will be gone from Malverne much more quickly than you."

Sarla looked up to see Letta walking toward them. "By that smug look on her face, I don't think Merrik has yet told them to leave."

Laren wanted to keep her temper and she knew she would lose it if she remained. She heard Sarla whisper "Coward!" but she kept walking away, more quickly now, until she heard Letta call out, "Stop, slave! I wish to speak to you."

She sighed, then turned. "What is it you wish now, Letta?"

"My father is with Merrik right now. He is bargaining over your purchase price. He wants you, for he believes you have some worth as a skald, but to have a murderess in his longhouse distresses him. He fears you might became angered at him and kill him."

Laren just stared at her.

Sarla said, "That is nonsense, Letta, and well you know it. You will hold your tongue. You are a guest here, nothing more, and you will cease strutting yourself about as mistress. You will cease tormenting Laren."

"Tormenting her! Ha! She has a hide tougher than that boar you were skinning."

"It is just that your torments are very childlike, Letta," Laren said. "You are too simple in your spite. Perhaps you will improve as you gain years. It seems you are walking in that path."

Letta opened her mouth, but Laren forestalled her,

saying quickly, her voice very mean, "Remember your pretty teeth, Letta. One by one. Do you understand?"

Letta paled, turned on her heel, and left the longhouse.

Sarla laughed. "Aye, she is on that path, but she can still be halted in her petty tracks."

Cleve walked to them, and he was shaking his head. "I waited until she had left you. Laren, Merrik is even now holding a meeting to discuss Erik's murder. Here they call it the *Thing*. It is what they do to determine guilt and search for fair answers. I came to tell you. Most still believe you guilty, but now, at least, they're discussing it."

Caylis came forward to stand beside Cleve. "I don't think you're guilty, but if you hadn't come here, Erik wouldn't be dead and my son and I would be safe."

She was right, but Laren said only, "I'm sorry, Caylis, but believe me, I did not kill him. I can do nothing about my presence here, for Merrik controls that."

"Aye, but Caylis is right," Megot said. "Because you came we will become as nothing. Perhaps Merrik will even give us to his men to be used at their whim. I pray that Merrik will make us his mistresses, but I know that he now takes only you to his bed. I heard him and Erik once speaking of such things and Erik said Merrik was stupid to want what their parents had shared. He told Merrik that he would come to understand his wish was as flimsy as a dream once he had wedded Letta. He said Merrik would leave her soon enough and search out other women to bed."

All of this in front of Sarla, Laren thought. She supposed it was much the same amongst her own people, but she'd been too young to notice such things. There was no expression on Sarla's face. None at all. Laren chanced to look at Cleve. She went very still. He was staring at Sarla, the look on his scarred face so tender, so very helpless, that she wanted to cry.

There came a cry from outside the longhouse, then there was shouting and loud arguing. Then there was utter silence. Gradually they could hear the voices resume, heard the low rumblings of arguments, but controlled now. Then they heard Merrik's voice but they couldn't understand his words. Other voices were raised in question.

"What is it?" Sarla said, and rushed toward the doorway.

Oleg appeared in the entrance. He looked at each of them until he found Laren. He said quietly, "You'd best come now, Laren. Merrik has reached a decision and all will abide by it."

16

MERRIK WATCHED HER walk to him, Oleg at her side, Sarla on her other side. He waited until she was standing before him, then said very quietly, "You will come with me now."

He took her hand and led her away. She heard the men's voices, some clearly angry, others simply questioning. Then she heard Oleg say loudly, "It is right and just. Merrik is the lord of Malverne now. We will all heed his wishes."

What wishes?

He continued silent until they had walked down the wide path to the fjord. He motioned to the pier. They walked out to the end and he pulled her down beside him, their feet dangling over the end of the pier. The water below was a calm light blue. She could see small ripples created by fish swimming just below the surface.

The sun was bright overhead, the air soft and very warm. She couldn't imagine snow covering everything. A cloud slid in front of the sun, but just for a moment. She waited silent.

"You have two choices," he said at last.

She cocked her head to one side, staring now at his profile. Still he didn't turn to face her.

"You will wed with me and remain here at Malverne." He turned to face her as he spoke. "Why do you look so surprised? Why do you shudder? Very well, then. If being my wife displeases you so very much, why, then, you can select the second choice. I will see that you are returned to your family. However, Taby will remain with me. I am making him my son."

"No!"

"No what?"

She just stared at him, shaking her head back and forth. He supposed he was pleased that for once he'd taken her utterly aback, but more than that, now he wanted her to tell him that she wanted to wed with him, that she—

"I cannot wed you."

"Oh? You cannot or you will not?"

"I cannot."

"Are you already married? I don't think it was Thrasco who was the hopeful husband, was it? Or perhaps before you were a slave you were married off as a child?"

"No, no, nothing like that."

"No, of course you weren't married. You were very much a virgin when I took you. Ah, I see. I am too beneath you to consider as a husband."

"No, never."

"More puzzles, more mysteries. Very well, Laren. Don't forget you are my slave. Regardless of what you were before, now you are nothing more than a slave, one that many of my people believe also a murderess. I offer you the moon and the stars—at least that's how a slave would see wedding the master of a large holding such as Malverne."

She jumped to her feet and stared down at him. "You cannot keep Taby."

"I can and I fully intend to." He rose now, more slowly, to face her. He took her upper arms in his big hands. "Will you marry me or no?"

She looked into the fjord and saw a school of herring racing through the water, very close to the smooth surface, leaping above, like darts of silver. She felt she could reach into the water and catch one, so close they were. She looked up at him now. She wanted to smooth the frown from his forehead, as she said very calmly, "I cannot marry you because I was promised to Askhold, heir of Rognvald, king of the Danelaw."

He jerked back as if she'd struck him. What she said was madness, surely . . . He stared at her, then at her loose-fitting gown and overtunic, not old or ragged, for it was Sarla's, just very plain and too big for her, not garb the future queen of the Danelaw would wear. Something violent moved within him, something he didn't understand, but accepted, just as he'd accepted her and he knew he'd accepted her for a very long time now, for probably longer than he realized. He believed her, tamped down on the fury raging deep within him, and said mildly, "The truth at last. Tell me the rest of it."

"Taby is indeed a prince. He and I were abducted from my sleeping chamber two years ago, and sold to a slave trader in the Rhineland."

"Who is your father?"

"Our father, Hallad, is dead. However, Taby is the second male in line to succeed his uncle."

"His uncle, Laren?"

She drew in a deep breath. "I haven't said his name aloud in two years. Our uncle is Rollo, called the first duke by the Frankish king, Charles the Simple. As you know, he ceded Normandy to Rollo so that he would defend France against the raids of other Vikings."

This time he didn't feel as if she'd struck him; he felt as if he'd been kicked by a horse. "The famous Rollo," Merrik said more to himself than to her. "I was raised on tales about the brave and ferocious Rollo. He is truly your uncle?"

"Aye, my father was his older brother. Rollo was wedded to a girl from a royal family in Spain. He loved her, so I have been told. She bore him some six children, three of them boys. However, only the second son, William Longsword, lived to manhood. Thus, Taby is second in line after William. His older brother, Hallad, my father, had four children, three daughters and one son, Taby. Unfortunately our mother died when Taby was only a year old. Our sisters, by my father's first wife, are much older. They are wed to men of high rank and all live in Rouen at my uncle's palace. Someone betrayed us. One or both of my sisters, or their husbands. I don't know who. William Longsword was out of Normandy at the time of our abduction, at the Frankish court in Paris. Also, I trust William. He would no more harm Taby or me than he would harm his own father. He realizes Taby's importance in the scheme of things. He, too, has a wife, but she has borne him no children as yet and they've been wed for five years. At least this was true when we were abducted. Perhaps by now he has a son. Perhaps by now Taby isn't so very important. But until we know, Merrik, Taby is very important to Rollo, very important to Normandy."

He said nothing for a very long time. Then, "At least they didn't murder you out of hand."

"No, that is why I believe it must be one of my sisters, or both of them, or their husbands. It would salve their consciences were Taby and I only to be sold as slaves, not killed outright. They surely must believe that they have won, Merrik. They haven't, unless William Longsword has died leaving no son, but I have heard naught about it. If there is no direct heir, why, then one of the husbands would become the heir to Rollo."

"That is what you meant when you told me you understood vengeance."

"Aye, I have lived with the thought of it strong and sweet in my mind. Aye, and on my tongue. I can nearly taste it. As long as I'm alive they haven't won."

"No, they haven't. You have spent the last two years surviving, keeping Taby with you, keeping him alive." He looked back up the winding path to Malverne, now his farmstead, enclosed within its mighty wooden palisade. He saw smoke rising from the hole in the roof of the longhouse. Then the barley, hay, and rye fields, surrounding the palisade, the crops nearly ready for harvest. An endless cycle. "Life is not at all what a man expects it to be. I suppose it is better that way. My parents are struck down by a plague, my brother is murdered, the assassin still unknown, and now the child I want as my son is in line to the great Rollo." He paused a moment, looking down at his brown feet. "It is almost more than I can accept."

"And I am his niece. It is all true, Merrik."

"Aye, I do not doubt you. But I do doubt myself. I went to the slave market in Kiev to find a comely female slave for my mother. Instead I found you and Taby. As I told you, you have made my life a confusion. And now I learn you are Rollo's niece. I am impressed with your lineage. Who you are will convince my people that you could not have murdered Erik. Your blood is too purified, too noble, to stain your hands on a man of Erik's station."

"You will now return me to Normandy? With Taby?"

He became very still. He looked down at her, at the shifting expressions on her face, his own face unreadable to her. Finally, he said, with no emotion in his voice, his eyes flat, not meeting hers, "If it is your wish."

He watched her scuff the toes of her leather shoes against the pier. They were an old pair belonging to Sarla. He could see a hole along the side of her foot. "Ah, then you don't wish to wed me now."

"I didn't say that."

"Then what do you want, Merrik?"

He clasped her left hand in his and flattened her palm over his chest, laying his hand over hers. "I won't return Taby to your uncle Rollo until I have found out who betrayed you. The danger is still there. To return both you and Taby there now would simply result in your deaths this time, doubt it not. I will not take that chance."

"Perhaps, but still, I must go back. I will find out. Uncle Rollo will punish my sisters, if it is they who had us abducted. If it is their husbands, they will be killed. I would protect Taby as would Uncle Rollo. Taby could be the future duke of Normandy, if something happens to my cousin before he breeds an heir. He must go back. My uncle grows no younger. He must train Taby, teach him, just as he did William."

"I had not expected this," Merrik said slowly, now looking beyond at the distant sheer cliffs, her hand now clasped in his at his side. "I hadn't expected you to be an innkeeper's daughter, however. I just didn't imagine that you would be royalty. I imagine that your Danelaw prince, Askhold, believes you long dead. I imagine he is wed to another by now."

"Aye, it is possible. He needed a wife to bear him children."

"What is he like?"

"I don't know. I never met him, but I heard my sisters talking about him. They said he was thirty and his first wife had died, and she had given him five daughters. He wanted a young girl. He thought I would produce sons for him. Uncle Rollo and the king negotiated the alliance."

"I do not want you for his reasons. You know me. I have saved your life. You have given me your virginity."

"Aye, that is true."

"This prince wouldn't want you if he knew you were no longer a virgin. That is the way of things."

She could only stare at him. "Aye, you are probably right."

"Surely you had already thought of this before you came to me. You are not stupid, Laren."

A cormorant flew low, its thick dark wing a brief shadow over her face, then gone. She said as she looked after it, "I wanted you, and I didn't want to think about a future that had no more texture than those clouds yon. I wanted to know what it was like, this joining between a man and a woman. You are a beautiful man and you have been more kind to me than not. Aye, I wanted you to show me what it was like."

"You are blunt and it pleases me. I haven't liked the deception between us. No, don't disagree with me. I understand why you refused to tell me about you and Taby. There was much at stake, too much. You are like the slave who was captured by Rolf the Viking, in your skald's tale. I will keep my word always, Laren. Do you trust me completely now?"

"Aye, I do. I must, but I'm afraid, Merrik."

"There is no reason now." He fell silent, just looking down at her hand held in his. He looked down at her silently for a long moment. Then he began to rub his hands rhythmically up and down her arms. "Do you want me to discover if this Prince Askhold still needs a wife?"

She stood on her tiptoes and kissed his mouth. He was so surprised he simply didn't move, didn't respond. She smiled up at him. "I would wish him thrice wed, all three of his wives malleable sheep who will give him more children than he can count, more children than a sultan in Miklagard, all of them female. There can be nothing more wondrous than kissing you, Merrik."

"Then you give your loyalty to me? You will wed me?"

"Aye."

"And if I wish to keep Taby with me, as my son?"

He was testing her, but it was only right. She'd tested him enough. Now it could only be the truth, nothing else. "I must return his birthright to him. He must be trained by Rollo to be the future ruler of Normandy, to be the heir, if something happens to William. You know well, as do I, that death is over your shoulder every moment of every day. The future of Normandy is important. There must be heirs. As for myself, surely what I choose to do isn't all that important."

"It is to me." He kissed her then, lifting her until her feet dangled above the wooden pier, and drew her close. He kissed her until she was frantic with need, until she was arching against him, pressing and pressing even more.

He said even as he laughed against her warm mouth, "Do you promise that once I have meat back on your bones, you will not become fat?"

Her laughter rang out and she kissed his mouth, his nose, his cheek, her hands cupping around his head, her fingers smoothing his thick eyebrows. "I swear," she said between kisses. "Since I am such a good cook, do you promise your belly won't stick out over your belt?"

"I swear it. Now, do not worry about Taby. All will be well, it is my vow to you."

She believed him. He was a man like her uncle—

strong and intelligent, a man of honor, a man to trust, a man to embrace in all ways. She remembered her father, Hallad, the same way, yet he had killed her mother and fled. She flinched at the memory, as she always did.

"Do not worry about my people not accepting you. We will find out who killed my brother and all will be well."

And she believed him again.

"You are the niece of Duke Rollo," he said, shaking his head in wonder even as he said the words again.

"Aye, but I was also a slave."

"You were doubtless a much better niece than a slave."

"And now I will be a wife," she said with a good deal of relish. "It is strange, Merrik. But I think it will be enjoyable, with you as my husband."

"Under my tutelage you will make an excellent wife, despite your illustrious blood. Were you unpleasant, Laren, when you were Rollo's niece? Were you spoiled and capricious? Could you have given Letta lessons in pettiness?"

She punched his arm, then immediately began to caress where she had hit him. He grinned down at her.

"Nay, all my time was spent with Taby, for he was my son as surely as he was my brother."

She wanted to kiss him right now, right here, in the middle of the longhouse, standing near the fire pit, with all his people here, doubtless looking at them, looking, nay, staring, at her, the niece of the mighty Duke Rollo of Normandy. Did they truly believe her?

"Will you continue to be my skald?"

"I brim with new tales, even now, at this very moment, and all of them are about you, my lord, and your splendid body and your beautiful eyes."

"You once told me that all Vikings looked alike, that we were boring with our fair hair and blue eyes."

"I was wrong. Your eyes are unique, the blue is softer than the blue of a robin's wing yet as bright as the sun-drenched sky in mid-morning, as—"

He clapped his hand over her mouth. "Your skald's mouth is spewing out nonsense."

He felt her kiss his palm. He drew his hand away, but continued to look at her, wondering for a moment what was in her mind, then he knew, and said, "Stop looking at me that way. Tell me of your father instead."

"I will also tell of your noble heart."

"I will retch if you mention such a thing."

She laughed and shook her head, saying, "It is difficult to tell you of serious things knowing that Letta would rather be gulleting me with a knife than preparing to leave Malverne. Her father is still looking at me as his skald. He doesn't believe me to be Rollo's niece. What did he say to you, Merrik, when you told him who I was?"

"He laughed, a great belly laugh, and wiped his eyes, and reminded me I was master of Malverne and had no need to weave tales so unbelievable."

"Does he believe you now?"

"He must. Am I not to wed you in two days?"

"I cannot wait for them to be gone from here."

"Tomorrow. Now, tell me about your father."

She dipped a wooden spoon into a barrel of mead and poured it into a cup. She handed it to him and watched him drink it down. "You wish me drunk?"

"No, it is just that I would put off the telling. It is painful, you see."

"It can wait," he said, and lifted her hand. He studied her fingers, the short blunt nails, the red chafed flesh. A slave's hands, used to endless hard work, his wife's

hands. In two days. He turned and smiled a welcome
at Sarla, who looked hesitant to approach them.

"Come, sister, and tell my betrothed that you will
drink mead with us at our wedding feast. She fears
Letta will try to gullet her before she leaves."

"I will drink and dance and sing, Laren. I am pleased.
I would have been just as pleased had you not been
Rollo's niece. Now I am not certain how to behave
around you."

Laren said nothing. She merely walked to Sarla and
wrapped her arms around her. "You are my sister. You
have been kind to me since the moment I arrived here,
and I was naught but a slave. This is your home. Please,
I am still the same."

Merrik was pleased. He started to tell her so when
he looked up to see Taby, rubbing his eyes, wearing a
loose tunic that flapped around his feet, standing there
yawning and looking around. He saw Merrik and
smiled, a big sleepy smile, and made Merrik feel like a
king, not just a simple duke. He went down to his
haunches and opened his arms. "Taby, come," he called
out.

The child ran to him, wrapping his arms around his
neck. Merrik nuzzled the child's cheek, breathed in his
child's sweet scent. He'd known him for such a short
time and now he would lose him again.

Laren said to Sarla, "Once we return Taby to Uncle
Rollo, Merrik won't see him except when we pay them
visits. It will hurt him deeply. It hurts him now just to
think of being parted from him."

"Aye, but you will have your own children."

Laren stilled. Then she smiled hugely. "I hadn't
thought of that."

Sarla grinned at her. "Perhaps it's time you gave it
full consideration. Oh goodness, here comes Letta. Now

that you will be mistress of Malverne, you have nothing to worry about. Do you wish to enjoy yourself, Laren?"

"I just wish the girl would keep her mouth closed. She hasn't much sense, Sarla."

"She is jealous, very jealous of you. She wanted Merrik and Malverne. She believed both in her grasp."

Laren said nothing. She had been cooking and there was a stain on the front of her overtunic. Her face was heated from the fire pit and her hair was wet on her forehead with sweat. Letta's very ample bosom, she saw, was heaving.

Laren saw Sarla turn away to attend to the woman Thyre's little boy, who had crawled too close to the fire pit. She took the child in her arms and hugged him, softly singing to him. Laren knew she would stay close, in case. In case of what? Letta sticking a knife in her heart?

"So," Letta said, coming to stand in front of Laren. "You have won. You have blinded Merrik to the truth, mayhap given him a potion to dull and confuse his mind."

"Nay. All his dullness and confusion are his very own. I have done naught."

"Now you insult him. But you are careful to be certain he is not close to hear you laugh at him."

"You have no humor, Letta. You should consider finding some."

"You are a whore. My father is furious. He wanted to buy you from Merrik."

"Now that is humorous. Listen, your father can take Deglin with him. I doubt he wishes to stay here."

"Deglin is a whining pig. I don't want him. All he will do is complain. He hates you more than I do."

"You can clout him, Letta. Under your tender care he will improve. There is no reason to hate me."

"Ha! You have Merrik. Once he knew that you were Duke Rollo's niece, he had to have you."

"No, he asked me to wed with me before I told him who I was."

"That's a lie. All know that it is your family that has turned him from thoughts of revenge for your murdering his brother to marriage and a more mighty alliance than with the Thoragassons. I no longer want him. He has no honor. He turns from his obligations too easily. He is not a man to trust or to follow."

"You will be quiet, Letta. I will allow no such words to be spoken about Merrik."

"It is true! He is an oath breaker and there is no more vile a thing."

"I could have held my temper had you only insulted me. But you spew your venom on Merrik and that I will not tolerate. He never agreed to marry you. He would never break his oath." Very calmly, Laren set her hands around Letta's neck and shook her. "No more. Your father has accepted Merrik's decision. You will as well and you will keep you mouth shut. Do you understand me, Letta?"

She felt his strong hands close over her wrists, gently tugging her fingers away from Letta's throat. She didn't let go.

"You defend me well," Merrik said close to her ear. "Release her. She must oversee preparations for their departure on the morrow."

But Laren felt rage still boiling in her and she said to Letta, "You will never speak of Merrik again, do you hear me? I will kill you if you dare to insult him thus."

Letta very slowly nodded, her own fury momentarily tamped down because of her aching throat. Laren saw Merrik's face, saw the stern set of his mouth. But she also saw the near laughter in his eyes. She wanted to kill both him and this miserable slut with her too strong fingers.

"Nod your head again, damn you, for I won't release you until you do." Laren shook her again for good measure.

Letta nodded again, her eyes dark with anger. Slowly Laren eased the pressure of her fingers. There would be marks on Letta's white neck, she saw with satisfaction.

17

"I WON'T BE your guardian, but I will be your brother, just as Laren is your sister. Surely that binds us just as close or even closer."

Taby looked from Laren back to Merrik. "Why do you sound sad, then?"

Merrik wanted to smile, but he couldn't find it inside him to do so. "There will be changes, Taby. You know you are something of a prince, don't you?"

The child nodded his head slowly. Suddenly he looked scared. "I don't have to be, Merrik. I can just be me and your little brother."

"Sometimes," Merrik said very slowly, "there are circumstances that we cannot change. You are a prince, Taby, actually you could become the heir to the duke of Normandy, the illustrious Rollo. Do you remember him? No? Well, you will probably recognize him when you see him again. If you don't recognize him, it won't matter, for you will come to love him and respect him. Laren tells me that he spent hours with you before you and she were taken away."

"I don't like this man Rollo."

"Taby, one day you will be a man and a very important man at that, even if you don't become the duke of Normandy. When that day comes, why, I will bow down before you and kiss your hand. If you are not pleased with me, you can make me eat with the pigs. What do you think of that?"

"I know you, Merrik. You love me but you wouldn't ever want to bow down to me or anyone."

Merrik ran his fingers through Taby's hair, a rich, thick thatch of deep reddish brown. He was a beautiful child. He would be a handsome man. He felt pain deep and deeper still. Still, it was right that the child take his place, that he become the man he was meant to be. After all, Merrik thought, he had the sister. He said, "It won't be for a while yet. First your sister will wed with me and then I will go see your uncle Rollo. Perhaps I will also meet your cousin, William Longsword. Laren tells me she trusts him and that he is honorable. How old is he, Laren?"

"William is only twenty-two, nay, now he is twenty-five, about your age, Merrik."

"And he has been wedded for five years?"

"Aye. Heirs are important."

Taby said, scuffing the toe of his leather shoe in the hard-packed earthen floor, "I don't remember him, Laren. I don't remember this Rollo either. I don't want you to go to him, Merrik. If he doesn't like you will he stick his sword in your stomach?"

"I trust not. Why would he when I will come to tell him our boy is alive and well?"

Taby was silent then. He looked at Laren and smiled. "Do you love Merrik, Laren? As much as you love me?"

"Oh yes, Taby." She never hesitated, not for an instant, nor did she look at Merrik.

"All right," Taby said and pulled out of Merrik's arms. He didn't look back, merely ran to where Kenna and several other boys were playing with feather-stuffed leather balls and making figures out of strings.

"Do you really, Laren?"

She still didn't look at him. "It is what I told Taby."

"Will you tell me?"

"No."

"Why not?"

"It will give you power over me."

He smiled. "I already have sufficient power over you. I have no need of more."

"You bray like a goat, Merrik, and you grin shamelessly whilst you do it. I will help Sarla. We will be wedded this afternoon, forget you not."

"Goats don't bray, only asses. Is that what you believe me to be, Laren?"

"Nay, you are a man, Merrik."

"Then why are you holding your hand over your mouth? To keep your laughter behind your teeth? Don't answer me more, woman. Think about tonight, for then I will take you again. I have missed holding you at night, Laren."

"It is right and proper that you miss me. It is also right and proper that you not practice on Caylis or Megot. I want you to lie in the bed and think about me. Only me."

"I cannot even think of Caylis or Megot?" He laughed. He looked at her, then laughed harder. Then he left the longhouse, shaking his head.

The ceremony was brief and in the Viking tradition. All the men stood beside and behind Merrik, the women beside and behind Laren. All wore their finest clothing and jewelry, the women in vivid linen gowns of scarlet, made from oak gall, bright blue, made from woad dyeing, and Laren's own gown, a beautiful saffron linen made from the bulbs of autumn crocus and presented to her by the women of Malverne. Two freewomen of

Malverne knew how to dye wool and linen to perfection and provided all the colored cloth required. Laren had never seen such beautiful colors, even at the court of her uncle Rollo. She wore a woven crown of white daisies. Her hair seemed even redder under the early afternoon sun, shining like a sunset curling nearly to her shoulders.

Taby stood beside Merrik, his small hand tucked securely in Merrik's. He was scrubbed clean, his face shining, his eyes bright. He was no longer thin. Just to look at him made Laren want to cry and to laugh with the relief and joy of it.

Merrik looked at her and smiled. He took a step toward her. He held out his other hand and she put hers in it. He looked at all his men, then the women and children. He said in a loud clear voice, "There has been much sorrow at Malverne, with the passing of Harald and Tora, and the violent death of Erik, my brother. There has been much change as well. I know it is difficult for you to accept me as the lord of Malverne. I hope that in time you will come to do so easily. Today I take this woman to be my wife. She is the niece of the great Rollo, but her life is here now, with me, with all of you." He paused a moment, then released Taby's hand and took both of hers.

"Laren, daughter of Hallad and niece of Rollo of Normandy, this day, before our gods, I take you as my wife. I pray to Freya to grant us long life and many children. I pray to Odin All-Father to see that we keep honor and good faith between us. I defend you with my strength and my sword. All that I own is now yours as well. I will be your husband in all seasons and I will be with you until breath leaves my body."

Laren had spent several hours preparing what she would say. She hadn't told anyone that she was a Christian, for Rollo had agreed to accept the faith when he had made the treaty with King Charles, and that included all his family with him. She realized clearly now that Taby would be raised a Christian and she would become a Viking woman in all ways.

So she had thought of what a Viking woman would say. Oddly enough when she was spinning a tale, she knew no fear, only excitement, but now she was nervous, her mouth dry. She was afraid she would shame him, for although she knew the names of most of the Viking gods, she wasn't certain which ones were most important at a wedding. She looked up at him and realized that he knew of her fear, even though he couldn't know its cause. He smiled at her and squeezed her hand. Still, she was silent. He said quietly, "Vow that you will send me to the pig byre if I dare look at another woman."

She laughed, a pure rich sound. She said then, "I vow to hold you close to me, Merrik, lord of Malverne. I vow to defend you with voice and deed, and to cleave to you on days of darkness as well as on days of joy. This I promise before all our people and before our gods."

"You did well," he said, pulling her to him. "Once I got your tongue to move again. Now you must kiss me."

He lifted her to her tiptoes and kissed her mouth. She heard the men and women cheering, even heard Taby's voice calling out. She felt his warmth and his strength and wondered what would happen to them.

He released her, but held her a moment longer, simply looking down at her. Then he called out, "Let us go to the feasting now."

A dozen long tables had been set outside, each one holding platters of boar steaks, baked cod and herring smothered in cloudberries, and salmon in boiled maple leaves, stacked loaves of rye bread and flatbread, pots of cabbage, peas, sliced apples, roasted onions. There were barrels of mead and barley beer, even dark rich red wine from the Rhineland. The women had done well, more than well, really, and Sarla stood there smiling at her, knowing that she was overcome with it all.

Laren, who had held steady and strong for two years, looked at all the men and women around her, at the magnificent tables of food, and finally at her new husband. She lowered her head and sobbed into her hands.

Merrik chuckled as he pulled her tightly against him. "Aye, 'tis too much, isn't it? Our people are good. This is now your home and this is your welcome."

She hiccuped and raised her head and wiped her eyes with the backs of her hands.

Merrik turned to shouts of "Let us drink to the bride and groom!"

"Hear, hear!"

It was nearly sunset. The wedding feast, begun hours before, had long since lost its respectable and inspiring beginnings. It was still joyous though, Laren thought, too joyous, as she watched Merrik and Oleg break up another fight. He'd told her to eat and drink lightly; it was their duty to watch all their people drink themselves into a stupor, and when they fought instead, it was their duty to keep the men from killing each other in their drunkenness. Vikings, he remarked, liked their celebrations boisterous.

Laren ate a piece of goat cheese. It was tart, even sour, and she quickly drank down some warm ale. She felt a lurch of dizziness and grinned down at her empty cup. She felt wonderful. She looked toward Merrik who'd pulled Roran off Eller, the small man whose clothes she'd worn on their way home. Home, she thought, looking around. She heard Merrik laugh, saw him lift Roran into the air and toss him toward Old Firren, who just ducked and watched him fall into a mess of meat bones.

He was a beautiful man, she thought. A good man. She watched him walk to a group of children whose leader was Kenna. He was stumbling about, aping his elders, and the children were laughing and trying to guess which man it was he was pretending to be.

She laughed when Sarla poured her another glass of ale.

"Merrik said I should remain sober, that it was very nearly a law, for we were responsible to see that no one got a broken head."

"I will be vigilant for you," Sarla said.

"And I as well," said Cleve, who stood behind Sarla.

For a moment, Laren saw them as one. She shook her head, but still, they were so close to each other that they seemed to merge. She said slowly, "When will you wed?"

She watched them start, then stare at each other, consternation on their faces, at least she thought it was consternation. She drank a bit more ale. "Cleve saved me. He is a fine man."

"I know," Sarla said. "Please, Laren, you mustn't speak of it. Erik is still too close, he still preys too much on my mind and on Cleve's. Someone killed him. It wasn't you nor was it Cleve or me. But it was someone and that person is here, close to us. I'm afraid."

Cleve took her arm and gently squeezed it. "Hush, Sarla, it is Laren's wedding day. We will find out who killed Erik and then we will be free. At least none believe it to be Laren, not with her royal birth. Hush now, sweeting, hush."

But who did kill Erik? Laren sipped at her ale and stared at the men and women who were shouting at each other, telling jests that had no meaning, not now, after hours of drinking, kissing and caressing each other, all in all, oblivious of the world around them. She looked at Ileria, the weaver, so drunk she was just staring into a plate of stewed fish, just staring, saying nothing, doing nothing. And there were Caylis and Megot, both with two of Erik's men. The men were young and comely, as were most Vikings, their faces flushed with too much mead.

She felt warm breath in her ear. "I thought I told you that it was your duty to keep your wits together."

She turned her head, found herself an inch from his face, and grinned. "I fear I have drunk too much ale, Merrik."

"Am I to bed a drunken wife?"

"Oh dear, I better stop," she said, tipped up the cup and downed the rest of the ale.

Merrik laughed at her and called out, "Behold your influence. My bride of four hours can barely hold herself straight. What am I to do?"

Oleg shouted, "Have her tell us a story! 'Twill sober her wits!"

"Aye, a tale, a tale!"

"Well, Laren, are you able?"

"A story," she said, as if marveling that such a thing could possibly exist. "Aye, a story." She stood then, stepped onto the bench, then up onto the wooden table. "Attend me," she shouted. "A story you want, a story you will have!"

There was cheering mixed with an equal measure of laughter.

"She'll fall and break her leg!"

"Better than her tongue. I want stories from her, many more stories!"

Laren stamped her foot and nearly slid off the table

on a piece of oatcake. Merrik was there to steady her, clasping her by her knees to hold her steady. "Go ahead, I've got you now," he said.

She tried for some dignity, failed, and said on a giggle, "I will tell you about Fromm and Cardle, two men who became the husbands of sisters in a royal family, Helga and Ferlain. Fromm was a bully and vicious, Cardle was a man who lived for learning, a man not really of this world. Helga saw immediately that her groom, Fromm, would be easily led by her, even though he was mean and petty. She told Ferlain to measure the strength of her groom, Cardle, and so Ferlain did and discovered there wasn't all that much strength there to measure. Then they met in the tower of the king's fortress and compared what they'd learned. They decided that through their husbands, they would be able to take over the kingdom. Unfortunately they first had to rid themselves of the king's heir, but he was grown and was away from the city. Ah, but there was their little half brother named Ninian and he was next in line after the king's son. Surely they could begin by ridding themselves of Ninian.

"But this wasn't so easily done, for little Ninian had a magic friend."

Laren stopped, frowned, then demanded, "More ale for the skald, if you please, husband. My wits are near parched dry of words."

Merrik gave her a full cup of ale, then clasped her legs again to keep her steady.

"What happened to the husbands?" Oleg called out. "Come along, Laren, tell us before your wits take flight into oblivion."

"Who was Ninian's magic friend?"

She frowned from her height on the table at Oleg and then at Bartha, a big-bosomed woman who had dyed the beautiful saffron gown Laren wore. "Ninian's magic friend was a Viking warrior who appeared only when the child was in danger. He was as cunning, as wild, as fearless, as a *berserker*. He wore bearskins like a *berserker*, but he didn't howl or scream out to the gods, or roll his eyes when he met an enemy. No, the Viking warrior was silent as a spirit. Once, when Ninian had lost his nurse in the forest close by the king's fortress, a wolf attacked him. The Viking warrior appeared as if spun from the smoke from a fire, tossed Ninian up onto a tree branch, and turned to face the leaping wolf. He gutted the wolf with his sword. Then, slowly, the warrior turned to the child and said, 'You may be the king one day. I was sent to keep you safe. Come down now and go back to the fortress. Your nurse is frantic with worry for you.'

"He lifted Ninian back to the ground, patted the child's shoulder, and then he just seemed to fade into the thick green trees. One moment he was there—solid and strong as the oak trunk, a huge man, his sword covered with the wolf's blood—and the next moment, he was gone, simply disappeared. The child stood there, not understanding, but not afraid.

"A dozen soldiers burst into the small clearing. They saw the dead wolf, saw the child standing over it, and they were struck dumb.

"And thus the legend began of Ninian, the king's nephew, who, when still a small child, killed a wolf. That the wolf had been gutted with a sword was dismissed and forgotten. The more thoughtful knew that the child couldn't have lifted a sword, much less smote the wolf a killing blow. The king marveled at this small being. The small being himself marveled. He tried to tell his nurse of the Viking warrior, but she was in no mood to believe that a spirit could have slain the wolf.

No, she would prefer Ninian to be the magic one, the special one, the one chosen by the gods to follow the king.

"The sisters decided they would kill the child. They didn't believe he killed the wolf, for Helga had powers herself, and she had watched Ninian, and seen none in him. Thus they convinced themselves that a man had come along, seen the child was in danger, killed the wolf, then quickly left before the soldiers came.

"Aye, they would kill the boy. Helga cast a spell in her tower room. She called up the demons of fire and ice and desert sands. She bade them use their powers to rid them of the child. The demon of fire appeared and said, 'I cannot kill the boy. He is sworn protection by one far more powerful than I. Leave him alone.'

"Helga cursed him and sent him back into the netherworld. She called up the demon of ice. He said, 'I cannot kill the boy. A higher power than I guards him. Leave him alone.'

"Helga still would not accept the demons' words. She called forth the demon of the desert sands. He said, 'You are a fool, woman, to call up the coward demons of fire and ice before you called me. You wish me to kill the child. I will kill him and I will enjoy it. Then you will be in my debt.'

"The demon disappeared in a swirl of thick black smoke. Helga rejoiced and told her sister that the child would soon be dead. They told their husbands. They all waited. One day Ninian was found missing. The king and all his soldiers couldn't find him. Everyone in the land searched for the child, but he wasn't to be found. He was gone, disappeared with no trace."

Laren looked down at Merrik and said, "I am going to be sick." She jumped down, trusting him to catch her, then broke away from him and ran through the open palisade doors and into the bushes around the path.

Oleg slapped Merrik on his back. "Perhaps she will not be groaning overmuch this night or racing from your bed to be sick. There is still hope, Merrik."

Merrik grunted. "Perhaps, but give me leave to doubt it. She will be very unhappy on the morrow."

"I want to know what happened to Ninian," Oleg called.

"Aye," Roran yelled out, "I want to know who the Viking warrior was."

"I hope she doesn't puke away the story with her guts," Bartha said, "else I won't dye her another gown."

"And I," Merrik said, gazing through the open gates of the palisade, "wonder if my bride will even remember the Viking warrior or me on the morrow."

"With all that royal blood," Old Firren said, and then spat, "surely she can recover quickly from the ale."

And she did. It was near to midnight when Merrik, convinced she was back to herself again, took her hand and raised her from the bench. He said to all his very drunk people, "There is no rain coming, for Eller hasn't smelled anything."

"He can only smell the foul odors of savages!"

"That's true enough," Merrik said, laughing, "but the night is clear. Stay here if you wish and keep drinking. I will take my wife to my bed."

They were given advice in the marriage bed, all of it very specific, all of it accompanied with laughter as both men and women played their parts as the bride and groom.

Merrik believed her embarrassed until they stepped inside the sleeping chamber and she said, "I trust you took note of all they said, Merrik."

"Aye," he said, and pulled her against him. "I heard everything."

"I think," she said, leaning her forehead against his shoulder, "that I'm still afraid. This is all very new to me, Merrik, despite all that I've seen in the past two years, and I have seen more than I should."

"I know, sweeting, but it isn't important now. What is important is us. I won't hurt you. I could never hurt you."

"I know," she whispered. She felt the allure of him, the temptation of him, and what he would give to her. Still, she just looked up at him, waiting.

He smiled at her and sifted his fingers through her hair, pulling loose the tangles. "Trust me," he said, "just trust me." He leaned down and kissed her, slowly, easily, as if there were nothing more he wished to do. He lifted his face.

"The night is long before us," he said.

18

THE FOLLOWING MORNING Laren stood beside Sarla, who was stirring the porridge. Very few men were upright, many more were sprawled on their backs, appearing quite dead save for the occasional moans and snores. The women, more stoic, went about their chores, more slowly than usual, but still they worked, looked at the men, and shook their heads. The children, not stupid, spoke quietly whilst in the longhouse.

"That was a wonderful feast," Sarla said. "I wish to hear the rest of the story tonight."

"Aye, you shall," Laren said. "Where is Taby?"

"He is with Kenna and the other boys outside. They are practicing with their swords, Oleg their teacher."

"Oleg isn't holding his head and moaning?"

"Oh no, Oleg never suffers when he drinks too much mead. Nor do you, I see."

"I don't know. Last night was the first night in my life I have drunk so very much."

"You felt all right when Merrik took you away last night?"

"Aye, I felt wonderful."

"You look wonderful this morning. You look very happy, very pleased with yourself."

Laren didn't say anything. She was looking toward

the entrance of the longhouse. Merrik stood there in the open doorway, the brilliant morning sun behind him, and he looked a golden god with wet hair from his bath. He saw her, stepped forward, and smiled.

She felt the impact of him, relentless and commanding, irresistible and growing stronger, she could feel it, stronger and deeper, pulling at her, luring her, claiming her, and she saw herself the previous night, her bare hand clasped between his two larger ones, her legs between his, the slide of his hair smooth and vibrant against her flesh, her breasts against the rich golden fur of his chest. The image was softly blurred in her mind, but the remembered feel of him was stark. She'd not lied to him. She'd been afraid, for there had been pain that first time with him, and she had tried to twist free of him and his invasion of her body.

He was walking toward her, his stride that of a man who knew himself to be the master, coming to her, a woman who was his and his alone, a woman he now knew, a woman he was studying thoughtfully, his brow furrowed even as he smiled.

She saw another smile of his in her mind, clear as the soft summer air, the curve of his mouth when he'd raised his head from her belly, and seen her gasping, her breasts heaving, as she'd tried to calm her breathing, and he'd known the immense pleasure he'd given her with his mouth, was pleased with her for yielding to him, trusting him with herself, and now he wanted more, he wanted to come inside her and she wanted him there as well, deep inside her, become part of her, melding with her until they were inseparable. His smile stopped then as he'd raised her legs and spread them and come between them, staring down at her woman's flesh, touching her, and she'd felt the slickness of herself on his fingers, saw his eyes close briefly

as he'd felt her, resting his fingers there for a long moment, just feeling her, and then he was easing into her
and she'd felt herself shudder with the strength of the
feelings that washed through her and she'd wanted
more and more and he was there, over her, always giving even as he took, always there with her, never leaving her, even in that instant when his own pleasure had
gripped him and he'd thrown back his head and yelled
his release. She'd held him tightly to her, reveling in
what she had brought him to, so grateful that he had
found her, and that he was the man he was.

Laren hadn't realized she was standing there, staring
at her husband, not moving, just staring, her lips
parted, her eyes wide on his face.

He stopped in front of her, and lifted her chin in his
palm. "It is only the beginning," he said, leaned down
and kissed her mouth. "Only the beginning."

"Will you always be thus with me?"

"Aye, as you will be with me as well." He kissed her
again, gently, lightly, his tongue tracing over her lips.
"I should have taken you to the bathing hut with me.
Next time I shall. I'll hold you on my lap with you facing
me and raise you so that you can take me inside you. I
think you will enjoy that."

Her breasts ached. She leaned into him, all that she
felt writ clear in her eyes, and he wondered how he had
deserved such good fortune. "You did well last night,
wife. You pleased me mightily." He lightly touched her
breasts simply because he had to, he had no choice in
the matter, then quickly stepped back.

"There is the matter of practice, Merrik," she said,
trying to smile, but desire held her now and all she
wanted was to have him hold her and stroke and kiss
her. To feel his mouth on hers, to feel his tongue lightly
touching hers, made her lean forward again.

He sucked in his breath, grasped her upper arms in his hands and held her still. "I cannot please you now, but I want to, the gods know I want to very much."

Oleg was there, some feet away from him, waiting. "When you are ready, Merrik, we will speak with each of our people. We should not wait too much longer, for memories blur and people forget."

"Aye," Merrik said, kissed her once more and left her.

"They are questioning everyone to see where they were when Erik was killed," Sarla said.

Laren didn't say anything. She was suddenly thinking that the man who had struck Erik with the rock wouldn't simply blurt out his guilt when confronted. No, he would have thought about this, reasoned it out and devised a story that would be reasonable. Or a woman, she thought. A woman could have struck Erik down.

She looked after her new husband, striding tall and determined beside Oleg. She tasted the warmth and sweetness of him on her mouth, the delight of him throughout her body. She cooled suddenly, her mind sharp and clear. She felt deep fear of the unknown man or woman who had passed her on the trail, looking down at her, knowing she would be blamed. And then, quite suddenly, she realized she hadn't been completely unconscious when that man had passed her. She saw him lean over her, staring down at her, then rising, smiling. No sound from him, just that smile of his. If only she could see him. Ah, but she knew now it was a man, for that silent smile sounded yet in her mind.

She had to find Merrik.

Whose laughter?

" . . . Prince Ninian was gone with no trace. The king was beside himself with grief. He took to his bed, refusing to eat or to drink. On the third day, he lay weak and uncaring about himself, about his kingdom, guilt overcoming all. He had lost Ninian and thus he had failed and didn't deserve to live. He hadn't kept the child safe and he knew Ninian was the future and now that future was blighted and it was all his fault.

"Suddenly, he saw a faint shadow form behind the candlelight. He stared at it, his mouth opening in awe and fear as the shadow grew and grew, becoming more and more solid, until finally, it was a man. It was a Viking warrior, huge sword in his hand, garbed in a rough bearskin, a pounded gold helmet on his head, his eyes a beautiful startling blue. The warrior stared at him, then said, contempt lacing his words, 'You will cease your grieving. You are the king. You will act the king. If you do not, your daughters will force themselves into power upon your death, placing their sodden, weak-willed husbands on the throne. Indeed I know that it is Helga's husband, Fromm, who will take your place. Helga's magic is greater than Ferlain's. Ferlain and her husband, Cardle, will both die from poisoning.

" 'Rise now and resume your duties. Eat and drink and regain your strength. Bathe and robe yourself. Become once again the man you are supposed to be.'

" 'But Ninian, my beautiful boy, what of him?'

" 'I will fetch him now. When I return with him, I will see to it that your daughters and their husbands receive the punishment due them.'

" 'Ninian is not dead?'

"The warrior shook his head, the gold helmet catching the light of the candle flame, brilliant and dazzling as the midday sun.

" 'But who are you? How do you know these things?'

"The Viking warrior said, 'Rise and be ready to receive Ninian. You will deal with your daughters and their husbands. Beware of Helga. She called forth the demons to kill Ninian. She will try to kill you as well.'

"The king leapt out of the bed. He felt young and incredibly strong, his days of privation forgotten. He wanted to touch the Viking warrior, but even as he walked toward him, the warrior seemed to retreat from him, though the king knew he hadn't moved. The air was still and warm and the warrior just seemed to grow dimmer until he was a veil spun of the finest silk, then he was naught but a brief shadow, then nothing at all.

"The king stood there, fear curdling in his belly. Then, because he was the king, indomitable and decisive, he yelled for his servants. After he had supped and drunk his fill, he returned to his vast chamber to await the return of Ninian and the Viking warrior.

"He had not long to wait. One moment he was alone, hopeful in his solitude, and the next, there stood Ninian, alone now, dirty as a village urchin and looking healthy as the day he left. His clothes were torn, his knees scraped, but he was smiling, by all the gods, he looked very well indeed. The king dropped to his knees and gathered the boy to him.

"It was a joyous reunion until the king realized Ninian was somehow different. He drew back, tracing his fingertips over his beloved face, and said, 'Where have you been? What befell you?'

" 'I have visited the netherworld that lies beneath the desert sands far to the south and east of here. I stayed with the demon of the desert sands, an odd title, Father, but that is who he said he was. He told me that I would remain with him forever, that I would become his heir. I told him that I couldn't remain with him, that I belonged here, with you, here with all our people, that I was needed.

" 'He would not listen to me. I told him that he had

to return me or the Viking warrior would come and hurt him. He laughed, Father. He laughed loudly, then, suddenly, he choked. His face turned blue and he clutched his throat. Then, the Viking warrior was there and he was not laughing. He raised his hand and the choking stopped. He watched the demon regain his breath, then told the demon of the desert sands that even though he was his brother, what he had done was against all their rules. He told him that he had the agreement of all the higher demons and that he would be forced to remain buried in his netherworld for one hundred years as his punishment. The demon of the desert sands begged and pleaded with the Viking warrior, but he just stood there, shaking his head. He raised his sword and the demon cowered away from him and left us alone.

" 'Then the warrior held me against him and suddenly I was here, Father, with you.'

"After the king had visited with his son, he gave him over to the servants to bathe him and garb him well. Then he called for his daughters and their husbands. Helga and Ferlain believed they were being called to their father's deathbed to receive his blessing. Imagine their consternation when they saw him, hale and strong, seated on his throne, garbed in his finest silks. Their husbands, Fromm and Cardle, stood back, not understanding why their wives looked pale and ill. They bowed to their father-in-law, bidding him good day. They remarked to him that he looked in excellent health, contrary to what they'd heard. They trusted he'd come to accept that Prince Ninian was dead.

"The king merely smiled at them and bade them seat themselves on a bench against the whitewashed wall of the huge chamber. Then he said, 'Helga, come here.'

"She did, forcing herself to smile, but surely nothing was lost yet. So he looked healthy, so perhaps he was resigned to Ninian's death. She would see to it that he sickened soon enough. She wondered if he had asked them here to announce that now because Ninian was gone from them, Fromm would be his heir. That made her smile in truth now as she approached her father.

"She bowed before him. 'You look well, Father,' she said.

" 'Aye,' he said. 'All of us look well.'

" 'We are all very sorry for Ninian's disappearance, Father. We pray you are not too distraught.'

" 'Nay,' the king said. 'I am very well, as I told you.'

" 'Do you ask us here to proclaim that our husbands are now your heirs?'

" 'Oh no,' the king said. 'I bade you here to welcome back your brother.' He called out and Ninian came from behind the thick crimson draperies behind the king's throne.

"Helga shrieked. 'It is a demon! A witch!'

" 'Nay,' said the king. 'It is you who are the demon and the witch, both you and your weak sister. As of this moment, you are no longer my daughters. Your husbands are no longer my sons-in-law. All of you are banished as of this day. Go and be damned, all of you!'

"Helga felt fury wash over her. She raised her arms to the sky and shrieked, 'Demons, come to me now! Strike down the man and the child! Kill them!'

"But no demons appeared. The Viking warrior was there, standing suddenly before them, radiant and shimmering, as if the sun were shining behind him. Helga cried out and stepped back.

"The warrior raised his sword high, kissed its finely worked iron handle, then said, 'What is due you, Helga? You are the evil one, Ferlain is only weak, her powers enhanced only by yours. As for you men, you wretched husbands, you are pitiful. What should I do with you?' "

Laren quieted and looked down at her feet. There was utter silence. She slowly raised her head and looked at Merrik. "If you were the Viking warrior, what would you do, Merrik?"

"I would kill Helga and banish the other three."

Laren smiled. "Do you agree, Oleg?"

"Aye, spit the witch on his sword!"

"Aye! Aye!"

Even the women yelled to kill Helga.

Laren waited until they quieted again. "All of you are right, in a sense. The warrior didn't spit Helga on his sword. He walked up to her, stared down at her, and spoke softly, very softly, strange words that even she had never heard. It sounded to the king like a strange benediction. The warrior's voice was so very smooth and steady. He raised his hand over her head, just held his hand there. She didn't move, didn't say a word. It was as if she were turned to stone. In the next instant, she began to fade away, growing dimmer and dimmer until naught remained but an armlet of solid gold that suddenly fell to the floor, thudding loudly. No one said a word, even her husband, Fromm.

"The king once again told the others to leave and so they did, grateful that they hadn't been made to disappear like Helga. The Viking warrior walked back to the king and Ninian. He said, 'I have gained my freedom now. I will return to you, Ninian, but as a man. I will still guard you, but it will be with a mortal's life and a mortal's strength. Look for me, Ninian, for I will come back.'

"With those words, the Viking warrior, just like Helga, paled into nothingness, at last simply clear air against the whitewashed wall."

Laren raised her hands and said finally, "It is over."

"But did the Viking warrior return as he promised?"

Laren grinned toward Merrik. "Aye, he will return, and he will protect Ninian."

When Merrik lifted the woolen blanket and eased down onto the box bed beside her, he said, "Are their names really Helga and Ferlain?"

"Aye."

"I am the Viking warrior."

"Aye, you are."

"Why didn't Taby say anything?"

"I told him not to."

"Ah. Do you truly believe it is Helga behind your abduction?"

"I don't know. Her dislike of Taby and me was the most obvious. The husbands aren't quite as stupid as I made them out to be, or as innocent. Fromm is a huge man, ugly and vicious. Cardle is weak-chinned with stooped shoulders. He whines when he doesn't get his way. No two men could be more unalike than they."

"I will see, won't I?"

"Aye, we will see together, Merrik."

He held silent, frowning into the darkness. "Nay, you will remain here at Malverne. It is now your home, your responsibility. Besides, I would keep both you and Taby safe. It was my vow to you."

"Nay, I must come with you. You do not know these people. I do. I could protect you. We will leave Taby here."

"You will obey me, Laren. You are my wife. You will obey me. I do not need your protection."

"Stubborn man," she said under her breath, but knew he'd heard her. Before he could reply, she rolled over to him and grabbed his face between her two hands. She

kissed him, missing his mouth, then finding it in the
darkness, kissing him hard until he parted his lips, and
she slipped her tongue within to find his and feel the
warmth and sweetness of him.

"You think to seduce me," he said, his voice bemused,
for she was innocent, yet she had no thought to hide
from him, to play the coy maid, or allow him alone to
direct their lovemaking.

"Aye, of course I do. Now be quiet. I love how you
taste, Merrik."

He smiled and she felt the softening of his mouth
against her lips. "You won't change my mind, Laren, no
matter what you do."

"This I do for myself," she said, and came over on top
of him, her loose hair spilling around their faces, an
erotic veil that made Merrik quake beneath her. She
was still wearing a linen shift, but it didn't remain on
her for very long. He stripped it over her head, then felt
the soft weight of her body on top of him, her breasts
pressing against his chest, her legs atop his, his sex
hard against her woman's flesh. And she was kissing
him all over his face, her tongue lightly touching his
ears, her fingers a light whisper over his brows, his forehead, his nose. Then she began to move over him as she
kissed him and he laid his palms flat over her hips and
pressed her down hard against him even as he thrust
upward. He moaned and she caught the warmth of the
sound in her mouth and parted her legs.

He thought he couldn't hold on much longer. His
hands were all over her now, tangling in her hair, pulling her back so he could kiss her breasts.

He rolled over atop her, coming up to catch his
breath, for surely if he didn't, he would spill his seed on
the woolen blanket and not deep inside her. His chest
heaved and he shook with his need to come into her,

but he held himself still, aware finally that she'd stopped squirming against him and was lying there beneath him, waiting, wanting him. He drew her legs up and brought his mouth down to her, his fingers tightening on the soft flesh of her thighs, knowing vaguely that she would be bruised, but not caring, for she was arching upward, and keening softly into the darkness, calling out his name, again and again, and the wanting in her voice, the urgency and fervor, made him feel things he'd never before known existed.

He gently closed his hand over her mouth when her cries erupted from her throat, giving her the freedom to yell if she wished to without the others in the outer chamber hearing her.

And when he was stroking her with his mouth, easing her and calming her, she was tugging at his shoulders, urging him upward, and he came up to his knees and then guided himself into her. He closed his eyes at the feeling of her, the smallness, the eagerness of her to bring him closer and nearer to her.

"Merrik," she said, and clasped his back to bring him even deeper. He couldn't hold back, though he wanted to. Once, then again, he came deeply into her, then nearly withdrew until he was shuddering with the frenzy of his need, then he was heaving over her, crying out, his arms stiff as he held himself over her, and she said his name again and again, accepting him, taking all of him, and he didn't want it to stop, ever.

They lay close, her right leg over his belly, her cheek against his heart, her hair damp from her urgency, fanned out over his shoulder. He kissed the top of her head, tightening his arms around her. "You give me passion," he said. "I wish I could have seen your face when you reached your pleasure."

Her knee moved downward just a bit until she covered his groin. The scent of him was rich and dark in the night air, filling her nostrils, and her scent was mixed with his.

"Cease your movement or I will take you again. You must be sore from me, Laren."

She leaned up a bit and kissed his chest, his shoulder, his throat. She sucked at the pulse in his neck, then kissed his mouth. "It was a man who struck Erik."

He stilled. She came up onto her side, her fingers smoothing the hair on his chest, lightly stroking him.

"How do you know this?"

"I remembered that he stood over me, smiling in triumph. I wasn't completely unconscious. He stood there, Merrik, saying nothing, just smiling. He didn't try to help me, he did nothing save smile that loathsome smile. It's just that I can't see his face, yet I know he was pleased that I was there, pleased because I would be blamed for killing Erik and none would suspect him. I cannot be certain that he did murder Erik, but it does seem likely, does it not?"

"You are certain?"

"Aye."

He cursed then, soft and long, and she felt the tension coming into his body and hated it. She should have waited to tell him, but now it was too late.

"Oleg and I learned very little today talking to each of our people. But you know something, Laren, I have been thinking that this man must have followed you up the trail to the point. Perhaps he meant to kill you, but when Erik came, he waited to see what would happen. All knew my brother wanted you. When you escaped my brother, he struck Erik down. When he saw you unconscious on the path, he knew he'd won. You would be blamed."

"There is but one man who would do that."

"Aye. But we must be certain, very certain."

She kissed him again, unable to stop herself, and that kiss led to another and yet another and her hands were soon wild on him, stroking her palms over his chest, downward to his belly and into the thick hair at his groin. When she touched him, she breathed in and said into his mouth, "The way you feel, Merrik, 'tis nothing I could have ever imagined."

"Nor I," he said. "Nor I."

19

DEGLIN GULPED DOWN his ale and wiped his hand
across his mouth. "It's hot out here," he said as he
poured himself another cup from the barrel beside him.
He frowned as he looked up to see three women washing clothing in the big wooden tub set on wooden planks
beneath a full-branched oak tree. "Aye, it's as hot as
she is, the cold bitch."

"As who is?" Oleg asked, looking toward the women.

"That bitch, Laren. I tell you, Oleg, she is nothing,
nothing at all." He drank down more of the ale. "She
bewitched Merrik, then whored for him. Aye, she pre-
tended she was hot for him, as hot as that damned sun
baking my flesh."

Oleg merely nodded, keeping his head down, sipping
only at his cup of ale. He didn't want Deglin to see his
growing rage. He wanted him to keep talking. Deglin
had already drunk a good half dozen cups of the strong
ale. At least now he was speaking of Laren. Oleg kept
his features carefully blank. He waited. He suddenly
had a clear memory of Laren lying over Merrik's thighs
while his friend cleaned the blood from the welts on her
back. He wondered if Merrik could have possibly imagined that this thin pathetic girl would become his wife.
He listened to Deglin speak of the worthlessness of both

Laren and Taby, how they'd taken over, how they'd turned Merrik against him, how they deserved retribution, aye, and he would see that there was punishment for the bitch. The summer sun was warm on Oleg's head, the breeze soft and sweet, filled with the scents of the ripening barley just beyond. He didn't think it was too hot. He felt his skin warming and flexed his shoulders. He looked at Deglin then and drew back at the stark anger he saw on the man's face, aye, and there was more. There was misery, deep pain that Oleg refused to see, misery he didn't want to acknowledge or to understand. No, he wanted to take Deglin's skinny neck between his two hands and squeeze the wretched life from him, but he didn't. He sat there and listened and nodded and tried to look thoughtful from drink, a silly look, he knew.

Deglin, restless, his fingers fisting then relaxing, continued, his voice as bitter as the frigid winds of the winter solstice, "Aye, she's a bitch and she should die. Look what she did to Erik and all have absolved her and just because she claims she is Rollo's niece! By all the gods, it is madness to believe her, naught but a slave she is, and Merrik found her in Kiev. A slave, and that little brother of hers is probably her own child, a bastard and a slave."

"You don't believe she's Rollo's niece?"

Deglin spat on a pile of bones then kicked them. "She is a liar, and now she has won. Merrik has proven himself a weakling, easily led and gullible, not the man I believed him to be, not that he ever showed he was as brave as his poor brother, aye, he failed all of us, taking that viper to wed. I will leave. I should have gone with Thoragasson. He begged me to go with him, but I said I had to remain with Merrik, that I owed my loyalty to his family."

Oleg wanted to tell him that all knew Thoragasson had decided he didn't want him. If he couldn't have Laren, he didn't want to settle for Deglin. Thoragasson had said, his voice as cold as the Vestfold winter, "The man's lowness offends me. I have to suffer my own daughter's pettiness, Deglin's I do not." Oleg had wanted to tell him that Deglin should wed Letta and let them berate each other, but he'd been smart enough to keep quiet. Oleg said now, "Erik wanted the girl Laren very badly. It is obvious he followed her up the path to the peak. Did she strike him to protect herself? She says not. Even if she did strike him, why it would be to defend herself, would it not?"

Deglin suddenly looked austere, and it sat strangely on him since he was so drunk he could scarcely stand. "She is a slave. Erik could have raped her until his manhood rotted off. It was his right."

Oleg just shrugged. "It matters not, for Merrik believes she didn't kill Erik; most of the people believe her for she is Rollo's niece and thus a lie wouldn't be in her nature."

"Ha! She killed Erik because she knew she had Merrik. Erik would never have set aside Sarla, so she had no choice but to kill the man who stood master of Malverne before Merrik. Aye, she wanted Malverne and now she's won."

"But she was unconscious. She'd knocked herself out hitting her head against a rock. I myself saw the lump on the back of her head."

"Aye, she was unconscious, but that was after she'd struck Erik. She was running, panicked and heedless, to escape her crime."

"I have wondered," Oleg said thoughtfully, staring into the dregs of his ale at the bottom of the cup. "Aye, I have wondered if perhaps Erik was struck down so that Laren would be blamed for it, that she was the object of the hatred, not Erik. What do you think, Deglin?" With those words, Oleg looked directly into Deglin's eyes. The man looked at once feverish and pale, deathly pale.

"Some dislike her, don't trust her," Oleg continued. "You, Deglin, hate her above all others. Did she not take what was yours? You have been skald here for five long summers. And now you are nothing. Aye, she stripped you of what belonged to you. Did she not also abuse you, make you feel less the man? Did she not make Merrik burn you when she accidentally fell into the fire?"

"Aye," Deglin shouted, pounding his fists to his skinny thighs. "Aye, she did. I'll tell all of it now. I have protected Merrik with my silence. But now I will speak the truth. It is time the bitch got her comeuppance, her punishment for her crime. No more protecting this family. I owe them nothing." He drew himself up, straightened his thin shoulders. There was a pleased glitter in his eyes. There was no drunken slur to his words now, no clumsy movements. It was as if he'd suddenly become miraculously sober. "I saw her strike down Erik. Then she saw what she'd done and she ran. Aye, she knocked herself unconscious, but she killed Erik nonetheless. I swear to it. I saw it all happen. It wasn't to protect herself from his rape, for she wanted him, and after she'd had him, when he was sated and lulled, she struck him on his head, killing him. Aye, I saw it all, I saw her murder Erik and I will swear to it."

At that moment, Laren appeared, her face pale as the raw wool on the loom. "Why do you lie, Deglin? Why?"

"You faithless bitch!" Deglin yelled and bounded to his feet. "You have ruined everything! I had prestige and respect until Merrik found you in the slave ring. You stole everything that was mine, everything! You killed Erik. I saw you kill him, strike him hard with that rock, when he was still on top of you, his sex still between your legs, his reason still swamped with his lust. Aye, you killed him after you whored for him just as you do for his brother. You killed him because you wanted Malverne. Will you kill Merrik as well?"

She just stared at him. The violence of his hatred was numbing. She wanted to tell him that the two of them could have both told stories, that there were surely enough people to listen to both of them. Instead, all that came from her mouth was, "Why do you hate me so much?"

"I should have killed you when I saw you lying there, aye, I should have—" Deglin rushed at her, his hands outstretched, curved inward, as if already digging into her throat.

Oleg rose slowly, hurling his cup to the ground. His right hand shot out and he grabbed Deglin by his neck, raising him slowly, staring at him even as Deglin scratched wildly at his hand to free himself. "You would strangle Laren, you puling snake? You lie," Oleg said directly into Deglin's face. "You lie and now I know it and Merrik knows it. You killed Erik because you wanted Laren blamed. She remembered you standing over her, and you were smiling in triumph, for you had just come down from killing Erik. You are a fool, Deglin. Your jealousy and your malice have twisted your mind."

He dropped the skald, dispassionately watching his knees buckle as he thudded hard to the ground. He was panting to gain breath, his hands rubbing wildly against his throat. Oleg raised his foot, but Merrik said, "No, Oleg, 'tis enough."

Deglin looked up and saw Merrik. He felt the weight of the trap, felt all he'd ever known crumbling around him. He tried to speak, to defend himself, but his throat was bruised and he could only make small mewling cries. The pain brought tears to his eyes. He felt as though he were collapsing in upon himself.

"He deserves to die, Merrik."

"Aye, Oleg, he does. He murdered my brother, his motives so base, it borders on madness. Take him to the blacksmith's hut and have Snorri chain him near the fire pit. Let him bake in his own sweat."

"No! I didn't kill Erik. Aye, 'tis true that I saw her lying unconscious there on the path, and I was pleased for I had seen that Erik was dead. But she must have killed him. I know that she did!"

Laren watched Oleg drag Deglin away, his hands still clawing at his bruised throat, still trying to speak.

"It is over."

"Aye, now I will ask you, my skald wife, what shall I do with Deglin?"

She was silent, looking over his left shoulder to the rich barley fields and the several blackbirds that were eating the crop. She saw a slave banging an iron pan with a heavy stick, startling the blackbirds, sending them squawking into frenzied flight.

"Not only did he kill Erik, he did it for the most base of reasons."

"Aye, 'tis true. But I do not understand him. Why didn't he simply kill me? He had no hatred for Erik. Why?"

"Because I would have flayed the flesh from his back without even asking him a single question. He believed by killing Erik, you would be blamed and he would still gain what he wanted. He could sit back and laugh at all of us, watching us perform as he'd wanted."

"I am very sorry about Erik."

"Aye, to die to have another blamed. I miss him sorely. Now we have the guilty man. I have sent a messenger to my other brother, Rorik, on Hawkfell Island. He and his wife, Mirana, will come, I doubt it not. Answer me, Laren. What should I do to Deglin?"

She said slowly, "Perhaps I would send him to my uncle Rollo. Let him serve up justice and punishment."

Merrik's nostrils flared. "Aye, it would be fitting. Rollo would have Deglin ripped apart by four horses or he would have him hung upside down next to a wolf. Your uncle isn't known for his clemency or his forgiveness."

"No, he is not, particularly toward those who attempt to hurt those he loves. No Viking is known for clemency. I would kill him, but not so crudely."

"And what would you do?"

"I think I would take him deep into the forest, give him a knife, and leave him. He is proud of his wits. Let him save himself if he can."

"Perhaps he would save himself. I cannot bear for him to live. It would offend the gods and all our people."

She sighed then. "You are right. Kill him." She paused a moment, then added, "He didn't really confess to killing Erik."

"He killed my brother."

"He swore only that he saw me unconscious, and that is what I remember, Merrik. There is no doubt now in your mind?"

"None at all."

All the Malverne people agreed that Deglin was guilty. They all had heard him speak ill of Laren, heard his bitterness, his rage at her seizing of his position. The men told of how Deglin, in his jealousy, had knocked Laren into a campfire, badly burning her leg. All of Deglin's silver was given to Merrik as Danegeld for Erik's life. It wasn't enough, there would never be enough to pay for Erik's life, but it was custom and Merrik bowed to it. No one wanted him taken to Duke Rollo in Normandy, they wanted him dead, the sooner the better. Thus it was that Merrik would wield the knife, as was his right. He planned one quick blow. He wanted it over. He would execute Deglin at dawn the next morning.

The morning was chill, clouds lying low. Everyone stood in a circle, waiting for Deglin to be brought out. But when Merrik, Snorri the blacksmith, and Oleg went into Snorri's hut, Deglin was dead. He'd managed to free himself and thrust a knife in his heart. It was one of Erik's old knives, there to be repaired, then to be given to Merrik.

"By all the gods," Snorri said, infuriated, "I should have remained here in the hut last night! But I didn't want to hear him pleading and begging me for his release. And now he is dead, by his own hand."

All complained that his death was too easy, too quick. Merrik wondered why Deglin hadn't tried to escape. Others wondered as well. Surely dying in freedom was better than knowing death was certain in captivity. Surely dying in freedom was better than taking your own life. But it was done.

Merrik merely shook his head and had Deglin's body dragged into the forest. He did not deserve a Viking burial. Laren watched him wipe Deglin's blood from the knife pulled from Deglin's chest. He stared silently at it for a long moment, then handed it to Snorri.

They planned to leave for Normandy and the court of Duke Rollo after the harvest. That would give them enough time to return before the first winter storm struck Vestfold.

One week after a farmer had come across Deglin's body in the forest, little left of it save bloody rags, there was much shouting and yelling and arm waving from the pier.

Merrik's older brother, Rorik, had arrived at Malverne.

Laren was on her back on the floor, laughing and trying to avoid the huge dog's hot tongue that lapped her face, grainy and nearly painful on her flesh. She gripped his thick fur and pulled and pulled, but it did no good at all. "Don't just stand there," she yelled, "help me!"

"Kerzog! Off her, you stupid hound! Get off!"

Kerzog took one final lick, then bounded up, his huge paws landing on Merrik's chest, nearly dropping him to his knees with the force.

"I see that Kerzog still admires a beautiful woman and remembers how my little brother fed him more meat from his platter than he himself ate." Rorik smiled toward the gigantic hound still trying to swipe Merrik's face with his tongue.

"I must wash my face at least six times a day," Mirana said to Laren. "Kerzog is as loving as is my husband, and he is considerably stronger."

"Six times?" Merrik said to his smiling sister-in-law. "I should say he is far more loving than any mortal man could be, including my brother."

Rorik Haraldsson grinned at Laren, and said, "Your new husband has enough wit for the entire family. You, I understand, are a skald. That is unusual. Both my wife and I are eager to hear a tale."

"And our sons as well," Mirana said, pointing to two little boys who were utterly identical, both with hair as black as their mother's, and eyes as light blue as the sky, just like their father's. They were beautiful. They were eyeing Taby, the three of them circling each other, wary, yet interested.

"In a few minutes, they will be rolling on the ground, wrestling and yelling," Mirana said comfortably.

Mirana was right. The boys were the best of friends within the next ten minutes and fighting like the worst of enemies. As for the brothers, they were speaking quietly together, and Laren knew they spoke of Erik. She watched them leave the longhouse and she knew they were going to Erik's grave. And to their parents' graves as well.

"So much trouble," Mirana said, shaking her head. "I am sorry that you have had to bear such dissension. At least Sarla has held fast to your friendship."

"Aye, she is like a loving sister to me."

"And you are the niece of the famous Rollo of Normandy!"

Sarla said, smiling, "Aye, but she still only has three gowns, Mirana. Ileria is weaving madly so that the mistress of Malverne does not embarrass us with her lack of finery. None of us want her to return to Normandy looking less than flawless. Have you yet changed Merrik's mind, Laren?"

She shook her head. "He still believes he is keeping me safe by leaving me here. But don't worry, this is too important for him to continue in his confusion."

The women laughed. Kerzog woofed loudly, and ran right at Mirana. She shrieked and ducked behind Laren. The huge hound knocked both of them over, barking and waving a thick violent tail that could break an unheeding arm.

When Rorik and Merrik returned to the longhouse, silent and each alone with his thoughts, his own memories, they were greeted with laughter. Each man slowly smiled. Life once again overcame death and all its pain.

The longhouse bulged with people. The men had hunted, bringing down a deer and a boar. Many others had fished, and the rich smells of the venison and the boar mixed with the baked herring and salmon, filled the air, covering the ever-present smell of men and women pressed too closely together. Laren looked upon the row upon row of bodies, each wrapped in a woolen blanket, along the far wall. She looked down at a tug on her gown to see Taby, rubbing his eyes with his knuckles, wearing only a linen tunic.

She dropped to her knees and drew him to her. "You were asleep, Taby. You had a bad dream?"

He nodded. "How can Merrik be my Viking warrior if he comes back here to Malverne? The Viking warrior stayed with the little boy, to protect him, to keep him safe. I'm not stupid, Laren. I know that this other place is far away from here."

She'd made up the Viking warrior. She felt tears sting her eyes. She'd given a child a hero and now, because they lived not in a skald's tale but in the real world, the hero would leave him, and so would she. She couldn't bear it.

"I don't know," she said against his soft hair. "I don't know, but we will do something."

She saw Merrik then, standing close to them, watching, saying nothing.

"I don't want to leave you or Merrik," Taby said against her neck. "I don't care about being a prince."

Merrik came down beside her, lightly stroking the child's arm. Taby turned, his eyes still dulled with sleep, but there was a quiver at his mouth that made Merrik's gut cramp. He drew in his breath and said slowly, "Taby, you remember I told you that who you are means many things have to happen that none of us can change."

Taby nodded, but said, "I don't care."

"I know, but I have to do the caring for you. I cannot allow you to be other than what you are meant to be. It is possible that you will someday be the duke of Normandy. There is no choice."

The child drew up, jerking out of Laren's arms. "I hate you, I hate both of you! You just want to get rid of me!" He turned and ran back to the children's sleeping chamber, this night filled with at least eight small bodies all pressed together in the single box bed.

Laren jumped to her feet, but Merrik held her still. "No, let him go. He is very young, Laren, but he must realize that there are duties, endless responsibilities, that direct each of us."

"He is very young, too young to remember. The last two years have been very hard for him. He's not known kindness or stability. He fears the unknown, for it is all he's had for far too long."

"And his sister as well. Now, we will go see him in a little while. Tell me what you think of Rorik and Mirana."

"She is more beautiful than Caylis or Megot."

He laughed at that. "Once I hated her, believed her evil, for her half brother, Einar, was a more black-hearted scoundrel than the Christians' devil. All that black hair of hers and her white flesh, aye, I believed her a witch. I was wrong. By all the gods, it is difficult to be young. Nothing appears as it really is, and your mind twists and bends and sees snakes where there are rainbows. And what do you think of my brother?"

"Rorik is like all Viking men. He is beautiful, well formed, stout-hearted."

Merrik just stared down at her, a dark blond eyebrow cocked. "And?"

"And his dog is going to sleep in our bed with us to-night, I doubt not. He has discovered that I'm not as strong as Mirana and thus he can lie on me and lick me until his tongue is dry."

Merrik grabbed her about her neck, leaned down and kissed her hard.

They planned to set sail for Normandy when the moon had reached its half phase some fourteen days later. Merrik would leave Oleg in charge of both the men and Malverne's defense. Sarla would continue as mistress of the household. Taby was sullen. He had been sullen since his outburst. On the morning of their departure, he allowed Laren to hug and kiss him, but when Merrik went down on his haunches in front of the child, Taby turned away from him.

Laren saw the pain on Merrik's face. Raw anger shot through her. She grabbed Taby's arm and jerked him back to face her. "How can you act so to the man who saved your life? The man who also saved my life? The man who will restore you to your proper position?"

He kept his head down, scuffing his bare toes into the hard earth.

"Answer me, Taby! You are of royal lineage and yet you behave like a thrall's get! What is the matter with you?"

"He doesn't love me, Laren."

She jerked back, momentarily stunned. "What did you say?"

"He doesn't love me. If he did, he wouldn't leave me, he wouldn't go tell Uncle Rollo where I was."

"That is quite enough. Listen to me, Merrik loves you more than he loves anyone on this earth."

Taby shook his head. "No he doesn't. If he did, he wouldn't leave me. He's even taking you with him."

"Well, that is different. He finally came to realize that without me, he would have a difficult time convincing Uncle Rollo of anything. I know all the people in Uncle Rollo's court. I can help him. He needs me. He's leaving you here so he can be certain you'll be safe, nothing more. He can't be worried about you, else he would endanger himself."

"He doesn't worry about you?"

"Not overmuch. I have proved I can survive."

"So have I, Laren."

"Ah, but you're a stubborn little pullet." She ran her fingers through his thick hair. "Listen to me, Taby. Merrik takes me because I will be useful to him. He doesn't take you because he loves you and doesn't want to take any chances with your being hurt."

"He doesn't care if you're hurt?"

Even as she shook her head, she knew he did care, but it was nothing compared to his feelings for Taby, feelings she knew he didn't understand, but so strong nonetheless that he was helpless against them. She accepted that and with the acceptance she felt a lurching of pain deep inside her.

"I won't be hurt," she said, rising. She kept her hand on Taby's shoulder. "I want you to go to Merrik now. Do not use his love for you against him. I expect you to act the man you will one day become."

Taby looked at her for a very long time. Then he looked toward Merrik who was speaking to Oleg and Roran, his body stiff with silent pain.

He walked slowly to him. When Merrik turned to look down at the boy, the blanked pain in his eyes turned to delight and relief. He clasped the child to him and closed his eyes, even as he spoke quietly in Taby's ear.

What was he telling him? Even when Merrik found his release with her, even when he laughed with her, he had never looked at her with such joy and tenderness. For the first time in her life, Laren found herself jealous of her little brother. She felt sour resentment roil in her belly, and she swallowed, forcing herself to turn away.

She sought out Sarla, to hug her good-bye once again, for there was really no other reason. As they walked side by side down the winding trail to the dock, she told her how to combine cloudberries with mashed hazelnuts to flavor venison-and-onion stew, something she'd already done two days before. Sarla looked earnest and nodded.

20

"A TALE, LAREN, a tale!"

"Aye," Roran said. "You, mistress, you sit there with nothing to do, doubtless dreaming about that smiling sod, Merrik, whilst we break our backs at the oars."

The wind had picked up and the men had rested their oars. They all turned about on their sea chests to face her. She smiled and said, "I will tell you a true story. Listen now. Duke Rollo's lieutenant, Weland, tells of how Charles the Third, the Frankish king, ordered my uncle present himself in Paris to swear fealty to him. Charles commanded Rollo to kneel before him and kiss his foot in homage. My uncle Rollo indeed went down on his knees, with all solemnity, you understand, but he didn't kiss the king's foot. No, he grabbed his foot and jerked upward, sending the king toppling over the back of his throne to land flat on his back."

Merrik and his men shouted with laughter. "And what did the king do?" Old Firren asked, then spat over the side of the longboat.

"His men picked him up and held their breaths. They were scared he would order them to kill Rollo. They weren't stupid men, and they knew many of them wouldn't survive such a contest of sheer strength. King Charles stood there, dusting off his beautiful robe of

purple wool, and just stared at Rollo. The men shuffled
their feet, their fear growing. Then, to their joy, King
Charles smiled. Then he threw back his head and
laughed. He told them all that he was pleased by Rollo's
insolent violence because it proved to him that the Viking overlord would control any marauders who dared
to sail down the Seine and plunder the towns. He is
called Charles the Simple, you know, a name he does
not merit, at least in his dealings with my uncle. He
gave all the northwest lands to Rollo in exchange for
protection. There have been no raids of any seriousness
in five years. All the Danes and Norwegians respect and
fear my uncle, for he has many well-trained men and
is also building fortifications and manning them. The
Franks under King Charles live in peace for the first
time in many, many years."

Oleg scratched his four-day growth of beard. "I heard
it said that your uncle refused to go to Paris to swear
fealty. I heard he sent a message to the Frank king
telling him that 'We know no master. We are all equal.'
Then he spat upon the message and rubbed his thumb
in it."

"If my uncle said that, I don't know of it. It sounds
like him though. He is ruthless and arrogant; he fears
no man. He did go to Paris, I do know that for certain.
Also I never knew Weland to lie. Otta, my uncle's minister, also tells the same story." She paused a moment,
then added, "Perhaps Rollo was wary of King Alfred of
the Saxons a long time ago. But Alfred has been dead
now nearly two decades so there is no one to disturb
Rollo's sleep, even his relatives, the earls of Orkney,
who occasionally send him threats that they will destroy him if he doesn't give them some of his vast holdings. Aye, the earls of Orkney are a vicious, nasty lot."

"So it is true that Rollo comes from the Orkneys?"

"Aye, it's true. Uncle Rollo told me once a long time ago that they were a savage clan."

"How savage?" Roran called out.

"They're so savage they even piss in their long-houses." She let the men's laughter warm her, then turned her face to the southern breeze off the longboat's port side. It was very calm now, the water a deep blue, the whitecaps small and lazy. They sailed just beyond the coast, always keeping land in sight. They would reach the river Seine by nightfall, if the wind held and the rain kept to the north of them.

"The giving of land to Rollo and making it a duchy— it is the poacher turned gamekeeper," Merrik said, as he picked up his oar and rhythmically pulled on it. The other men soon joined him. "No, this Charles the Third isn't at all simple. He gave to your uncle what he already occupied. He is a wise man."

"You make it sound as though my uncle were a naïve child to be led about by the nose."

Merrik laughed. "Nay, acquit me, Laren, of speaking thusly of the sainted Rollo. He is a man to fear and to respect. Your uncle wanted permanency and he assured it. Aye, he saved himself much trouble and got what he wanted for his people and for his heirs. If you wish to farm and settle, it makes no sense to want to make war on your neighbors. Tell me more about this Otta and Weland."

"Otta has been at my uncle's side since Rollo was outlawed from Norway by King Harald. He is younger than my uncle and very smart. Weland, my uncle's lieutenant, grew up with my uncle. They fought together, wedded at the same time, and their wives died at nearly the same time. They are all very close."

The men fell to speaking of other matters. Laren sat back beside Old Firren, who held firm to the rudder, letting the afternoon sun warm her face. She slept. When she awoke the sun was no longer on her face. Merrik stood over her, his hand outstretched. "We are coming now to the Seine. We will continue south down the river. We will make camp outside of Rouen. I wish us all to be clean and well garbed when we go to your uncle's palace."

Laren thought of the three new gowns Ileria had woven then sewn for her. All of them were of the softest linen, all now neatly rolled in Merrik's sea chest. Aye, she wanted to face all of them looking the best she could.

They pulled the longboat from the water onto a deserted stretch of narrow beach, bordered by thick beech and maple trees. The evening was warm, insects were flying madly about, the water lapped against the shore. There were no villages close by. All was peaceful.

Merrik turned to Eller. "Keep your nose awake to smell out any trouble."

"I shall, Merrik, have no worry."

Merrik was worried, though not about enemies coming upon them unawares. He was worried because he'd allowed Laren to come with him, bowing to her quite logical arguments that her uncle might just as well dismiss him out of hand rather than listen to him, that he might be enraged by his unlikely tale and have him killed. All the reasons made good sense, but it still didn't make him like the situation.

He wasn't worried that Rollo would kill him even though he'd wedded his niece, who had been destined for a dynastic marriage with the king of the Danelaw's heir. No, he imagined the man would bow to that. He was worried about the traitor who'd had her and Taby abducted. Was it Helga? It seemed possible, and Laren, in her skald's tale, seemed convinced she was the guilty one. However, Merrik hesitated to believe in the obvious, for in his experience, what appeared obvious in reality proved many times a devious and wrongful path.

He turned onto his side and gathered Laren into his arms. The scent of the warm wolf fur and the feel of her soft flesh against him made him harden instantly. He licked back the tendrils of soft hair and kissed her earlobe. But he didn't wake her.

He was on the edge of sleep when she screamed. She was frantically struggling against him, her breath coming in short painful gasps, and she was crying, helpless cries that made his guts churn even as he shook her hard.

"Wake up, Laren, come, it's a bad dream, nothing more."

She blinked at him, shuddered, and sniveled, trying to still her tears.

"The same dream?"

She nodded.

"You haven't had the dream for a very long time. It's about the men who took you and Taby?"

"I can see their faces very clearly, Merrik. Do you think they're still in Rouen?"

"No, not those same men, but others. Aye, there will be others. By all the gods, I shouldn't have listened to you. I should have left you safe at Malverne." He cursed long and fluently.

"I will be safe with you. Doubt it not. I'm sorry I woke you, Merrik."

"Do not be sorry. You will be safe with me, dammit. If men come after you, I will kill them. Hush now, the night is still upon us."

She nestled against him, seeking the heat of his body. She whispered against his chest, "Do you miss Taby?"

"Aye, overmuch. It is a sorrow and a joy I will have

all my life. Were it not Rollo to hold claim to him, I would keep him with me."

"You have an excellent eye."

"What do you mean?"

"He was a sniveling, filthy little boy and yet you wanted him the moment you saw him. You saw what he really was and accepted what you saw immediately, regardless of the other."

" 'Tis true, though I had no thought to his parentage. You were just as filthy and so thin I could have snapped your neck with my hand, yet I also took you and saved you and made you into a skald and married you."

She raised herself on her elbows, trying to see him in the darkness of the tent. She felt his warm breath on her face. "You are a good man, Merrik."

"Is that all I am to you?"

She shook her head, kissing his chin, saying, "Nay, you are also my lover, even though it is said that you need more practice."

His hand was on her buttocks, lightly slapping her, then quickly caressing instead.

She arched into his hand, saying, "What will happen to Sarla? I do not know your customs for a widow. Uncle Rollo would marry her to another man of his choosing, use her for his own gain."

"But that is not my way nor was it my father's. A woman may refuse to wed any man. It is true that fathers arrange matters and negotiate for goods and a dowry, but the woman may still refuse, the man as well."

"I am relieved to hear that. You forget that Uncle Rollo became a Christian when he swore fealty to King Charles. He says often that he doesn't mind this heathen religion for it grants him many privileges he didn't have before. And all the Christian monks bless him for actions the Viking gods would never allow."

"Such as treating women as chattel and as puppets to gain what he wants. Your uncle is a smart man and a very ruthless one." There was admiration in Merrik's voice, and Laren punched him in his belly. He grunted, then grabbed her hand and brought it to his mouth. He kissed each of her fingers, then her palm. She stilled. Gently, he drew her back down against him. "If Sarla wishes it, I will return her to her family."

"She loves Cleve and he loves her."

He tensed. "I hope you aren't right about that. It would mean that she betrayed my brother and that I cannot allow to pass. My brother didn't deserve to have his wife betray him."

She rammed her fist against his arm, this time in anger. "Betray him! By all the gods, Merrik, your brother took both Megot and Caylis to his bed—in front of Sarla's nose! You speak of betrayal, what of him?"

"A man can take women unto himself. A woman cannot take a man other than her husband, for if she conceived, then the child born could be a bastard. It isn't allowed, Laren. Did Sarla bed with Cleve?"

"No, I am certain they did not. They are both honorable. They feel guilty about their feelings, but they won't act on them, not for a long time."

"I will have to ponder this. It is disturbing. I like Cleve very much, but he has nothing to bring to Sarla. Aye, I will have to think about this."

"You won't take other women, will you, Merrik?"

He kneaded her buttocks, saying simply, "Erik believed I would. Who knows? After all, thus far you have proved yourself to be a cold woman, with little care for the pleasure I would offer you. You endure me, nothing more. You sigh with boredom when I am moaning with pleasure. It makes my man's rod shrivel."

She laughed, sent her fist lightly again into his belly, then immediately flattened her palm and caressed him. She felt his muscles tighten, felt him suck in his breath in anticipation. She smiled into the darkness, but didn't allow her fingers to go lower. " 'Tis true," she said, her voice as sad as a merchant's who had just lost a valuable barter. "I cannot even bring myself to give you any pleasure. Look at my hand. By the gods, it won't move downward to your shriveled manhood. I can't seem to make it move. What am I to do?"

He laughed, then grabbed her hand in his and pressed it against him. "Ah," he said. "Now you needn't do anything, at least until I direct you to."

She found that her fingers did move. She wanted to stroke him, to feel him lurch and quiver as his need grew.

His need grew quickly. She was laughing until he came into her fully. Then she closed her eyes against the power of him and what he made her feel and she drew him deeper and deeper still. She groaned into his mouth, pushing upward, then yet again, until she cried out her pleasure. He kissed her until she calmed and then he found his own release.

"You pleased me, Merrik," she said, her voice still raw and breathless. "Aye, you pleased me." She bit his shoulder, then said, "Next time I will please you more."

He wondered how that would be possible, but didn't question it. He said, "We will bathe the smell of me off you. I wouldn't want your uncle to kill me before he believes that we're married."

"Leave the smell of me on your flesh."

He shuddered at her words and came into her again.

"We must sleep soon," Merrik said when his heart had once again slowed. He rolled onto his back, Laren pressed against his side.

"Aye," she said, and kissed his chest.

"I cannot stop thinking of my brother. He was so very alive, Laren. He loved life, he wanted everything he could get from it. You saw him acting the bastard, unfair and arrogant. But I knew him before."

"Did he change so much?"

"Aye, I believe he must have chafed sorely against my father's authority, for my father was master of Malverne and none other, even his eldest son who was his heir to Malverne. After my father's death, he gained too much power too quickly. Aye, it changed him, made him unmindful of others, made him unwise in his arrogance. There was no one like my father there to temper his vanity."

"He hurt Sarla very much."

"I saw the bruises on her face. That wasn't well done of him. She is a gentle girl, kind and giving. Still, to die in such a way, I would have wished it otherwise."

"Deglin is dead, and that is something."

"Aye," he said, kissed her forehead, and pressed her cheek against his shoulder.

Weland, Duke Rollo's first lieutenant, a man who had been at Rollo's right hand since they'd both been boys, a man so strong he could pull a sapling oak from the ground, was grinning like a hyena.

"I have a great surprise for you, sire, a very great surprise."

Prince Rollo, as he was called by his people, even though his lands were called a duchy and thus he was only a duke by grant of the French king, was taller than any sapling Weland could pull from the ground. He turned his dark eyes on his man and said, "Aye, Weland, what is it this time? You bring me a Nubian maid to warm my old bones? Mayhap a magic potion to

stop the grinding pain in my joints? A stallion tall
enough so my feet don't drag the ground?"

"Nay, sire, I bring you a gift beyond any weight of
silver. Laren has come back."

Rollo just stared at Weland. "You jest," he said at
last. "She and Taby are dead, long dead. I forgive you
most things, Weland, but this is too much. Do not trifle
with me."

Weland just shook his head, still smiling like a fool,
and called out, "Bring them in!"

Rollo saw only the slender girl with her glorious red
hair, nearly curling to her shoulders, the way he'd always liked her to wear it when she was younger. He'd
hated her braids because they'd dimmed the beautiful
color, the exact same shade as his older brother Hallad's hair. She was too slender, he saw as she walked
closer, ah, but she'd become a beauty, and more than
that, there was more of life in her eyes, and more shadows, but there was also joy and confidence that the child
had lacked. She was gowned beautifully in a soft blue
linen that was belted at her waist. She wore finely
wrought silver brooches and silver armlets. She was
almost of his loins, this graceful creature, and now she
was here, alive, with a man striding beside her.

He said her name softly, just the saying of it making
her real, very real. He rose, towering over even the back
of his throne.

"Laren!"

His shout reverberated throughout the chamber, and
she laughed aloud and ran to him, and he caught her
up in his arms, lifting her high off the floor, and squeezing her and laughing with her now.

"By the gods, you're taller," he said, and kissed her
on both cheeks, back and forth, squeezing until she
groaned with the force of his strength.

"I am home, uncle," she said. "Ah, you are still so very handsome. The two years are as nothing with you, my lord. You haven't Weland's grizzled gray hair. I am also pleased you have not grown taller, bless the gods."

He lowered her to the floor, and just held her hand, then pushed her a little bit farther away from him, and continued to stare down at her. "You are the same yet you have changed more than I can begin to imagine."

"Aye, it's true."

Suddenly his eyes clouded. She knew he was thinking about Taby but was afraid to hear that he was dead. She said quickly, "My lord, Taby is well and healthy and safe."

"Ah," Rollo said and raised his voice heavenward. "I will make sacrifices to all the gods, even the Christian God. We searched everywhere for you and Taby. Your cousin William led scores of men throughout the countryside and even into Paris. There was no trace of you. Tell me, Laren, tell me what happened to you."

"I will, my lord. First you will meet the man who saved both Taby and me, the man who is now my husband. He is the master of Malverne, a wealthy farmstead in Vestfold, and his name is Merrik Haraldsson."

Weland said, "Go to His Highness, Merrik."

Merrik walked slowly to the mighty Rollo, a man he'd heard unbelievable tales about all his life. Now this man was of his family, this man whose legs were so long Merrik imagined that he would need a horse at least seventeen hands high to keep his feet from touching the ground. It was said he walked most places, his men riding beside him. That would be a sight indeed, Merrik thought. Ah, but his was a royal bearing, even though the years had dragged a few strands of white through his dark hair and etched lines in his cheeks and forehead. But his eyes, dark as midnight, were bright with intelligence and, Merrik saw with some surprise, with humor. He had all his teeth and his jaw was firm and stubborn. A man to reckon with.

"My lord," he said, coming to a halt in front of Rollo. He would not bow. A Viking bowed to no man.

"You saved Laren and Taby."

"Aye. I was in Kiev and found them both at the Khagan-Rus slave market."

"Slave market!"

Laren laid her hand lightly on her uncle's richly embroidered woolen sleeve. "It is a very long story, my lord. Quickly put, Taby and I were abducted from my bed two years ago and sold as slaves south in the Piedmont. We have lived as slaves ever since."

Rollo just stared at her.

"I dismissed the guards, my lord," Weland said into the immense silence. "Laren said she wanted only you and me to know she'd returned. And Otta, of course. Only Haakon knows besides us. He is seeing to Merrik's men. He is saying only that they are your visitors from Norway, naught else. There is betrayal, my lord. We must take steps before it is known she and Prince Taby are returned to us."

Rollo said finally, "Where is Taby?"

Merrik said, "He is at my farmstead, Malverne, lying some half day's inland sail from Kaupang. He is safe and guarded well."

"Ah, and when we know who had you abducted and sold as slaves, then you will bring Taby back to me?"

"Aye, my lord, but not until then. I love the child. I won't chance his being hurt again. I would ask that none save you, sire, and Weland here know that Taby is alive. I won't take any chance with his safety, no matter how unlikely."

"I agree, Merrik. However, he must come back to me,

for my only son, William, as yet has no heirs that have survived their mother's womb. Taby is important to me, important to Normandy."

"That is the only reason I am here, sire."

Rollo looked at the Viking more closely now. "You are Laren's husband," he said. "Did you wish to wed her before or after she told you who she was?"

Merrik took no offense. "Before, sire. However, I care not about this Danelaw prince. She is mine now and the mistress of Malverne."

Rollo made no move, merely continued studying the man who'd saved his niece and Taby. For that, he owed him more than he could imagine, as did his son, William, for William knew it vital for a man's line to continue, and continue it would. This man Merrik Haraldsson looked to be a man of fine parts—big and robust, bursting with youth and good health—no pain in his damned joints!—and he had the handsome looks women admired, that doubtless Laren admired. He would see. Aye, he would study this man closely before he decided if he would keep Laren with him or let her hold to this marriage.

He said to Weland, "For the moment Laren will remain with Merrik. He will guard her better than any of our men, but keep men close to their sleeping chamber nonetheless." Rollo turned away and smote his palm against his forehead. "Ah, why did I listen to those damnable women? They told me they'd heard of plots and evil men who wished me dead, and through Taby and you, Laren, to eventually destroy my dynasty. There are always plots, always evil men, particularly that vicious lot from the Orkneys, and thus I believed them. I have kept William safe but I failed with you and Taby. By all the gods, Helga's tongue is smoother than an adder's, and Ferlain's manner is as innocent and guileless as a damnable Christian nun's. I will kill the bitches."

"We must have proof, my lord," Laren said. "I cannot be certain, even though it seems very likely. As you said, there are always evil men, even the Franks who owe their allegiance to their Frankish king, Charles."

"More than likely. I will speak to Otta about this, but I will not tell him about Taby, no matter that he deserves to know. I don't know where he is. Weland, where is Otta?"

"He, er, is in the privy, sire. He will attend you soon."

"Otta and his damned belly," Rollo said. "His belly is always paining him, always sending him to the privy. Well, Merrik, let me tell you that I was nearly to the point of deciding that one of their husbands should follow if something happened to William. Well, I was not completely ready to do it. I am not an ancient graybeard just yet. I would have waited perhaps another year or another score of years. William's wife is breeding. We pray to the Christian God for a live boy. If it happens to come out a girl, then we will see—"

Merrik interrupted him smoothly, "And what if they tired of waiting and poisoned you, sire, or William?"

Weland said, his wide brow lowering, "Aye, 'tis likely what they would have done, you have the right of it, Merrik Haraldsson. Otta has spoken about that as well. He is forever worrying that Rollo and William will be poisoned. He many times tastes Rollo's food before he allows him to eat."

"Aye," Rollo said, laughing. "Then he hies himself to the privy as if he had really just eaten the poison."

Merrik grinned, then grew quickly serious. "What do you wish to do, sire?"

Suddenly Rollo smiled. It wasn't a nice smile. It was filled with rage and intelligence and determination.

Merrik saw in him the immense strength of will and the unending ambition that had made him a man above men, that had led him into more battles than any man should survive, ah, but Rollo had not only survived, he'd conquered an entire land and was now its ruler. And, Merrik thought, he would rule until the gods determined his time had finally come to an end, then his son would rule, his grandson after him. He saw this, believed it, and prayed it would be true.

21

Rollo kept her close, always within his reach—his hand on her shoulder, lightly touching her face, squeezing her fingers. And he marveled at how she'd become a woman, of what she'd endured, how she'd survived, keeping both herself and Taby alive, how very proud her father, Hallad, would be . . . His thoughts stopped there, he always forced them to stop, for life continued, so many times in unexpected ways, and in this case he'd won, he'd changed damnable fate. He grasped Laren's wrist and frowned as he felt the still prominent bones.

They'd eaten in Rollo's private chambers, a sumptuous meal that made even Merrik sigh in contentment. Neither Otta nor Weland were present. Merrik had yet to meet Otta. "Laren is a good cook, sire, but I'm not certain if she could best this."

"The venison is beyond delicious," Laren said. "Nay, husband, I fear my skills do not exceed what you have already eaten by my hand." Her uncle was looking appalled, and she added quickly, "One of my owners, an old woman, taught me to cook. I learned well."

Rollo said slowly, "It is almost more than I can comprehend. My niece a slave. There is knowledge in your eyes, Laren, and sadness, but more than that I also see the happiness there brought to you by this man."

This man was looking at the two of them. He smiled. "I have tried, sire, to please her. Did you know she is a skald?"

Rollo stared at her in some amazement.

"Aye," Laren said. "It was my plan to gain silver from the telling of my stories, and buy Taby's and my freedom from Merrik. However, I had no idea how I would return to you even if Taby and I were free. There was Cleve, of course. He had to come with us."

"Cleve," Rollo repeated. "Tell me about this Cleve."

When Laren had finished, Rollo said, "Send him to me. I will see that he never wants again in his life."

"He is now free," Merrik said. "He told me that he wanted to stay in Norway."

Rollo frowned at that, for in his long experience any man offered a chance to come to him would have murdered his own brother to gain it. He said, "He doesn't know yet what I have to offer him."

"There is a woman, my lord," Laren said and Rollo sighed, throwing a meaty pheasant bone to one of the huge hunting dogs who were surprisingly calm and quiet.

Rollo said, as he took a handful of honeyed walnuts, "Tell me about the old woman who taught you to cook."

And she did, the story coming alive, for she was a spellbinder, and when she told of the old woman tasting her seasoned onions baked in honeyed maple leaves with peas, Merrik could nearly taste it himself, at this very moment.

Rollo would never have enough, Laren thought, as he said now, "Tell me about this merchant Thrasco who bought you."

She did, her voice curt now, and she left out the beating, but Merrik wouldn't allow it.

"He believed her a boy, sire," Merrik said, his voice

hard and rough. "He was going to give her to Khagan-Rus's sister, Evta, a woman who liked boys. Laren was frantic to get back to Taby and thus she spoke with insolence to him. He beat her quite savagely. Fortunately he did not discover she was a girl."

"But you saved me, Merrik," she said, seeing the red flush on her uncle's face, seeing the gnarled blood lines that veined his neck swell and pulse. She wouldn't ever want to be his enemy.

"Nay, not really. I merely caught you." He wanted Rollo to understand the horror she had endured, but he didn't want him so enraged he wouldn't listen to reason. He said now to Rollo, "She had managed to escape Thrasco's compound when I came along to rescue her. She'd already rescued herself. She is of your seed, sire, she would never give up."

Rollo laughed, thank the gods, he finally laughed, Laren thought.

"She is a woman to reckon with," Merrik said when Rollo had become still again.

Laren didn't stare at Merrik, though she wanted to. Did he really believe these wondrous things he was saying about her to her uncle? He'd never said naught about her being a woman to reckon with.

"She always was, even as a little mite," Rollo said. "I knew she could tell stories—but a skald! It is an amazing thing."

Their talk went on into the late hours. Rollo wanted every incident, every detail of the past two years. Finally, Weland was allowed into the chamber. He said, "Sire, we must speak of other things. By tomorrow, Helga and Ferlain will have heard about these guests and wonder about them. Even now there are scores of questions about the twenty Vikings who are now here and treated well by you. Aye, they're not stupid. And their husbands have men loyal to them, doubt it not, particularly Fromm. I know he pays dearly for his traitors."

Rollo was stroking his chin with his joint-swollen fingers. It was odd, but his joints didn't ache like the Christian hellfires this night. No, he felt renewed. He'd been given more than a man deserved. He knew it and marveled that either the Christian God or his Viking gods had granted him his greatest wish.

"Aye," he said finally. "We must talk."

"I have a plan, sire," Merrik said, leaning forward on his elbows.

Ferlain paced to and fro in front of her sister, Helga, but Helga paid her no heed She was mixing a potion and the measures had to be precise.

Ferlain said for the third time, "Who are these Vikings? There is also a girl with them, but none know who she is. Who is she, Helga? You must do something. Look at me! Ask your miserable smoke concoctions! Look into that silver bowl of yours."

Helga finished her measuring. Only then did she look up at her sister. Then she looked down again and began to gently stir the thin mixture in the small silver bowl. She said in her low, soft voice, "I can see why your husband avoids you so much, Ferlain. All you do is screech and whine, all to no account, and worry and fret. It is tiring. Sit down and hold your tongue behind your teeth. I must finish this or it will be ruined."

Ferlain, tired and worried, sat. They were in Helga's tower room where servants were forbidden to enter. None came in here save Ferlain, not even Helga's husband, Fromm. He didn't like it, either, always raged about it, but Helga held firm. He could do nothing. Indeed, Ferlain thought, staring at her sister's intent ex-

pression as she stirred one of her vile potions, he was
afraid of his wife, 'twas the only thing that stilled his
vicious bully's hand against her. She wondered what
the potion was.

Perhaps a poison for Rollo, damn the old man for continuing forever and ever. Why wouldn't he simply die?
He had lived fifty-six years, but still, despite his painful
joints, he appeared healthy as a stoat, his teeth strong,
his head covered with thick hair, his back straight.

No, it wasn't poison. It had to be a potion for Helga's
own use. Ferlain looked at her older sister and knew
that she looked much younger than she, Ferlain, did.
There were no wrinkles on her face, and her flesh was
soft and resilient. Her hair was rich and full, so light a
brown that it was nearly blond. And her waist hadn't
thickened over the years. She was nearly thirty-five
years old. Ferlain was twenty-nine and she looked old
enough to be Uncle Rollo's wife, not his niece.

Ferlain started to jump to her feet, to pace again, just
to move, but her sister looked over at her in that moment, and she stilled. Her fingers began violently pleat-
ing the folds of her skirt. She couldn't bear not to be
moving, to be doing something, ah, but it was difficult
now because she was so very fat. All those babes she'd
carried, and all of them dead, leaving her nothing save
the unsightly flesh that weighted her down and made
her ugly. "Are you finished yet, Helga?"

"Aye, I am." Helga straightened, eyed that damned
potion of hers that looked like nothing more than a light
broth, and smelled of nothing at all. "Now," she said,
picked up the potion and drank it down. She wiped her
hand across her mouth. A spasm of distaste distorted
her features, but just for an instant. Then she lightly
touched her fingertips to her throat, to her chin, and
finally to the soft delicate flesh beneath her eyes. Then

she said calmly, "All right, Ferlain, we have strangers visiting. Rollo and that fool Weland aren't telling anyone who they are. Even Otta is resolute in his silence. Is that correct?"

"Aye, who are they?"

Helga shrugged. "We will know soon enough. Why does it bother you?"

"I know it's her."

"Her? Who?"

"Laren, Helga. Don't pretend you don't know who I was talking about!"

"Laren," Helga repeated quietly. "Odd. I haven't thought of the child in a very long time. Do you really believe it possible that the girl survived? That she's actually returned? How very interesting that would be. But Taby wasn't with her, at least you've said naught about a child. He would only have six years now, aye, still a child, and you know how very fragile children are. A puff of a dark wind, and the child sickens and dies. Aye, such fragile creatures they are. So if it is indeed Laren, why do you care?"

"I hate you, Helga! You act so smart and so above all of us. I hate you! If it is Laren, she is back to brew more trouble for us, more trouble than you can concoct potions to counteract."

Helga smiled and shrugged. "Let her brew up all the mischief she can. We know naught of what happened to her. Calm yourself. You are looking even fatter, Ferlain. You must see to leaving off all those sweetmeats you keep next to your bed. And Cardle is so very thin, the poor man. His chest looks as if it's next to his backbone."

"Damn you, Helga, I have carried eight babes! A woman gains flesh when she carries a babe."

But Helga had no interest, for she had lived through

each of her sister's pregnancies, each of her failures.
She said, shrugging, "I do hope it is Laren, our long-
lost half sister. Such a quaint child she was, always
running wild until Taby was born and then she became
such the little mother to him, so much more so than her
own mother, the faithless bitch. I wonder what Laren
looks like now. She is eighteen now, or close to it. Aye,
what does she look like?"

"Will you do nothing?"

Helga stared through the narrow window that gave
onto the rolling hills behind the city. The land was rich
with summer though it was well into fall now. The hills
were still covered with trees and grass and blooming
daisies and dandelions. She forced herself to look at her
sister. It wasn't a pleasing sight, but she was her sister,
after all. "Naturally I will do something. We must now
just wait and see if this unknown girl is Laren. Then
we will see."

Laren wore a pale saffron linen gown, Ileria's favorite, she'd told Merrik, as she smoothed the material free
of wrinkles. A saffron ribbon threaded in and out of
three thin braids artfully pulled back from her forehead
and looped behind her ears. She wore two armlets, both
given to her just that morning by Rollo.

She looked like a princess, Merrik thought, and felt
a sharp pang in his belly. She looked as though she
belonged here. There was a new confidence in her walk,
in the way she spoke. For the first time since he'd carried her away with him from Kiev, he felt a lack in
himself. He hated it.

"Are you scared?"

"Aye," he said without pause, then realized she
couldn't have known what he'd been thinking. "Scared
about meeting your half sisters and their husbands?"

She nodded, then took his hand.

"You've told me so much about them that the fear of the unknown is long gone. No, not that. Other things bother me." He looked down at her hand, now held in one of his, adding quickly before she could question him, "You slept deeply last night."

She smiled up at him. "I didn't expect to. It was my old sleeping chamber. The men took Taby and me from that same bed. Nothing has changed."

She was silent, only her fingers closing and opening in his hand telling him that she was nervous. They were waiting behind Rollo's throne in a small chamber hidden from the huge outer hall by a long scarlet hanging.

They could hear men's and women's voices, the curiosity, the questions, the speculation.

"I've never before seen such richness," Merrik said. Again, he felt that curious lack, and immediately felt disgusted with himself.

She nodded, distracted.

He smiled, shaking his head. She'd been a slave, then his wife, and now she was returned to her opulent beginnings. But it didn't seem to matter one whit to her.

They stilled. Rollo spoke in a rolling deep voice that brought everyone to immediate and instant silence.

"I asked you here to announce the return of my niece Laren, daughter of my older brother Hallad of Eldjarn."

There was pandemonium, then the scarlet drapery was pulled aside and they stepped forward to stand beside Rollo.

Then voices were saying, "It is Laren, just look at that red hair!"

"She's a woman now. How old was she when she disappeared?"

"Nay, 'tis a girl who just looks like Laren, she isn't here. Laren is long dead. Whoever took her killed her."

"Aye, 'twas the earl of Orkney, the vicious sod, who took her and Taby."

Rollo held up his hand. "My niece. Welcome her."

Laren looked out over the assembly of people, most of whom she'd known all her life, and said, "I am home again. I see you there, Mimeric, do you still play the lute like one of the Christian angels? And you, Dorsun, do you still shoot your bow as far as before? I remember you nicked the wing of a bird some four years ago, and the bird was in flight. Ah, and Edell, you have gained flesh, my old friend. I remember that you liked overmuch the honeyed bread the cooks gave you when no one was looking. All you had to do was smile at them, and they gave you whatever you wanted."

She paused then and waited. Merrik watched the people's faces change from disbelief to uncertainty to astonishment. There was a deep rumble then bursting calls of "Laren! Laren!"

Rollo allowed the fiftysome people to continue in their calling and yelling for some more minutes. Then he raised his hand. The hall was instantly silent again.

"My nephew Taby is not here. He was but a babe when he was abducted and all know that a babe, even well tended and protected, cannot always survive. But do not fall into grief. There has been too much pain already." Rollo turned to Merrik, and drew him forward. "This is Laren's husband, Merrik Haraldsson of Norway, cousin to King Harald Fairhair. I have known of him now for some time. Now he is here, for I bade him come and take his place."

Merrik grinned down at her, saying quietly, "I am a distant cousin, 'tis not all fabrication. Of course, many in Norway are distant cousins to just about everyone else."

"Here is the man who will rule if my son William

Longsword dies before he produces an heir. Welcome Merrik Haraldsson!"

It was baldly said, no easing into it, no smooth explanation or justification, just Rollo booming out his announcement in his smooth deep voice. Even Laren sucked in her breath, and she'd known what he was going to do. The shock was clear on every face in the huge outer hall.

"Good," Merrik said to her with relish. "Now I am the one who is the threat, not you."

"I don't like this," she said again, and not for the first time since the preceding evening when Merrik had given his plan to Rollo. "It is not your place, Merrik, to throw yourself into such danger. Look at everyone. They don't know what to do. It is a shock beyond what they've ever known. Where are Helga and Ferlain?"

She'd argued with him endlessly and he'd listened and nodded, but never wavered. Now he only smiled at her, still staring out at all the faces staring back at him in blank consternation. "They will show themselves in due course. As for the others, I will play the valiant hero, and show them as much ruthlessness as they are used to seeing in Rollo, and show them that I seethe with honor, so much honor that I can barely hold up my head with the surfeit. Perhaps Rollo will come to admire me so very much, he will beg me to remain in Normandy and rule beside him, then beside William. What do you think?"

"I think you are mad."

"Mad, am I? Do you not believe I can be an heir to Normandy to everyone's satisfaction? Do you not believe me skilled enough to persuade all the people to believe in me?"

"Aye, you know that you can. In that, you are mad."

"Will this madness continue in our children, do you think?"

She stared up at him, for the moment, all else forgotten. "I don't know of such things," she said.

"You have not had your woman's bleeding since I first came to you."

She turned as pale as the white of her undershift.

At that moment, Rollo, smiling, turned to Merrik and held out his hand. "My lord Merrik, come forward, and greet my people. Perhaps they will be yours someday."

At that moment, Laren swayed, her eyes bewildered and wide on her husband's face, even as she said, "I am not well." He caught her and lifted her into his arms.

There was again pandemonium, and Rollo, scared to his toes, leapt to his feet and shouted, "By the gods, what is wrong with her?"

Merrik said loudly, "She has but fainted, sire. She isn't ill. She is carrying my heir." He lifted her high in his arms and his voice rang out deep and strong in the huge chamber, "Aye, she carries the son who just might rule Normandy one day."

Helga said quietly to her sister, the wide smile on her face never slipping, "Perhaps she will not carry anything for very long. Perhaps she is like you, Ferlain, and her womb is diseased."

"She has our father's hair—a girl shouldn't have hair that color, 'tis sinful, all that miserable red."

"Our father looked very handsome in his red hair," Helga said. "A pity he killed that faithless wife of his and ran away. But then I have always wondered if he did kill her. She died so quickly, you know, and there didn't seem to be violence. Aye, such a pity that our father believed he would be blamed and disappeared. More a pity that the bitch gave birth to Laren and Taby before she succumbed."

Ferlain felt the cold of the grave, a cold so profound that it numbed the body and the mind. She thought of her eight dead babes, aye, they were in cold graves, every one of them, naught but scattered tiny bones now. She stared at her sister, who had now turned and was saying to her husband, Fromm, "So, husband, what do you think of this Merrik Haraldsson?"

Fromm puffed out his chest, a habit he'd learned from Otta, only when Fromm did it, it was annoying. He said, "It is obvious he is cunning. He has taken advantage of Rollo's advancing years, showing Rollo only what the old man wants to see, saying only what he wants to hear, doing only—"

"Aye, I know," Helga said, not bothering to hide her irritation. "I think him handsome. He wears his youth splendidly, does he not?"

"Do not give me your smooth spite, Helga." Fromm turned from her to his brother-in-law. "Cardle, I will speak to you once Rollo dismisses us."

Helga laughed now, overhearing her husband speak to Cardle. By all the gods, why would he want to speak to that pitiful fool? Ask his advice on how to kill Merrik? Laren?

Helga turned to listen yet again to Rollo as he calmed the crowd and spoke of the Viking's character and his honor, of the advantages they would gain allied to the king of Norway. Rollo did not mention that it had been that same king who had outlawed him some years before. Merrik had carried the still-unconscious Laren through the thick draperies behind Rollo's throne. Helga didn't listen to Rollo, it was all nonsense in any case. She listened to the questions put to Rollo from high-ranking families, but she was picturing the Viking in her mind. He was a beautiful man.

Was she not a beautiful woman?

Was his wife not pregnant, fainting like a weakling and probably vomiting up her guts in front of him? Laren was also still too thin, scarcely looking like a female, save for the red hair in those stingy braids. Surely no man could willingly wish to bed such a stick as she was. Surely she had not the skills to please such a man as this Merrik Haraldsson.

Why, Helga wondered, listening to that ass, Weland, respond to Raki, a man of little intellect and great strength, nearly as great as Weland's, hadn't Rollo told them what had happened to Laren? She herself was very interested. She wanted to know how this Merrik had met Laren. Had he killed Taby once he'd learned who they were, guessing that he could take the child's place in Rollo's plans?

She looked back at Rollo, seeing him as a man, not just as her uncle. He was still handsome, still more forceful and stubborn as a pig, but he was old, so very many years sitting on his still-broad shoulders, too many years. She wondered idly what she would do.

22

MERRIK HELD HER head as she vomited into the basin. She was shuddering with the effort, her skin clammy and cold. She'd eaten little that morning because she'd been so nervous, and now she was heaving and jerking, but there was naught left in her belly save the twisting, grinding cramps.

"I shouldn't have told you," he said as he pulled her sweat-damp hair from her face. "You were feeling well in your ignorance."

"Aye," she said. "I would bless both you and my ignorance if only it would return."

He gave her a mug of ale. She washed out her mouth, moaned and clutched her stomach again, then, to his relief, eased. "I don't like this," she said, looking at him with less than adoration. "You did this to me."

"Aye, it is a man's duty," he said, grinning at her. "Come." He lifted her to her feet and then into his arms. He carried her to the wide box bed and laid her down. He straightened the beautiful gown Ileria had made for her, not wanting to wrinkle it overly. He sat beside her, wishing indeed that he'd kept his mouth shut. How could her suddenly knowing she was carrying his babe make her ill? It seemed incomprehensible to him, yet she'd turned white and fainted dead away, in front of all Rollo's people.

If he could have planned it, it couldn't have been done better.

She opened her eyes as he covered her with a woolen blanket. "I don't like you at this moment, Merrik."

He leaned down and kissed her nose.

"How do you know so much about babes and such?"

"When a man can take a woman for weeks without having to stop, she is either too exhausted to say him nay, or pregnant with his babe."

She sent her fist into his arm. He grabbed her fist, smoothed out her hand, and kissed her palm. "Thank you, Laren, for my child."

"It is my child."

"It is my seed and without my seed there would be no child."

"I take your seed and nurture it into life. Without me there would be no child."

He smiled at her. "You are right."

"You're just saying that because I feel so wretched."

"Aye. Get well again so that I can argue freely with you and not suffer guilt."

She said suddenly, sitting up, "I feel fine now. Isn't that odd?"

She fell silent, queried her body, then said, "Aye, 'tis true, there is no more faintness, no more illness. My belly is happy."

"I hope it stays happier than poor Otta's." He pulled her into his arms, and held her, kissing her ear, smoothing the tangles from her hair with his fingers, pressing her cheek against his shoulder. "All will be well, you will see. Trust me in what I am doing."

"I don't like it," she said again. "You are now in danger, Merrik. I cannot like that."

"You can protect me when you're not on your knees with your face in a bucket."

She chuckled and it made him feel immensely relieved. He was kissing her when Rollo came running into the sleeping chamber. He was so tall he had to bend to get through the doorway without hitting his head.

"Is she all right?"

Laren looked over Merrik's shoulder. "I am fine, uncle. I am sorry for disturbing your announcement."

"Nay, don't be. I am more than pleased." He paused a moment, then said easily, "Your half sisters tell me they're concerned about you. Ha! Helga fears you might be cursed with Ferlain's womb. They wish to see you, they claim, both of them more serious than the Christian nuns, to welcome you home again."

"That is very kind of them," Laren said. "I will see them shortly."

"Aye," Merrik said, "I wish to meet them as well."

Helga looked about Laren's small sleeping chamber, the same one she'd slept in all her life. She hoped Laren had nightmares. She smiled at her half sister, thinking she looked pitiful and so very pale. It was afternoon and yet she'd vomited again. Poor Laren, she looked close to death. So very close. Carrying a babe was a dangerous thing, all knew that. A woman's life was so fragile, more so than a man's, curse the sods. Yet Ferlain continued to flourish after carrying eight babes. Helga wondered if her sister would carry yet another babe.

She smiled as she walked to the box bed and held out her hands. "Laren, it is really you. Even seeing you in the great hall I couldn't be certain, for I was so anxious that it be you, but I couldn't trust myself. You look lovely, dearest. Welcome home."

"Thank you, Helga. Ah, here is Ferlain. Hello, sister."

Ferlain couldn't bring herself to smile. Unlike Helga, she saw a very slender girl with magnificent red hair and a complexion that only youth occasionally granted, brilliant blue-gray eyes, and even white teeth. She hated the girl. She felt very old, and she was Laren's half sister, not her damned mother. It galled her. She said, only a slight tremor in her voice, "I have missed you, Laren. A pity that Taby had to die so that you could survive."

Merrik arched a dark blond eyebrow. "You sound as though Laren left Taby in a ditch somewhere so that she could have a better chance to live."

"Did I? Surely I couldn't mean that. Helga, I didn't say that, did I?"

Helga gave a small laugh and moved a step closer to Merrik. He was tall, this Viking, and he smelled delicious, a man smell that was uniquely his, a scent both dark and musky that made her want to touch her fingertips to his mouth, to his shoulders, to the thick hair at his groin. "No, Ferlain," she said, abstracted by him, "you love Laren, as do I. Naturally, she wouldn't kill Taby to save herself."

Laren could but stare at the two of them. Odd, but Helga seemed to look younger than she had two years ago. Ferlain looked older, petulant, downward lines about her mouth, streaks of gray in her once rich brown hair. She was fat.

She felt Merrik stiffening beside her, but just smiled. "No, of course, neither of you would ever think I would not guard Taby with my life. Merrik, would you like to pour some of the sweet wine for Ferlain and Helga?"

He nodded, and walked to the low table that was near the doorway. He poured the wine into ivory goblets, beautifully made those goblets, like none he'd ever seen before. And the heels of his boots thudded on the wooden floor. He was used to pounded earth floors, as were most normal humans. This was noisome and he didn't like it. If he had no boots on he would have splinters in his feet. He gave each of the women a goblet of wine.

He felt the heat of Helga's flesh when she took the goblet from him, and there was that same heat in her eyes, dark eyes, deep and mysterious.

"Where are your husbands?" he said, his eyes mirroring the same hunger in hers. He didn't look away from her even as he slowly walked back to stand beside Laren.

Helga gave him a long, slow smile, nodding slightly as if she recognized and accepted what had happened between them, and said, "Fromm is doubtless practicing with his sword. He is a very strong man, you know—"

"He is a bully," Ferlain said, took a large gulp of her wine and fell into spasms of coughing.

"Aye, he is," Helga agreed easily. She looked over at Laren. "So you carry Merrik's child. It seems you are as fertile as your poor mother was. Such a pity that she died so soon after Taby was born."

Laren couldn't remember her mother's face, but oddly, she could remember her singing, her voice firm and strong and off-key. And her father had strangled her, all had seen the imprint of his fingers around her neck. She nodded, then said quickly, "Uncle Rollo spoke of how everyone believed it was his blood family from the Orkneys responsible for Taby's and my abduction. What do you think, Helga?"

"What I think," Helga said slowly as she sipped her wine, her eyes on Merrik, "is that whoever it was felt some mercy. After all, you did survive, Laren."

"Aye, I often wondered why Taby and I were spared.

I never thought it an act of mercy though. Nay, I believed the person responsible wanted both Taby and me to die slowly, to suffer, for what reason I don't know."

Ferlain said, "I always believed it was your father, come back to take you and Taby away. He knew he would be put to death if he remained after murdering your mother, and thus he went away until he could capture you and Taby."

"*Our* father," Laren said flatly. "And it wasn't Hallad. I cannot believe that you would think that, much less say it."

"I do wonder what happened to him," Helga said. "He was never the warrior Uncle Rollo was, but he was a nice man, a good father until he married your mother. Doubtless he was killed by outlaws. But enough of that. It is long in the past. You are home now, and you have brought the man who will be one of Rollo's heirs. I wonder what the Frank King Charles will make of all this. A man who is a stranger, becoming a possible heir to the duchy of Normandy."

"I will go pay homage to the king," Merrik said. "Aye, and he will bless our union, doubt it not. But not just yet." He rubbed his hands together then, and there was an opulent pleasure in his eyes, and unmasked greed, but just for the barest moment, not longer.

Helga said slowly, her eyes never leaving his face, "Ferlain and I will leave you now, Laren. We will dine with you this evening, if you are not vomiting again."

Laren silently watched her two half sisters leave her sleeping chamber. She leaned her head back and closed her eyes. "You are most convincing, Merrik."

"Aye," he said and chuckled. "Most convincing. Helga believes herself irrestible and I showed her not only my interest in her but also my boundless greed. It should prove interesting. Now we will wait and see."

"Helga is smart though, I do remember that. You will be careful, husband."

That night after a feast that lasted until well after the dark hour of midnight, Merrik left the palace, for he'd been given a message from Oleg, spoken softly into his ear by a small boy. He walked beneath an archway and called out, "Oleg, it is I, Merrik. What goes?"

There was no answer, nothing. He heard people speaking, but from a distance, not near here where the boy had told him to meet Oleg. The guards were some distance away. He could hear them wagering on the throw of the dice. He smiled into the still shadows around him. He prepared to wait. He looked relaxed, ill-prepared, mayhap even drunk, but he was not. He began to whistle, a man with no cares to bow his shoulders, a man to whom the world had been freely given.

When the attack came, Merrik dropped gracefully to the ground and rolled. He came up, leaping backward even as he came down solidly on his booted feet.

There were two of them, big men, garbed in coarse bearskins, their faces covered with thick beards, heavy silver bands around their upper arms. He saw the intent in their eyes even in the dim light given off by the distant rush torches and the sliver of moon overhead.

They both had curved knives like the ones Merrik had seen in Kiev, used by the Arabs, sharp knives, the silver gleaming.

He drew his own knife and tossed it from his right hand to his left then back again, his rhythm steady. His legs were planted firmly, spread. He smiled at the men.

They were coming toward him, splitting up now, and they were more silent than starving wolves in the middle of winter, stalking their prey.

He laughed aloud and called out, "You are slow and I grow weary of waiting for you to prove your prowess.

Have you any skill, I wonder. You look like savages to me, naught more than slaves released just this night to kill me. You, there on my left, hopping about like a virgin maid on her marriage night, what will you do? Sing me a song? Play the lute for your friend here to chant me a story? You puking coward, come on, cease your dancing!"

The man howled, and rushed at Merrik, the other one just an instant behind in his lunge, but it was enough, and Merrik knew it was enough. He struck the big man's throat with the flat of his hand, then spun him about. He looked at his face as he eased his knife into his chest. The man dropped without a sound, but Merrik didn't see him, for the other man was on him, and this one was smarter, perhaps, for he wasn't rushing in so quickly.

"I'll see your guts in the dirt," he said, and leapt, his balance keen, his eyes on Merrik's eyes and the knife that still Merrik gently tossed back and forth from left hand to right hand, taunting.

Merrik took two quick sideways steps and slashed out with his knife. The other man jumped backward, the tip of Merrik's knife only slicing through the outer bearskin he wore.

He looked down at the clean knife-cut through the skin, then back up at Merrik. "You'll not gut me, you bastard. I'll kick your guts out of your belly and grind them into the dirt for cutting my bearskin."

Merrik didn't like the image of that. He skipped sideways until he was standing just behind the fallen body of this man's friend. Slowly, he kicked the man's ribs, pushing him forward. Then he spat on his body.

It was enough. The man roared as he leapt forward, screaming curses at Merrik, screaming what he would do to him with his knife. He was fierce and he became a fool only for a moment. When Merrik's knife came up underhand to his belly, he jerked his entire chest inward, nearly bowing his body. He did a complete turn, then brought down his knife in a swift arc, slicing Merrik's arm.

Merrik felt the sudden cold of his split flesh, then the blessed numbness that followed. The man wasn't as careless as his friend had been. He felt the warmth of his own blood, knew the bleeding wouldn't stop, and in that, he knew he would win. He made a pained sound and staggered, his head down, grabbing his wounded arm in his other hand.

The man rushed in, his knife raised. When Merrik could breathe in the man's rancid smell, he smashed his bloody arm into his face, rubbing his eyes, the thick warm blood momentarily blinding the man.

The man tried to turn, tried to escape, but Merrik now wrapped his good arm around his throat and spun him about. He pressed until he knew the man could scarcely breathe.

"Who is your master?"

"I have no master. Kill me. I have failed."

"Aye, you have. Tell me your master and I will let you live."

Merrik lightly touched his knife tip to the man's throat. Gently, he shoved the tip inward. "Tell me," he said.

"It is Rollo, aye, the great Rollo. He wants you dead."

Merrik was so startled that he loosed his grip. The man lurched forward, ripping himself free. He staggered and ran full tilt into the darkness.

Merrik let him go. He stood there, clutching his arm to his chest, panting. He wanted to chase the man down but he doubted he could catch him anyway. He would probably fall flat on his face. His arm was no longer numb. It was on fire, the pain making him grit his teeth. He ripped off the end of his tunic and wrapped it around the gushing wound.

Oleg was impatiently pacing the length of the sleeping chamber. When Merrik entered, he said quickly, "Don't worry. Laren is with Rollo and her sisters, telling them a story. Helga and Ferlain didn't want to hear it, but Uncle Rollo gave them no choice."

"She's not here then," Merrik said. "Good."

It was then that Oleg saw his arm. "By all the gods, Merrik, you bleed like a stoat! I should have gone with you, dammit! I shouldn't have listened to you."

Merrik just smiled wearily at him, not bothering to interrupt his cursing. He unwrapped the wound on his arm and stared down it. It was bleeding only sluggishly, but he knew it needed stitching.

"Get Old Firren. Tell him to bring his needle and some thread."

Not long after Oleg had helped Merrik to sit on the edge of the box bed, Old Firren walked into the sleeping chamber, looked around at the opulent hangings, grunted, and started to spit in the corner. He looked disgusted, saying, "I can't spit, Merrik. It will sit on the damned wood like a spot on a woman's face. I don't like all this—it makes a man feel as if he's walking on live coals. What did you do? Cut yourself, that's what Oleg said, the lying sod. Give me your arm and let me see how bad it is."

Old Firren studied the arm, pinched the flesh, ignoring Merrik's pallor, and said, "The knife was very sharp, nice and clean the slice. Hurts, huh?"

"I'll kill you, old man, if you don't shut your mouth and get on with it."

Laren came in, yawning. Old Firren had finished, and was now studying his long row of stitches. She looked at her husband lying on his back, his arm extended, all the blood-covered rags on the floor, and said, "I will surely kill you for not calling for me."

"It isn't bad, mistress," Old Firren said quickly. "You were telling a fine tale. Oleg didn't want to interrupt you, for surely your uncle wouldn't have been pleased. He loses himself in your stories, Merrik says, believes himself young and strong again. Don't worry about your husband. Merrik will survive, he always does. He's a hardly lad."

"I will kill him and you and Oleg," she said.

She walked slowly to stand staring down at Merrik. "I am your wife. It is my responsibility to stitch your wounds."

"You would use a different color thread?" Merrik said, trying very hard to make her smile.

She placed her palm on his forehead. His flesh was cool and dry. She said to Old Firren, "Leave Oleg to guard the door. You remove all this blood and yourself."

"Aye, mistress," Old Firren said, carefully spat into the basin of bloody water, grinned at Merrik, and shuffled out of the chamber.

"What story did you tell everyone?"

"Don't try to distract me, Merrik. You got yourself attacked, didn't you? You had a plan, I knew it from the way you were acting—all nonchalant, laughing overmuch, looking at me as if touching me would make me vomit. I won't have it, Merrik. I told them a story about a high lord of Egypt who sold his wife into slavery to an Arab trader from the Bulgar. He had a dozen other wives, you see, so one wouldn't be much of a loss to him, and he needed the silver she would bring him. Now, I will ask Helga to give you a potion so that you won't sicken. Perhaps she has something for the pain as well."

He just stared at her, his expression bemused, saying nothing as she walked from the chamber.

He awoke to see Helga sitting beside him. She was staring at him, her eyes hot. He wanted to tell her that she was the last woman on earth he would willingly touch, but caught himself in time. He tried to smile at her, an effort he hoped she appreciated.

"You are awake," she said, and touched her fingertips to his face, caressing his cheek, his jaw. "I have looked at your arm. It is clean. I have made a potion for you. Here, let me help you."

He drank slowly until all the potion was gone. It tasted sweet, and that surprised him.

"In a few moments you will feel no more pain."

"Where is Laren?"

"The poor child is with Rollo. He can't seem to let her out of his sight, the silly old man. You will rule shortly, Lord Merrik, doubt it not. Is there more pain?"

He shook his head. "What did you give me?"

She shrugged, her hand now stroking over his throat. "Ah, a bit of sweet basil, some barley water, hemlock—"

He sucked in his breath, and she added easily, "Just a bit on the end of my finger. Scarce enough to kill a fly, but not a man like you, Merrik. Other things whose names you don't know. Ah, and a dollop of honey to make it taste good."

"I feel no pain now," he said, and was surprised.

"Good," she said and leaned over him. She kissed him, her mouth soft, her breath sweet and warm. He felt her tongue gently pressing against his closed mouth, and he allowed her entrance. He responded to her, knowing there was no choice really.

The man had said that Rollo had wanted him dead.

He brought up his good arm and pulled her closer. Her breasts were full and very soft against his chest.

Why would Rollo want him dead? Surely the man lied. Aye, he lied, and Merrik was back to having nothing, and thus he continued kissing Helga, letting her do as she wished with him. When her hand smoothed down his belly to touch him, he stayed her hand. "Nay, my wife. I know not where she is. She is Rollo's niece. I am her husband and one of Rollo's heirs. Is it true that William Longsword is a paltry young man?"

"I have always believed so, but then I also believed that Laren and Taby were dead. I have been wrong about many things. If William has his father's wretched longevity, why then, he won't die until the next century."

She kissed him again, her tongue warm and searching in his mouth.

When she finally raised her head, he said, "You must leave me now, Helga. There will be another time."

She smiled at him, kissed him lightly once more, and rose to stand beside the box bed. "You will be fine, Lord Merrik. Whoever tried to kill you wasn't good enough."

Suddenly he saw coldness in her eyes where there had been such heat but a moment before. The coldness was stark and hard and real, but gone so quickly he wasn't certain that he hadn't imagined it. He said nothing.

She smiled again, and left him, saying over her shoulder, "It is very late. I will come back to you tomorrow."

It was near to dawn when Weland came to their sleeping chamber. Merrik was awake, thinking, Laren asleep, pressed against his bare shoulder. He felt very little pain and blessed Helga for her medicinal skills if for nothing else.

"My lord," Weland said quietly.

"Aye, what is it? Rollo is all right?"

"It is Fromm, Helga's husband. He is dead."

23

IT WAS JUST past dawn. Rollo was still in his huge bed, piled high with reindeer furs from Norway, golden fox furs from the Danelaw, and thick white miniver from the Bulgar. Otta stood back, watching Rollo shake his head, yawn deeply, then turn his dark eyes on his face. Weland said then, "Fromm was afoot in Rouen with some of his drunken friends. I'm sorry, sire, but he's dead. There was a fight—"

"There are always fights," Rollo said, rubbing at the swelled joints of his fingers. Even at this early hour he knew it would rain, for the air was heavy and thick, making his joints swell, and he was already suffering from it, the moment he awoke, he suffered. By all the gods, he hated the betrayal of his body, but then again, he was still strong, he still had all his teeth and all his wits. What was a bit of pain in his joints?

He sighed, then thought, so, that bully Fromm is dead. He was much younger than I yet he is dead and I'm not. Will anyone care? Certainly not Helga. He'd made a mistake with Fromm, he'd acknowledged to himself long ago. The man had been a miserable son-in-law, giving nothing, preening and strutting about because he was now kin to the great Rollo of Normandy. He'd not even given Helga any children, but perhaps that wasn't his fault. Rollo said to Otta, his voice emotionless, "Fights over women, over honor, over nothing worth anything. Why would Fromm die in this one? Did he not attack men smaller than he? If he didn't, he was more careless than usual."

"Nay, sire, there were many men smaller than Fromm, but none of them were hurt. Nonetheless, somehow, he was killed, stabbed through the throat, he was. We will bury him tomorrow if you wish it. I recommend it. We don't want his spirit to hover here. His would be a malignant ghost."

Rollo gave his minister an ironic grin. "You forget that you are now a Christian, Otta?"

Otta actually paled, his hands went to his belly, and Rollo laughed. "Aye, we're all Christians, but we'll pray that damned Christian God understands our heathen ways for a while longer. Aye, we'll bury Fromm on the morrow. I wish Weland to question all these small men who were in the fight and managed to come out of it unscathed."

He paused when Merrik and Laren came into his sleeping chamber.

"Sire," Merrik said. "We came quickly. Weland told us about Fromm's death."

Rollo stared at Merrik's arm, bound in soft white linen. "I find it odd. Do you not find it odd, Otta? Both Merrik and Fromm were attacked. You were the lucky one, Merrik."

"Nay, he is simply a better fighter, uncle."

"You are his wife and women are a fickle lot. Naturally you would believe so, at least now, at the beginning."

Laren was startled by the testiness of his voice. Rollo looked old this morning, smaller somehow, burrowed down in all the furs that were piled high on the bed.

His skin was deeply seamed, the veins bulging in his throat above the rich woolen bed tunic he wore. His hair was tousled, making him look faintly ridiculous. He sounded and acted like an old man with an old man's rheums and querulousness. Ah, but it was his joints that pained him, made him peevish, all the rest of it wasn't real, it couldn't be.

She said carefully, despising herself for her unkind thoughts, "What will you do, uncle?"

"I will bury the damnable bully and find Helga another husband. She is looking quite fit for a woman of her years. Aye, another husband it is to be."

"A man wants children. She is too old to bear children, sire," Otta said.

"Aye, I am convinced that she never birthed a child because of her wicked potions. Ah, and poor Ferlain, birthing eight dead babes, none of them coming from her womb breathing. And my seed now as cold and dead as all of Ferlain's babes. But no matter. I have William and the son his wife will doubtless birth. And I have Merrik and Laren. The man who takes Helga will be richer than he is now. Who knows, mayhap he will breach her potions and plant a babe in her womb."

"One hears that she is distraught," Otta said and plucked at his sleeve, his pale gray eyes on the spot of porridge spilled there just an hour before. He frowned at it. He disliked looking unkempt. His belly was always cramping and burning and forcing him to run many times to the privy. At least he could look flawless on the outside.

Rollo said, his voice peevish, "Aye, one hears many things. Leave me now, all of you save Laren. I wish you to tell me the rest of the story. You left Analea in the hands of that king in Bulgar."

Laren smiled toward her husband, and said, "Aye, uncle, I will tell you the rest of the story."

She was sick again, pale and sweaty, and she hated it. She rose slowly to her feet, stared down at the basin, and felt her belly knot and cramp again. She eased down on the box bed and tried to relax. The cramps continued. She tried to breathe through her mouth, slow, shallow breaths, and it helped.

Her old nurse, Risa, bent, thin, and quarrelsome, came into the sleeping chamber, clucked over her, thankfully said nothing, and took away the basin.

Laren slept. When she awoke it was nearly dark. The sleeping chamber was cast into deep shadows, and the stillness was oddly frightening. Suddenly there was no comfort here. This was a place of violence, a place of fear. The sleeping chamber was again as it was two years before.

She raised herself on her elbows, calling out quietly, her voice raw as a cold night, "Is anyone here? Merrik?"

There were whispers of sounds, surely there was something she heard, but no, there was only stillness and it seemed to grow, and with it the shadows, the encroaching darkness. She swallowed, but her throat was dry and it hurt. Then she heard it. A small noise, of little account really, but it was over there, in the far corner of the chamber, a noise that was like a wounded animal.

She held herself very still.

It came again, only closer this time. She wanted to cry out, but there was only dryness and pain in her throat. "Merrik," she said, and wondered if his name was only in her mind for surely there had been no sound from her mouth.

"Who is there?"

She swung her legs over the side of the bed, felt her

belly knot and churn, and bowed her head, trying to keep from vomiting. Where was Risa? Why was she alone?

But she wasn't alone. There was that sound again, so very soft, yet distinct, unlike any sound she'd ever heard.

"Who is there?"

It was different now, a rustling sound, no longer soft, no longer muted, and it was close. She looked toward the doorway. It seemed far beyond her, that doorway, the only way to escape this chamber and what was in this chamber and growing closer to her. When something touched her shoulder, she screamed, whirling about to see Ferlain beside her, her face as pale yet as distinct as a cold winter moon framed by utter darkness.

"How very strange you are, Laren. Why are you shaking? 'Twas you who startled me."

There was black amusement in her voice. Laren tried to calm herself. It was but Ferlain, fat and slow Ferlain who whined and carped, but who was harmless, certainly no one to fear.

"You frightened me. Why is the chamber dark?"

"I don't know. It was dark when I came in. I am only here to visit you. How do you feel?"

"Let us light a lamp."

"Very well." Ferlain held the oil-soaked wick next to a burning coal in the brazier near the box bed. Soon it burst into a small flame.

"I prefer the darkness, you know," Ferlain said, staring at the flame. "But you don't, do you? When I was your age I didn't like the darkness either, but things change, you know. Always change, always grief and sorrow. But enough of that. Now you can see everything. Nothing is the matter, is it?"

Ferlain, such a common sight, comforting, the gray
streaks of hair, the fat smooth hands. Surely there was
nothing frightening about Ferlain. Laren said, "No, not
really. I suppose when I wake up suddenly I remember
that horrible night two years ago when the men came
and took Taby and me."

"Aye, that would be frightening. Helga is right. It was
an act of mercy that you weren't killed. Well, Taby died,
didn't he, but not you. No, you are safe and pregnant
with that Viking's babe and everything will be yours, if
you survive the birth, that is. If your babe survives. I
know that many babes never survive, Laren. Many
babes are dead before they know life. My babes all died,
you know." Ferlain looked at the gleaming hot coals in
the brazier, then back at her half sister. "Only it is not
the same as it was before. You were to wed the prince
of the Danelaw but you didn't. He wed a Danish princess. Of course he would have taken you away from
here, wouldn't he? He would have made you live in the
Danelaw. We hear that there is trouble there now, that
soon the Danelaw will fall to the Saxons. The Wessex
king is strong and growing stronger. Soon there will be
no more Viking kings and the Danelaw will be ruled by
Saxons again. The prince and his wife will lose everything. Mayhap you should have stayed away, Laren."

"I couldn't. Were you the one who hired the men to
take us away, Ferlain?"

"I? My dear girl, why ever would I do that?" She
laughed then, a fat merry laugh, but somehow it wasn't
funny, that laugh. Laren wished desperately for Merrik, for Risa, for anyone.

"I don't know. I wish to leave the chamber now."

"Oh, not just yet, Laren, not just yet. I wanted to
speak to you, to warn you." She leaned close, her heavy
fingers closing about Laren's upper arm. "Listen to me,

Laren, for I have your best interests at heart. It is Rollo who is your enemy. He is old and bitter and he hates all of us, including you, including that Viking husband of yours. He hated Taby most of all because he was of Hallad's seed and not his. He sired but one male and one female whilst Hallad's seed was wild in its potency. Aye, Rollo hated his own brother. Did you know that he wanted your mother? Aye, 'tis true, and Hallad discovered that she, the faithless bitch, wanted to be the duchess of Normandy. Thus she wanted our father dead. She wanted Rollo. Did our father kill her? It seems very likely, does it not? Our father did run away, disappeared. But beware of Rollo. He is quite mad and he became madder still after she died and our father left. Aye, Laren, you should leave too."

Laren stared up at her, felt her belly heave, and ran for the basin. She heard Ferlain laughing behind her as she retched and retched.

Fromm was buried with many of his favored belongings in a deep mossy grave on a hillside overlooking the Seine. His old slave was killed and laid beside him, his arms crossed over his chest, a rough wooden cross in his hands, a token sop to the Christian God, Rollo said. All of Fromm's weapons, his clothing, and his prized chair posts were wrapped carefully and placed into the grave with him.

Helga was a magnificent widow, tall and beautiful, her face set and still, aye, a tragic brave figure. Fromm was buried quickly, despite the Christian tenets, for the Vikings believed deeply in the return of the corpse's spirit as a ghost, a monster, who would bedevil them. And Fromm hadn't been a good man when alive. What could his spirit be upon his death but a malicious ghost?

"It is over," Rollo said, and turned away from the

heavy mound that held no marker, no adornment, as was again the Viking way. When grass covered it once again, no stranger would know that it covered a body and riches. There would be a marker, but it would be placed near to the palace, where people would see it and know of all Fromm's good works and bravery.

Rollo looked at Helga and Ferlain, then at Laren who stood close to Merrik. "I dreamed of Hallad last night," he said. "I dreamed he came back and that he was angry at me. He wasn't old, but as young and strong a man as I once was. Odd, but he even looked like me, and that isn't right, for Hallad was very different from me, you remember that, don't you, Helga? He wasn't strong or fierce. And his hair was that damnable red, and thicker than a mink's pelt. Ah, but the women loved Hallad, all of them, even those—"

Rollo looked down at his fingers. He began to rub the joints. Weland said quietly, "Sire, it is time to return to the palace. There is a man, a blacksmith by trade, who has asked to see you. It seems he knows about Fromm and the fight. I questioned the other men and none admit to any knowledge, just the violence and it was over quickly and Fromm was dead, nothing more than that, they all swear to it."

Rollo nodded and followed his lieutenant. He said over his shoulder, "My sweet Laren, you and Merrik will dine with me, just you two. I would speak to Merrik about King Charles and his sly ministers, pigs all of them, so William tells me. Merrik must know all of this before he travels to Paris to meet William and the Frankish king. Otta knows many of them for he has spent much time in King Charles's court in Paris."

Merrik smiled down at his wife. "How do you feel, sweeting?"

She listened inward for a moment, then laced her fingers through his. "Your babe is sleeping, thank the gods."

"I spoke to Helga. She said that this illness will not last many more weeks. She said the sicker you are now, the more the signs say that you will birth a boy. But I care not, Laren. I just want you smiling again, or yelling. Then I can argue with you without worry or guilt, and you can shout at me and insult me."

"Aye, that I would like, for you are growing very settled in your ways. You are too confident in your own opinions since I am too busy retching to gainsay you." She touched her fingers to his sleeve. "There are other things I miss as well, my lord."

His eyes darkened and she knew that look, that need in him that brought him so very close to her. For those moments, he was hers and only hers. She could pretend that he loved her, for he was generous in the giving of pleasure, and the words he spoke to her in his passion moved her and brought her to her own pleasure. Aye, the deepness of his voice moved her unbearably and the movement of him over her and within her as he spoke to her. She wanted him desperately.

Not long thereafter, in their sleeping chamber, Merrik walked her toward the box bed with its magnificent miniver spread. He eased her onto her back and unfastened the brooches at her shoulders. He quickly undressed her, saying nothing, just watching his fingers as they removed her clothing, watching his fingers as they touched her bare flesh. When he caressed her breast, balanced over her on his elbow above her, she arched up into his palm.

"Your nipples are larger and darker," he said, and very gently took her into his mouth. His tongue, hot and skilled, scraped over her flesh, making her gasp at the pleasure such a simple action could bring her. She finally cupped her hands around his face, pulling at him. He lifted his head and looked down at her, his mouth wet, his eyes deep and bluer than she'd ever seen them. He was beautiful, this man who was hers, at least here, when he wanted her.

She said clearly, "Give me your mouth, Merrik."

He did. He kissed her and caressed her until she thought she'd surely die from the delight of it, but she didn't, of course. Her body was alive with wanting and she knew more would come, even that ultimate pleasure that would catch and hold her, blurring what was real and what wasn't, just leaving the two of them, clasped together.

She urged him with her hands, parting her thighs, tugging at him, saying his name again and again, and he just smiled at her, but didn't yet come to her. He lay on his back instead and lifted her over him. He came up into her slowly, so very slowly, not allowing her to take him deeply inside her, holding her above him as he moved upward into her. And when he was touching her womb, his fingers found her and she stared down at him, frozen in that instant, feeling the slickness of her flesh, the rough softness of his fingers, and then, without her knowing that it was near, her body exploded into pleasure.

As she heaved over him, her pleasure swamping her, wanting more and yet even more, arching, then folding inward, her hair spilling onto his face, he thought of his child within her and his breath caught in his throat and his body shook, tensed, and he believed in those moments that there could be nothing more to match this, but then there was, and he couldn't believe the intensity of the sensations that were binding him to her. He yelled, his hips jerking upward, his body trembling and shaking, and she took him even more deeply and caressed his face with her fingers as his release took him.

It was over, yet he knew it wasn't, it would never end, this sorcery between them. And he was content.

It was then, in the fading afternoon light, that his vision cleared and he looked up to see Helga standing at the edge of the shadows, gazing at him, her lips slightly parted, her eyes avid on his face.

He went still as a stone in shock. Very slowly, Merrik shook his head at her. She turned then, looking at them one last time, and disappeared from his sight. He felt his heart pounding, not from the wildness of his release, but with the utter fury he felt. Helga had watched them, had watched him bring Laren atop him, watched him slowly thrust upward into her, watched Laren yell in her pleasure as his fingers caressed her, watched his face turn bloodred as he reached his own release.

He wanted to kill the bitch.

"Merrik?"

"Aye?"

"You are all stiff. What is wrong?"

He forced himself to ease, forced the muscles in his arms to loosen, forced his legs to sprawl. She raised herself atop him again, placed her hands on her hips, and smiled down at him, a superior smile, one filled with satisfaction. "Now I know how it is that you feel when you are above me, the one who decides when one is to do what and for how long."

"Do you really believe that, sweeting?" As he spoke, his hands stroked up her legs, upward until he was touching her and himself still inside her. He felt the dampness of her and of his seed and closed his eyes a moment against the deep, deep joy it brought to him. Then he touched her again and she lurched over him and sucked in her breath.

He laughed. "So, you still believe that you are the one who controls?"

She said nothing. Then she leaned forward, splaying her hands wide on his chest. She kissed his mouth, then his chin, his throat, downward to his chest. She raised herself, felt him swelling within her again, and grinned as she came down on him very slowly. She raised herself again, then came down on him even more slowly.

Merrik's eyes nearly crossed. He moaned. His hands tightened about her hips as it began again, only this time, after letting her do as she wished, he lifted her off him and came over her, to cover her and stroke her and kiss her until he was deep inside her once again, and he brought her again to pleasure. He held her, feeling the sweat on her soft flesh, the giving of her, and he managed to forget for a while longer that Helga had been there, watching.

Merrik sat with Otta and Rollo in the private chamber set apart from the great hall. He and Laren had dined with Rollo, then Rollo had sent Laren to await him in his chamber. Now Otta was to tell Merrik about the court of King Charles.

Merrik listened carefully to Otta as he said, anger lacing his voice now, "There are factions in the court, and I wonder still how the king controls them."

"Wonder not, Otta," Rollo said and laughed deeply. "The king acts stupid, it's that simple. He looks blankly from one set of opinions to the other, and smiles and nods, as vacant as a longhouse at the night of the summer solstice. I thought you understood that."

"I understand that he is stupid, but it is not a ruse, sire. Sometimes he is lucky, that is all, just lucky."

Rollo stared at Otta, surprised that he dared to gainsay him, but then he only shook his head, looked bored, and rose. "I will leave you two together now. I wish to have Laren continue the story of the mighty Danish king, Gorm, and how he lost his life only to gain immortality as a god."

Otta watched Rollo leave the chamber. He looked troubled. Merrik said nothing, but he wondered. Did Rollo really have no interest in this? Were his old man's wits gone begging? Was it true what the man had said? Had Rollo hired him and his friend to kill Merrik?

No, he couldn't, wouldn't, believe it. It made no sense. And what about Fromm? An accident? Merrik doubted it. There were so many strange currents running here, emotions smothered then let loose, so many things he didn't know, couldn't begin to guess. He leaned back in the chair, his arms on the beautifully carved posts, and listened to Otta drone on about a king Merrik would never have a bit of interest in. He was no closer to discovering who had been responsible for Taby's and Laren's abduction. His wounded arm began to throb.

He slowly opened the thick narrow door to Helga's tower room and looked inside. It was a strange chamber, octagonal in shape, strange scents lying strong in the still air. She was standing beside a long bench that held numerous pottery bowls and glass containers. She looked up and smiled at him.

"I have waited for you to come to me."

"I have been told that you allow no man here in your tower chamber. However, I did not believe you would forbid me to enter." He paused as she smiled more widely at him. "You looked at Laren and me. I do not like that. Why did you do it?"

She only shrugged, not at all alarmed by his show of

male anger. "I never take a man before I know if he is
sufficient to fulfill my needs. You are, Merrik Haraldsson, indeed you are."

"Did you take men before Fromm was killed?"

"Fromm," she said, and then repeated her dead husband's name yet again and then a third time. "Fromm.
We were wedded for many years. He wanted a child so
badly, and I did as well, for I saw my son as Rollo's heir
after William. But my belly never swelled. Rollo and
Fromm blamed my potions for it, but that isn't true.
Then, just when I gave up, I became with child. Poor
Ferlain had just birthed the fifth of her eight dead
babes. The gods know that I feared for my babe as well.
He moved strongly within me, my beautiful son, but I
held silent, not telling anyone. I was afraid to."

"What happened?"

"The babe came from my body much too early. I was
out collecting herbs and roots in the forest to the north
of Rouen when the cramps began. There was so much
blood. I never imagined there would be so much blood.
I buried the little scrap of a babe there, in the depths
of the forest."

"Why do you tell me this, Helga?"

"I didn't pay those men to kill you. I have always
wanted to tell someone about it." She looked away from
him, staring into the distance, yet there was no distance, for the chamber was close with fall warmth and
the smells of the potions held in the pottery bowls and
basins. "It was after that I began to make potions that
enhanced my beauty, that brought youth back to my
flesh. I wish to take you as a lover, Merrik Haraldsson.
You are strong, I admire your man's body. Many men
care not about a woman's pleasure. You do, for I saw
what you did to Laren, and she, ah, she didn't even

realize that what you do is different from most men. She doesn't appreciate what you give her. I want you. What say you?"

"I cannot think of why I should agree. I am one of Rollo's heirs. Surely it would be dangerous for me to betray my wife and Rollo's favored niece by plowing your belly, as soft and white as it may be."

"On the other hand," Helga said very quietly as she set down a slender glass goblet on the bench top, "it is possible that I will give you more pleasure than a man dreams of, that I might even be able to tell you who was responsible for Laren's abduction two years ago."

Merrik looked at her for a very long time, saying finally, "I can take your white throat between my hands and squeeze until you tell me those who are responsible."

"Aye, you could," she said.

He walked slowly toward her. She smiled at him and pulled the high top of her gown away from her neck. "Come," she said. "Kill me."

24

"My lord Merrik! Don't," Otta yelled from the doorway. "Don't hurt her!"

Merrik merely smiled down at Helga, then slowly turned to face Rollo's minister. "You move silently, Otta," he said easily. "Perhaps you were waiting outside? For a signal? Perhaps you hoped to find me on top of her rather than my hands itching to close about her throat?"

"You mock me, Viking," Otta said, and came into the room, his pace slow, for he wasn't a fool, and he knew that a man like Merrik Haraldsson could erupt into violence in an instant of time. "I am not a spy. I did not know you were here with Helga. I merely wished to see her."

"You see her," Merrik said, smiling, a cruel smile that made Otta want to leave, and very quickly.

Helga laughed. She smoothed the tunic over her throat again, then said, "Otta, what do you wish? Another potion for Rollo? I cannot make the pain lessen in his joints. I have tried."

"It isn't that," Otta said. "I must speak with you."

Merrik looked from the woman to the man. "Do you wish to take Fromm's place? I should consider it carefully were I you, Otta."

"I consider everything carefully, Lord Merrik. That is why I am Rollo's minister."

Merrik merely smiled and left the tower chamber. He walked down the winding wooden steps out into the palace courtyard. There were deep wide gashes in the black earth, filled with muddy water from the heavy rain the day before. There were horses tethered together in a long line, a long trough of hay in front of them. The air was rich with their scent. He nodded to the threescore soldiers who lolled about the compound. They eyed him warily, knowing well who he was, knowing that he could be their master after Rollo's death. Each wondered if William knew of the Viking's existence.

Merrik continued on his way, his mind taken with the duke. Laren had told him about Ferlain, how she'd come quietly into the sleeping chamber, scaring her nearly witless, then telling her that it had been Rollo who had had them abducted. He hated them, had wanted Laren's mother, Nirea . . . It all seemed too fantastic. It made no sense. Ferlain had sounded mad from what Laren had told him. And Helga? If Merrik went to her bed, would she truly tell him who had been responsible for Laren's abduction? He shook his head, looked up, and saw Weland detach himself from three men who were wrestling on a wide patch of ground covered with thick hay.

He was sweating and smiling, massaging his bare shoulder as he strode toward Merrik. The man was old, it was true, but he looked stronger than the oak sapling at the edge of the courtyard. There was a man on the ground, groaning. Had he been one of Weland's opponents?

"Ho! My lord Merrik. I have a message for you from Rollo. He visits an old man who owns a farmstead northward on the Seine some five leagues from here. He wishes you and Laren to join him there."

"Why?"

Weland looked at a loss for a moment, but his smile didn't slip. "The old man predicted Rollo's rise to his present position many, many years ago, I'm told. He is a wizard of sorts. Rollo wants you and Laren to meet him there, for the old man to examine your future, to predict your success. He says it's for the benefit of the people, so that when he dies, if you are to be his successor, there will be no challenges to your succession."

"I see," Merrik said, but he didn't believe any of it for an instant. Weland was lying to him. Was it truly Rollo who had sent Weland to lie to him? Was the duke mad? Eaten by hatred and jealousy? Too old now to realize what he was doing? He had seemed magnificent when they had first met him, the Rollo of legends, but now, he seemed to have changed.

"Have you yet spoken to Laren?"

"Aye, she awaits you at the stables. Several of my men will lead you to the old man's farmstead. I must remain here. You will return to the palace with Rollo."

"Very well," Merrik said. He wished he had his sword. He carried two knives. He would take a sword from one of the soldiers, but it wasn't the same as having his own, the one he'd bloodied at the age of fourteen, the one forged for him by his grandfather's blacksmith. Nor did he want Laren with them, but how to avoid it? "Send the soldiers to me and let us go," he said.

He had no chance to speak to Laren, to convince her to become ill and vomit and thus remain here, safe. But was she safe here? He wanted nothing more at that moment than to bundle up his wife, collect all his men, and leave this wretched place. He wanted to go home. He wanted to keep Taby with him and forget Rollo, any possible succession by Taby, which seemed highly unlikely to Merrik in any case, and all the miserable secrets that festered here.

Then he realized yet again that Taby belonged here. It could so very easily become his birthright, all this immense rich land that already held great wealth and granted great power. Life was fragile, it was true, and any man's or child's life was easily forfeit. Aye, and this duchy would grant even more power in the future, its dukes would vie with the Frankish kings for even more control, he knew it. He had to resolve this mystery and do it now. Thus, he had no intention of acting suspicious around the soldiers that would accompany him and Laren.

He saw Oleg and Old Firren. He smiled at them and called out, "You remember how much Erik likes to wrestle? When you return home, tell him I will visit him soon and I will rub his nose in the dirt. Tell him that, Oleg. Tell him that it will require at least six of his men, not less than six of his strongest men, to aid him if he wants to bring me down."

"Aye," Oleg said slowly, studying his friend's face, "aye, Merrik, I will tell him."

Old Firren spat in the mud at his feet.

Merrik gave them a small salute and turned to follow the four soldiers to the stables.

Laren breathed in the soft autumn air, the scent of the yew bushes and hedgerows, the wild daisies, and the tangy smell of the Seine. They rode past fishermen plying their nets, others spearing the larger sea bass as they bent down from atop massive black rocks that clustered above the river. The road was rutted from all the rain, but the sky was cloudless, as blue as Merrik's eyes.

She was humming, smiling to her husband. There were four soldiers, two of them riding in front of them and the other two at their backs.

She said gaily, "My lord, we should have brought some of Uncle Rollo's sweet Rhenish wine. A gift for this old wizard friend of his. What think you?"

Merrik agreed that it was a good idea, if only they had thought of it earlier. Weland's second in command, a rough man with a sharp eye, whose name was Rognvald, said over his shoulder, "Aye, the Rhenish wine is good, but we must concern ourselves with outlaws and robbers who, it is said, hide in these woods. Weland doesn't wish to take any chances with your safety, mistress, or yours, Lord Merrik."

"I am vastly relieved that you are with us," Laren said, and smiled at him.

"You now carry a sword, Merrik," Rognvald said, eyeing the sword in a way Merrik didn't like.

"Aye," Merrik said easily, "one of your soldiers saw that I had need of one. As you say, there are many outlaws. It is wise to be prepared."

Rognvald nodded, then kicked his stallion forward to speak to the two men who rode ahead of them.

Merrik pulled his stallion closer to Laren's mare. "Listen to me," he said quietly, trying to look loverlike and doubting if he was succeeding. "I—"

"Ho! Lord Merrik, look yon. 'Tis a group of monks the Frankish king has thrust upon us. Rollo was forced to give them a monastery—it's called St. Catherine's and is only two leagues from here. It is set atop a promontory. The prospect it gives is spectacular."

Merrik pulled away from Laren, and called back to Rognvald, "Monks make me want to go immediately to a bathing hut. Their stench offends me."

Rognvald laughed. "Aye, 'tis true. The beggars never

bathe and wear those long robes that are never washed. They are always itching from their own filth, lice, and the wretched coarse wool."

"I can no longer accept a god who wants his subjects to be filthy," Laren said, knowing that the Christian God was forever lost to her, and accepting it.

And so their journey continued. For another hour, they rode close to the shore of the Seine, alert for outlaws.

But there was no attack. One of the soldiers shouted and pointed just ahead to their right. Atop a small hillock that overlooked the Seine stood a rough sod house with a small hole in its roof through which poured a thin thread of blue smoke. In front of the dwelling stood only one horse. The rider was not to be seen.

It was Laren who said, "I do not see Uncle Rollo's horse, Rognvald. I wonder where Njaal is." She turned to Merrik. "Njaal is a huge beast, some seventeen hands high. It is the only horse to carry my uncle without his feet hitting the ground."

"Well, Rognvald?" Merrik said, staring at him, his hand going down to his sword handle.

Rognvald was frowning mightily, then suddenly he looked vastly relieved. "There the stallion is, over there, beneath that oak tree. Aye, 'tis Njaal."

"Come, Merrik," Laren said gaily, "let us go meet this wizard."

She climbed from her horse without aid and hurried to the entrance of the small dwelling. Merrik wanted to shout to her but he held his peace. He dismounted, tossed his horse's reins to one of the soldiers, then followed his wife into the farmstead. He had to lean down not to hit his head on a beam, blackened from too many years of soot. It was dark within, and it took several moments for his eyes to adjust. When he could see well enough, he winced. It was a wretched place, and it smelled, the air rancid with old food, unwashed bodies, and closely packed animals. He saw an old man seated by a fire pit in the very center of the single room. He had a long white beard and he wore a surprisingly beautiful white robe. It was clean. He looked up as Merrik entered.

"You are her husband?" he said.

"Aye, I am Merrik Haraldsson of Malverne."

"In Vestfold," the old man said low, and stirred the embers in the fire pit with a skinny stick. "It is a beautiful land, Vestfold. Harald Fairhair will rule even longer. Know you that, Viking? He is as long-lived as Rollo."

"I have never doubted it, old man."

"You have gained yourself a wife blooded of valiant men and women." He didn't look at Laren, who stood opposite him, obviously fascinated, staring at the old man, but saying nothing. Merrik took another step forward, but the old man held up his hand to stay him.

"Nay, stay there, Viking, else you will disturb the embers. All these flames, licking about the new twigs I just laid in, they show me things."

Merrik came forward in any case. "You will tell me, old man, where is Rollo?"

"He came and left."

"His horse, Njaal, is still outside."

"He is swimming in the river. I gave him a cream for his joints, then told him to bathe it off. He is at the river."

"Now you will tell me who you are."

"I?" The old man lifted very bright dark eyes to Merrik's face. "Ah," he said, and laughed, a rusty sound. "You do not trust me. I do not blame you, Viking. Look

at your wife. She doesn't trust me either, but she is
more subtle about it. She watches closely and doubt not
that she carries a knife in the folds of her gown."

"You are right," Laren said coldly. She raised her
hand to show him a long thin-bladed knife that would
easily sink through a man's chest and show its bloodied
point out his back. Its handle was exquisitely carved
ivory. Merrik had never seen it before. "You will not
harm my husband. If you attempt it, I will kill you."

Merrik simply stared at her. He hadn't guessed that
her suspicions ran as deeply as his, for he had been so
very worried that she believed this to be different, to be
safe, to be . . . He had underestimated her and he
vowed he would never do it again. He walked to her
side.

"She also carries a babe," the old man said, seemingly
not bothered by her threat. "Aye, a knife without and a
babe within. You have grown fierce, Laren, and loyal.
Rollo told me that Taby lives. He was a beautiful babe,
fat and smiling, always smiling, showing his toothless
gums, and I loved him deeply. He always held out his
arms to me. I was besotted with him. But then everything changed and I was forced to flee. It was Rollo's
idea that I become as you see me now."

Merrik was aware suddenly that Laren had grown
very still. He saw that her face had paled and he immediately held her against his side. "Do you feel ill?"

"Nay," she said, never taking her eyes off the old
man.

Suddenly, the old man rose from the rough stool and
smoothed out the folds of his white robe.

Laren said very quietly, "It is you, isn't it?"

Merrik stared from her to the old man. "What do you
mean, sweeting?"

"It is my father," she said, pulled away from him, and

walked around the fire pit to stand in front of the old man, an old man who seemed not so old now, for he was taller now and very straight.

"Aye, daughter, 'tis I."

She sobbed softly and threw herself into his arms. "When you disappeared I couldn't bear it. First Mother and then you."

"I know. I know." Hallad held her close, stroking her beautiful red hair. He looked at Merrik over her head. "I had to see her and to see you as well, Merrik Haraldsson. You are distrustful of me, as was she. Why?"

"Because we do not know as yet who was responsible for her and Taby's abduction," Merrik said. "I believed this to be a ruse to get us both away from the palace and relative safety. You know that Fromm was murdered? That I was attacked?"

A deep voice spoke from a dark corner of the hut. "Aye, I told him."

They both looked up to see Rollo striding toward them, his face grim. He was no longer a querulous old man, thin graying hair brushing his shoulders. No, he looked more like the Rollo of legend, strong and decisive, a man to fear and a man to trust, the man they had first seen upon their arrival.

"Aye, I am here, Merrik, and it is no trap unless others have made it thus for their own benefit. Hallad wanted to meet you and to see his daughter again. I have told him that soon, with your aid, we will discover who killed his wife and your mother, Laren. I didn't kill Nirea nor was I her lover, as I know you've been told. But Hallad was blamed for her death and I knew I couldn't allow him to be killed for it. Thus he became an outlaw, but I couldn't allow that to continue. Two years ago, shortly before your and Taby's abduction, he become the old wizard who lives here, supposedly, and provides me with prophesies and advice. This abominable hut stinks, a pit of filth, I know, but Hallad only uses it to discourage any men who would come here to rob him. He lives in the monastery of St. Catherine's. You passed it on your way here. When he is there, he is a Christian monk. It has worked well, this ruse of ours. Show yourself to your daughter, Hallad. I will see that the men stay out of here."

Hallad set Laren aside. He pulled off the thick white wig and the heavy beard. Brilliant thick red hair freely laced with gray sprang up. The red was just the color of Laren's. His eyes, dark as his brother Rollo's, were vibrant with life. Standing side by side, there was a resemblance, surely, but that red hair, it was like a beacon. He was a handsome man, a man Merrik was very glad hadn't died, and he was an old man, too, even though he had fewer years than his brother, Rollo.

Hallad seemed to guess his thoughts. "Aye, Merrik, Rollo and I both are old men. I can see it in your eyes. But we are blessed with years upon years of life."

"You both carry the years well," Merrik said. He turned to Rollo. "This becomes even more of a tangled skein, sire. I have men arriving shortly, Oleg leading them. I truly believed this to be a subterfuge, that whoever was responsible for attacking me and killing Fromm would try to kill us this time."

Rollo smiled and rubbed his hands together over the orange flames. "Will your men gallop up like an invading hoard of Vikings or will they hide amongst the trees and wait for a signal?"

"They will wait for a signal."

"Good. My men will wait outside, too, well hidden in the trees. There is only one horse outside, all the others are in the woods. We will have some mead now."

"And wait as well?" Laren said, and hugged her father again.

"Aye," Hallad said, kissing the top of her head. "We will wait as well."

"Ah," Merrik said. "You have planted seeds and watered them."

"Aye, I am a great leader, Merrik Haraldsson. My mind and my body forged this land. You expect that I wouldn't protect it and those I love with all the cunning I possess?"

Merrik laughed, and Hallad, to Merrik's surprise, punched his brother's arm. "He is always braying like a damned mule," Hallad said, and punched him again. "He will soon begin to believe that he is a godlike figure, a myth to survive the centuries. He will soon believe all the incredible stories credulous fools tell about him."

Rollo laughed, a deep booming laugh. "And you, graybeard, what of you? Making me visit you here in this filthy sod shack, making people believe you've nearly reached the status of a Christian's holy man, an old ass who gives me advice by looking into the flames in this wretched fire pit? Ha, Hallad!" And he laughed again. He said then to Hallad, his voice deep and serious, "The children do not understand all of this, brother, particularly my old man's irritation and bile. My show of an old man's foolishness."

"It surprised me," Laren said, "when you behaved as though you were doddering on the edge of your brain."

"Good," Rollo said. "That means all others saw it and believed it as well."

Hallad struck a thoughtful pose and said, "I wonder if he was truly playing the role?"

"I pray so, Father," Laren said.

Merrik said to Rollo, "You are certain our villain will show himself today?"

"Aye," Rollo said. "Aye. I have told several men of Hallad's presence here, how he was pretending to be like a holy man and of my visit to him here today. I told them all that he sent me a message telling me that he had discovered who had killed Nirea and abducted Laren and Taby."

"Including Weland and Otta?"

Rollo nodded, a flash of pain in his dark eyes. "Aye," he said after a moment, "today we will know our enemy."

"Finally," Hallad said. "Finally."

Helga rode beside Otta and his score of well-armed men. He'd told her that her father was still alive. He wanted her to see him for herself. Helga didn't believe him for a moment, but Otta was a man she was considering as a new husband, despite the foolish pains in his belly that none of her potions could cure, and thus she didn't consider it wise to flay him just yet with her tongue.

She would flatter him and show him she believed his fine tale. She could laugh at him after he was her husband.

When they drew close to the squalid dwelling, she wrinkled her nose. "You say that my father lives here? That is nonsense, Otta. My father would never soil his fingers, much less live in a sod hut like this. It is impossible."

"Nonetheless," Otta said, not looking at her, "it's true. I have it from the great Rollo himself. He told me of it just this morning. Do you wish to see him or no?"

"Oh aye, but have him come outside. I have no wish to dirty myself."

Suddenly, with no warning, Otta grabbed her arm and jerked her off her mare's back. He hurled her to the ground. Helga lay sprawled on her side, gasping for breath, staring up at him.

"Perfidious bitch," he said, smiling, and dismounted, standing over her. When she tried to rise, he kicked out his foot and caught her in the ribs. She yelled and fell back. "Stay there," he said. "I like you there, on the ground, helpless for once, and silent. By the gods, at last you are silent. And you are helpless, Helga, even more helpless than Fromm was, so drunk he could barely fight back for even a moment. I have wanted to kill you for a very long time now. All of you, this entire cursed family."

She stared up at him, then looked at his men, who were trying hard not to look at her, no expressions on their faces.

"There have been many men here, your brave uncle Rollo amongst them, but they are gone now, and the only one here will be your father, a murderer, a man who will finally be brought before the people to be judged for his crime."

"Uncle Rollo won't allow my father to be hurt, if he is indeed inside the hut, as you say he is."

"I know it," Otta said. "I know it well. Rollo hid him here. Rollo didn't tell me as a man would another man he trusted. Nay, he has recently become older and more of a foolish old man as each hour passes. He speaks when he should hold his own counsel. He mumbles and rambles. Thus I know it is true. Hallad is here. Both of them will die soon, very soon. This is the beginning of his downfall. When I have taken care of Rollo, I will travel to Paris and kill that miserable son of his. I asked that Charles do it, but he tried and failed. No, I will see to it myself. Then the Frankish king will place me in his stead and I will be the second duke of Normandy. Aye, William will be assassinated under my direction, his pregnant wife with him, and none will grieve. Charles knows that I can guard this land from marauding Vikings better than that doddering old man, better than any of his damnable progeny."

In a very soft voice, a man said, "Otta. I cannot say that I am overly surprised. Nay, I am only surprised that you would be so stupid as to tell Helga as well as all these men exactly what your plans are and why you have acted as you have. The more people to know what you think and plan, the more likely it is that you will fail. You are not a leader, Otta. You are naught but a foolish man. You will never take my place. You have failed, Otta."

Rollo stood proud and tall, looking as strong as a warrior, armed with his knife and his sword, wearing a rich, thick bearskin like the one he had worn in his youth. His gray hair was tied back with a leather thong, no longer lying limp and grizzled about his face and shoulders. He looked a different man. He looked, Merrik realized with relief, like a man who would well teach a young boy to become a leader of men. Aye, Taby would be safe with him and with his father, Hallad.

Otta was held only a brief instant in shock. He yelled to his men, and drew his sword. "You bastard! What happened to you? Nay, I see it now, you tricked me, lied to me! Kill him! Kill them all!"

His soldiers drew their swords, ready to do Otta's bidding, but they didn't have a chance. Within moments, they were surrounded very suddenly by men who moved as stealthily as forest beasts. Otta froze, now silent as a tombstone, staring at the man he'd believed was nearly riddled in his brain.

"Sire," Merrik said, striding forward. "He paid to have me killed. It is my right to challenge him."

Suddenly, Helga leapt up from the ground, saying

softly, "Father? Is that really you?"

"Aye, daughter, 'tis I. Come here."

She ran to him, closing her arms tightly about him. "You haven't changed," she whispered into his neck. "You are as you were. The red of your hair is still as bright as it was. Oh, I have missed you, Father."

"It has only been three years, Helga," Hallad said. "I become old, aye, it is true. I have missed you, too, daughter, but your uncle tells me that you have become something of a witch, spinning riddles and mysteries for credulous ears, mixing potions to terrify people and make them afraid of you. Aye, and that damnable tower chamber, filled with the noxious smells of that swill you mix and boil. But you have enjoyed taunting poor Laren, have you not? Hinting that it was you who had her and Taby abducted? You tried to make yourself important, Helga, you made mischief and caused pain. I am not pleased with you. It wasn't well done of you."

"It is true, Father, and I am sorry. There was nothing else for me to do. There was Fromm and he would have killed me if I hadn't frightened him. I learned long ago that to survive I had to have power over people, thus my magic." She stared up at Hallad. "But how did you know all of this?"

"Your uncle told me, who else?"

"But he—" She shook her head, knowing that she hadn't seen the truth of him.

"Come away from your men now, Otta," Rollo said. "It is over for you. There is much you owe, to me, to Merrik, even to Hallad as well."

Otta didn't move. He looked from Rollo, still unwilling to see him as the man he was now and not the sniveling old fool he'd left just this morning, to Merrik, seeing clearly the cold fury in the young man's eyes and knowing that if he fought him, Merrik would gut him as quickly as he would a fish. And Hallad, alive, truly alive, even though he hadn't wanted to believe it, but Rollo had assured him it was true, and Otta had seen it as more proof that the old man's mind was nearly gone, spilling out secrets to him. Helga stood pressed against him, his arm around her shoulders. At least her gown was filthy and he knew he'd hurt her. He knew she must feel pain from the kick in the ribs he'd given her. That pleased him for a brief moment.

Otta didn't want to die. He was a man with a noble and proud destiny awaiting him. He'd been patient, endlessly patient, his belly growing more painful by the year. But he'd borne it. King Charles had assured him that his destiny would come to pass. He looked at Laren, hating her even though she'd just been a child and he hadn't known her, hadn't paid her any heed. At least the little brat, Taby, was dead. If only she hadn't come back, if only she hadn't married the Viking warrior . . .

"Let me tell you something else, Otta," Rollo said. "Taby is alive. Merrik saved him. Of course, it was Laren who saved him for two years. She protected him with her life. Aye, Taby is alive, and he will serve William loyally and faithfully. But if fate decrees it, then Taby will become the second duke of Normandy. You have lost mightily, Otta, everything. Your dishonor sickens me. I will see that your death is more painful than the pain you have caused all of us."

Otta began to tremble. "Bitch!" he screamed at Laren. He drew his sword, raised it above his head and, yelling like a madman, jumped onto his horse's back, kicked it hard in the sides and ran directly at her.

25

AT THE LAST instant, Otta jerked his stallion toward Rollo. There was fury and death in his eyes, and Merrik knew in those few moments that Otta accepted his own death if he could kill Rollo.

Merrik threw Rollo to the ground, blocking him with his body. His sword was drawn and up.

Otta was yelling, the language of the Franks that Merrik didn't understand, but Merrik knew Otta fully intended to kill him to get to Rollo. Otta was on him, the stallion rearing back, snorting frantically, his hooves lashing out.

Quite suddenly, Otta's yell became an obscene gurgle. He dropped his sword nearly at Merrik's feet and grabbed his throat. A slender knife was bedded to its hilt through his throat, its bloodied tip protruding from the back of his neck.

He stared from Merrik to Rollo, who'd risen and was standing between his brother and the damned Viking, then to Laren, who was staring at him, pale, her hand still raised.

"You killed me," Otta said, blood making his voice slur. "You're but a woman, yet you killed me. I should have strangled you two years ago and thrown your body

in the forest for the animals to ravage. Aye, I should
have killed you and that puking little brat."

"Aye," she said, "you should have." She said nothing
more, just stood there and watched him try to pull the
knife from his throat, watched his face turn a sickly
gray, watched the blood gush from his mouth and well
thick and hot from his throat. He slid off his horse, dead
before his body thudded to the ground.

Rollo stood over Otta's body, staring down at him dispassionately. He smiled then at Laren. "I am glad it
wasn't Weland who betrayed me. I don't think I could
have borne that. Aye, I am more relieved than I can
say. Your throw was straight and true, girl. It's obvious
I taught you well."

"You?" Hallad said, striding forward, his long white
robe brushing the low-growing grass. "I taught her, do
you not remember? She was but a little nubbin of a girl
when I put a knife in her hand and began to teach her."

"Nay, your wits are more addled than you would like
to think, Hallad. Attend me, for I am Rollo, the first
duke of Normandy, and I never remember things awry.
I taught her and I will teach Taby as well. You are
naught but an old graybeard. What do your trembling
hands know of knife-throwing?"

"Ha! Heed me, Rollo, I had to live with those
wretched Christian monks at St. Catherine's. I had to
stoop my shoulders and mumble all the time so they
would believe me holy. But no longer. No, it is I who
will teach my son as I did my daughter."

Laren looked at Merrik. She shook her head at the
two men trading insults that would surely lead to some
pounding.

"Let them argue in peace," Merrik said. He looked
down at Otta, sprawled on the ground. "That was a fine
throw. Perhaps it was I who taught you."

She laughed, looking up at him with all the love she felt clear and shining in her eyes. Merrik stared at her, saying nothing. He raised his hand, then lowered it. Laren shook herself, then said to Helga, "I am glad you did not betray me or Taby. I am glad you didn't try to kill Merrik."

Helga merely nodded, then walked to Otta's body. She looked down at him, her mouth twisted with fury. She drew back her foot and kicked his ribs so hard she must have broken enough of them to make him scream, had he been alive to feel it.

Rollo, who had just hit Hallad in his belly, turned and said, suddenly serious, "Aye, Helga, you are innocent and that pleases me as well, for I had believed you guilty. You have not been an easy woman. I told only Weland and Otta of Hallad and where he was. But I knew that the guilty one did not act alone. I knew that you or Ferlain had to be working with the guilty one."

"It is not I, Uncle Rollo."

"I know," said Hallad. "It isn't you, Helga."

Ferlain stood impatiently in her sleeping chamber, her hands fisted at her sides as her husband, Cardle, paced in front of her, carrying on about the damned now-dead King Alfred of Britain. She looked as if she had been saved when Weland and two of his men came into the chamber.

"But you can't take her," Cardle said, startled by their sudden appearance. "What are you doing here? What do you mean, her uncle wants her? This cannot be right. I was just telling her of my studies of the great Charlemagne. Or was it Alfred? No matter, they were both great men, men of courage and men of vision. Can this not wait? Cannot Rollo wait to see her?"

Weland looked from the bent scholar whose seed had

birthed eight dead babes. The man's rod was his only connection to this world. Weland said quietly, "You will see her later, Cardle. Rollo wishes to see her now."

"He knows," Ferlain said very quietly.

"Aye, Ferlain, he knows."

"Knows what?" Cardle said, and scratched his head. "What is this, Ferlain?"

"Continue your study of Charlemagne, Cardle. I will return soon. Or was it Alfred? By the gods, I really don't remember nor do I care."

She heard Cardle gasp behind her and smiled. "I have wanted to tell him that for a long time," she said to Weland, then became silent, her head up, her shoulders squared as she walked beside him.

"I could order you killed right now, Ferlain, but I wanted to hear you speak. I want to know why you have betrayed me. You are my blood and yet you deceived me, deceived all of us, with Otta. Do not bother to lie, for we know everything."

Fat, plain Ferlain, with coarse white strands threaded through her dark brown hair, threw her head back, and said, her voice loud and strong, "You would have been next, Uncle Rollo. You have become a fool, a doddering old man who does not deserve to rule this mighty land." She paused, frowning at him. "What has taken place here? You have changed again. What has happened to you? You were mad just this morning, I saw it, and knew your time was near, for you were deranged and knew not what you said. Otta assured me it was true. He assured me that now was the time to act, to rid ourselves of all of you. Aye, I expected to see you drool as you spoke your nonsense, yet here you are, hale and stout and you act like a man once again."

Rollo merely smiled at her, remaining seated in his

massive throne with its carved raven posts, a throne constructed higher than any other throne, for Rollo's legs were so very long. Merrik and Laren stood to his right. The only other person in Rollo's chamber was Weland, and he was staring down at the wooden floor covered with rich crimson wool rugs.

Rollo said finally, very quietly, "It was a ruse, Ferlain, naught but a ruse."

"Where is Otta?"

"He is dead. He meant to kill me, but you knew that, did you not?"

"Aye, I knew it. He told me there was some tale you had told him of my father being alive. I did not believe it. I still do not believe it. My father killed that foolish bitch, Nirea. He is long dead, for he is nearly as old a man as you, uncle."

"Aye, 'tis true I am old, daughter, but I still breathe. I still walk and I can still reason."

Ferlain sucked in her breath, but she didn't move. She showed no fear, no elation at Hallad's sudden presence. She stood there, staring at her father as he strode toward her. "I didn't kill Nirea and you know it. She was a sweet girl, not the faithless bitch you created in your own mind."

Ferlain merely shrugged. "Then it was Helga. She hated Nirea and she has even bragged to me once about sticking a thin knife into her neck. She didn't mind that you got blamed for it. She hated you because you wed Nirea and kept producing children. Neither of us wanted you to have more children, yet you wouldn't listen."

"Helga is beyond foolish but she didn't kill Nirea either."

Laren said, "You told me that Uncle Rollo was in love with Nirea, that he was mad with jealousy, that—"

"Be quiet, you stupid girl!"

Laren stared at her half sister. Never had Ferlain raised her voice, never had she heard such venom.

"By all the gods, I was stupid. I should have had my men kill you and that brat our father sired off Nirea. But no, I let the men sell you to slave traders from the south. I wanted you to suffer as I suffered and I wanted you to know pain and hunger and hopelessness. Otta wanted to kill you but I didn't let him. By all the gods, he was right."

"We did suffer, Ferlain," Laren said, but Ferlain wasn't listening to her, just continued over her, saying, "They told me they didn't gain much with your sale to slave traders, but with what I added, the villains did well enough. Otta then killed them, for he didn't trust them to keep silent. He never gave me my silver back."

"Why, Ferlain, why?" It was Hallad and there was pleading in his deep voice, and such sorrow that Laren couldn't bear it.

Ferlain held silent. She was smiling, taunting them with her silence. "I didn't do anything. It was all Otta. I am innocent. I am like Helga, making myself important by teasing you with half-truths. I am more a skilled skald than Laren is. Aye, I am innocent and that is all there is to it."

"You are as innocent as an asp and as deadly," Rollo said. "Why did you kill Fromm? Why did you send men after Merrik? Why, Ferlain? You have always gotten what you wished from me. Your dead babes, it was always a tragedy, but these things happen. Women don't turn into monsters because of dead children."

"All of them died," Ferlain said, her voice calm, too calm, staring now beyond Rollo, at the thick crimson draperies behind his throne. "Dead in my womb, all of them. Not a single cry when each of them emerged. All dead." She turned back to look at him. "I believed it was Cardle's fault, all my dead babes, and thus I took Fromm to my bed, and he sired the last three, but they were dead too. My body killed them, all of them. They rotted in my womb until I thrust them out. The pain, uncle, the pain would have bowed the strongest man, but I wanted a babe to live, so very badly, and that babe would have come after you, and I made myself thrust out those dead and rotted scraps, praying each time that there would be a cry of life, that there would be arms and legs that would move, eyes that would see something other than death, and I endured the pain and made myself try again and again."

"Ah, Ferlain, I am so very sorry," Hallad said. "I had no idea."

"You wonder why I killed that miserable bully Fromm? He threatened to tell you he had bedded me. Even now, after two years, he threatened to tell you. The fool was jealous when he found out I had taken Otta to my bed. He made no sense. 'Twas he who told me after that third and last babe died that I was fat and ugly and he didn't want me anymore. Why would he care what I did? Ah, but he did because he was afraid I would find Otta more to my liking than I had found him. Not that Otta did much of anything, the braying fool. He could not even sire a dead babe. All he did was hold his belly and whine of his incessant pain. Or perhaps now it is my fault and not Otta's. Perhaps now I am too old to plant more babes in my womb."

There was anguish on Hallad's face. He went to her. She looked at him and the dazed expression was gone instantly from her face to be replaced by a rage so deep, so raw that Hallad flinched back from it. "Stay away from me!" she screamed at him. "You perfidious bastard, why didn't you die? You killed my mother with

your lust, and then you wed that bitch Nirea who was
no older than I and you let her birth Laren and then
Taby, aye, the vaunted heir, little Taby who was so very
perfect, who was beloved by all, especially by Uncle
Rollo who would teach him and love him and make him
one of his heirs. I wanted to kill him and you. And I
killed that bitch Nirea, but by the gods, not in time. Not
in time, for there was Taby! And there would have been
more babes, more little boys, so I did stop her, I had to
and I did."

Hallad said slowly, "You have naught but hatred and
bitterness in you, Ferlain. Nirea never did anything to
you. She was fond of you and Helga, and she tried, the
poor girl tried to befriend you. She was so very innocent.
And yet you killed her. Was it poison? Aye, I believe it
was. I was accused of strangling her for there were finger marks about her white throat. But I didn't touch
her, would never have hurt her, even though we argued
that day and were overheard. You took your chance and
all believed me guilty and thus I had to escape to keep
Rollo from having to execute me. I think you dug your
fingers into her throat after she was dead. But you
know, Ferlain, Rollo never believed me guilty. He hid
me and then I became the old wizard two years ago. I
survived. I am sorry for you, Ferlain. I would kill you
if Laren and Taby were dead, but they survived. At
least you spared them, though your reasons for doing
so are wretched. What will you say now, Ferlain?"

"I say this, old man. If you hadn't been accused of
murdering that bitch wife of yours, then you would
have wed another girl within weeks, aye, not more than
several months, for you are a lustful fool for all your
years, and this one would have probably been much
younger than Helga or me. Then she would have
birthed more boys, would she not? You always flaunted

your virility before all of us. And there was Taby and then all these others, aye, you would have continued to sire babes—all of them alive and breathing and yelling the instant they came from their mothers' wombs—and I would have had naught."

"You have naught now," Rollo said. "You have lost everything, Ferlain."

"I still have Cardle."

"Aye, he is a harmless man, a faithful man. He never knew that you had bedded with Fromm, did he? Or Otta?"

"He wouldn't know anything if I didn't tell him," she said, her voice filled with contempt. "You, Rollo, you wed me to that imbecile. He would not even bed me unless I took him in my mouth and brought him to a man's size. I had to thrust him into me, uncle, for he would just gaze at me, and I knew his mind was in the past, thinking of all those miserable Romans or King Alfred or that gallant fool, Charlemagne. At least Fromm and Otta were men with men's appetites and men's knowledge. I would that you would die, Uncle Rollo, but you will not. You will continue forever, I know it."

Very slowly, she slipped to her knees. She bowed her head and held her arms around her, slowly rocking back and forth.

"Why did you try to kill Merrik?" Rollo said, quiet now, his voice oddly soothing. "He did nothing to you, nothing."

She was silent for a very long time. Rollo started to ask her again, when she raised her head and looked toward Merrik, as if he were a stranger. "He would have been another damned heir. If I couldn't produce a son, I wouldn't allow the possibility that he would rule, his son after him."

"He would never rule, Ferlain," Rollo said, and his voice was that of the ruler of Normandy, cold and decisive and no one would gainsay him and live. "He will never rule. Taby is alive. Your father told you but you didn't heed him. Aye, Taby is alive and happy as a child should be. He is safe in Norway, in Vestfold, at Merrik's farmstead."

Ferlain jumped to her feet. "No! You lie! It is Merrik who now holds your favor, it is he who will—"

"Taby is alive. Merrik found both Laren and Taby at the slave market in Kiev. I would that I could have sired a son like Merrik, for he is honorable above all things. But then so is William, and it is he, Ferlain, it is William my son who will rule after me. Taby will be at his side, loyal to him and brave, his arm and his mind strong and sure."

Ferlain said nothing. She merely stared first at Rollo, then at Laren and Merrik. She didn't look at her father.

Finally, Rollo said, "Weland, return her to her sleeping chamber. Post two soldiers near. We will decide what is to be done with her."

It was Helga who came to their sleeping chamber late that night. She didn't look as young in the dim shadows. "Come quickly," she said, shaking Merrik's shoulder. "Come."

Rollo and Hallad were there before them, looking down, both silent. Ferlain lay on the box bed, a soft pillow beneath her head, an exquisite embroidered robe covering her, smoothed by loving hands over her body. Her face was smooth with renewed youth in death, her eyes closed by gentle fingers. Her hair was brushed until it shone and braided very neatly, the long ropes lying over her breasts. Her arms were at her sides, palms up.

"Cardle is gone," Rollo said to Merrik and Laren. "She

has been dead for a long time."

"How did she die?" Laren said.

"I do not know," Rollo said. "There is no blood. Her face is without pain, without struggle. Helga came to visit her early this morning and found her thusly. The guards said she hadn't tried to leave the chamber. Cardle left late last night. They had no reason to stop him."

"Bury her," Hallad said suddenly. "Leave her be and bury her now, this morning."

Rollo slowly nodded.

"What of Cardle?" Helga said. "He killed her, he did it. What will you do, Uncle Rollo?"

"I will tell you soon," Rollo said. "Aye, I will tell you soon."

26

Taby was sitting on the bench next to Cleve, tying a knot under his direction. There was sudden loud commotion from outside the longhouse. Taby raised his head like a young animal trained to the sound.

"Is it Laren?"

"Let us see," Cleve said and took the boy's hand. But he couldn't keep up. Taby scampered away with Kenna and both boys bounded through the now wide palisade gates, through the fields now flat and dull, their barley and rye harvested, past the slaves who were mending the palisade walls with tight cord, wet and then dried three times over for added strength, and down the path to the fjord.

Taby saw Merrik, shouted at the top of his voice, and hurled himself at him. Merrik, laughing, caught the child in time and threw him high into the air, then caught him and held him tightly against his chest. Laren watched from behind him, saw him close his eyes as he buried his face against Taby's hair. She felt the familiar bittersweet longing as she watched. Then Taby raised his head, kissed Merrik's cheek, a loud smacking kiss that made him laugh, then saw his sister.

"Laren!" he shrieked. She was then the one to have

his child's arms around her neck, his wet kisses on her face.

"You are like a puppy, Taby," she said, knowing tears were in her eyes and trying to swallow them back. "Stop wriggling so. Soon you will be licking my face like that massive beast Kerzog. Will you grow as big as that monster?"

The child laughed at that. All was as it should be.

"I have something to tell you," she said to Taby and set him on the ground. "Our father is alive. Hallad came back here with us."

The child grew very still, his eyes wary. "No, no, Laren. I don't remember my father, Laren. Merrik is my father."

"Oh no, sweeting. Merrik is your brother. Do you not remember? No, here is your father and my father as well."

Hallad hung back, staring at the little boy who looked up at him, his expression suspicious.

"You are nearly six now, Taby," Hallad said, then wondered where that had come from. He hadn't seen his son since he was a babe. Now a little boy stood in front of him, a sturdy little boy who looked just like him when he'd been young. He watched the boy take a step back and stop when he hit Merrik's legs.

He saw Merrik's hand come down to the boy's shoulder and gently squeeze. He saw Merrik come down to his knees and look at Taby, all the love he felt shining in eyes the brilliant blue of the autumn sky. Merrik said, "Your father lives and I have brought him back with me. What happened to him is better than any tale Laren can weave in her skald's voice. Aye, and he will tell you about such things as he has seen when you return with him to Normandy. Come now, Taby, and greet your father."

Hallad saw the pain in Merrik's eyes when he gently placed Taby's small hand into his. "This is your father. Bid him welcome."

"I welcome you to Malverne, sir."

Merrik shook his head and laughed. "He is a stubborn little mite and loyal to his finger bones. Come, Hallad, let us go inside and have some of Sarla's fine ale." He lifted Taby onto his shoulder and marched up the path, back through the fields scythed flat of their crops.

It was difficult for Hallad, Laren knew it. It was difficult for her as well, and Taby was her brother. She watched her father try to remain impassive, a smile on his face, but his little son was curled into a ball against Merrik's chest, sound asleep, his small fisted hand clutching Merrik's tunic.

"They love each other very much," she said to her father. "It is very odd really. As you know, this fat merchant, Thrasco, had bought me, and they'd pulled me away from Taby. Merrik saw Taby and wanted him. It is that simple and it goes that deep."

"You were both very lucky," Hallad said. "The woman, Sarla, she is comely, very comely. And so very gentle. You told me she was married to Merrik's brother, the former master of this farmstead?"

Laren nodded. "He was killed. His former skald, a jealous man named Deglin, killed him and tried to blame me, for he wanted me gone. Many believed that I did it, for Erik wanted to bed me. I did not like Erik, for he was cruel toward his wife and arrogant in his actions, but to die because Deglin wanted me blamed, it is horrible."

"What will become of Sarla?"

Laren smiled as she sipped her cup of sweet mead.

"I may be just a few years older than she," Hallad said sharply, eyeing his daughter, "but I am not dead.

No segment of me is dead, daughter. I am still a man of many fine parts. Do you understand me?"

"Aye, Father, I understand you quite well," Laren said solemnly.

"You should since you are carrying Merrik's babe in your womb." He was clearly irritated and she couldn't help herself, she giggled. Merrik looked up and smiled widely. It had been too long since there had been lightness in her. He was enchanted, and he told her so later that night when they were finally settled beneath a soft woolen blanket in their box bed.

"If I enchanted you then I must be a witch."

"Aye, you may be my witch. It has been a very long day," he added and kissed her ear, then licked lightly inside.

"Aye, but we are home, Merrik. How glad I am to be home at last. And alive."

"Your father was asking me questions about Sarla, how well placed her family was, what I planned to do with her. I told him that she would do as she pleased, that she was welcome at Malverne forever if she wished it."

Laren came up on her elbow above him. "My father is a man of fine parts, that each of his segments was working. He told me so. Do you think Sarla would like to marry my father? Live with him in Uncle Rollo's palace? Be a great lady?" She giggled again, nestling her face against his shoulder, and he felt her warm breath, and squeezed her tightly against him.

"I do not know. You told me that she and Cleve were growing close. Indeed you told me they loved each other."

"Aye, but now I don't know." She sucked in her breath, all thought of Cleve and Sarla forgotten. "I like your hand there, Merrik."

"Do you?" He gently cupped her breast in his hand, leaned down and began to caress her with his mouth. When she moaned, arching into him, he raised his head and smiled down at her. "You have not been ill for a week now. I am relieved. You were growing too thin again. Ah, but not here, not here."

"You are a man," she said, and kissed his warm mouth, "and a man likes to caress a woman's breasts. Ah, Merrik, I do love you. More than you can begin to imagine. I will love you until I die." She'd said the words, she didn't regret saying them even though he was still beside her. For just a moment he was very still, and silent, then he was kissing her frantically, his tongue stroking her mouth, his hands wild on her breasts, then his fingers were moving to her waist and belly, gently probing there, searching for a sign of the babe, then going lower still to find her and caress her.

"It has been too long," he said as he eased her down over him. "Far too long. By all the gods, Laren, you give me so very much."

The pleasure he brought her momentarily made her forget the truth of things, and that truth was always there and would always be there, even after Taby and her father left to return to Normandy. Taby would always be in Merrik's heart, closer than any other man or woman or child. She thought of the child she carried. Merrik would love the babe, surely he would love his own son or daughter, but not so much as he loved Taby, never so much as Taby.

She cried out in her release, shaken by its power and its sweetness as she always was, then held him to her as he took his own pleasure.

"You please me," he said, his voice low and deep, for he was sleepy now and sated. She felt him leave her, felt the wet of his seed, and eased down beside him. He kissed her forehead, caressed her shoulder, then he closed his eyes.

She loved him more than she could imagine loving another human being. She would love him forever. He was her husband and in that, he would always be hers.

"My father has been here with you, has he not, Sarla? Do you know where he is now?"

Sarla smiled as she stirred the mutton, cabbage, and onion stew. "Aye, he was here and he made me laugh. He is a very valiant man, Laren, your father. Perhaps he is outside now, speaking to Merrik. Or perhaps he is yet again trying to gain Taby's affections. Do you think I should add some mashed lingonberries?"

Laren agreed, waited for Sarla to say more, but she didn't. She went outside to the privy, then to the bathing hut. Merrik and her father and Taby were all within, their shouts loud, making her smile. When they emerged, all of them wet and well scrubbed, she saw that Taby was in his father's arms, not Merrik's. She looked quickly to her husband. To her profound relief, he was smiling. There was no hurt in his fine eyes, no sign of shadows.

"Laren," he said to her. She ran to him, flinging her arms around his back. He laughed as he hugged her to him. He continued to hold her close, waiting until Hallad and Taby were farther away. "Taby begins to accept him," he said, and now she heard the ache in his voice, but also his acceptance. "It is the way it must be. I've known it for a very long time. Aye, all will be well. You and I will visit Rouen and see him and your father and Rollo. Now, sweeting, I must see Cleve. He will tell me what has happened at Malverne whilst we were gone adventuring. And I must know what it is he wishes to do now that he is a free man."

"You remember that Uncle Rollo told us that Cleve was welcome to come to him. He said he would see that he was rewarded."

"I will tell him that. Stop looking at me like that, Laren, and take your hands off me. Go now, sweeting, else I'll take you back in the bathing hut, lather you with that sweet-smelling soap Helga made for you, and keep you there until neither of us can speak or walk."

She laughed and said, "I would like that better than stirring mutton stew, my lord." Slowly, unwillingly, she released him. She stood there, watching him stride toward the fields, his hair fair and bright beneath the sun, his body strong and brown from the sweet summer.

Merrik found Cleve chopping wood with a fine old axe that had belonged to Merrik's grandfather. Its blade was as sharp as ever, the grip smooth from the scores of years of men's hands gripping it. Merrik waited, watching him. He was stripped to a loincloth and he saw him now as a handsome man, well made, his golden hair glistening with sweat and health beneath the bright sun. Even the scarring on his face no longer detracted. He wondered if Sarla would take him as her husband. Cleve or Hallad, an old man, but rich and powerful, a man of wit and learning and kindness. No man could know a woman's mind. Suddenly Cleve looked up.

"That pile of logs will last us a week this winter," Merrik said. "I came to thank you, Cleve, helping Oleg look after everything here at Malverne."

"Naught of anything happened," Cleve said, gently cleaned the axe blade on his tunic, and strode to where Merrik was standing beneath an oak tree that was as old as the fjord. "The crops are safely stored, the goats and cows and children are fattening well, and Taby learned to ride the children's pony, Ebel. Your farmstead is a fine place, Merrik. You are blessed with sufficient arable land for your needs."

"Aye, I know it," Merrik said. "But you also know, Cleve, it was never destined to be mine. It was Erik's. It feels strange to me to be the lord here. Did Taby miss me and Laren?"

"Aye, but he forgot you soon enough on Ebel's back." Cleve laughed and punched Merrik's arm. He drew back instantly, a flare of the old slave terror in his eyes.

"Nay, my friend. You are free. Indeed, I come to ask you if you wish to return to Normandy with Taby and Hallad. The great Rollo himself wishes to reward you. Whatever you wish is yours. Whatever life you choose to lead, he will see that you gain it. He is a good man, a man to admire and follow. You would have a good life there, Cleve."

"I shall think about it, Merrik. I thank you."

"Tell me what you think of Hallad."

"He is a good man, despite the richness of his blood. He is also a very lucky man. His brother believed in him and protected him for three long years. And now he has returned to what he knew and he has his son and daughter as well. Aye, a very lucky man is Hallad."

"He is those things, it is true. However, Cleve, he is not young and strong and filled with health and a young man's vigor and eagerness for life. He is an old man. If he were to breed a child, he would probably be dead before the child reached his boyhood years."

Cleve grew very still. "Perhaps," he said at last. "I trust so, Merrik, but life is always uncertain, is it not?" He looked away from Merrik, into the distance at the stark mountain peaks on the opposite side of the fjord. "There is much to consider."

Merrik began to stack the logs Cleve had cut. "Tell me about what you did in my absence. Tell me how many fights there were, how many men are now just growling at each other."

That night Laren took up her duty as Malverne's skald once again. She told the story of an Irish merchant whose son, Ulric, was a bully, a vicious coward, and could never be trusted to act with honor. "Aye, our proud bully wanted to be a chieftain. One day he chanced upon a strange lady, and even though he was a spiteful ruffian, he wasn't stupid. The lady was stuck in a bog and couldn't free herself. Ulric managed to rescue her. He even decided not to rape her, such was his goodwill that day. It was a good thing, this goodwill of his, for then she told him she was a fairy and that she would grant any wish he asked for. He wanted to be chieftain, he told her, all puffed up, his eyes gleaming in his greed, for he believed her. Ulric said, 'I want to rule all the people in all the lands hereabouts for as far as I can see.'

" 'That is great deal of land and a good number of people,' the fairy told him.

" 'Aye,' he said. 'As far as I can see. That will be my dominion. You promised.'

"She smiled at him and gently raised her arms to the heavens. She called upward, her voice as sweet and strong as Malverne's honey mead, 'Grant this man, oh mighty Odin All-Father, grant him all the land that he can see.'

"There was a loud rumbling of thunder, flashes of lightning filled the afternoon sky.

" 'It is done,' she said, smiling upon Ulric. 'All that you can see is yours.'

"Then she disappeared. Ulric rubbed his hands together. He thought of the men who were his enemies. He thought of the girls who had managed to escape him, and said, 'But it is night now and that is strange, for it was a bright afternoon when I saved you. Grant me the sunlight again so that I may see my dominion.'

"Alas, there was no one there to hear him. The fairy was gone, but the night remained. Always."

Laren stopped. She said not a word more, just stood there and waited. The groans and hisses came quickly. Merrik laughed and rose to stand beside her. "It is the babe that makes her tales less courageous than before. The babe in her womb makes her moralize. She gives me sermons each night, and endless instructions on what she wishes me to do, and—"

Laren grabbed him by his ears and pulled him down to her. She kissed him loudly.

27

TWO DAYS LATER, late in the afternoon, Laren was
seated in front of the longhouse, loading a shuttle with
thread from her distaff. Once the thread was woven into
cloth, it would be a soft blue, just the color of Merrik's
eyes. She could already see the tunic she would make
for him. She was humming softly, the everyday sounds
so familiar to her that she scarce paid them any heed.
No heed until she heard Taby yelling at the top of his
lungs. She dropped the distaff and jumped to her feet.

He was running toward her, his face utterly white,
his bare legs filthy and bleeding from cuts from bramble
bushes.

"Laren! Where is Merrik? Laren!"

She raced to him, dropping to her knees in front of
him and grabbing his arms. "What is the matter, Taby?
What have you done?"

He was panting and for a moment he couldn't catch
his breath to speak. She held him, his urgency flooding
her now, and she felt her heart begin to pound faster
and faster.

"Tell me," she said, shaking him now. "What is
wrong?"

"It's Cleve," Taby gasped out. "He will die, you must
hurry, Laren. A rope. Hurry!"

He wrenched free of her and turned to run, screaming over his shoulder, "Hurry!"

Merrik was there suddenly, carrying a line of herring, Old Firren beside him.

"Come quickly!" Laren yelled at him. "Something has happened to Cleve! Bring a rope!"

Merrik called to Oleg and a dozen other men. They were all running after Taby. They caught him quickly. Merrik raised him to his shoulder, saying calmly, "Tell us where to go, Taby. Easy, lad, tell me."

Taby was sobbing with fear by the time they had claimed up the narrow path to Raven's Peak to the very top where Erik had been struck down by a rock.

"Over the side," Taby said, his voice small and shaking, yet Merrik understood. He set him on the ground, then raced to the edge of the cliff. He saw Cleve some fifteen feet down, his body tangled in an outgrowing bush, unconscious.

"By all the gods, he has fallen."

Oleg quickly unrolled the rope. "I will get him," Merrik said as he tied the rope about his waist.

Oleg grabbed Merrik's arm. "Listen to me. That bush doesn't look very strong and you are very big, Merrik. Best to let Eller go."

Merrik nodded slowly. Then he shouted, "Quickly, Eller, quickly."

Oleg and Roran held the rope as they eased Eller down the sharp face of the cliff.

"The bush is pulling free," Laren said, staring down.

"No," Merrik said. "The bush will remain until we have freed Cleve." And she believed him. She fell to her knees and took Taby in her arms. "You did well," she said to him as she kissed his filthy cheek, stroking her hands up and down his back. "Can you tell me what happened? Did Cleve fall?"

Suddenly Taby stiffened in her arms. He lowered his head.

"Taby?" It was Merrik. "What happened?"

"I don't know," Taby said, his face still buried in Laren's neck. She felt his tears on her flesh.

Merrik looked baffled. He shook his head, frowning in some bewilderment down at the boy, then walked to the cliff edge. Eller was balanced, just barely, and was tying the rope around Cleve's waist.

It was slow, agonizing work. Eller looked none too happy to hold on to that scrubby bush, knowing that if it gave, he would plunge some three hundred feet to the rocks and fjord below, but he worked quickly, his fingers steady and calm. Finally it was done. It was Merrik who grasped Cleve beneath his arms and dragged him over the top of the cliff. "Quickly," he said, "get that rope back to Eller before he shames himself and pisses in his trousers."

Laren was at Cleve's side. There was blood on the side of his head, over his right temple. He was still alive, thank the gods, but just barely. "Do you think he tripped and fell over the edge?" she said.

"I don't know," Merrik said. "What was he doing up here alone? What was Taby doing here?"

Merrik lifted Cleve into his arms and they began their slow descent back down the long steep path to the longhouse.

Cleve remained unconscious until late that evening. Then he was addled in his mind, crying out in a strange language, then begging for someone not to leave him, pleading until Laren thought her heart would break. She forced broth down his throat as Sarla gently bathed his face with cool water to keep away the fever.

There was much talk, much speculation, voices not low now, for all remembered that it was there Erik had been found, dead, a rock having smashed in his head. They had all believed that Deglin had done it. Had someone else then struck Cleve and shoved him over? And what of Taby? All wondered about Taby and what he had seen, but the child wouldn't say anything, even to Merrik.

That night, Laren and Sarla took turns staying by Cleve's bed. But it was Taby who refused to leave him at all, curling up beside him to sleep through the night.

Hallad tried to coax his small son away from Cleve, but Taby remained stubbornly silent. He would say nothing nor would he leave Cleve.

"He will awaken, I know he will," Laren said to Sarla, who was so pale Laren feared for her health. "Go sleep now, and I will stay with him."

"Nay, 'tis you who are exhausted. You also carry a child and I do not. You go rest now, Laren, I will stay with Cleve."

Laren looked into Sarla's shadowed eyes and slowly nodded. She gently shook Taby's shoulder. "Come, little sweeting, we will go to our own beds now. If you like, you can sleep with Merrik and me."

Taby was awake immediately. He didn't blink or yawn. He looked from his sister to Cleve to Sarla.

He shook his head. "No, Laren, I wish to stay here, with Cleve."

She started to pull him off the box bed, but the look in his eyes stayed her hand. "Very well, but remain quiet. He is very ill."

"I know." The child curled up against Cleve, his small palm over Cleve's heart.

"Sarla will become ill," Hallad said. "She is too pale and there are shadows beneath her eyes. She is very quiet, even withdrawn. None of it is her fault. I do not understand why she is so struck with this man's accident. Speak to her, Laren."

"Father, I believe she and Cleve were becoming close even before Merrik and and I went to Normandy."

Hallad just stared at her. Slowly, he raised a cup of ale to his mouth and drank deep.

"I could be wrong, for when we returned they seemed somehow distant. I don't know. He is a good man, Father, and he was there with me in Kiev. He tried to save me at the risk of his own life."

"This man is naught but a slave, or at least he used to be. Sarla is so wondrous kind she feels pity for him, nothing more, just as she would for any of the people here at Malverne. Perhaps if he recovers he will come back to Normandy with us."

She cocked her head to one side in question. "Us?"

"Of course I mean Taby and me," he said, but Laren didn't trust that tone of voice she'd heard men use before. It was false in its sincerity, gentle in its sarcasm. Ah, yes, his voice was smug, that was it.

"Laren!"

She turned to see her husband striding toward her. In his hand was a rock. When he thrust it at her, she saw the dried blood on it. "Cleve didn't fall by accident. Someone struck his head with this rock and shoved him over the edge. Here is the proof of it."

"Just as Deglin struck Erik," Laren said and shivered. "I don't like this, Merrik. It means there is another at work here, since Deglin is dead."

"Nor do I like it. I had to know if Cleve had simply lost his footing. I searched and searched, Oleg and Roran with me. Roran found the rock thrown behind a bush halfway down the path. But this time, the man who struck down Cleve wanted us to believe that it was an accident."

For the first time in many days, Laren ran from the longhouse and vomited. As Merrik held her head, stroking back her hair from her forehead, she knew it wasn't from the babe in her womb. No, it was from fear. She was very afraid.

Taby had changed, utterly. He was no longer happy and carefree. Now he was silent, sullen, wary of anyone who spoke to him. He even avoided Merrik. He looked drawn and thin. In just a day, he had lost the glow of health from his small face. He refused to leave Cleve. Finally, Merrik pulled the boy into his arms and hauled him out of the small sleeping chamber. He carried the kicking little boy out of the longhouse. He didn't say a word until they were well beyond the palisade wall. He eased Taby down, then held him down as he sat beside him on a huge smooth boulder. "When I was your age," he said easily, "I would come here and think. If my father had cuffed me for some wrongdoing or I had hurt someone, or I was just uncertain about anything, I would come here to think and to ponder. It is a good place, Taby." He said nothing more, merely held Taby's hand so he couldn't run away.

"Your father is distressed because you avoid him," Merrik said at last, not looking at the child, but speaking calmly as he gazed out over the fjord. "He believed you dead for two very long years. Then he found you again and now you avoid him. It is very strange and he does not understand.

"However, I believe I do understand, for you are closer to me than to anyone else. I have thought about this. You saw who hit Cleve with the rock. You saw who shoved him over the side of the cliff. This is why you refuse to leave Cleve, because you fear the man will come again and try to kill him. You are a brave boy,

Taby. I love you deeply and I want to help you. But you must tell me the truth for I cannot begin to guess who this man is. Do you also realize that it could be the same man who killed Erik? That Deglin was innocent of his murder?"

"It wasn't a man."

Merrik jerked at the small voice, thin and liquid with fear and dread.

Merrik waited. He could do nothing more.

"She said she would kill Laren if I said anything. She said Laren was a fool and didn't deserve to be mistress here at Malverne. She said life had not dealt fairly with her, not until my father came. She said that was why she had to act. She said after she killed Laren, she would kill you. I couldn't say anything, Merrik, I couldn't."

It was so very clear then, so very clear. Merrik said quietly, "Sarla."

Taby shuddered and pressed against Merrik's side. "She will kill Laren. She will kill Cleve, for he is helpless, Merrik. He is helpless; he has not regained his wits. I must go back to him. You will take care of Laren."

"Aye, I will, and I will take care of Cleve as well. Come, Taby. We will return now."

"I am afraid, Merrik."

Merrik smiled down at him. "For once, I am not afraid."

He told Taby to remain with his father. "Aye, you have done the right thing. Now it is my turn. Stay here, Taby. Soon Laren and I will come to you."

He heard Laren's jubilant voice as he neared Cleve's small sleeping chamber. "He is awake, Sarla! Thank the gods, Cleve is finally awake. Now we can learn what happened."

Merrik slowly drew back the thin bearskin pelt from the doorway. He saw Laren leaning over Cleve, a smile on her face. He saw Sarla standing behind her and now she was lifting a heavy oil lamp from the floor.

"Do not even think to do it, Sarla," he said very quietly. "Put the lamp down."

Sarla whirled around to face him. "No," she said. "No, Merrik, you misunderstand."

Laren turned. "Cleve is going to be all right, Merrik. Come and speak to him. Now we will learn what happened."

"I know what happened, Laren. But not all of it. Sarla will tell us all of it, will you not, sister-in-law?"

Laren straightened very slowly. She studied Sarla's pale face, her dulled eyes. But Sarla shook her head, saying again, "You do not understand, Merrik. It is not what you believe. Cleve, ah, it was an accident, I swear it."

Laren said slowly, incredulously, "You, Sarla? You struck Cleve?"

Sarla said nothing, just shook her head.

"But why? I don't understand. He loved you. I saw it in his eyes before we left to journey to Normandy. And you were coming to care for him as well, were you not?" Laren stopped. She looked wildly at Merrik as she whispered, "Erik? She killed Erik as well?"

"Aye, she did. I suppose she killed him because he was betraying her yet again, this time with you. I suppose she killed him, too, because she wanted Cleve."

"I saved Laren from dishonor. Surely you will acquit me, for I saved her."

"That was a consequence, surely," Merrik said, "but do not make yourself into a heroine, Sarla, for the truth does not fit itself to you. Why did you try to kill Cleve?"

His voice was low, filled with pain. "Tell him, Sarla.

Tell him the truth or I will."

"Oh, Cleve, you are back again." Laren whirled about to hover over him, protecting him now, Merrik saw, for she was standing between him and Sarla.

"Be quiet, you fool! You are a liar, say nothing!"

Cleve said quietly, "Move away from me, Laren. She will not strike me again. Merrik, she carries my child in her womb, and, aye, we were to wed upon your return. Only you brought Hallad back with you. He looked at gentle, kind Sarla and wanted her. Sarla wanted to wed with him then, for he is rich and powerful. She would have power and jewels and slaves. What am I? Nothing at all, at least to her now. Thus she had to convince Hallad that it was his child she carries. I told her I wouldn't betray her, I swore to her that I loved her, but I would not give up my son to another man, a son he would believe was his. She struck me down." He'd never taken his beautiful eyes off Sarla. "You have lost your beauty, Sarla. It is odd but true. Your beauty was in your sweetness, your gentleness, but now you are showing to the world what you were on the inside for a long time. I remember when you claimed before all that you had killed Erik, but no one believed you, did they? They all believed that you were protecting Laren, protecting me."

Merrik stared at her, a woman he'd grown so very close to, or at least he thought he had, a woman he would have sworn to the very gods themselves was pure and honest and good. He said slowly, "Did you kill Deglin as well?"

"I will say nothing more," Sarla said.

"I always wondered about that," Merrik continued. "How did Deglin get loose? Why didn't he try to escape? Where did he find that knife? The blacksmith simply accepted that the knife must have been in his hut, left by one of the men, waiting to be repaired. But it wasn't. You fetched it and you killed Deglin. You took no chances, Sarla, none at all."

Sarla straightened to her full height and said to Merrik, her voice proud and tight, "I wish to return to my parents' farmstead. I wish to leave very soon. This man is lying. His jealousy of Hallad has twisted him. He is pathetic with his scarred face. How could any woman love such an ugly man, a man who was nothing more than a slave? He is lying, about everything. I spurned him and now he wishes to destroy me. I wish to leave this place."

Cleve forced himself up onto his elbows. "You will bear my child, and then you can leave. What say you, Merrik?"

"It is not your child!" she shrieked at him. "It is Erik's! If it is a son, he will be the heir to Malverne!"

Cleve just shook his head. "I am sorry, Sarla, but it is my babe. I will swear that your woman's flow occurred after Erik's death."

"Liar!"

"But he isn't, is he?" Merrik said. He bowed his head and was silent for many moments. When he spoke again, he said, "I am glad you survived, Cleve. I am very sorry for all this."

Epilogue

IT WAS TWO days after the winter solstice. A blizzard raged outside the longhouse. Inside, it was warm, the air thick with smoke, the smell of broiling venison steaks, and the ripening smell of the two goats and two cows. The horses were, thankfully, safe from the storm in the end of the stable, plenty of hay piled in the troughs for them.

Laren occasionally looked up from her needlework to see Merrik still speaking to the messenger from Rollo. The tunic was nearly done and he would look splendid in it, for the blue was darker this time, but just one shade darker than the beautiful blue of his eyes. It would be the third tunic she'd sewn him of varying shades of blue. Their people were beginning to notice and to hurl jests at him. Merrik just laughed and shook his head.

The child moved suddenly within her and she jumped and smiled, her hand going automatically to her growing belly.

Merrik came to her then, dropping to his knees beside her chair. He began to caress her belly. "I saw you jump and then smile. My babe moves?"

"Aye, your babe moves. Has the messenger told you more of anything?"

"Cardle is in Britain, at the Wessex king's court. Rollo decided not to have him killed. He said that after all those years with Ferlain, he deserved to think about his Saxon kings and his Greeks in peace."

"That is good."

"Also, Cardle sent Rollo a message that he planned to spread tales of Rollo's greatness throughout Britain. Perhaps this is one reason your uncle decided to let him live. Also, your father has wedded a girl your age. He says that he is getting no younger, therefore his haste in wedding again. She is a daughter from one of the men of King Charles's court. Aye, you've the right of it, I can see it in your eyes. His wife—your stepmother— is already pregnant." He looked over at Sarla as he spoke. Once she birthed her babe, he would send her back to her parents' farmstead. He'd said naught of her actions to anyone, nor had Laren or Cleve. If any of them had told what she'd done, doubtless one of Erik's men would have killed her. As it was, all treated her as they always had, even Cleve. But it was his child he guarded, Sarla knew it, but no one else did. All wondered why they didn't wed since she was carrying Cleve's child. All finally came to believe that she didn't wish it because Cleve, after all, had been a slave. No one, however, was brave enough to ask.

Laren, unaware of her husband's thoughts, laughed at the news, she couldn't help it. "My father," she said helplessly, and shook her head. "And now he does it again. What is my new stepmother's name?"

"Bartha, an ugly name, but the messenger says she is passing fair."

"I hope Taby likes her."

"Nay, not particularly. Evidently he ignores her. Rollo finds it all vastly amusing. Our Taby grows more by the day and his skills increase by the day as well.

Helga is less a witch now than she was. Aye, I see the doubt in your eyes, Laren, but she has wedded with Weland. Evidently he allows her none of her former tricks. What think you of that?"

"I think you have just made me prick my finger, Merrik. You jest, do you not? You try to outdo me in weaving strange and bizarre tales."

" 'Tis the truth, I swear it to you. Now, sweeting, shall we retire? I am weary of all this commotion and all this smell and all the arguments."

"Aye," she said, giving him a smile that made him instantly hard, "the night is young, Merrik. Have you the strength, do you think, my lord?"

"We will see. Since my lust for you is nearly as great as my love, then I believe I can please you until you deign to ask me to cease."

She very slowly put down the needle and the beautiful soft material. She began to stroke the cloth, not looking at him, merely said in a whisper, "Do you truly love me?"

He took her chin in his palm and raised her head. He looked at her, silent for a very long time. He leaned down and kissed her mouth. "Aye," he said against her warm lips, "I love you more than you can imagine. I am your husband. How could you doubt it?"

"You never told me until now."

"I know. It was difficult for me, but I have felt it, Laren, for a very long time."

"Taby," she said. "It has always been Taby you loved."

"I will always love him, but he is a child and my brother. He is not the woman who will stand beside me until we are both dust and ashes. You are. I love you as a man loves a woman, as my father loved my mother. I have found you and never will let you forget what you are to me." He grinned as he kissed her again. "I grow boring with my seriousness. I have nearly made you fall asleep repeating myself. Now I wish to take you to my bed and hold you and come into you and make you a part of me. I wish to hear you tell me you love me. You have said naught of affection for me since that long-ago night. It is important for a man to hear this often from his wife."

"Aye," she said, "it is very important. But like you, I said nothing. These are very powerful things I feel for you, Merrik. It is just that I feared that you didn't want to hear such things from me."

"You were wrong. Tell me again that you love me and let us go to bed."

"I love you, Merrik. However . . . " She paused, then grinned widely up at him. "Not just yet. I really wish to finish your tunic before I come with you."

He looked at the tunic folded neatly beside her, lifted it and tossed it to Oleg. "Take a needle and finish this garment, Oleg. As you can see, it is another blue tunic. My wife knows but one color for me." Oleg, who was holding Megot in the crook of his arm, stared with horror at the tunic, opened his mouth, could think of nothing to say, and closed it.

Merrik carried his wife from the huge outer chamber, the sound of his people's laughter in his ears. He felt the bulge of her belly against his heart, the warmth of her breath against his throat.

All was well. With any luck life would continue sweet if the gods weren't angered, if other Vikings didn't lust after Malverne, if illness didn't . . . His thinking stopped. Life was fragile, fraught with chance, but now, at this moment, the sweetness of it was something he would never forget.

He said to his wife, "When will you finish the tunic? The color pleases me mightily."

Author's Note

ROLLO, THE FIRST duke of Normandy, was also known as Rolf the Ganger. He was such a large man that he could sit very few horses without his feet dragging the ground. Unfortunately not much is known about him. What we do know is that he and Charles III, the French king, formed an alliance in 911 at the chapel at St. Clair-sur-Epte. Rollo agreed to keep other invading Vikings at bay, thus saving Paris from further sacking, and the payment of Danegeld, a great sum of silver to bribe marauders to stay away. Charles III granted Rollo the vast rich lands that included Rouen and the surrounding countryside, land which the Vikings already occupied and controlled. Rollo lived for seventy years, turning the reins of government to his son, William Longsword, only three years before his death in 930.

I created a brother, Hallad, his brother's son, Taby, Hallad's daughters, Laren, Helga, and Ferlain. I made Taby very important to Rollo, because life then was as fragile as death was final and always nearby, and thus one heir wasn't ever enough, particularly if a man wanted to create a dynasty, which Rollo did. Indeed, William the Conqueror, who conquered England in 1066, was his direct descendant.

Rollo, first duke of Normandy (derived from the word *Northmen*), is buried in Rouen Cathedral. His face carving shows quite a handsome fellow.